Magical Midlife Dating

Also by K.F. Breene

LEVELING UP
Magical Midlife Madness
Magical Midlife Dating
Magical Midlife Invasion (coming soon)

DEMIGODS OF SAN FRANCISCO
Sin & Chocolate
Sin & Magic
Sin & Salvation
Sin & Spirit
Sin & Lightning
Sin & Surrender

DEMON DAYS VAMPIRE NIGHTS WORLD
Born in Fire
Raised in Fire
Fused in Fire
Natural Witch
Natural Mage
Natural Dual-Mage
Warrior Fae Trapped
Warrior Fae Princess

FINDING PARADISE SERIES
Fate of Perfection
Fate of Devotion

Magical Midlife Dating

By K.F. Breene

Contact info:
www.kfbreene.com
books@kfbreene.com

CHAPTER 1

"JUST JUMP. YOU'LL never know unless you try." Mr. Tom stood beside a gaping hole in the third floor of Ivy House, looking down at the cold emptiness below.

He was trying to get me to jump out of the trapdoor that I'd first discovered almost thirty years ago when I visited Ivy House as a kid. Staring down from that height had given me a sense of foreboding way back in the day, and at the time no one had been pressuring me to jump out of it in the hope a pair of magical wings I wasn't positive I had would snap out of my back and save me before I went splat.

"Niamh is circling just out of sight," Mr. Tom said, motioning me forward. Frigid air blasted through the opening and tousled his stringy comb-over. He grimaced and smoothed the gray strands across his scalp. As a protector of Ivy House, he'd gotten the strength and vitality of youth when I accepted the magic, but he hadn't received any visual benefit, including growing back his hair. I'd made that choice for him, and for the other protectors, Niamh and Edgar and Austin, by deciding to keep my own appearance, and I'd learned pretty quickly that it was a point of contention for some of the others. Mainly Mr. Tom.

Thankfully, he didn't mention it now.

"Okay, but…" I shook my head, focusing on my breathing. "Are we sure she's waiting down there?"

"The house has put out a summons to its protectors, insisting that we support you in your training today. It would require an incredible amount of willpower to resist or wander away. She will circle until called off; Ivy House will make it so."

"Except…Austin didn't show up."

"Yes. He clearly has incredible willpower."

I shook my head, staring down at the green grass and the small shape of Edgar, his arms raised.

"He can't possibly think he could catch me from this high of a drop," I murmured.

"He's not playing with a full deck of cards. The magic returned his strength and prowess, but there is only so much magic can do for the mind. That vampire only has one oar in the water, so to speak."

As if Mr. Tom could talk. Tom wasn't even his real name! He'd made it up when he first met me. I didn't even want to get started on his habit of naming weapons and his absolute refusal to let me burn down the doll room. Mr. Tom was clutching to reality with nothing but his fingernails.

"I need a drink," I murmured, fear running through my blood in cold shivers.

"Nonsense. Drinking is for the weak. You don't want to turn out like that wretched woman, do you, reduced to throwing rocks at strangers and allies alike and forcing dry sandwiches on unsuspecting folk?" He meant Niamh. The two didn't see eye to eye on many things. Or *any*thing, really. "No. You will jump, your logic will deduce that you need to fly in order to save yourself, and thus your wings will extend from your back."

"Uh-huh." I edged forward, the toes of my runners scuffing the wood floor. The cold wind crept along my bare arms, raising goose pimples. My shirt did little more than cover my front, looping around my neck and upper waist, exposing my back so that my wings wouldn't be hindered.

Presuming I had any.

"Yes, using them will be as natural as you please. I never told you, but I was a late bloomer. It took me forever to get up the willpower to attempt flight. Finally, my father just threw me off the edge of the cliff. All I needed was a little shove!"

"Your wings just knew what to do, or…?"

"Well, no, at first I couldn't quite get them to work in sync, so I accidentally careened back into the cliff face and eventually spiraled down into the water, but on the third try, I had it! Nothing to it."

My flat stare wiped the supportive smile off his face.

"Your wings will be dainty," he rushed to say, patting my shoulder. "Much easier to control."

My body shook, and I wasn't sure if it was because of the cold or because of the fear.

"Just because you are trying a new thing, doesn't mean you need to let go of what you've already learned," Mr. Tom reminded me softly. "You should not feel the cold. Remember?"

Barely having to think about it, I reached for the heat deep in my gut and *pulled* it out until it covered my body. As Mr. Tom had promised, learning this magic had so far been second nature. Edgar would read instructions for controlling body heat or whatever from an ancient volume only he seemed able to decipher, and barely at that, and the knowledge would burst forth as though it had been tucked in my brain all along. Sometimes it was even easier—I'd just think about something and, without knowing how, make it happen. My situation wasn't exactly a science at this point.

Edgar said the recall ability had been built into the

magical transfer because there were often large time gaps between the chosen, and it wasn't a given there'd be anyone around to train the new heir. The unconscious magical ability was the same situation, only more uncontrolled.

So why hadn't I already jumped?

According to Edgar, certain higher-level abilities would be more difficult to master. No one knew if flying was the run-of-the-mill type of magic that I'd pick up easily, or the harder version that would take extensive practice.

"Are you sure I even have wings?" I asked, dangerously close to whining. "We've seen no evidence."

"Ivy House chose you. It gave you the magic. Tamara Ivy was a female gargoyle, so wings are part of the package."

"Youth was supposed to be too, and we don't have that."

"That was your misguided notion, not the fault of the magic. Trust me, if you didn't have wings, Ivy House would slam this trapdoor shut right now to prevent you from falling to your death. It will protect its chosen at all costs."

I held my breath, looking at the heavy steel of the trapdoor leaning open. Given Mr. Tom's pause, I could tell he was doing the same.

After a few quiet beats of no activity, I whispered, "Damn it," and blew out a breath. "Why not try a window on the second floor? That way, if nothing happens, I might just break my leg instead of my neck."

"You need falling time to figure things out. If you jumped from the second story, you'd probably break your legs just as your wings extended, and you'd almost certainly crush Edgar when he got in your way trying to save you. Besides, I doubt you'll kill yourself jumping from the third floor. It's not *that* high."

It certainly seemed that high.

"Okay, fine. Okay. *Fine.*" I shook out my hands. Wind whipped around me. I didn't see the flutter of Niamh's black wings within my limited scope of sight. I'd have to trust she was there, and was close enough to swoop in and grab me should things go pear-shaped.

I had every belief things would go pear-shaped. How the hell was I supposed to believe I could fly when just a couple months ago I didn't even believe magic was real? I thought I was doing a pretty good job of acclimating to the fantastic, but this was pushing it. Wings magically sprouting from my back? And I was counting on being able to use them instantly, something even baby birds couldn't do without practice.

"This is stupid. What the hell am I doing? I'm going to kill myself." Clenching my fists, I barely stopped myself from edging backward. My toes hung over the lip. The world swam in front of me.

I thought about jumping. Maybe even just tipping forward and falling.

But, oh God, what if I started spinning or flipping in the air, and my wings did pop out, but I was ass over end and couldn't right myself, and—

I clenched and unclenched my hands, trying to still my mind. Trying to get into the mindset to jump. My legs felt like jelly. My stomach pinched and energy buzzed through me, soaked through with fear.

Austin's voice drifted through my head, remembered encouragement from one of the many pep talks he'd given me.

Take life by the balls, Jess. You are strong and confident. You are powerful with or without that magic. You have things to say, and this world needs to hear them. Grab life by the balls and make it yield.

"Yes, indeed. Exactly right." I gritted my teeth and nodded, leaning forward over the large drop.

"What?" Mr. Tom asked.

"Grab it by the balls…"

"Who?" Mr. Tom covered his crotch.

"Just grab…" Wind swirled my hair. Edgar reached up a little higher, ready. He seemed to think the job of saving me would be left to him. He always had the utmost faith in Niamh, and yet he was acting like she wouldn't come through.

My mind buzzed. Fear beat a drum in my chest. My stomach flipped as I prepared to jump.

How was Niamh going to grab me without hands? Her other form was a freaking flying unicorn. The best she could do was swoop down under me, but if I was spinning around, I'd just glance off her, go careening, and slam into the ground anyway. There was no way I'd have the presence of mind to grab on to her, and even if I did, she didn't have a saddle. What was I supposed to hold on to?

"Screw it. Grab life by the balls. Now or never—"

CHAPTER 2

I LIFTED A foot to jump, my stomach now in my neck, and a strong gust of wind slapped me. So intense it felt solid, it shoved me back, away from the opening. I unconsciously put out my hands to ward it away, and the steel trapdoor swung from its position and crashed down, bouncing on its frame.

A pulse blasted out from the center of me, reverberating through the house and shocking into the grounds beyond. From there it kept traveling, not losing steam, until it drifted into nothingness.

Mr. Tom looked at me as though waiting for an explanation.

I wasn't sure if I should ask, "What was that?" or just randomly shout for no reason. Really no losing between those two options.

I chose, instead, to just stare back with what I knew was a dumb look.

The silence felt gooey around us, suffocating the natural creaks of the house. I realized belatedly that I was creating it.

I tore the magic away, accidentally lifting the magical heat keeping me warm. Goosebumps returned along my arms.

"Dang it," I said softly, trying to balance everything out.

"Well. I guess we'll see what kind of help you're looking for." Mr. Tom straightened up, sniffed, and walked from the room.

I eyed the closed trapdoor. It appeared Ivy House didn't think I was ready to take that part of life by the balls. *Thank God.*

"What do you mean, the kind of help I'm looking for?" I followed Mr. Tom out of the room and down the hall toward the stairs. "What did I do?"

"You called for aid, which is well within your rights as the mistress of Ivy House. It seems you don't think myself, Niamh, and Edgar are enough. That's fine. You know best, after all." His nose was lifted when we reached the ground floor. "Tea? Coffee? Something to take the edge off the horrible guilt you're sure to feel once you've come to your senses?"

Edgar and Niamh met us in the kitchen, each wearing a pair of white cotton sweats, Edgar's rumpled and with a yellowed stain that I didn't want to think about—fearing it was a blood source of some kind—and

Niamh's with dirt and grass speckled on one side.

Mr. Tom had been in charge of choosing the house sweats when "at work," a.k.a. changing forms, and it was no surprise his were the only ones that stayed clean.

"What went wrong there?" Niamh asked in her thick Irish brogue as she sauntered into the kitchen, her hair still short and white, her face baby soft but with deep creases of age, and her step light and spry, compliments of Ivy House. "Earl, put on a cuppa tae, would ye? I'm absolutely dyin' with the thirst."

Earl was Mr. Tom's real name. As usual, when she used it, Mr. Tom pretended he couldn't hear her. It was why I'd buckled early and just resigned myself to calling him by his chosen name.

"Earl, ye insufferable gobshite, I know you heard me," Niamh said, ruled by her own weirdness. She wasn't put off by his silent treatment. She was also so ancient that, even though she always retained her accent, she went in and out of various countries' slang and choice of words. "Is this why that other family you worked fer shoved ye out the door, is it? Couldn't do a simple thing like—"

"Ah yes, how I missed your soft, dulcet tones these last few days when we trained Jessie in close combat, independently of you," Mr. Tom said sarcastically, moving to the kettle. "What a treat to have us all

11

together again."

"You're no feckin' picnic yerself, sure yer not," she muttered, heading to the table. She noticed the dirt and grass clinging to her leg and bent to wipe it off, sprinkling it onto the floor. Mr. Tom's mouth pressed into a thin line, but he held his tongue.

"Did you lose your nerve?" Edgar asked me, his brown eyes soft.

"Didn't you feel the summons?" Mr. Tom asked, pulling down the tea set covered in yellow and orange flowers and placing it on the granite island. Porcelain clinked and shook as the pieces settled. It was the ugliest tea set I'd ever seen in my life. "She is calling in reinforcements."

"Of course we felt it. The whole world probably felt it," Niamh said. "It nearly blew my hair back. 'Bout time, too. There's only so much carry-on we can handle from Edgar while he hems and haws over that terrible excuse for an instruction manual."

"It is not an instruction manual," Edgar said patiently—the guy never seemed to lose his temper. "It's an ages' old magical artifact that remains lost until a new chosen is selected, and then is miraculously found. Given I was the one who found it in the garden, I am the one able to decipher its mysteries." He scratched his head, and small flakes drifted toward the counter.

"Edgar, *please*." Mr. Tom slid the tea set further away from him. Porcelain clattered. "Use some Head & Shoulders or visit Agnes. She can probably concoct a potion to get rid of that…issue."

"It's my nails. I need to cut them." Edgar looked at his pointed, claw-like fingernails.

"Mysteries, me arse." Niamh shook her head and looked out the window onto the sunny but cold afternoon.

"The summons wasn't connected with the minor setbacks I've had with deciphering the book," Edgar said, "though you'd think the house would make it a *little* easier for its chosen to read it. The summons was for help with flying, or maybe just help in general, wasn't it, Jessie?"

I sat opposite Niamh at the round table and pulled my laptop in front of me. "I don't know, honestly. I was just about to hurtle to my death when a gust of wind pushed me back and the trapdoor closed by itself."

"You did those things," Mr. Tom said, dropping a tea bag into the pot. "Half the things you do are still subconscious; you know that. Which is to be expected, of course. Your magic is designed to respond to your needs. If it weren't, you wouldn't be able to use half of it. Not without proper training, and, as we've seen from Edgar's efforts, you do not have that."

"I thought I was doing okay," Edgar muttered, reaching up to scratch his head again. He paused with his hand halfway there, caught Mr. Tom's severe look, and slowly dropped it.

I frowned at Mr. Tom. "I was preparing to jump, though."

"You only think that. What you were really doing was psyching yourself up to shut it all down and call for help." He lifted his nose and pulled bread out of the cabinet. "It seems you have an idea of the kind of help you need, and we are not it."

A grin spread across Niamh's face. "She has twelve spots in that Council Room for her staff, but you thought if she had ye, she wouldn't need to fill them all up, is that right? You thought an old, fired butler with too few marbles rolling around in his head was all she needed to conquer this incredible new magic? Well, don't ye think the world of yerself, boy." She leaned back, chuckling. "You know yerself that she needs all twelve in that circle. She certainly needs whoever is meant to fill the number one spot."

When she paused this time, I couldn't help a rolling wave of unease in my gut. No one had yet explained to me *why* I needed a council. What I was meant to do with the incredible magic I'd eventually wield. Was there a larger purpose for me, or was that council just meant to keep me alive if anyone threatened me? I didn't know, and I was too chicken to ask.

Niamh entwined her fingers. "That is the way of it. It's the way it's always been, hasn't it, Edgar?"

Edgar beamed. "So you *do* listen—"

"She should've sent out that call before now," Niamh continued. "Elliot Graves has already shown his interest in her. Given that she now rules Ivy House, he'll be thinking on how to get her to join his faction. He's the best mage in the world—he's watched by his peers. Even if people don't have a clue what Ivy House is, they'll certainly get curious in a hurry. If you think they won't come knocking, trying to poke the bear and see what all this is about, you're a thickheaded dope, so ya are. They'll pick a fight just to see what she can do. I'll tell ye what, too, we'd better hope she's a helluva lot better at the magic than she is now. She's mostly *use*less right now."

"Thanks," I said sourly, shifting the screen away from them as I clicked into an online dating app for (non-magical) mature singletons that was supposed to be best for thirty-three and up. How they'd landed on thirty-three, I had no idea, but I figured that since my magic made me a target, it was best to start with someone more my speed, hence the non-magical.

On the one hand, I wasn't sure I wanted to head

into the stormy waters of dating. I liked being on my own for the first time, able to come and go as I pleased without having to answer to anyone other than an old butler who just wanted to make my life easier and make me snacks. Becoming a giant starfish across the bed was a rare treat after sharing with someone for half my life. It felt pretty great, actually.

But the need for intimacy gnawed at me. Toward the end of my marriage, my libido had started ramping up, but Matt's version of foreplay had been moving into position and going for it. By the time I was warming up, he was ready to go to sleep. It was more frustrating than gratifying, and I didn't really have anyone to vent to—it was something people my age didn't seem to talk about. At least not women.

Part of the problem had been me, of course. I hadn't demanded he try a little harder or learn the things that would have worked better. Resentment had kicked in, and sex had become the equivalent of *one more chore* at the end of the day. One more thing that pleased him and not me so much.

I wanted to change that so badly. I wanted my fresh start to be inclusive of physical intimacy again. I used to love it. I loved kissing and making out, holding hands and taking walks. I loved *love*—at least the idea of love. I wanted to experience that again. I wanted to experience the rush of falling headfirst, and the anxious but not unpleasant fear of the floor dropping out from under me.

I just needed to find someone to do that with. Super easy, of course, given I hadn't dated in a dog's age, didn't know how to flirt without being awkward or creepy, and didn't have the first clue how to meet someone in the wild. Like, did you just walk up to a rando and start a conversation? That wouldn't go well for me. Small talk was my nemesis. Did you give *come hither* eyes and wait to see if they did? How was I supposed to manage that without giving a deranged serial-killer vibe?

All unknowns. I'd decided to get my feet wet with online dating. I'd be taking the plunge for the first time later tonight.

Maybe I should've jumped earlier. My inevitable injuries would have given me an excuse to cancel.

"I wonder if there is an adult bookstore in this town," I mused, because the only way I was likely to get some action was if it was from myself.

All conversation stopped.

My face instantly heated and I slammed my laptop closed out of pure embarrassment. Liking some boom-boom time was one thing, but broadcasting what I planned to do if it was not readily available was a different thing entirely.

"I mean... What I *meant* was..." I stammered.

"First things first, Jessie—we need to square away business," Niamh said, completely unperturbed. Edgar's wide eyes said he was not so blasé about the whole thing. "After that, we'll get ye enough bells and whistles to have ye singin' the Lord's name. Ye won't want to come out've that room for a week, so you won't."

"That's... No. What I'd meant to say was—"

"Austin is practically beside himself with preparing for whoever might come calling," Niamh went on. "That poor fella is actin' like he'll be the only one defending this town against 'em. We need backup we can trust."

"How do we know we can trust them?" I asked, face still blazing like a furnace as I pretended to be as mature as my age.

Niamh gave me a long look. "That's your department. The house will help, I believe..."

"Yes." Edgar entwined his fingers as he neared the table. Surely the gesture was meant to keep him from scratching his head, but Niamh's *look* made him pause and retreat to the other side of the kitchen. "The summons should call all the able-bodied that your magic deems worthy. You will need to choose who works for you and who doesn't. This will just be the first wave, I believe. The first summons. As you progress, you'll send out more, the first few accidental, like now, and then on purpose as you fill in your team. It is expected that you be choosy. Very choosy, if you want to. Downright picky—"

"We get it," Mr. Tom drawled, putting the finishing touches on the sandwiches. "Edgar, you don't want a sandwich, do you?"

"No, no." Edgar smiled, his long canines looking ghastly in his gleaming smile—he'd been using whitening gel on his teeth, a subtle hint that he clearly wished Ivy House had spruced the color up a bit. "I stunned some trespassers I caught sneaking around in the woods before the house called us in. I'll just go tuck into them."

"You don't…" I cleared my throat. I'd asked this before, but I always worried the answer would change. "You don't plan on killing them, right?"

"Oh no, of course not." Edgar laughed. "I only kill for sport. No, I'll just take enough to tide me over. Don't fight today, save it for another day."

Niamh shook her head. "You've missed the mark on that cliché."

"Right, well." He nodded at me. "Probably best you didn't jump. There was a possibility of Niamh running you through with her horn. You might've healed from that, but then what if I didn't catch you? A horn *and* a splat? That might've been too much for even Ivy House magic to patch up."

"Run her through, me arse," Niamh grumbled. "I would've gotten her. The height was tough, though. We should find a higher point to drop her from. That way I'd have more time for maneuvering. You know, since *someone* is too afraid to miss and drop her." She gave Mr. Tom a pointed look.

I let my jaw drop, looking at each of them in turn. "Really? You were all thinking this and didn't bother to mention it?"

"If we'd mentioned it, you wouldn't have jumped," Mr. Tom said, coming around the island with the plate of sandwiches.

There were no words.

"Now, about this dating—let's see what you've got there." Niamh moved around the table and motioned at my laptop. "Who's this fella you're goin' out wit' tonight, then?"

CHAPTER 3

I HAD TOLD them all when I confirmed the date. I'd even broken down and told my son on our last call. Surprisingly, Jimmy had wished me well. The others had mostly ignored me. Given I hadn't canceled the date, something I was sure Mr. Tom hoped I'd do, since the guy wasn't magical, clearly Niamh now wanted some specifics.

My stomach rolled over. "I found him on a different site. I was just checking this profile…"

"Sure, yeah, fine, let's have a look. Come on." She stood behind me.

A second opinion probably wasn't a bad idea. I hadn't been incredibly choosy on the guy I'd agreed to meet tonight, not really knowing what to look for in a dating profile, let alone which not-as-obvious red flags to avoid. He was about my age, somewhat in shape, based on his profile pictures, and said he liked to stay active. I figured that was a good start.

I inched the laptop open and clicked into my account again. "I've only posted a profile on this site. I haven't talked with anyone yet…"

My voice trailed off and my eyes widened at the number of messages waiting for me.

"How long has that profile been up?" Niamh asked, leaning closer.

"The chosen of Ivy House dating?" Mr. Tom placed the plate on the table and huffed. "Ridiculous. With your prestige, you'll have your pick. It's as I've told you: you need but wait."

"I don't want someone who's after my magic," I said. "Besides, anyone interested in my magic is going to assume I've been turned young again. They might be put off that I'm not."

"The only thing they'll be put off by is your social awkwardness." Mr. Tom turned and headed back to the island. "Eventually they'll warm up to you."

"He's a real treat," Niamh said, reaching over me and touching the message icon on the screen.

"This isn't a touch screen," I said, clicking in. "The profile has only been up for a few days. There's no way I should have—*Oh my God!*"

The very first message was an erect member of the male persuasion. Grainy and angled, obviously taken as a still life in the heat of the moment with a bad-quality camera, it was one of the worst dick pics I'd ever seen.

And I would know—I'd seen quite a few since entering the world of online dating. "I *hate* this part of dating sites." Disgusted, I trashed it and moved on to the next. "Come on, really? Two in a row? Why do they do this?"

Niamh leaned a little closer, examining. "You've got this all wrong. It's best to see the willy up front. This way, ye don't have to go through all the rigmarole to check out the equipment. Good size? Well then, sure, let's try it out. Too small or big? Keep moving, my dear, I haven't the time."

"It's not the size of the vessel, it is the motion in the ocean," Mr. Tom said.

"That's only what women tell you, ye old goat. They're trying to make you feel better about yerself," Niamh said as I trashed the pic and moved to the next. Yet another one. *Trash.*

"In my prime, they were too speechless to say anything at all." Mr. Tom puffed up in pride.

"I think I just died a little inside," I groaned.

"This many photo peep shows can't be normal." Niamh clicked into the profile section.

"What do you know about it?" Mr. Tom asked, pouring hot water into the teapot.

"I've done a great many of these dating sites for Edgar. Before he got his vitality back, we had to lure his food in under false pretenses. It's easier to get guys on board, o'course, so I did the profile for a younger me." Niamh blinked at the screen, then moved back a bit. "I keep forgetting that Ivy House fixed my eyesight. I'm a new woman."

"Still wretched, sadly," Mr. Tom muttered.

"Ah. Here." She pointed at my list of favorite ways to relax. "You put 'watch Netflix and chill.'"

I nodded. "I figured saying 'watch TV' was dated, Prime isn't as popular, and I just don't see the point in Hulu—Netflix seemed like the obvious winner."

Niamh leaned to the side so she could see my face. "Are ye *jokin'*?"

"What?" I asked.

"'Netflix and chill' means you are looking for sex," Mr. Tom said as though that were common knowledge.

"What's this now?" I asked, staring harder at the words as though they might morph before my eyes.

"Single sex, group sex, dirty sex—"

"Yes, we get it, Niamh." Mr. Tom brought the tea over. "Let's not get carried away."

"Well, clearly she doesn't get it." Niamh hooked a thumb at me.

"That explains the plethora of dick pics," I said softly, trashing the whole lot and clicking in to edit my profile.

"Nope, don't do it that way." Niamh shook her head as she moved back around the table and took her seat. "You'll want to start over. You've ruined the algorithms. They'll send your stuff to the wrong people, now."

"Are you sure?" I asked, hesitating.

"You should trust her," Edgar said from the corner. He'd been so still and quiet that I'd forgotten he was there. "She did a great job of luring men to her. They were so excited, they didn't even notice me sneaking up behind them."

"Edgar doesn't realize that, unlike Janes, Dicks are rarely afraid that a stranger will attack out of the blue," Mr. Tom said, setting the tea tray down on the table. Janes and Dicks were what magical people called non-magical women and men.

"Yes, true." Niamh poured milk into her mug before reaching for the teapot. "Janes are used to being prey. They often have their guard up. Dicks, however—la-dee-da until they have a vampire attached to their necks. They're asleep before they even react."

"Not like our Jessie," Edgar said, beaming with pride. "My eye hurt for the rest of the night. I thought I might lose it."

He was talking about the night he'd bitten me to keep me from discovering the magical world too soon. I'd gouged him in the eye before I succumbed to the sleeping agent of his bite.

"What is all this *shite* in me sandwich?" Niamh nudged the lettuce and tomato off her turkey. "Where's the butter? I bet you didn't put any Irish butter on it, did ye?"

"I used mayonnaise, like a sane person," Mr. Tom said, "and that is a variety of vegetables that enhance the sandwich and are good for even you, you miserable cow. If you're going to eat over here, you're going to eat like a civilized adult."

"Oh now, come on, what have ye got here?" Niamh inspected the inside of the sandwich. "What is this, *mustard*?" She dropped the bread and leaned back. "Thank ye, no. I will not be poisoned. I'll be getting back."

"If only I'd known getting you to leave was as easy as making a *good* sandwich," Mr. Tom said.

"It's actually as easy as pushing your company on me." She headed toward the door. Before she went through, she turned back to me. "You told yer date that you'd meet him at the bar, right? So's I could meet him?"

My stomach flip-flopped again. "I just said we'd meet for a few beers to get to know each other. He's coming from a town over, so it's just an informal meetup. I thought that was—"

Niamh nodded, waved me away, and disappeared into the hall.

"—best for my first time out of the gate," I finished before bending to my sandwich.

"Don't mind her, Jessie, she is a little rough on etiquette. She's out of practice." Edgar smiled at me, gliding to the table. He replaced the bread slice over the turkey, left off the vegetables, and headed for the door. "I'll just take this in case those trespassers are awake. They'll probably stick around if I offer them a refreshment."

Stick around? They were likely trapped in his cottage somewhere. I doubted a sandwich would erase the sting of having been transported to a stranger's house without their knowledge. At least it wasn't a cave, but still.

Mr. Tom shook his head sadly as Edgar left the room. "He means well." He presented his hand, at the end of which, resting on his bare fingers, hung a limp slice of Swiss cheese. "Niamh isn't the only one out of practice. He used to be an excellent hunter. Now he's... Well, Niamh will probably have to return to the dating site for him. I'd forgotten she used to do that." He bent to look at the computer. "Or maybe they can just use your throwaways." After a moment, he shook the cheese at me. "Well? Here. I forgot the cheese. Just tuck that right in there."

No matter how long I was here, things never quite bent toward normal.

I CHECKED MYSELF in the mirror before heading down to the front door. My little black clutch matched my little black dress, which fit much better than I remembered. I'd done my version of a smoky eye, which really just looked like dark eye shadow and ill-placed liner, paired with nude lips and only a touch of blush. My shoes were flat, because I planned to walk and honestly couldn't be bothered with a heel. There was only so far I was willing to go for fashion. Stilts had not made the cut.

Hair messier than I'd like, I put on a shawl (for appearances; I could have been perfectly warm naked in the middle of winter) and set out down the stairs.

"Miss." Mr. Tom met me there, his tux wrinkle-free, his wings hanging down his back like a cape, and his expression still perturbed because I'd unintentionally called in reinforcements (add that to the grievance of not granting him the appearance of youth, and a real list was forming). "Shall you be requiring refreshments this evening?"

He always asked me this when I went out, but this time, I discerned a tone.

"No. It's just a meetup. I won't be bringing him

back with me, Mr. Tom."

"Whether you do or do not is no business of mine. If you do, however, you must remain cautious. Just because you can no longer contract diseases doesn't mean you will not get pregnant. You are not too old to conceive."

My mind stutter-stopped. "What do you mean I can't contract diseases?"

"Magic. It cleanses the blood, in a way. You can't get diseases of any kind. You won't get cancer, you won't get…whatever else Dicks and Janes contract with their weak immune systems."

"But…Niamh said she lost one of her breasts be-cause of breast cancer. You know, before Ivy House magic brought it back."

He gave me a long-suffering look, which he seemed to reserve for discussions with or about Niamh. "She was not being honest. She lost it in the Battle of Five Spades. The enemy pierced her armor, and the golden sword tip lodged in her breast—gold is to her kind what silver is to shifters. Lethal. Losing her mammary gland saved her life. She lopped it right off, I've heard. After killing the enemy, of course. She never mourned its absence. No one else in town shared her view, especially when she walked around downtown wearing a thin white T-shirt, while braless, in the rain. The show she gave was apparently more than anyone cared to see, though I suppose it wouldn't have mattered if she'd had one or both mammary glands in that instance." He straightened up and put an arm behind his back like the ancient butlers in a place like England. "Should you decide to reduce yourself to a Dick's level, there are condoms in the drawer of your never-used night table, the one on the guest's side. Let him put it on—you're clearly unused to the practice and would probably do it incorrectly. There are more in the bathroom. You have plenty to be getting on with, but if you need more, I can go—"

"Oh my God, I'll be fine." I hastened to the door. "I'm good, Mr. Tom. We don't need to be so much in each other's lives."

"As your protector, miss, I must—"

I shut the door. Edging into middle-aged dating was uncomfortable enough; I didn't need help from my ancient, wacky butler. I had to draw the line somewhere.

As I started walking, nervousness coiled within me. Wow, it had been a long time since I'd gone on a first date. A long, *long* time. I had no idea what to expect. The guy I was meeting was a few years older than me, with a couple of teenagers and a steady job as a winemaker, and lived one town over. We had similar interests, and though he was apparently big into crime shows, he also enjoyed comedy. If we went to a movie or something, we'd probably be able to find some common ground.

That was about the extent of what I knew, though. I supposed I could've exchanged a bunch more emails with him before taking the plunge, but I didn't much like getting to know someone via electronic communication. Inflection was missing, as was tone. I had a large propensity for sarcasm—I couldn't have someone mistaking that for genuine concern, because then where would we be?

The windows of Austin's bar shone up ahead, the honeyed glow spilling out onto the sidewalk and highlighting a couple of Harleys parked out in front. A flicker of light caught my attention to the right. A man leaned against a thin tree trunk in front of the closed candy shop, his head bowed over his phone, the light not reaching his face. He glanced up as I passed, his face concealed in the shadow of a flat-billed baseball cap.

A familiar warning sensation crawled down my scalp and over my skin—something I felt whenever I encountered a male stranger lurking in the shadows. I pulled my gaze away, lest he took that as a challenge or as interest, watching instead for movement out of the corner of my eye. I held my breath as I increased the distance between us, speeding up just enough that I'd get out of there faster, but not enough that he saw I was scared and decided he liked chasing prey. I might not technically be prey to people anymore, but old habits died hard.

In a moment, though, he dropped his head back to his phone, uninterested. I let out a relieved breath. He was probably waiting for something, bored, and had decided to check out the chick in the dress as she walked by.

My relief was short-lived.

Up ahead, hanging out outside the bar, sucking on a cigarette and checking out the Harleys, stood my nemesis. He kept trying to annoy and antagonize me in subtle little ways, something he did despite knowing Austin would punch him off his barstool (literally) if he talked trash to me. It had happened on my very first night in town, plus another handful of times in the two or so months since. The guy's name was Ryan, but he didn't deserve the respect of being called his real name, so I'd dubbed him Sasquatch for his shaggy hair and bushy beard, which probably held crumbs and fleas alike. He was clearly as dumb as rocks, and if his vendetta weren't so tragically annoying, it would be hilarious.

He grunted as I neared, the amber of his cigarette

glowing across his bushy unibrow. "What are you doing here? You don't come in on Thursdays," he said.

"Funny, I'd hoped the same thing about you."

"I come in every day."

"Maybe if you had a friend, you wouldn't have to."

"Well, maybe if you had a friend…" His brow furrowed and a constipated look crossed his face. "You'd… You wouldn't…"

I smirked. "Need a little more time for that comeback? Should I check in later and see if you were able to think of anything?"

He flicked his cigarette at me, sparks shedding as it sailed through the air.

"Oh my God, what the hell?" Pain flared on my palm as I slapped it away, a flurry of sparks following its progress. "You've got problems, dude. That hurt."

"You're magical now, apparently. You'll heal."

"Just wait until I know more of my magic. Hopefully you *won't* heal."

He chuckled. "Fat chance, terrorist."

I could do nothing more than stare at him for a moment, shaking my head. What did you even say to that? It had exactly no grounding in reality.

Giving up on our not-so-snappy repartee, I continued on toward the door. At least I wasn't scared of him anymore. Thanks, Ivy House. And thank you, Mr. Tom, who had been teaching me close combat with a knife named Cheryl. It was the same knife I currently had tucked away in my clutch, a light, sleek, spring-loaded blade that required very little pressure to bring springing forth from its lovely teal casing.

Before I could get through the door, Sasquatch stepped in front of me, halting my progress.

"Really?" I asked dryly, half inclined to take Cheryl out for a spin right now.

"Ladies first, which is why you're going last," he said.

"Great, yeah, real snappy put-down, jackass."

"How do ya like me now?"

I gritted my teeth, wondering what I could do. Magically shove him out of the way? Shank him? Wet willie? All were terrible, but I didn't want to start a fight this close to Austin's bar. It was rude, for one, and two, I wasn't one hundred percent positive I would win. I mean…I *thought* I could, but a lifetime of being weaker than my possible attackers made me hesitate. I had a lot of past conditioning to work through before I was ready to start a bar fight. Besides, Austin quelled violence in his bar, regardless of who started it.

Sasquatch took slow, heavy steps, intentionally holding me up, swinging his weight too far from one foot to the next. He'd be easy to knock askew, and then, when he was getting his balance back, probably flailing his arms, it'd be easy to stick something sharp into one of his soft places.

Wow. I'd really retained Mr. Tom's teaching. Clearly I had a violent streak somewhere inside of me, no doubt bulldozed in my twenties so I could better fit in with the mothers and wives and women around me.

Did social conditioning bulldoze away their interesting bits too? I wondered as I followed Sasquatch into the bar, careful to breathe through just my mouth. There was a funk wafting off him that I didn't want invading my world. Maybe we'd all had a fire inside of us, clawing to get out, and we'd kept it at bay to fit into someone else's mold of what we should be as women.

I chewed my lip, thinking. Digressing. I kinda wished I could go back in time and strike up some very different conversations with a few of them.

Maybe we could have encouraged each other to approach life differently, to let out some of that fire. Because it felt pretty damn good, and I couldn't wait until I no longer had to rely on Austin and the others to protect me. Someday I would be the only protection I needed.

"Goals," I muttered, drawing the notice of a younger guy sitting at a small table off to the side. I shrugged. "I only talk to myself when I need an intelligent conversation," I told him, continuing on.

"Nut job," Sasquatch said.

"You should talk," I replied, barely stopping myself from giving him a dig in the ribs.

Sasquatch peeled off to the side, finally getting out of my way. I caught sight of Austin behind the bar, his large shoulders straining the confines of his gray cotton shirt. The fabric stretched down over his robust chest, pulling tight between his pecs and loosening a little over his flat stomach. His cobalt gaze noticed Sasquatch before darting to me—and then back to Sasquatch. His easy posture and relaxed air changed in an instant, and suddenly every muscle in his very impressive body was flexed. He straightened up slowly, and cold shivers zipped down my frame, screaming of danger. Telling me to leave Cheryl where she was, forget my magic—it wouldn't be enough—and race the hell out of there.

Chatter and laughter died down until Austin's presence extinguished it completely. His face—high cheekbones, straight nose, planes and angles that ended in lush lips—morphed from something handsome into something that might be the last thing his enemy saw on Earth. That enemy, at the moment, was Sasquatch.

Sasquatch froze. He tensed for a beat, clearly feeling a challenge, and just as clearly thinking about answering it.

I could feel the whole bar holding its breath. I'd seen Austin in action in wide-open spaces. He was strength and power and incredible brutality that, if set loose in this confined space, would ruin the bar.

I started edging backward.

CHAPTER 4

S ASQUATCH LET OUT a breath...and about-faced. Picking on me wasn't worth facing Austin. He muttered an apology as he made his way out the door. Austin couldn't possibly know what Sasquatch had done, but it was clear he'd identified that *something* had happened, and it was Sasquatch's fault. Suddenly I was glad I hadn't attempted to retaliate.

His silent decree carried out, Austin's demeanor melted back into that of easygoing bar owner, steering his ship and slinging his alcohol.

"You don't need to do that," I said as I approached an open space at the very end of the bar. He met me there, his gaze roaming my face before slipping down over my body.

"You look beautiful, Jess."

"Thanks." I smiled at him, suddenly flustered that the hottest man I'd ever known had complimented me. "Turns out the only nice things in my closet are, like, ten years old. Fits, though, so that's a win. Thanks, Ivy

House."

"Big win. You're going to knock 'em dead." He winked at me.

Face heating and trying not to show how nice that was to hear, I checked the time on my phone. I was only a tiny bit early. I had a feeling my date might already be in the bar.

The Sasquatch incident had temporarily derailed my anxiety, but it returned stronger than before. I stopped myself from looking down the bar, afraid of what I would find.

"You don't need to scare Sasquatch—I mean Ryan—out of here," I said.

"Yes, I do. He was going out of his way to be rude to a lady. He knows better than to do that in my bar."

"Well, if you let him keep it up, maybe he'll get stabbed one of these days…"

A smile wrestled with Austin's lips. "This is true. Can't allow it in the bar, but maybe if you hung around in a less-populated area, like in the shadows along his route to the bar, you could surprise him and I wouldn't be the wiser."

"Meaning…you wouldn't feel pressured to keep the alpha's law and order in this town?"

The grin dripped off his face. "I'm not the alpha of this town."

"Yes, yes, I know, but you know what I mean. If you didn't know about my randomly attacking a member of this town, you wouldn't feel obligated to punish me…"

Confusion and unease stole over his expression. "I don't think I could hurt you if I tried."

"Oh." I twisted my lips to the side, guilt lodging in my gut. "Because of the Ivy House magic?"

His eyes were deep and troubled. He didn't comment.

"Honestly, Austin, I'm trying to find a way out for you. I really am. We all know you were trying to protect me and not the house. Ivy House knows that, too. She—or it, I guess, but I think of it as a she now—can communicate with me after a fashion. She knows she pulled a fast one. She's being a real stubborn butthead about the whole thing, but I'm positive that I can break your attachment to the house once I learn more of my craft. I know I can. You won't be trapped by the magic forever, Austin, and then you can thump on me like you thump on everyone else, don't worry. I'll be super scared of you, just like every other normal Dick you meet." I grinned to show my jest.

He shook his head, a tiny movement that I barely noticed. It was the snap of his magic that had me clicking my teeth shut without meaning to, feeling the command of his power, his presence. I couldn't remember him doing that to me before.

He grimaced. "Sorry, I didn't mean to use my magic just then. I haven't quite mastered controlling my magic around you when it compels me to assert..." He let the thought drift away.

"Your dominance?" I narrowed my eyes. "Not cool, man. I don't want to be ruled any more than you do. One day I might accidentally react negatively to that silent command, and you won't be pleased with the result. Or will you disown me when I have more power than you?"

"You already have more power than me. I can feel it brimming within you, which is why my magic tries to react. It's muscle memory."

"I mean, when I know how to use more power than you."

"My ego isn't fragile, Jacinta. I don't give a damn how much power you have." He paused for a moment, staring at me. I swallowed, not ready for his sudden intensity. "I know that you might accidentally react with magic, which is why I'm trying to train myself. I don't want to set you off when you're not sure what you're doing. I felt that...summons earlier. That's what Niamh called it, anyway. Not the one from Ivy House, which I also felt, but the one from you. I would've texted to see if you were okay, but it didn't feel like it was meant for me…"

"Yeah, that was more unconscious magic. I was gearing up to fall to my death, apparently with the possibility of being run through by Niamh's horn and then smooshing Edgar, when I felt that happen. I thought the house had done it. Mr. Tom is annoyed with me for calling in help, did Niamh tell you? His list of grievances is growing. He's also upset that I'm dating Dicks. The guy is not super pleased about my life choices at the moment, I'll say that much."

Austin grinned, and then his humor drained away. "Listen, Jess, I will continue to ignore Ivy House. I did not agree to work for it, so I won't come at its beck and call. If you need help, though—if *you* call me—I will be there, okay? All you have to do is ask."

"I know," I murmured, warm inside. "I didn't bother you because I didn't think you'd be much help with the whole flying thing. Though…you'd certainly be better at catching me than Edgar."

Austin's brow quirked. "I thought you were jumping from up high?"

"Yeah. Third floor. Edgar thought he'd be able to save the day if my wings didn't show."

"But…" He paused with a semi-open mouth and a confused expression. Whatever question he had, though, dissolved, and he shook his head. I agreed—*no words.*

"Anyway," he said, "I'll try to walk on eggshells until you've got your bag of tricks under control."

"And after?"

"After you have complete control?" A smug grin pulled at his lips and his blue eyes glittered. "I won't pull any punches. We'll see who comes out on top."

Excitement sparked deep within me, coursing through my blood. That was a challenge if ever I'd heard one. He didn't want to be ruled, I didn't want to be ruled, but trying to rule each other?

"You're on," I said with a grin to match his. "Say goodbye to your king-of-the-mountain status. It's time for a queen around these parts."

He huffed out a laugh. "We'll see. Anyway, we can talk about how I'll dominate you later…"

A flash of unfettered heat stole my breath. I looked away, not ready for it.

Most of the time, I liked being in the friend zone with Austin. He had his hang-ups, and I had mine. He wanted to live a solitary life, and I didn't want to embarrass myself with the hot local bar owner that I would see all the time. Both of us needed a good friend—a close friend that we could be open with—and we'd each found that person in each other.

Sometimes, though, his hotness blasted through all

my defenses and seared me alive. He would be a wild ride. A wild, scorching-hot, sweaty-sheeted, delicious-bodied ride…

"You okay?" he asked.

I fanned my face. "Yep. Just nervous about my date. Is he here, do you know?"

His glance down the bar said it all. He pushed away, grinning, and moved to help someone.

"Crap," I muttered, checking my watch again. Now five minutes late. Time to officially show up.

I tapped the bar with my nails and thought about pulling a runner. Mr. Tom was right. Me and this guy would never work—I was now magical and he was not. Our worlds were different, and that would never change.

I had to start somewhere, though. He was level one in my dating life. If I chickened out this time, I'd have to start at the same level—I couldn't jump to level two.

Leaving wouldn't accomplish anything. But that didn't mean I had to go in totally blind.

"Austin," I whisper-shouted across two middle-aged guys with their hands wrapped around their brown bottles. They halted their stilted conversation and leaned back uncomfortably. I leaned with them so as not to be seen by anyone at the other end of the bar. "Austin!"

Austin took a twenty from someone down the way and glanced at me. I gestured him closer.

His saunter looked loose and confident, like he had a line on a horse that was going to make him a millionaire. That, or he knew of a joke that he couldn't wait to see play out.

I was the joke. I hoped to hell my date wasn't the punch line.

"What's he like?" I asked as he came closer, still mostly whispering.

Austin leaned against the bar with one hand, his muscles popping out through his plain shirt. "He's exactly what you'd expect from online dating."

I grimaced. I didn't know what that meant, but I assumed it wasn't good. "What sort of guy is he?"

"And ruin the surprise?" He winked, that action always upping his level of hotness. I was certain he knew it, just like he understood the impact of his muscle shows. The plain shirt made his very opposite of plainness more noticeable.

I met that wink with a scowl. "He's not dangerous, right? Nice guy?"

"Not dangerous, no. You would've been fine without the magic." He turned toward the cash register. "Middle of the bar. Blue dress shirt."

"Good luck," the guy next to me said, and lifted his

beer in a salute. His buddy followed.

"Right, sure, yeah. Thanks." I stepped back from the bar and cautiously headed to the middle, looking at the backs as I did so. Since this bar was mostly full of magical people, most were in good shape. They might not do much fighting these days—Austin had ensured O'Briens was a safe haven for magical misfits—but they apparently lived in a state of readiness in case their pasts came back to haunt them.

...wide back in black...thin but muscular back in red...toned female back in purple...a little padding covering a powerful body in a very bright orange sweater that would fade after the first wash...

I stopped as I reached the blue dress shirt loosely draped over a much softer body than I remembered from his profile pictures. Gray-white hair created a horseshoe around a balding, shiny head that also did not match the pictures I'd seen, his hair different in both color and plenitude. Large love handles worked to escape the straining brown belt on the gray slacks.

This person did not scream "middle-aged and in great shape" like he'd very clearly identified himself on his dating profile and showed in his—obviously quite dated—profile pictures. I wasn't expecting a bodybuilder, but "athletic" seemed to mean something different to him than it did to me.

Two seats beyond him, Niamh glanced back at me. Without a word, she shifted back toward the bar. I didn't know if that was good or bad. Maybe she was just giving me my privacy…for the first time ever.

"Um…" I inched closer, scanning to make sure my date couldn't be anyone else. No one else wore a blue dress shirt, but maybe Austin had been confused. I could only hope. I inched closer still. "Gary?"

The man straightened up and half turned, revealing loose jowls and a collection of wrinkles. His dull, watery eyes brightened when he saw me, and his gaze did a sweep, similar to Austin's.

"Oh, wow." His yellowed smile revealed crooked teeth, yet another discrepancy from his profile. What else hadn't he mentioned? Knowing how to work a little magic with Photoshop?

He struggled off the stool, his movements stiff. "Hel-lo!" He laughed and moved in for a hug.

"Oh…" I tried not to grimace as his arms encircled me. I patted his back, stiffening.

"You look even better than your picture! You don't see that very often," he said with a toothy grin, gesturing to the open stool next to him. "I'm so used to women lying about their weight, you know? They say *fit*, but…" He gave me a long look as he struggled back into his seat, indicating these women clearly didn't live

47

up to his expectations. Once seated, he sighed and looked around. "Boy, am I relieved. I figured, since you wanted to meet at a bar—*sit* at the bar, no less—that you must be one of *those* women." He widened his eyes, his brown peepers swimming in white for a moment. He must've seen my "confused, bordering on annoyed" expression. "Bar bunnies, you know? The kind at the end of their rope, grasping at straws, desperate for a man..." He laughed. "But that's not you at all, is it?" His grin said we were sharing a joke of some kind.

I couldn't even form a response. This madness was coming at me so fast that I wasn't sure what to do with it. Surely there were a few sarcastic remarks I could've fit in there somewhere, but first I had to come to terms with the fact that he'd chosen to talk like this to anyone, let alone to a perfect stranger on a first date.

"But no, look at you," he said, more seriously, his gaze appreciative. The needle on my creep-o-meter started waggling toward the red zone. "You're nice and trim. You keep yourself up." He turned to flag a bartender, waving at Paul, a guy in his mid-twenties who seemed timid for a shifter. "That's important. So many women your age let themselves go. It's tragic."

Still trying to unpack all of this, I stared at him in disbelief. This guy was worried about finding a woman who kept herself up, but he clearly didn't hold himself to the same standard. What, he expected to find a girlfriend with no tummy and probably great tits while he sported a big tummy and matching tits? Like…who was he trying to kid? Talk about throwing rocks in a glass house. I hoped the shards struck his jugular.

Was it too late to pull that runner?

"She's just gotten here and already this date has gone tits up," Niamh said.

So much for respecting my privacy.

"Say the word, and he ends up in an unmarked grave," the man between Niamh and me, a guy I had never met, said softly, facing straight ahead. Very sly. "I'm good to help, if you want. Say the word. That guy is a joke. You should invite him outside and then ring his bell. Dicks just don't get it."

My date's elevated voice rang out across the bar, authoritative and demanding. He was clearly annoyed he hadn't already been seen to regardless of the fact that both Paul and Austin were helping other people. Either that, or he was trying to show off for me.

If it was the latter, boy was he in the wrong bar. I didn't dare warn him, though. I kind of wanted to see how it would all play out, while also wanting to knife myself to escape this horrible foray into dating life.

"Hey," he barked, "can I have another gin and tonic here, and a…" He turned to me as Paul finished up and hurried over.

"Glass of Pinot Noir," I murmured.

"Which one?" Paul asked. "We have two now, since you like that kind so much."

"Oh…" I pulled the wine list to me, looking for the options.

After a silent beat, Gary moved his hand in a circle to hurry me up. "Come on now, don't take all day. Women!" I glanced up in time to see him rolling his eyes at Paul exaggeratedly. "They can never make up their minds."

His condescending chuckle drop-kicked something deep inside of me. How many times had I been minimized because of my sex? How many times had a man reduced me to some clichéd version of an indecisive female, or a bad driver, or a hysterical woman, because I didn't have a penis to swing around and constantly fiddle with? They had always done it as if to say, "Aren't they all the same? As men, we just have to humor them. It's our lot in life, sadly. Can't live with them, can't kill them, am I right?"

I hated the grating laughter that always seemed to follow. Laughter like this clown was currently exhibiting. It seemed to establish a *them versus us* mentality, with me on the outside. Me as the *lesser*.

Fire kindled in my belly.

Grab life by the balls. Raise your voice until you are heard.

Only, I had no idea what to say. I had no idea how to combat something like this, aside from knifing him. I'd always been taught to react to such "jokes" with a silent smile, to act like *boys would be boys* even though the belittling made me quail inside.

"I got hers, Paul," Austin said as he approached. He placed a clean wine glass in front of me, his gaze heavy on mine. He was checking in, I knew. Ever my knight, my guide when I didn't know how to be strong. I couldn't tell by his expression if he knew I was thinking about the burly guy's offer and Cheryl's willingness...

Austin pulled the cork out of a bottle and reached for the glass.

"Whoa, whoa." My anger and annoyance momentarily took a back seat. Sometimes wine sat around forever in this place. He'd poured me the equivalent of grape vinegar a few times. "How long has that been open?"

A blue-sleeved arm reached into my vision, and Gary's damp hand grasped my forearm. "I'm sure it's fine," he said. "Just take it."

I knew he was reacting to Austin's natural predatory dominance, sensing the hierarchy and falling in line so as not to upset the rather large man with lots of muscle and crazy eyes, but his attempt to subdue me just added coal to my locomotive.

I gritted my teeth and sweat coated my forehead. My fingers tingled and I wasn't sure why, but I *was* sure his hand was in the wrong place, as was the muzzle he was trying to place on me.

Before I could turn—before I could even speak—Austin leaned forward with such unspeakable malice that I, strangely, felt a little relief from the furnace raging within me. His gaze beat into Gary's face as he somehow poured the glass without looking. Add that amazing party trick to his long list of talents.

"Opened when you sat down," Austin growled, the roughness of his voice spreading a crazy, primal fear through my body.

Run! Run now! it screamed.

Out of the corner of my eye, I could just see the burly guy next to me get up and walk off toward the pool and bathroom area. Beyond him, Niamh had both hands clasped on the bar and a determined expression on her face. She felt Austin's power and was actively trying to ward it off.

"Yes, well, th-that's wh-why I told her to take it," Gary stammered. "Did you hear me? I told her—"

"I heard you. It is not a man's job to police his date. It is his job to make her comfortable and show her a good time. So far, you're failing. Try harder." Austin turned away. Not a drop had been spilled.

Paul landed in a moment later with the gin and tonic. "Sir," he said, and then scampered off.

I reached for my glass as Gary turned to me, face red with anger and embarrassment from being put in his place. Austin's ego might not be fragile, but this guy's sure was. "Well, now do you see?" Spittle slapped my face.

That was about all I could take. Time to see what I was made of, and how quickly I could make him run from this bar. If he wanted a kiss good night, that kiss would be from Cheryl's spring-loaded blade.

CHAPTER 5

"JESSIE, YE GOTTA walk away now," Niamh said before I could let him have it. "You're on the edge, girl. The whole bar can feel it, just you trust me. If ye accidentally do another summons for help, I'm not sure we'll like what shows up from this send-off. Walk away. Let Austin Steele sort this out. This type of thing is what the big lummox is good fer." Her voice reduced to a mutter. "Lord help us if someone is sneaking around Ivy House tonight. That el' house will feed off your mood and flay those poor bastards alive. Edgar will go hungry, and then he'll wander around the town with his weird smile and hunched body and the cops will come callin'. I couldn't be botherin' with them tonight, sure I couldn't."

I hesitated, because I knew Niamh was speaking in my best interest (and also her own). Usually she'd egg me on, hoping for violence. Given she was forgoing a show and talking about Ivy House getting violent because we were connected, and Edgar *did* say it fed off my emotions…

"If you'd just taken the wine like I—"

I held up my finger, and when Gary wouldn't stop muttering about my perceived shortcomings, I talked over him.

"It was nice meeting you. I think we both know this isn't going to work, and it's not just because you seriously lied on your profile. Update your pictures, bud. This is one step away from catfishing. If you weren't doing such a bad job of it, I'd wonder if you were trying to land someone for your vampire friend—"

"And that's your cue, Jessie," Niamh said.

"Yup." Couldn't talk about vampires to normal folk. Whoops.

"Just one minute, here," Gary started, but I was already walking away.

It wasn't until I was to the end of the bar, almost to the opening that separated this part of the bar from the pool table area, that the true nature of the situation dawned on me. I slowed, Gary's shocked and frustrated chatter fading into the background.

The bar area had all but cleared out, only a few people lingering at the edges in booths or at tables, their eyes down and bodies hunched over their mostly empty glasses. Drinks littered the bar surface in various stages of fullness, abandoned by their owners. Even the two guys at the other end had walked away, leaving their beers behind.

So focused on Gary and the horror show of my first date, I had somehow missed the mass exodus.

Blinking in confusion, I resumed making my way out, leaving Austin to sort it out as Niamh had requested. I had a suspicion he wasn't the only one who'd lay into the guy. Niamh would want her say, I had no doubt.

A crowd loitered in the pool room, watching the balls roll around the green felt. When I entered, most looked up, then quickly back down, as though some gunslinger had entered the saloon and they didn't want no trouble.

"Sorry," I muttered, knowing I was to blame for Austin's second assertion of dominance in less than an hour.

"Hey…" The burly guy that had been sitting next to me shrugged his meaty shoulders, standing off to the side with his hands in his pockets. "If you got it, flaunt it."

Those around him shifted from side to side and murmured their assent, heads bobbing.

If I got it…flaunt it?

I checked my boobs as I turned toward the bathroom. The cut of my neckline barely plunged, showing next to no cleavage. Sure, I had spaghetti straps, but so what? Last I checked, a little shoulder didn't drive anyone crazy. My hem stopped right above my knee, very modest. It was a *Mom's night out* dress if ever there was one, down to the fact that it didn't fit exactly right. I wasn't flaunting anything.

I was clearly missing something, but at that moment, I didn't care what it was. I shook my head and pushed into the bathroom, taking my place behind two women in jeans and flannel.

"Excuse me." The woman in front of me moved out of the way.

"Oh." I pointed at the two occupied stalls. "You're not waiting?"

"No, no. Go ahead." She gestured me on and fell in behind me.

After a step forward, the woman at the head of the line gave me a tight smile. "Here." She stepped out of the way as someone came out of the larger stall.

"Oops. Sorry! I didn't mean to take so long." A younger woman, who *did* have a plunging neckline and a hem that lazily tapped her very upper thighs, quickly scooted out of the way.

"No worries," I said, admiring her sparkly sequins as I slipped past.

For the first time in...*years*, I actually wanted to try

something like that. Something a little loud and a little *look at me, world, here I am!* I used to wear stuff like that all the time when I was in my twenties. After my body had morphed into a holding cell for a human and then refused to bounce back, I'd gravitated toward darker clothes and blacks for the slimming qualities. I'd started aiming for modest attire, something I thought better suited my age.

But if Niamh could walk around town braless in a white T-shirt in a rainstorm, not at all worried what people thought, why couldn't I opt for some color? Black was great, but so was the sparkly sequin extravaganza on that woman. I'd need it a little longer because I didn't have the presence of mind to watch myself as I bent over (I'd flash the whole world, repeatedly), but what was stopping me from going for it? People's reactions?

An uncomfortable feeling coiled in my belly as I closed myself in the stall.

Honestly, yes, it was people's reactions. It was the fear that I'd get condescending looks if I stepped out of my lane or shrugged off my mantle of midlife modesty. That I'd get judged or sneered at or maybe even pitied if I showed off a little cleavage, a little leg, and a lot of personality. "Look at that woman, Janice! Good Lord, she is too old for a dress like that. Poor dear is trying too hard to cling to her youth."

Time to be brutally honest with myself. The fictional jerks I was imagining weren't the problem. *I* was the only one holding me back. So people might think I was too old to have some style—so what? I didn't give two craps what people thought about me when I dressed like some sort of swamp monster. Why should I hesitate to wear the equivalent of a sexy disco ball?

I shouldn't, that was the bottom line. I shouldn't let the Garys of the world push me down or treat me badly, and I shouldn't cave to people's expectations of women my age. Distinguished with a side of crazy fabulous, here I came!

When I worked up the confidence, that was. Rome wasn't built in a day, after all.

Finished up, I exited the stall to find the same women who'd let me in front of them. One of them, now the next in line, gave me a tight smile and passed me into the stall. The other waited for whoever was taking their time in the occupied stall.

Had they let me go first because they feared (somewhat correctly) that middle-aged women couldn't hold their bladders? Except one of them was at least as old as I was.

Confusion growing, I washed my hands and made my way out. Gazes found me as I re-entered the pool room, which had essentially become a waiting room. Almost immediately, the gazes zipped away again.

The burly guy from the bar was leaned up against the wall on the opposite side of the opening.

"Do you know if the…Dick—the non-magical guy—left?" I whispered.

"Dick can be used in a couple ways with that guy. How the hell did you find him? He was a real gem."

"Clearly I am too gullible when it comes to online dating."

"Ah. Yeah, that explains it. Online dating can be a nightmare, I hear. The undesirables can hide their little peccadilloes until they get you in person." The burly guy stepped sideways, to the very edge of the door-frame, before curving around and looking through. "All clear." He gave me a thumbs-up. "Guess I don't need to go borrow a shovel from my neighbor."

I grinned as I sighed. This town did like to joke about unmarked graves.

"Cool." I looked around the room. No one moved. "What's everyone waiting for, then? Does Austin need a cooling-off period or something?"

The guy studied his shoes. "Don't expect so. He's pretty clean about taking out the trash. Austin Steele takes care of this stuff all the time."

"Right." I nodded, chewing my lip. "Sooo…"

"Jessie, wine's getting old," Niamh hollered from within. "It's turning to sludge before me eyes."

"Vinegar," Austin said.

"Sludge, vinegar, whatever. Would ye come on, Jessie? You must be chokin'. Come and get a drink."

I hooked a thumbs-up at the burly guy, which he probably didn't see, given he'd returned to studying his shoes, contorted my face in an expression that would have loudly declared my social awkwardness had anyone been looking, and returned to my stool.

Austin waited in front of a thankfully empty seat devoid of a gin and tonic and a guy I hoped to never see again. My wine sat where I'd left it, as did all the abandoned drinks from the people in the pool room.

"Austin, I have to hand it to you," I said as I hovered behind my stool. "You can really clear a room. You might give them the all-clear, though. They're just waiting in the other room, not drinking."

"Here. Jessie, sit next to me. Logan can move." Niamh pushed the burly guy's drink away.

"Oh no, I'll just—"

"It'll be grand," Niamh said. "He won't mind."

Austin studied me as he switched the positions of my glass and Logan's beer, again without looking.

"It's not my all-clear to give," Austin finally said as Niamh gulped down some cider.

I lifted my eyebrows as I switched seats. "Why? Does this fall on me because I invited Gary here? I said I was sorry when I went in the other room, but the guy— Logan—gave me a weird response." When they both stayed silent, I put up my hands. "I'm going to be honest, I'm lost. Did I cross a line by inviting a Dick here? Because I figured anyone was allowed in, and I just wanted—"

"*You* need to allow everyone back in the room," Austin said in a low, even voice.

"After that," Niamh said, "let's chat about exactly how utter shite you are about choosing dates online, because I have to hand it to ye—"

Austin held up his hand, and Niamh's mouth clicked shut, which meant she must have gotten one of Austin's whip cracks of power (I'd yet to find anything else that would silence her). Her expression crumpled into a scowl.

"Okay, I realize you mean magically," I told Austin, "but for the record, I'm still not clear on what's happening. I don't know why it's my job."

He braced himself against the edge of the bar, his arms flaring with muscle and his eyes fixed on me. "A wave of power swept the bar, urging—no, commanding—everyone to scatter. A magic unlike any I have ever felt called me to arms beside you. Called Niamh. Why

Mr. Tom—Damn it." A vein in his jaw flared as he gritted his teeth. "Why *Earl* hasn't come barging in, I don't know—maybe you kept it localized. It didn't seem to reach the people on the outskirts of the bar area. Whatever you did, Jess, you had everyone fleeing this space faster than I ever have in my life. They are waiting out there because that is where you put them—out of harm's way. Out of the action. There they will probably stay until you release your hold."

The world spun. My head felt light. I blinked into that steady cobalt gaze more than was natural. It was hard to believe him, because I hadn't felt anything, not a single thing. If I'd used that much magic, wouldn't I know? A strange pulse had come with the summons.

And then a memory surfaced of my fingers tingling. That was all I'd felt, just anger and tingling fingers. The implications were troubling—if I could pull off magic like that without even trying, without even knowing I was doing anything, what else could I do by mistake?

"Are you positive it was me?" I asked quietly.

"Yes," he said, just as quietly, comforting. "We're probably in the most dangerous time for you. I hope we are, at any rate. Unlike mages or shifters or most other magical beings, you didn't have the benefit of growing slowly into your magic—of learning it by trial and error in relative safety. Instead, you were given a large dose of magic upfront, are steadily working into a huge dose that will possibly trump all other magics in the world, and have zero instruction."

"She has plenty of instruction—we were talking about this earlier," Niamh said. "She has a senile vampire who found a magical book among the petunias that he can barely decipher. I'd say that's her sorted."

"You are reacting to your surroundings, as you always have," Austin said, "but now your feelings are manifesting magically. Thankfully, you have a shining character and a good heart, because you sent everyone to safety while you handled what you deemed a threat against you. It's what I would've done. Actually, this situation provided you with some good, low-stakes practice. A greater threat would have yielded a stronger reaction, and given you are not in direct control…"

"Anything could have happened, and we might not have been enough to set it to rights," Niamh finished.

"And here I was worried about dealing with annoying old dudes and wearing sexy disco-ball dresses," I murmured.

"You shouldn't worry about either of those things. One you handled just fine, and the other…" That vein flared again, and Austin pushed back from the bar, his eyes intense.

"Would look absolutely lovely on ye," Niamh said.

"That, or it'd look like a clown suit. But sure, I can see you pulling that off, too. Ye have the jokes for it, like."

I gave her a flat look. "Thanks."

"Let them back in, Jess, and we'll talk about it." Austin jerked his head at the pool room.

"Sure, yeah, except I have no idea how."

"Remember how you call Earl when he's in his stone form?" Austin said. "You just think about what you want from him, right?"

"Ye've gotten good at that one." Niamh pushed her empty glass forward for a refill. "That gobshite is changing in and out all the time these days, wantin' to fly for this and that. He's a little too excited, if ye ask me. It's gone straight to his head and corroded what's left of his brain."

"Give them the all-clear, Jess," Austin said, magic riding his words, a command hidden in their depths.

Instead of wanting to resist, like earlier, I fell into his power and command, letting him guide me. He might not have officially signed up for the alpha role, but he was a master at leading the people in this town. He could curb their behavior or bolster them, depending on what was needed to create a thriving magical society. I could learn a great deal from him, even if I just applied it to the current protectors of Ivy House. Getting Niamh and Mr. Tom to stop bickering would take all of what Austin knew, I was pretty sure.

I was lucky to have him for leadership, Niamh for battle strategy, Edgar for hunting lessons (I'd insisted he stick to theory) and reading that book's instructions, and Mr. Tom for managing the house (and me) and teaching me close combat. That was a great start, but I still needed someone who knew something, *anything* about the practical application of my magic. Someone who could guide me to use it in increments—like the people who'd grown up with magic had learned to use their abilities. And I needed a safe place in which to learn, away from a bar full of people I, thankfully, hadn't harmed *this* time, because in the future I might not get so lucky.

I'd always been a quick study. I was confident that with a little more insight and hands-on instruction, I could really roll with this thing. I *would* really roll with it. I'd stomp on the Garys of the world, I'd wear disco dresses with confidence, and I'd handle my magic like a champ.

Like I said, goals.

A blast of magic concussed the air and flowed out of me like a wave, rolling out of the bar and across the town and beyond, spreading out like the magical force from earlier. This one felt a little different, but I knew it was doing the same as the last. Summoning aid.

"Ah, Christ, she's after doin' it again." Niamh shook her head. "Don't tell Earl, or he'll moan something awful."

"He would've felt that," Austin said, his expression grim.

Those in the pool room started returning to the bar. At least I'd managed that bit.

"Yeah, I s'pose," Niamh replied. "Austin Steele, soon we're going to get visitors. Lord only knows what kind." She tapped her empty glass. "Get me a whiskey, will ya? I'm goin'ta get pissed. No need to face the future sober."

CHAPTER 6

AUSTIN SAT IN his Jeep at the curb in front of Ivy House, staring straight ahead with his hands on the wheel, his knuckles white. He'd gotten as far as shutting off the engine.

He'd sworn he would never answer a magical summons from this house.

And there'd been many of them since the house had claimed him as one of its protectors. He'd ignored every single one. It didn't matter how strong they were: if they were beating, or throbbing, or pulsing deeply within him, he'd shouldered his resolve and resisted the pull.

Until now, a week after Jess had shown up at his bar to meet the world's worst online date.

He stared down the street as the sunlight seeped from the sky. No snow covered the ground, but the dropping temperatures suggested a light dusting wasn't far off. No tourists sauntered down the sidewalk toward the old, Gothic-style house. Few people visited at this time of year, and those who did would prefer to drink inside than take walks in the cold.

Usually Niamh would still be manning her rocking chair on her porch, her pile of stones orderly and within arm's reach. That woman had great aim and good distance. The police had shown up dozens, maybe hundreds, of times to warn her away from throwing rocks at people...

It was a wonder they never arrested her for it, although she typically only targeted curious tourists (Earl being the exception). Most of the trouble in this town came from visitors, or at least the trouble the human police were expected to fix, so maybe the officers were grateful to her for scaring off strangers. Hard to say.

Niamh's absence meant she was otherwise occupied. Austin had come from the bar and her usual seat was empty. She didn't shop, preferring to pay people to deliver groceries, therefore she must be at Ivy House.

Had she gotten the normal command, the one he was so good at ignoring, or had hers been a plea, too? A desperate need for help.

Begging.

He let out a breath, willing himself to start up his Jeep and head out. He was nearly positive the summons hadn't come from Jess, but the change in potency, and the genuine worry he could feel riding the wave...

He let out an agonized breath.

It had sunk down deeply and grabbed the roots of him.

If Jess was in some kind of trouble, he wanted to help. She was fighting for her place in this life, and he'd be damned if he'd turn his back on her. He wanted her to succeed with everything in him. She'd been forced to start over, and instead of slinking away like he'd done, hiding in a small town that posed absolutely no challenge for his skill set and experience, she'd reached for the stars.

It was commendable. *She* was commendable. She'd shown him that life didn't end in the middle—chances could still be taken, new opportunities embraced.

Seeing her accept her new role, and all the baggage that came with it, had inspired him to make changes of his own. Once she was squared away and safe, whether the house released him or not, he'd move on and finally become the alpha he was meant to be. He'd start again, and this time he'd do it right.

The huge house sat within its magical shroud of shadow, pushed back from the street and laughing at him. It had figured out the right tactic to get him to do its bidding.

He hated that damn house.

"Is this the way to madness?" he asked himself in the quiet Jeep. "Is pitting oneself against a magical but ultimately inanimate object what made the others crack?"

Because cracked they had. None of the other guardians could be mistaken for sane, and he might be well on his way to joining them.

Another throb of desperation rattled through him from the house, from Jessie—or at least *about* Jessie—breaking him down beat by excruciating beat.

"Fine." He stepped out of the Jeep, still no doors or top regardless of the season. He never felt the cold. "You win this battle, but I will win the war."

And now he was talking out loud to a house.

Shaking his head, he muttered, "So help me God, if I start asking people to randomly call me by a different name, that's it. I'm out." He walked up the drive, glancing around to make sure no one was around to witness his one-sided conversation.

Blooming flowers leading to the large front door saturated the air with a lovely fragrance. Edgar's prowess as a vampire might've faded with time, but his green thumb surely hadn't suffered. Austin didn't think vampires had any magical growing power—if anything, it seemed like the opposite would be true—but no other flowers were blooming in town, it being winter. He must've done something to keep these in a constant state of springtime.

One foot on the tweed mat, he put his fist up to knock, ignoring the iron gargoyle-head knocker.

The knob turned, and the door slowly swung open. No one stood inside.

If tourists really knew what this house was capable of, no way would they come looking.

Fighting the heebie-jeebies, he stepped across the threshold and looked around the empty and silent space. Two doorways on either side led to front-facing sitting rooms, both empty. Beyond, two empty stairwells curved up to the second floor, forming an archway, through which an empty hallway led to the back of the house.

"Okay, then," he said into the hush. "You've let me in—now tell me where to go."

He waited a moment for something to happen. Regardless of the magic running through its veins, though, it was still just a house, not a person. It couldn't talk. It couldn't point.

"Thought so," he said, about to go find Jess when a sound from the second floor caught his attention. It sounded like small feet shuffling against wood, then carpet—and it was moving closer.

Something unseen crept down the stairs.

Uncomfortable shivers skated across his skin. He remembered the sort of defenses this house had enacted when they'd gone to battle to take it back. Maybe it couldn't talk and point, but it could certainly kill those who did.

He took another couple steps so the banister no longer obstructed his view.

"*Fu—*" He jumped and quickly scooted back when he saw what was hobbling down the stairs.

He hadn't seen these when they were first unleashed, and they'd been hidden away by the time he returned to the house. Now he understood why Jess was afraid for her life.

"Okay, okay," he said, backing up quickly. "You've proven yourself."

A large doll, its exact height hard to judge but probably topping out at his thigh, worked its way down the stairs. The little girl's face, made of a different material than the plastic of the limbs, had rosy cheeks and a pouting mouth, twisted up as if she were about to cry. It looked like someone had ripped a child out of the nineteenth century, shrunk her, and stuck her in a dreamscape.

Saying it was haunting did not do it justice.

He stood tall when it reached the bottom, showing no fear, as befitted someone of his rank. Its little face tilted up to him, and it was all he could do not to grimace and kick it away. The doll pointed down the hall.

"Overkill," he muttered to himself.

He got it. The house could point.

He took a step in the way the doll indicted, but it toddled forward, like a two-year-old. He couldn't hold back the grimace this time. This whole house needed to be set on fire.

Down the hall the doll hobbled, its little feet, stuffed in plastic white shoes, making soft clacking noises as it went. On the rugs he heard its pitter-patter and committed it to memory. He didn't know what these monsters were capable of, but if things ever turned, he wanted to be prepared.

Near the back of the house, he hesitated. He didn't have a clear map of this place, but he did know a few of the prominent rooms, one of which was the Council Room, a space for the house's heir to hold court, or so Earl had said. Jess would eventually lead her twelve chosen, the best and the brightest magical people in the world. Again, so Earl had said. Austin had no idea where she planned to lead them, or in what. The fact that Earl himself was part of the circle made the whole system suspect. Though Austin supposed only a person with a guaranteed spot would have been willing to loiter around the empty house for years, waiting for an heir who might or might not show up.

Austin had only glimpsed the room once, before Jess had come to town. He'd come over to check the place out, allowed in by Earl, but a terrible sickness had washed over him as soon as he crossed the threshold of this room. He'd barely made it outside to throw up. Earl hadn't been long in shutting the door after him.

Only pleasant feelings radiated through Austin as he approached it now. Warmth, acceptance, and welcome.

Jaw aching from how tightly he was clenching it, he followed the doll until it stopped at the door. It bowed to him, of all things, before retreating from the door and scooting past him.

He gave it plenty of room.

Standing in the doorway, not wanting to cross the threshold in case the house got any more notions regarding his involvement, he looked inside and saw Jess standing in the center of a circle of ornate, high-backed wooden chairs. She stared at the wall opposite him, utterly still. Her hair was in a high ponytail that had let as much hair escape as it had kept contained. Her formfitting jeans hugged her curves, and her red hoodie collected just above her muscular butt.

"Hi," she said without looking.

"Hey," he answered, drawing her eyes as she turned around.

She gave him a once-over, her gaze lingering on his

chest. "Nice shirt. That's a good look for you."

He glanced down at his snug white shirt. The only thing he could say for it was that it was clean and wrinkle-free. "Thanks. I was just escorted by one of your dolls."

She shivered. "I've managed to get rid of two of them, but Mr. Tom keeps catching me before I can burn them in the yard. Once I'm better with this magic..." She drew her finger across her throat.

A chuckle bubbled out of him. She was utterly serious about burning the horror-show dolls, and something about that tickled his funny bone. The mirth was short-lived. He'd been right to come. Something was bothering her, the worry of it creasing her face and hanging heavy in her eyes.

"Do you need me for anything?" he asked. "Are you going to try flying again soon?"

She sighed and trudged out of the circle of chairs, her back bowed in defeat. "You can't help me with flying. I'm supposed to train with Edgar and Mr. Tom this afternoon, but we don't need you for that. To be honest, I doubt we'll get very far with the book. Edgar is in the middle of a tricky passage that he can't quite make out. The book is written in all five languages that he knows, mixed together, with one of those being Sanskrit. It's such a stupid way to divulge information.

It takes him forever to translate, then make sense of it. In fairness, though, I doubt anyone else could do it. He's very patient. Regardless, I'll probably just practice close combat with Mr. Tom while Edgar scratches his head." She stopped at the window, not taking a seat in one of the two chairs facing a little wooden table, and looked out at the garden beyond.

"Not going well overall, huh?"

"No, which would be fine—I don't mind easing into all of this—but…" She shook her head. "I don't know."

"What do you need, Jess?" he asked softly, stepping into the room despite himself and standing at her side. "I'm here to help."

Her eyebrows rose and then fell. "Either you have excellent timing, or Ivy House finally got to you, huh?"

This was why he'd come. She didn't like asking for help, but she'd take it if someone offered. The house clearly knew that about her, too.

"What do you need?" he repeated.

She shook her head again and tucked a cluster of hair behind her ear. "At the moment, nothing, it's just…" She shrugged. "Remember when we first met and you said you were really good at reading people?"

"Yes."

"And remember those summons I sent out last week?"

"Uh-huh."

"Well…" She put her hands on her shapely hips. "It feels like they're coming. I can't explain how, it just feels… Honestly, it feels like danger. It feels like whatever is answering my summons is going to be dangerous."

"We'll handle it."

"Right, well, that's just it. I'm not worried about you handling the town. You've got that locked down. Whoever is coming is basically showing up to work with me. *I* need to handle it. I need to be strong enough to lead, or possibly combat, a dangerous person. Maybe dangerous people."

"And you're scared you won't be able to do it?"

"I'm scared I *can't*, Austin. You saw what happened in the bar. I have plenty of power, sure, but I don't know how to work it. It comes in random bursts, either by accident or when Edgar finally figures out a passage in that book. If someone dangerous waltzes in here, throwing their weight around, I'm not sure how I'll handle it. Niamh and the others can probably fight them off, if it comes down to that, but that's not going to win us any loyalty." She paused for a moment. "I know you can teach me about leadership, but there's just no time. This is happening soon, and I don't think I'm ready. The little magic I know probably won't be

enough for the type of presence I feel coming. I'm..."
She took a deep breath. "I'm not happy to admit it, but
since things might start heating up... I'm not so confident, Austin. I want to be strong and dominate my role
here, but...I'm nervous I won't be enough. That the
house chose poorly."

It hadn't. He knew she'd blow everyone away, but
she didn't need someone to tell her that. She needed
someone to understand. "It's okay to be nervous," he
said, "and it's okay to not feel up to leading yet. You
have to walk before you run."

"I'm still at the 'lying on my stomach' stage of development, actually. My next goal is crawling."

He rubbed her back, her warmth seeping into his
touch. "I'm here, okay? I have experience in leading.
Obviously you don't need my help with Niamh and the
others, but if new people show up, you can count on
me. I will put them in their place until you're ready to
step up and take over. You know my past—you know I
won't try to usurp power. Eventually, hopefully, I won't
be able to."

Her grin was slight, but she leaned into his touch,
taking the comfort he offered. Yes, this was why the
house had begged him. Jess desperately needed help and
hadn't felt comfortable enough to ask for it. He was
happy he'd answered the summons.

"I've been here for…what, three months? Less?" She leaned sideways this time, her shoulder fitting just below his armpit. He slid his arm around her and pulled her in tighter. "Suddenly I own a house with acreage, I have a staff, and I'm apparently filthy rich even though I haven't seen any money or bank accounts or anything. And, oh yeah, magic is real and I'm supposed to have a crapload of it that I don't know how to work." She sighed. "Anyway, after a huge life change, suddenly I have all of this new…stuff that I haven't a clue how to manage. And I don't have time to figure it out, because I summoned some magical people who are coming to join this backward, incredibly odd operation. I'm in way over my head, Austin. *Way* over my head. I tried to tell Mr. Tom, Niamh, and Edgar, but none of them would listen. They think I'll just miraculously know how to handle everything. I'm socially awkward and their minds are warped—how can we possibly have a chance in hell to make an impression on the magical world? If important people come to meet me or the house, expecting some sophisticated magical master with a well-oiled machine of a crew, and find this lot?" She shook her head. "I can't even handle those freaking dolls!"

"No one can handle those dolls," Austin said without meaning to. "No one."

"I just... Did you ever feel overwhelmed by everything?"

"I was too filled with rage, testosterone, and stupidity to feel overwhelmed when I really should have, and once I smartened up, I hid instead of trying to start over. I slunk into the shadows to lick my wounds and moan about the hand I was dealt. I realize that now. I wasn't overwhelmed because I settled for less than I should have." He squeezed her. "Your concern shows your responsibility. The way you always keep trying, despite everything, shows your courage. This house chose well. The more I see, the more I'm convinced of that fact. Don't underestimate Niamh and the others, either. They might seem like nut cases, but they have a lot of experience under their belts. A *lot*. They'll steer you true, and if anyone tries to throw their weight around and they can't handle it, you have me. Worst case, you have those dolls and this house. You're protected here, Jess. Trust in that, and allow yourself to learn and grow. You're only going to get better."

She nodded, still looking out at the garden. "Thanks. You always know what to say."

"I have no idea why."

She smiled at him, and as he looked down into those sunburst eyes, he knew one moment of vertigo. The ground dropped away and the world spun on its axis, up and down, right and left.

A moment later, when she moved away from him, he almost constricted his arm to keep her put. The woman was a beauty with a soft heart and fire in her core. This house had chosen its heir perfectly. This might all be new to her, but she would rise to the occasion easily, he had no doubt.

He just wished this house hadn't chosen him. That, or maybe he wished *he* were different. He hadn't defined himself enough for a woman like her. She was entering midlife like a fallen star hellbent on taking out anything in her path. He'd entered midlife asleep, hoping everything didn't crumble around him and wake him up.

"What's the matter?" she asked as she led them out of the room.

"I thought you said you'd learned to cut off your receptors to your team?"

Those receptors were yet another reason Ivy House's magic felt like a cage. Jess had a magical connection to the people who served the house, something that allowed her to read their feelings. She'd blocked her connection to him to preserve his privacy. She'd then blocked the others so as not to get more insight into their lives, apparently. He didn't blame her.

Ultimately, though, Jess had control over that—she

could reopen the receptors as easily as she'd closed them. He was trusting her to keep her word, a trust he wasn't used to giving.

"You look like you swallowed a toad," she said, pointing him toward an exit at the back of the house. "What's the matter?"

"Nothing. Just reflecting on my life choices."

"Aren't we all," she muttered, opening the door and gesturing him out. "Sir."

He reached above her hand and took hold of the edge of the door. "Ma'am."

She smiled and scooted out ahead of him.

"Think Gary would've held your door open?" he asked with a grin, unable to help it. He'd let Niamh do the teasing about Jess's terrible pick, mostly because he had never done online dating, and for all he knew, the guy had posted someone else's picture and lied about his personality. But man, that had been a shitshow from the word *go.* The second that guy had walked in, Austin had known exactly who he must be, and had been giddy at the thought of how Jess would handle him.

Granted, he couldn't have known she'd evacuate the whole bar with an incredibly potent burst of magic that had gotten his heart thumping, but regardless, her facial expressions throughout the encounter had made his year. If it hadn't been for the magic, he would've shushed Niamh so Jess could give Gary the wake-up call he'd so deserved.

Of course, Austin had been plenty happy to do it himself...

"Yes, actually." She veered right through the wide expanse of grass. "He wouldn't have seen holding the door open as a sign of respect, though, like most people."

"You think I respect you because I held the door open for you?"

She twisted around in order to give him a *you're so dumb* look. "Yes, but even if you didn't respect me, you still respect yourself enough to be polite. You have manners. You'd hold the door open for an enemy."

"I'd hold the door for an enemy because I'd want to be at his back, and also wouldn't want him at my back."

"Well...probably, yeah. It's different when you do it than when most men do, is what I meant. I noticed that when we went wine tasting that one time, do you remember?"

Of course he remembered. That was the day she'd reached into the center of him, dragged out his horrible past, blown fairy dust on it, and shoved it back in. She'd single-handedly changed his perspective on who and what he was. It was a moment suspended in time that he'd remember until the end of his days.

"Yes," he said, because he wasn't sure how to tell her all of that—or even if he should.

"I felt really safe with you. This probably sounds dumb, but it felt like you ushered me in front of you so you could guard my back. I don't know, it's hard to explain. My life was in flux back then, even more so than it is now, and my worldview was being turned on its head, but there was one thing I didn't have to worry about: my safety. I knew you had it covered. You see, as a woman, I need to at least keep some semblance of awareness about my surroundings, but that day...I didn't feel like I had to. It was a nice feeling. I mean, I did mostly pay attention, but... *Blech*. I'm babbling."

"You have it right. As the strongest, my job is to take the rear, to protect the most vulnerable. I'd do that for anyone in my territory."

"That's not your job."

"It's...my position."

"It *should* be your job. Ivy House is my job. These are my premises. The town should be yours. Officially yours. The people who come here should know they answer to you. Here, they answer to me." She pointed at the trees up ahead. The brush hid the elderly guardians from sight, but their bickering gave away their position, Niamh and Earl arguing about the best way to set things up. "Apparently we are training in the trees today. Lord only knows why. They never tell me. But given no one is in the air, they aren't planning on forcing me to fall as a means to fly today."

"Probably scared who else you'll call," he murmured, following her through the reaching branches.

The first of the guardians he saw was Edgar, crouched off to the side of the clearing and bent over a large volume with yellowed pages. A bicycle helmet adorned his head and a baseball catcher's chest pad was strapped around his body.

Austin stopped and stared at Edgar for a moment as Niamh and Earl glanced over. That old vampire was unparalleled in his oddness.

"Why should I create that distinction now?" he asked Jess, turning so he wasn't looking at Edgar. The situation was just too distracting. He'd have a hard time focusing on what she was saying.

She faced him, her expression serious. "As I said, it feels like I called something dangerous on that last summons. It's coming, whatever it is. Ivy House will help me on this premises, I can feel that. Figuring out the whole leadership angle is on me, but the house will baby me, and push me, and coax me until I reach my true potential. The problem is that it has no influence on the town. Austin, I told you, I'm in over my head. I know I said I would, but right now, I can't help you protect the town. I don't know enough yet. I'm afraid I'm about to create exactly the situation you feared."

"The people coming to help you won't tear up the town," he told her.

"Those who have chosen to help, no. What about those who don't make the cut? What about those who show up for the sake of curiosity? It feels like more than I asked for are coming. They're coming, and they'll lurk in the town, swinging their weight around and asserting themselves. Obviously this is all just a hunch, but…the feeling is growing increasingly…" She shook her head. "They're dangerous, that's all I'm saying. Danger is coming. I *feel* it.

"Right now, you're just a guy maintaining order. You have no actual authority. You're uncrowned. That means people who don't know you won't feel compelled to listen to you—most out of ignorance, and some out of stubbornness. You shouldn't have to fight for dominance every time someone oversteps. You need a sheriff badge, like in the old westerns. You need to be legit. Otherwise, it'll be mayhem."

The little clearing fell silent as he looked down at Jacinta's worried face. He infused his words with his magic as he gently wrapped his fingers around her upper arms. "For as long as I've been here, I've always been just a guy maintaining order. Trust me, Jacinta, it's more than I'll ever need. I *am* the sheriff badge, and I *like* fighting for dominance to prove it. Don't worry about the town—I've got it covered, no matter what comes."

CHAPTER 7

AFTER FINISHING UP my training in the trees a couple of hours earlier, mostly close combat, as I'd expected, and watched by Austin for the first time, I had excused myself to get ready for the date Niamh had set up. She'd taken over my online dating accounts because, in her words, I couldn't be trusted to choose decent candidates. I hadn't even argued—I was genuinely curious if she'd do a better job than I had. She couldn't do much worse.

I checked myself in the mirror and felt all the color drain from my face. I pulled my eyes away...then slowly let them drift back.

That pep talk I'd given myself last week after the train-wreck date had prompted me to go shopping and pick up some new dresses. I hadn't found any fun disco-ball outfits in my size, but I had picked a few dresses that showed off my curves and newly toned-up body— thank you, Ivy House, for tightening everything back up. Cheat to win.

Where the hell had all that courage gone?

I stared at the woman in the mirror, standing in a tight, bright red dress that showed popping cleavage, pushed out and up by a push-up bra, plenty of leg, and every single plane and angle of her body. She might as well have a sign that said, "Look at me, I'm sexy and glamorous!"

Which had seemed right up my alley when I was trying things on in a colorless dressing room and getting beaming nods of approval from Mr. Tom whenever I asked for his opinion. Now, ready to go into reality where strangers could see me, suddenly I wasn't so sure. As a forty-year-old divorced mom…I wanted to gawk at myself, laugh nervously, and then slip into my PJs.

"No." I balled up my fists, my face now the same color as the dress. "I'm sexy, damn it. I *am* glamorous. I will not swim around in frumpy black dresses as a means to escape attention. Oh crap, I'm showing a lot of boob."

I thought about switching bras, but honestly didn't want to fight my way out of this one, not to mention the dress. While the dress was actually quite comfortable, since the material stretched a little and the lace on the bodice and wrapping around my back wasn't too tight, I worried I might break the zipper or bust a seam or something. I didn't have the energy to pick out another outfit. Best to just go with it.

"I hope this guy is not a turd," I muttered, fastening on a sparkly diamond and ruby necklace. My ex had had his faults, but when it came to jewelry, he'd given amazing presents.

I clasped the matching bracelet, chose dangly diamonds for earrings, and did one last check of my hair and makeup. My smoky-eye ability was much better this time—thank you, YouTube tutorials. My hair…well, there was a *little* curl in the otherwise straight sheet that fell past my shoulders. Good enough.

I sucked in a breath, widened my eyes at my boobs, which now looked on the verge of popping out of my dress, and blew out my breath again. I must remember not to do that at the restaurant. I didn't know much about the kind of guy Niamh had chosen—I didn't want him to think my breathing was an invitation.

I was more nervous to wear this dress in public than I was to meet another potential romantic interest.

"You are a sexy, independent woman, Jacinta," I told the woman in the mirror. All dolled up like this, I hardly recognized her. "You look better than you have in years. You *feel* better than you have in years. Freer. Austin said he'll be around in case danger shows up. All you have to do is—"

A stranger touched down on the front walkway, followed by another. The visitors walked up the path slowly, their presence throbbing through my middle. This wasn't the danger I still felt coming, working its way to the house from afar. This was the result of the first summons, I knew. These people were answering my first call for help, the one I hadn't put any requirements on before sending out.

Without another thought, I put on a pair of thick-heeled strappy sandals so I wouldn't wobble (hopefully) and made my way down to the first floor. Mr. Tom stood in the doorway to one of the sitting rooms, his hand on the frame, looking at the front door.

"Can you see anything through the window?" Niamh asked from inside the sitting room.

"Quiet, woman," Mr. Tom hissed.

"Quiet? You're supposed to be using your eyes, not yer ears, ya muppet."

"Someone should get Jess," I heard Austin say. Relief washed over me—he hadn't gone back to the bar yet. He would help.

"She's here." Mr. Tom watched me finish descending as the two pairs of feet stepped up onto the porch.

The metal of the door knocker struck wood. The dull thunk reverberated through the space, quaking the very marrow of the house. I stopped at the bottom of the stairs, seeing a shadow fall over the sheer curtain covering the window beside the door. Bright tangerine light coated the porch, pushing back the darkness.

"How am I handling this?" I asked Mr. Tom, my hand on the railing.

"Goodness, miss, you look lovely. Excellent choice of dress for the occasion. You look just like the queen you are, ready to greet your new loyal subjects."

"Janey Mack, what is he on about now?" Niamh said. "Loyal subjects? She's going on a date, Earl, not retiring to her throne room."

"That is gargoyle magic at the door, I can sense it," Mr. Tom said haughtily, "and now she is the queen of our kind. You'd understand what I meant if any of your kind could stand joining your army of one."

"There aren't many of my kind, ye know that. Most of them have been killed off. The ones that are left are always on the whiskey. Mad as hatters. Horrible to be around."

"Yes, your kind typically are." Mr. Tom paused as the knocker struck again.

Austin appeared beside Mr. Tom, his mouth open to speak. But his gaze found me, and no words came out. He froze.

My stupid face flamed again.

"Earl, answer the door," Niamh called. "Jessie, come

in here with me. Let them ask for you."

Austin's gaze flicked up to my eyes, down again, and then back up. For the first time, I caught a little flush on his cheeks. His eyes stopped moving, as though he were focusing with everything he had on maintaining eye contact.

When he finally spoke, his voice was slow and deep and rough. "You are a showstopper, Jacinta. Stunning."

My stomach flipped and I smiled, relief washing through me. I moved in their direction, motioning Mr. Tom to the door.

He smoothed his tuxedo jacket and fluttered his wings. "This would be much more impressive if I were of a proper age and had a lovely thick, black, full head of hair, but beggars can't be choosers..." But the side-eye he gave me suggested otherwise.

"Well ye've certainly got an ear fulla hair, will that do?" Niamh called.

I smoothed my hands down my sides. "You don't think it's too much?" I asked Austin. "Or too revealing?"

"Not at all. It's perfect. You look absolutely beautiful." Austin turned and put out his arm for me to take, ready to escort me into the sitting room.

Niamh sat in a recliner with a beer in hand and her feet up. Edgar stood at the back, having showered and put on fresh white sweats with two mustard-colored stains near his collar. I really needed to have a word with Mr. Tom about changing the color of the sweats. White clearly was not working for the vampire. Mr. Tom was getting pissy about all the trips to the store for bleach and had slacked off. The result was not ideal.

Niamh whistled. "Well, look at ye. You shine up like a new penny, so you do. You look absolutely deadly. Fair play to ya."

Edgar smiled, his extended canines making the expression ghastly. "Very pretty, Jessie. You'll knock 'em dead."

Austin stopped next to a love seat and flared his arm, releasing me. I sat down with what I knew was a goofy expression, but it felt nice to be treated like I was delicate. Like I was royalty.

The front door opened as Austin took a seat beside me.

"Is this the danger you felt, do you think?" he asked as I distinctly heard Mr. Tom say, "You *rang*?"

"What an *eejit*," Niamh muttered. "He gets nervous and turns into a donkey. *More* of a donkey, I should say."

"No, I don't think so," I whispered, trying to hear who was at the door. "This must be the first wave—the people I summoned before the bar."

"Well, if Mr. Tom is right," Edgar said, having no problem with Mr. Tom's name change, "and they are gargoyles, then you'll have your work cut out for you, Jessie. They are some of the most stubborn creatures alive, not to mention they'll keep trying to mate you. They're like ants in that way. They'll be helplessly attracted to their queen, and they will feel it is their duty to help you conceive."

"That's only if she wants a child." Niamh waved the thought away. "If that's not her goal, they'll just try to shag her. Especially lookin' like that, eh, Jessie? Who wouldn't? You goin'ta let yer date have a ride tonight?"

My eyes widened and Austin stiffened before clasping his hands in his lap.

"No," I said, lowering my face to try to hide my embarrassment.

"Well, if you do, I know Earl has loaded up on co—"

"I know, I know, it's fine, I don't need them," I said quickly to cut her off. Why was Mr. Tom telling everyone he'd stocked up for some sort of sexual enlightenment? I planned to go on a few dates to get back into the swing of it, not bang the whole town. Good God.

"She is right in here, if you please." Mr. Tom entered the room at a slow walk, his chest puffed out and his wings fluttering behind him. He stopped just inside the door and peeled off to the side, his hand out. "She is about to leave. She has limited time. Very busy, as you can guess."

Two men followed him, one behind the other, in their mid-twenties or early thirties, with thick arms and chests, though not as robust as Austin. The first of the two, the younger one, had a broad face with a round nose and thick brows. His companion was taller, with a slightly thinner frame and piercing brownish-black eyes that settled on me like a punch to the face. Wings that looked like thick, shiny capes fluttered out to their sides, glimmering in the light.

They stopped just before the chair Niamh sat in, the one in back coming to rest beside the other, their presences imposing, the air about them intense. All the nerves I'd felt came rushing back. At the very least, they were intimidating. I wasn't even sure I wanted to be in the same room with them.

How was I supposed to *lead* them?

Mr. Tom scooted a little so the new entries could see him, trying to hold his puffed-up posture while only sliding his feet. He looked absurd. "Jacinta, this is Cedric"—the taller tilted his head down—"and Alek." The other tilted his head in turn. "Jacinta is the owner and magical heir of Ivy House. I'm sure you've heard of her."

The two didn't move or speak, their expressions severe. How could they have heard of me, given I was non-magical before this and Ivy House had been unclaimed for generations?

"Hello." I bent forward to get up, but my seams groaned. Any further and they might pop. This dress did not allow the freedom of movement of sweats.

Smile fixed in place, facing a conundrum, I scooted forward, holding down my hem so I didn't show everyone my underwear. If I kept this up, I'd fight Mr. Tom for the Most Ridiculous Award.

"Wait," Austin said quietly before standing, uncoiling from his position with lethal grace. The gazes of both newcomers snapped to him like rubber bands.

He bent and offered me his hand, which I gladly took, and helped me up.

It wasn't until I started walking toward them with a smile that the newcomers refocused on me, but judging by the tension in their bearings and their occasional glances at Austin, following at my back, his presence weighed on their minds.

"Welcome," I said, stopping in front of them. Niamh didn't bother to get up, but watched us with her head tilted and her beer in hand.

Both newcomers bent at the knee, their bows deep, their eyes continually flicking to Austin.

"This is Austin Steele, the peacekeeper of the town." I stepped to the side a little and motioned to him.

Austin didn't step or bend forward, like I had thought he might. Instead, he stared at each of them in turn with a flat expression, his eyes sparkling aggressively. He wasn't even trying to assume the commander of the house role right now—this was just his way. He did this posturing stuff in his sleep, which was why he didn't need to wear that sheriff badge, I guess.

"This is Niamh." I put out my hand to her. "She is one of the original protectors of Ivy House, as is Edgar there, in the back."

"Hello. Lovely to make...see you." Edgar bowed. "Your acquaintance."

"Fail," Niamh drawled.

"You've met Mr. Tom, of course." I put out my hand for him. "So...do you plan to stay for a while, or..." I motioned for them to sit.

"We stay so long you need us, Majesty." Alek bowed to me.

"No, no." I gave him a stop gesture. "Don't call me that."

"She likes to remain informal while at home," Mr. Tom said, stepping forward, his haughtiness knowing no bounds. "You may address her as 'miss.'"

"Yes, of course." Alek bowed again. It was clearly

his go-to move. "It is an honor, miss. Our people…" He muttered a collection of syllables I couldn't make sense of.

"Jealous," Edgar helped, clearly knowing whatever language Alek had used.

"Yes, yes, *jeal*-os." Alek bobbed his head. "We pick. They no. We the best. Proof."

"The tales of the Ivy heirs of the past all speak of her beauty and power…" Cedric put his hand on his chest. "They were correct. You are ravishing. A woman of experience, as well. I was expecting younger." I tensed, then widened my eyes when he went a direction I didn't expect. "This is a nice surprise. I look forward to your heightened sensual experience. It is said that a woman of your age is at her sexual peak, is it not?"

"Now. Aren't you glad I stocked you up, miss?" Mr. Tom's eyebrows rose and he zipped his eyes back and forth, as if to say, *See? Two younger guys to take a turn in the sheets with.* "They'll have excellent stamina. You'll be able to do away with all that online Dick-dating hoopla."

"Oh my God, what is his malfunction?" I muttered, mortified.

"Time check," Niamh said with a crooked smile. "Don't be late on account of the hired help."

"I'll walk you," Austin said, his hand touching down

on the small of my back.

"Right. Well." I smiled at the guys, trying to hide my embarrassment. "Mr. Tom will fix you something to eat and get you settled. We have plenty of room if you need a place to stay."

Austin's head snapped toward me, his gaze questioning.

"We...stay?" Alek asked.

Cedric turned to watch me exit.

"Yes, yes, she has some business to attend to." Mr. Tom took up his position in the doorway after Austin and I had passed. "She's very busy, as I said. She must not be delayed. Now, settle in and I will explain all the particulars. You need to know about her life leading up to this moment."

His voice cut off as I stepped outside. Having forgotten a shawl, I wrapped my magic around me for warmth.

My magic. It still sounded so crazy, but in some ways it had already become second nature.

"What is with Mr. Tom?" I asked, taking Austin's arm again. He chose a slower pace, more like a stroll, sauntering down the sidewalk toward town, where I would meet my date. "What is with those gargoyles just assuming they'd get laid?"

"Gargoyles are one of the more...promiscuous magical types, I think. You wouldn't know it because of their...gruff nature, but they do like to get down with whoever is willing. The female of the species is quite rare, and she often cycles through males at her leisure until she finds someone she wants to mate. The someone she chooses might not be a gargoyle, but I've heard it usually is. They are drawn to strength and power, and some gargoyles have that in spades."

"They're not going to just assume, right?" Fear and uncertainty coiled within me. "There won't be...consent concerns?"

His voice turned into a hard growl. "If they harm a hair on your head, Jacinta, I will rip them apart. Literally."

"That's all well and good, Austin, but that isn't going to help me avoid a bad situation. I don't want revenge; I want to not get hurt in the first place."

He covered my hand with his. "You're right. Sorry, I wasn't thinking. No, from what I've heard, that won't be an issue. Just be upfront and they should back down. You...could have your pick, though, if you wanted...practice."

That last sentence sounded as if it had been dragged out of his mouth. As though he was as reluctant to talk about it as I was.

"Yeah, let's not open that door for discussion," I

said, looking straight ahead. "I wish Mr. Tom wouldn't."

"That guy is such a trip. I always think I'm going to get used to him, and then he surprises me by upping the ante of weirdness. Edgar, too. It is…really unbelievable. That crew is honest-to-God the strangest group of people I have ever met in my entire life."

I was laughing helplessly by the time we got to the little bistro on the main drag, an Italian restaurant I hadn't been to yet but had heard was fantastic. He stopped by the door, waited for me to take my hand back, and then stepped back to give me more space.

"So," he said, holding my gaze.

"So," I responded, looking around the quiet street. Then I lifted my empty hands to—hug him, maybe? I wasn't sure, but it didn't matter because it made me realize something. "Damn it." I looked back toward the house. "I was in such a hurry to get out of there that I forgot all my stuff. We're supposed to split the bill. What time is it?"

He checked his watch, a large square of technology. "Five past eight. You're late."

"Dang it. Can you call Mr. Tom and tell him to bring it for me, please? With my phone, obviously."

"Here." He reached into his back pocket and dragged out a gold money clip pinching a dull green wad. "How much do you need?"

"Oh no, don't worry about it. I need my phone, too, so he can just bring the whole lot."

"I'll call, but just in case this date ends as quickly as the last one…" He slipped the folded pack of bills out as he glanced at the restaurant. "This place is pretty pricey." He leafed a few fives and twenties out of the way before sliding out a hundred-dollar bill, and then another. He handed them over.

"No, it's—"

"Jess, take it. If you don't need it, great, no biggie, I'll get it back from you. I'll ask Niamh to drop off your clutch on her way into the bar. She has to be less embarrassing than that clown Mr. Tom—damn it. Earl."

"Just give in." I couldn't help the giggles. "Just give in and call him Mr. Tom. You know you want to."

"No," he ground out, threatening a smile. He slipped the wad of cash back into his jeans, the material hugging his large package and muscular thighs. I didn't know if he bought them tight to show off on purpose, but they did a great job of drawing the eyes.

"Right, but where am I going to put it…" I held the notes in my hand, looking down at my tight dress.

Austin's eyes snagged on my bust.

"It's not going to fit in there," I said with a grin.

In the dim light, I just barely saw a flash of hunger in those deep blue eyes. "No, I guess not. Your shoe?"

I laughed, folded it, and threaded it into my bra. "Just kidding—there is always space for money."

This time I was sure of it—hunger, wild and ferocious, moved within his gaze. My body warmed, then pounded, my core tightening in response.

He didn't comment, nor did he drop his gaze.

"So," I repeated in a strained whisper.

"I'll see you"—he gritted his teeth, spared another glance for the restaurant, tense now, and stepped away again—"when I see you, I guess. Good luck."

"Oh, I forgot to ask," I called to his backside while admiring the view. The man must have been created in the mold of a Greek god. "What's the status of those guys? Did you silently sort out the king of the hill?"

"Of course," he said over his shoulder without stopping. "It's always going to be me."

CHAPTER 8

THE INTERIOR OF the restaurant was fashionably elegant, with white linens, flickering candlelight, and red carnations in dainty glass vases. Most of the tables within were taken, couples or families dining quietly. A small bar sat off to my right—room enough for four people, but only one seat was taken, a younger guy with a black collared shirt and rimmed hat.

The memory of my father reminding my brother to take his hat off at the table kept my gaze rooted to him, and in a moment, the attention was obviously noticed. His shoulders tightened and he turned in his seat. But instead of looking around for the source of his creepy-crawlies, he looked directly at me.

I should've shifted my gaze—I was the rude one in this scenario, staring at a stranger for no reason—but I couldn't. He had a fresh face that spoke of a guy in his early twenties, but something in his eyes felt...ancient. I couldn't see their color, or really any details from this far away in a dimly lit restaurant, but they carried the ennui of someone who'd lived this life three times over and was just waiting around for something different to happen. An old soul, clearly, or maybe just a guy in a small town desperate to get out.

"Can I help you?"

I jumped, not having seen the hostess walk up. After giving my name, I glanced over at the guy again. He was back to looking at his phone, a sweating brown bottle waiting in front of him.

"Right this way," the hostess said.

I held my breath as she led me into the back, to a table by the window where a man was already seated. He looked to be about my age, with a shaved head and a modest brown beard. His nose was long and straight, and his lips, partially hidden by the beard, were turned up in a large smile.

He stood when the hostess stopped by the table with a menu in hand.

"Hi. I'm Ron." He held out a hand.

Thankful he hadn't moved in for a hug, I offered him a relieved smile and shook hello. "I'm Jacinta. My friends call me Jessie."

"Please, sit." He gestured to my chair and sat, waiting for me to follow suit, and didn't speak until the hostess strode away. "Do you live around here?"

"I do, yes. Just down the street, really."

"Oh yeah? I've been to this town a million times for wine festivals and because I have some friends here. Which area?"

"Just…" I pointed in the direction of the house as the waitress showed up to take our drink order. "I haven't been here long. It's the court with the creepy house at the end. Usually people know—"

"Ivy House." The waitress smiled and nodded, ready with her pen and paper. "Right? You're talking about Ivy House?"

"Yes—"

"Right! I know that house." Ron paused for me to order a glass of wine before ordering the same for himself. After the waitress left, we started looking at our menus, and he said, "So that's cool, huh? Living on the street with that house? I heard the owner lives in Europe or something, and there's an insane old woman next door who throws rocks at people trying to check it out…" He laughed at the insanity of it all and held up his hands. "I'm sure there are a lot of urban legends surrounding that house."

I shrugged as the waitress came back with the drinks. "I don't honestly know. I've only been there for a couple of months. But the woman at the end…that's true. She really does that."

"No!" He laughed, delighted, and I found myself

smiling with him. He had a carefree, infectious laugh. "That's hilarious. I'd go check it out for myself, but I don't want to get hit by a rock!"

"Yeah, she's a really good shot." I chuckled, ready to order when the waitress returned.

When she left again, he said, "So how close do you live? Do you see ghosts or anything at night? I hear it's really creepy."

"It is creepy, and...I live *in* it, actually. I'm now the owner."

He paused for a moment, his glass half raised to his lips. "Wait...you live...*in* the house? You own it?"

"Yeah. I recently bought it. I like creepy old houses."

A crooked smile worked within his beard. He laughed. "What a trip." He squinted at me and turned his face to the side, mockingly suspicious. "Are you pulling my leg? You are, aren't you? You're poking fun because I'm so curious."

I put up my hands. "No, honest. I swear." I laughed, my tension from earlier dripping away. He seemed so normal. Non-magical, curious, no idea what went bump in the night... The most he had to worry about was a house payment or rent, bills, dating—normal life stuff. He didn't have to think about flying, or warding off advances from promiscuous creatures, or a crazy house, or learning magic. He didn't have to worry about the danger I felt drawing ever nearer, or whether Austin would soon find out the hard way that he was not, in fact, the biggest, baddest alpha on the block. Or wonder what would happen to the rest of us if our fearless protector fell.

I sipped my wine, relieved for this one moment. Relieved for this return to my old normal, if only for a night. *This* was one of the reasons I'd wanted to date a Dick.

"Wow!" He leaned back as our plates arrived. "I probably shouldn't ask this, because I don't want to open a can of worms, but…is it haunted?"

I told him about the room of dolls, obviously leaving out the detail that they came alive. Working through our dinners, we spoke about little things, the conversation starting and stopping as we navigated the waters of small talk, working around to hobbies and things we did for fun. It wasn't until we started talking about what we did for a living that the conversation came to a screeching halt.

"Oh…uh…" I laid down my fork and blotted my mouth, my plate nearly empty and my belly completely stuffed. "I actually came into some money recently, so right now I'm mostly concerning myself with…working on the house."

It wasn't a total lie. Working on my magic was similar to working on the house.

"Oh, yeah? Hmm." He nodded. "What…uh… Does it need much work, or…"

"Quite a bit, actually," I said. His eyebrows drew together in a troubled expression. "I kind of have to start from—What is it?"

I turned around to see what had given him such a constipated look.

Cedric walked our way, his dress shirt and slacks snug enough to show off his thick, corded muscle, his wings flaring out weirdly from beneath his thin jacket, and his expression hard as nails. His dark gaze pounded into Ron, clearly freezing him up and making him incredibly uncomfortable.

I put out my hand, facing Ron with a comforting smile. "That's just my…cousin. He's staying with me for a bit. You know, to sort out the house. I forgot my clutch when I walked out—he's just bringing it for me."

The clutch filled my waiting palm.

I smiled again and slipped it under the table.

"Thanks," I said to Cedric, giving him a fleeting glance. I did a double take when I caught his look of death, still pounding into poor Ron. The unveiled threat was plain, as was the effect—Ron's face looked ashen.

"Don't mind him," I told Ron, the lies coming faster now. "He's an MMA fighter." I said over my shoulder,

"I said thanks. *You can go now.*"

I barely caught Cedric shaking his head as he turned away. Movement by the door caught my attention before I could turn back—Alek. His stare was on Ron, too, his threat just as plain.

"My other cousin. They're—"

Mr. Tom's head leaned into the frame of the window, the shades not pulled, sadly. A bowler hat covered his head, wire-rimmed glasses circled his eyes, and the collar of his trench coat was turned up, partially obscuring his face.

Ron's head turned slowly until he locked eyes with Mr. Tom.

After one tense beat, Mr. Tom slowly leaned back out of the window frame.

"I, uh…" What the hell could I say about that one? "My family is…odd."

Ron's head turned back. He dropped his hands into his lap, moving ever so slowly as if worried a fast movement might summon one of my "cousins."

Gritting my teeth, I turned long enough to frantically wave Cedric and Alek away, then gave Ron a large, hopefully calming smile. "I'm so sorry about that. They're just…"

"Protective?" Ron asked, his gaze flicking toward the door before he glanced the other way, probably looking to see if Mr. Tom was peeping at us again.

"I was going to say overbearing. My…cousins only got here tonight. They haven't really acclimated yet."

"You're kind of old to have younger cousins scaring your dates, aren't you? I mean, that's something for teenagers." He gave a humorless laugh, playing it off as a joke, clearly having no idea how deeply those words stung. He dropped his napkin on his plate before blowing out a breath. "Are they going to be waiting outside with a shotgun, too?"

I could hear the tremor in his voice. I could see the unease written plainly on his face. They'd shaken him, he clearly wasn't used to it, and he was trying to make light of it.

"Honestly, I'm really sorry. I'd asked my friend— my *female* friend—to drop off my bag. They're just acting up, honest. They're young and dumb and bored."

"That's fine, but the creepy dude in the window—"

"You aren't going to believe this, but…he's a butler. He basically came with the house."

Ron's look was fixed and unflinching. The blinking was his tell—I should've gone with Mr. Tom being my uncle. But honestly, if he ever visited Ivy House, he'd know the term *uncle* didn't line up.

"He was like a caretaker for the old place, and I felt bad firing him," I added quickly as Ron made a sign for the check.

"Oh, gotcha. And…he…hangs out with your cousins, or…?"

Crap. "He probably just wanted to make sure they handed over my clutch."

"Ah." He nodded, reaching for the check when it came.

"Oh, here." I smiled as I held up the clutch. "Just in time, huh?"

"I got it." He slipped his card into the leather folder and pushed the whole lot to the edge of the table. "I don't want your cousins to break my legs or something." His smile was strained.

I couldn't think of any other way to apologize or explain, and even if I did, it seemed like he wasn't going to come back from whatever he was feeling. If he couldn't handle the new guys, how would he ever handle Austin?

"So…been online dating long?" I asked, leaning back in my chair, knowing when to throw in the towel.

"Not very seriously. I got out of a long relationship last year, and…" He shrugged. "Where do you start again, you know?"

"I do know. I'm recently divorced after twenty years. I'm in a new town, in a new house—a creepy one for funsies…" He laughed. "I didn't know where to start, either. Online dating seemed like the logical place."

"Except it is a minefield of crazy."

"Yes!" I put out my hands to him as the waitress whisked the bill away. "You're only my second date. The first guy... Well, that was a disaster. He set up a profile from yesteryear, and *surprise*! Basically a different guy."

Ron laughed. "I've had a few of those. Or women who say they are athletic and outdoorsy, so you make a date to hike only to realize they have an ailment they didn't tell you about, and suddenly your fun date is not possible. So you scramble."

"But why didn't she tell you that hiking was a no?"

"I do not know." He laughed as the bill came back and he left the tip. "Shall we?"

"I had him meet me at the bar," I said as I got up. "Apparently that made me suspect."

"Oh, the one downtown?" He stood up too but waited for me to go first.

"No, the one up the way? The Paddy Wagon?"

"Oh wow, you chose that one for a first date?" He shook his head and stalled at the front. When I gave him a confused frown, he gestured to the coat rack. "Don't you have something to wrap up in?"

"Oh. No. I was in such a hurry to leave the house

after my cousins showed up that I literally forgot everything. It's fine, I'm not bothered by the cold."

He followed me outside, disbelief clear on his face. "We can just wait inside for them to bring you a sweatshirt if you want? I'm prepared this time. I'll handle the intense scowls."

"No, honestly, it's fine. Seriously." I pushed through the door, immediately wrapping my magic around myself. "What were you saying about the bar up the way?"

"Oh, just that—you have to be *freezing*! Here." He shrugged out of his jacket and draped it over my shoulders.

"No, really, it's…" I sighed and let him finish. He was being a gentleman and wouldn't understand why I didn't need it. "Thanks."

"That's a really rough-and-tumble bar," he said. "I'd be nervous if that's where someone wanted to meet."

"Oh no, it's fine. My neighbor—the rock-throwing old lady?" He smiled at me. "She brought me there my first night in town, and now I know the owner. He makes sure everything is aboveboard. It's probably the safest spot in town when he's on duty."

"That big, burly guy?" Ron blew out a breath, pausing by the parking lot. "That guy, safe?" He shook his head with a smile. "That guy scares the whole town."

"That's just how he keeps order. Don't break the rules and he won't bother you."

He shivered but tried to hide it, the cold permeating his dress shirt. "Are you one of those thrill-seeking women or something?"

"No! Honestly, he's a really cool guy. He walked me here tonight."

"He…" He put up his hands. "Well, there you go. If he's on your side, you're all set."

"Let's hope, huh? If someone gets through him, we're all screwed."

"No one is getting through that guy. He's a tank. Hey, did you want a ride?"

"No." Cedric stepped forward from the wall down the way, utterly invisible one moment, and in plain view the next, the nearby streetlight washing down his body. "She will not get into a car with a strange man, no matter how weak he might be."

I rounded on him, incredulous, knowing his presence meant Alek and Mr. Tom were likely lurking somewhere nearby, too, using their gargoyle magic to blend into the building. The ability could be used with any kind of stone or cement.

"Get out of here," I yelled at him, pointing for him to retreat. "Mr. Tom, Alek, you better show yourselves if you're hanging around, too."

"You should not ask us to reveal ourselves, miss." Mr. Tom clasped his hands, suddenly appearing three feet behind Ron.

"Ah!" Ron sprang up and took a few quick steps toward the parking lot, creating some space for himself. "What the—Where'd he come from?"

"You have the power to unmask us," Mr. Tom said as Alek appeared at the far corner of the restaurant. No matter which way I might've gone, one of them would've been on my heels while the others caught up. "You have the power to feel presences. You should never be snuck up on again. We just learned this."

"Mr. Tom," I said through clenched teeth, "*get out of here*. All of you, go away!" None of these dates would ever go well if these idiots didn't learn to give me some space.

"You summoned us here. You are now under our protection. We cannot leave you with—"

I turned to Cedric with wide, crazy eyes and balled fists.

"Go," Mr. Tom said quickly and loudly, waving his arm through the air like he was calling off a fleet of jets. "Go!"

"I can take it." Cedric held his ground, but I could tell he felt the magic seeping out around me, just like Mr. Tom obviously did. I could feel it too, feeding on my anger and annoyance. Just this side of controllable.

"Are you sure?" I asked in a low voice.

Cedric's stare bored into mine, his body braced in stubborn indignation. He did not want to bend his will, and a part of me knew this was a hallmark of his species. Of my species, now. If I relented, or backed down, he wouldn't respect me as much. Worse, he'd see it as a green light to walk all over me. Guys like him, gargoyles, needed a firm hand.

Which was probably why Mr. Tom ruled my life and got all up in my business. I'd mistaken stubbornness for weirdness. In fairness, I hadn't been completely wrong.

"Go home. Now," I said, brooking no argument, wondering what I'd do if he refused.

He didn't move at first, a block of muscle facing me on the walkway like we were in a Wild West showdown. Finally, grudgingly, he nodded, shifted his weight to the right, and picked up a foot to move on.

"You too," I called behind me. Alek didn't need to be told twice, clearly the less dominant of the two. Their large backs draped in shadow and their wings fluttering down their legs, they headed in the direction of Ivy House. They did not look back, and they clearly were not happy about this turn of events.

"Very well done, miss. *Very* well done." Mr. Tom

nodded, then stepped back against the wall, waiting for me.

"You too, Mr. Tom," I said.

"Oh, don't be silly. Someone will have to walk you home. As soon as your date unfreezes from his fear-induced paralysis, he'll sprint out of here."

"I don't need someone to walk me home." I took a step toward Ron, who was watching my exchange with Mr. Tom with a pale face.

"I'm already here. I might as well," Mr. Tom said. "I just baked a lovely chocolate cake. Doesn't that sound nice?"

"Ron?" I gave him what I hoped was a disarming smile. "Sorry about that."

He shook himself out of his stupor. His smile looked more like a grimace. "It's getting late. I think I'll head out."

My heart sank. "Sure, yeah." I shrugged out of his jacket.

He held out his hand to stop me. "That's okay. It's a cold walk home. Keep it."

"Oh, but…"

"It was a nice time!" He jogged backward, hit a rock with his heel as the paved walkway turned into the dirty parking lot, and fell onto his butt. Dust puffed up around him. "Ha! Oops. Clumsy." He pushed to his feet, gave me a thumbs-up, and sideways-walked toward a Ford Explorer. "Okay, see ya. I'll call you!"

"He won't call," Mr. Tom said, watching the scene. "He's so desperate to get away, he's going to lose a thirty-dollar jacket."

"Yes, Mr. Tom, I am aware, thanks." My heart sank further and I sagged. "He was cool, too. He seemed like a really nice guy."

"It looked like someone hit him in the face with a two-by-four." Mr. Tom clasped his hands behind his back. "Repeatedly."

I tsked. "No, it did not! He was fine looking. Average."

"Ugly. C'mon, I know what will cheer you up. But first…" He peeled the jacket from my shoulders. "We don't know where this has been, dirty Dick. He might have fleas from that wild sort of growth on his face. I'll just leave it back in the restaurant." When he returned, he gestured me toward town, then turned us in the direction of the bar.

"Are you going to drop me off with Niamh?"

"No, as a matter of fact, I am going to have a drink with you. I can't wait to tell Niamh that she failed."

"She didn't fail—she picked a really good guy that I would've hit it off with if it hadn't been for the Doobie Brothers busting up the party."

"The…who?"

"Never mind." I sighed. "Back to the drawing board. At least this one leaves hope that there are decent guys on the online dating sites. I just need Niamh to find them for me."

"It doesn't matter who is on those sites. They'll never work for you, miss. All of your Dick dates are going to end like that." We'd reached the road crossing, but Mr. Tom held his arm out in front of my chest, like I was a child, waiting for a car to pass. Once the way was safe, he swept his hand wide and waited until I stepped off the curb to follow. He was in rare form this evening. "That isn't your world anymore, miss. You have to accept that. Neither will you get the privacy of your old life. You are the chosen and heiress of Ivy House. With that comes expectation and privilege. You will always be accompanied now. Our job is to protect you, and my kind"—he palmed his chest—"do that better than most. Don't worry, you'll get used to it."

"I haven't gotten used to you…"

"Lovely, it seems Niamh is rubbing off on you," he said dryly. "What joy is mine."

The bar was slow for a Saturday night, but the casual atmosphere and the faces I was starting to recognize cheered me up after the botched encounter with Ron. I found Niamh where she always sat, three-quarters of the way down by the support beam, hunched over her cider. The seat to her right was empty, and the one beyond that was taken by my dear friend Sasquatch.

Austin glanced up from a drink he was pouring, noticed Mr. Tom with me, and a series of expressions crossed his face so quickly that I nearly didn't catch them—regret, relief, surprise, apprehension. He dipped his face back down without nodding hello.

Paul smiled and met us near Niamh. "Hi, Jacinta. Wow, you look really pretty. That dress is nice."

"Well, lads," Niamh said, half turning. She looked at Sasquatch. "Wipe off that seat when you leave. It probably has a grease stain now."

"Yes, a bath once in a while would really work wonders on your mood, I think," Mr. Tom said, looking Sasquatch over. "I've always thought so."

Sasquatch frowned back at Mr. Tom and then glowered at me. "What do you want?"

"Now, Sasquatch, you hairy bastard, you know how this always goes," Niamh said. "You make a holy show of yerself, then Austin Steele knocks you on yer arse and chases you out in disgrace. Best get up and move that fat arse down a ways so we aren't tickled by yer presence anymore."

"I'll give you a tickle," Sasquatch muttered sourly.

"Grand. As soon as you can find yer wee willy, you

go right ahead and give me a tickle, that'd be fine. Now give us a little peace, and *move.*"

"He was there first," Paul said softly, his expression like he'd just eaten a bug. He did not like standing up to Niamh, but he apparently thought he had no choice.

"Nah." Sasquatch batted his hand through the air. "Last thing I want to do is listen to a bunch of chickens clucking."

"I beg your pardon," Mr. Tom said, puffing up in indignation.

"You heard me," Sasquatch groused, pushing off the stool and leaving the bar.

"You've really ruined his drinking habit since you came to town." Niamh turned back to her cider.

"What's up with you?" I asked Niamh as Mr. Tom pulled out my stool. "I'm fine, Mr. Tom, I can—"

"You're in a tight dress, miss, one it took us all day to find and a grisly fight for me to pay for. I do not wish for you to rip it trying to get onto this stool like some sort of cowboy straddling a horse. Now." He patted the seat.

No, I was never going to win a battle of wills with Mr. Tom. It would just never be worth the effort.

Once seated, which, to be fair, required some gymnastics on the part of Mr. Tom, Niamh answered me.

"I am knackered." She drooped a little more. "That

training today was more tiring than usual, but then dealing with Tom and Jerry throwing their weight around after you left and already trying to establish a pecking order in which they are on top…"

"They weren't trying to—"

Niamh silenced Mr. Tom with a raised hand. "No. No more. I cannot handle any more nonsense from gargoyles today. The lot of you are as *thick*!" She shook her head. "Stubborn bastards if ever there were any. They'll be staying in that house with you now, Jessie. Ye invited them in, and now they get a room each until you kick their big, dumb butts out. They won't make the cut, mark my words. That Cedric fella is going to get me foot in his hole, too, if he keeps on with how things *should* be. Well, I'll tell him how things *are*, and that will be that."

"What happened after I left?" I asked as Paul placed a bottle of cider next to Niamh's glass.

"Jessie? What can I get you?" Paul asked, smiling.

"The usual. Pinot Noir, whichever one is somewhat fresh."

"And for you, Earl?"

Mr. Tom leaned forward, his hand on the bar. "I haven't had a chance to tell you, being that I am not a lush like *some* people who often grace this establishment…"

"Keep it up, see how it goes," Niamh mumbled. "I'm not in any sorta mood tonight."

"My name is Tom now." Mr. Tom patted the bar, and Paul's brows pinched. "Mr. Tom." He smiled expectantly.

"O-kay." If Paul was looking at Niamh and me for help, he wouldn't get it. I shrugged, and she ignored the situation completely. "Uh...Tom—"

"Mr. Tom."

"Right. Mr. Tom, what can I get you?"

"A sherry would be nice, thank you."

"Hey." Austin sauntered over to us, wiping his hands on a white bar towel and giving me a tentative grimace. "So, how'd it go?"

"Well, tonight I was the Gary." I recounted the situation, noticing Mr. Tom's wings flutter, just slightly. The feeling of someone watching me tickled between my shoulder blades. A glance back and I saw why.

I groaned. "I told them to go home."

Cedric and Alek lingered to either side of the door, leaning against the wall, staring at me. The other patrons in the bar noticed, glancing furtively between the gargoyles and Austin, clearly wondering if these new guys were a problem.

"But you did not tell them to stay there, miss." Mr. Tom put his finger in the air. "As I said, their job is to protect you. Which they are doing."

"Their job is probably to help me fly." I took a sip of the wine. "That's what I was thinking of before the summons. I didn't expressly ask for help, but…" I shrugged. "That's my guess."

"And when are you going to attempt that?" Austin asked, dropping the towel onto the back of the bar. If he was annoyed by their presence, he didn't show it.

I heaved out a sigh. Something in me said flight was the cornerstone of my magic. Learning to fly would usher in the rest of my abilities and cement my role as the heir of Ivy House. It would prepare me for this new life.

Except I was starting to wonder if it would ever happen.

"Sooner the better, I guess." I shifted my gaze to Niamh. "That guy tonight was perfect—"

"She was way out of his league," Mr. Tom interrupted.

I gave him a flat stare. "He would've been great, if it weren't for this circus following me around. But they did help me realize it doesn't make sense for me to date non-magical guys. It was my way of holding on to the past, but it's probably time for me to own my situation and ease further into the magical world."

"How do you plan to do that?" Austin asked, his

gaze intense.

"I have no idea," I mumbled, and took another sip. "I have absolutely no idea."

CHAPTER 9

I REALLY WANTED to say today's situation was *déjà vu* of the last time I had tried to fly. I really did, but this situation was infinitely worse.

"Starting a new thing on a Monday is a terrible idea, everyone knows that," I told Edgar. The frigid wind whipped the words out of my mouth.

"This isn't a new thing," Edgar replied, raising his voice over the howling wind. He adjusted his bicycle helmet. "You tried a week ago, remember? Right before your first failed attempt at dating a Dick."

"Is the reason you're wearing that helmet, because you know I'm going to throw you off this cliff?"

"Thrown, jumped—what's the difference? At least you have wings. I'll have to get caught and carried. Or dropped and killed."

"The new thing I was originally talking about was jumping off an enormous cliff on the side of a mountain, high above a bunch of bone-crunching rocks. Now, however, I think the new thing is having you as my moral support to go through with it."

"Oh yeah, I'm well known to be terrible in these situations, but I'm the only one without wings. I can fashion myself into a swarm of insects, as you might remember, but that's more for hovering and moving quickly. I maintain a relationship with the ground. If there is no ground, I cannot sustain the form, have to change back, and go splat. This support role is the sole purpose I can serve when it comes to flying. I'm supposed to talk you out of running, but I don't really have to, since it's a long walk back to Ivy House. Fear-induced hide-and-seek is only a fun game for a little while, and then you'd have to come back and face the music. Though, I will say, it would take them forever to find you in the trees back there."

He hooked his long thumb over his shoulder at the dense trees on the mountain side, the incline slight for about a hundred yards before climbing rapidly again toward the peak not terribly far above us.

Niamh had chosen this spot, about an hour away from town. Only the most advanced rock climbers attempted the cliff, and it was likely too cold for that. Hikers wouldn't be able to see me through the thick canopy of trees below. Patches of glistening white snow clung to the rocks around us and dusted the leaves behind, not sticking to the ground way below us.

Way, *way* below us.

"It's a long way to fall," I said, my toes pushed up against the edge and shivers racking my body.

"Yes, it is. I don't much like heights, did I ever tell you that?" Edgar watched Niamh fly by in her nightmare alicorn form, deep shadows swirling in her wake while the sinking sun slid across her oily black feathers. "This is a little torturous for me. You know what they say, though—what doesn't kill you will haunt you for the rest of your life…"

"That's not what they say! Of all the people in the world that could be standing next to me in a supportive role, you are the absolute worst."

"Yes. Probably."

"I should've begged Austin to come."

"And have one of those young gargoyles fly him up here like a sack of potatoes? Hardly. He might've done it because he has a soft spot for you, but I doubt he would've been any better at this than me."

"He would've, trust me. He would've been so much better."

He shrugged as if to say *fair point*. "So, what's the plan?"

The brawny, purplish Cedric flew close to the cliff, his giant wings beating lazily at the air as he sailed by. Thick slabs of muscle coated his large gargoyle form, his lower half clad in flowing pants. I sure wished he and Alek would fit Mr. Tom for some of those pants. He typically stayed nude when he shifted.

Speaking of Alek, he flew by a little further out, circling in the opposite direction. Though his human form was shorter than Cedric's, their gargoyle forms were of comparable size. His body was deep brown, covered in chunky muscles, and his thick arms hung at his sides as his wings beat the air.

Mr. Tom, his form a darker brown than Alek's, almost black to match his midnight eyes, sailed below on a lower plane, his wings slimmer in breadth and needing more beats per minute to compensate.

"Alek and Cedric are really great flyers," I said, working on my courage. "Look how graceful they are in the sky. They were born for this."

"Gargoyles are born to fly, yes. Except for you—you were made to fly—and the females of the species have smaller wings. They will need to aggressively protect you when you're in the sky."

"They might need to catch me first." The canopy of trees beneath us butted up against a lovely garden of huge, jagged rocks that would break my fall should my wings not work. "They're going to have to catch me. My wings aren't going to work."

"Why do you say that?"

"Because I don't think I am ready for this life. I mean, I'm not even used to being single yet. I was living with the same people for half of my life, and suddenly I'm in a completely different situation in an unfamiliar, *magical* world. It's all too much. That's part of the reason that I wanted to date a Dick."

"Except...everything would have been new to you anyway, right? You were in a cocoon for the last twenty years. Dating has changed since you were last single. So what does it matter if the person you're dating is a Dick or someone magical? Either way, it's going to feel unfamiliar. The magic part is just one more thing to learn about the person, plus it'll be something you have in common. What do you do for a living? Oh, you are an international bounty hunter, fantastic. How's business these days? What brings you to these parts— not me, I hope." He chuckled. "See? I've even given you an icebreaker joke to start things off."

"How would I meet an international bounty hunter in this small town?"

"They pass through, like everyone else. Get Austin to hook you up with someone. Or, I know-you're familiar with shifters now, so maybe start there. Leave the bounty hunters for when you want a bigger thrill."

He did make a lot of sense, I had to give him that. Thinking about the whole magic thing as a job made it a bit less daunting.

"Thanks, Edgar, that actually helped."

"That's great! Might've been nicer to have that pep talk without the crushing fear of falling to one's death hanging over our heads, but beggars can't be choosers, as they say. You still haven't come around for tea. We'll have to get you over to my cottage one of these days. If we survive the fall, of course."

I sighed as Cedric sailed by again, looking straight ahead as though he had all the time in the world. He was not rushing me in any way, nor did he seem like he was wondering why I was taking so long. That took the pressure off a little.

"Okay, I gotta jump." I rubbed my hands together. "I've stalled long enough."

"Drat. I was rather hoping you'd refuse so we could play that game of hide-and-seek. I'm pretty good at it. Then maybe we'd just wander home on our own two feet."

"That would take forever."

"But at least we wouldn't slip through the claws of these creatures and plummet to our deaths."

"The absolute worst possible choice for support. The worst."

"Yes, you do have a point."

"Okay, wings..." I edged forward in a flurry of terror and adrenaline, breathing faster. "Here we go, wings..." I put my arms out to the sides for no reason—what was I going to do, flap them and play pretend? The wind whipped around me, yanking at my half shirt, the back open, and shoving at my loose sweats. "I can do it. Oh, hell, this is so high. This is so, so high."

I looked down at the trees and rocks way below. Then back up at the limitless blue sky, crisp and cold. I was never going to fly if I didn't take a chance. I had four people ready to catch me, three with actual arms. There was a long drop, so they'd have plenty of time to swoop in.

"They're asking me to put a lot of faith in a couple of strangers. Guys I've only just met." I wiggled my fingers. Cedric made smaller and smaller circles, glancing over at me now, still not trying to rush me, I knew, but preparing.

Mr. Tom worked in closer, too, and Niamh went low, probably the last resort.

Four people. They'd catch me if my wings didn't open. They would.

"Oh God!" Not bothering with any kind of count, I jumped out into the nothingness. My stomach rolled and another shot of adrenaline rocked through my body, tingly with fear. My exclamation turned into a scream I couldn't help.

Gravity sucked at me, dragging me down. My heart clattered and my chest felt light, my brain knowing I was falling, and tacking a *to death* to that thought.

My reflexes kicked in, but only my body's reflexes, not my magic. My spindly, featherless arms beat at the air, doing absolutely nothing to fix the situation. My feet kicked of their own volition, as though I were swimming against the current. My speed picked up, my body dropping like a sack of rocks. The ground—still far below, thank God—vibrated through my watery stare as my mouth cranked open to let out the sound of my fear.

"Help," I yelled. Electricity coursed through me. It blazed across my skin and curled within my hair. It felt like I'd grabbed a live wire, my body tensing up as the current flowed through me, infusing me with power. It pierced down to my core and then pulsed outward again, a peal of thunder commanding Mr. Tom or someone around me to come to my aid.

But just in case they hadn't felt the magic... "Help!"

I looked around wildly, my body lazily turning in the air, my head pointed toward the ground while my feet faced the sky, the position only increasing my speed.

"No. Oh God. Help! Catch me!" I sent another pulse, stronger, direr, an SOS. "*Why is no one catching me*?"

A little surge of magic reached me from Ivy House, not obstructed by the distance or any of the many objects in the way.

"Those you summoned are already en route. They will protect you."

She must've been talking about the second summons, because the guys from the first were around here somewhere *not* doing their job. Definitely not protecting me in my plummet toward the ground.

"I hope this next wave is better than the first," I said through clenched teeth, still flapping my arms like an idiot, hoping for those wings to sprout. I could really use them. "And I hope they've been en route for a while, because I'm running out of time!"

"I have sent help."

"I already have help! I have four helps. *Why aren't they doing anything?*"

Ivy House was now hearing every swear word I'd ever learned.

Wings thrummed near me. "Oh thank God." It felt like I had been falling forever.

I continued to rotate through the air and lost sight of the rocks rushing up for me. The jagged points that would break me into pieces.

A purplish body swooped down over me, arms

reaching. I stretched to grab Cedric's outstretched hand, but a streak of bright white light cut across my vision, slashing down his chest and blasting him away.

I screamed, looking around wildly, and the next moment my back struck something pliable, like an enormous spiderweb, only it wasn't attached to anything I could see. The sticky material wrapped around me and jarred me to an almost complete halt, but then the bottom ripped across my back and dumped me out, feet and butt first. Gravity clutched at me greedily, pulling me down again.

Another slash of light zipped across my field of vision. This one slammed into Niamh's side, the light swallowed by her inky black feathers. She flapped her wings furiously, fighting through the attack and continuing to head my way.

A blast shook me from my right and a shooting rainbow of color exploded into her this time, smashing her back.

"What's happening?" I gasped out, ever falling, thankful now for the incredible height of that cliff. If we'd done this at Ivy House, I would've been smooshed on the grass long before now.

But if we'd done it at Ivy House, we probably wouldn't have been attacked.

The rocks reached up for me, thirty feet and closing

fast.

"Oh no. Oh God, oh no."

Dark skin dove into sight, Mr. Tom with his hand held out. His wings beat frantically, and it was hopefully just my imagination, but it sounded like the echo hit the rocks below and bounced back up. Trees studded my peripheral vision.

"Edgar should've gone first. Wait, crap, I shouldn't think that thought right now, right before it's decided if I end up in heaven or hell…"

His hand just barely at my ankle, a searing light pierced his wing, cutting clean through. He wobbled in the air but didn't relent, his bony fingers wrapping around my ankle.

I didn't get a chance to say my thanks before he spun, whipping me around.

I opened my mouth to scream, but no sound came out. My hair barely slapped the very edge of a jutting rock before I was catapulted upward at an angle, end over end.

"Wings," I said, my stomach rolling, my bladder threatening release. "Wings!"

Electricity shocked through me, and I pushed it out, shock waves filling the sky. Ivy House answered.

"Almost there. I have you."

"I need my *wings!*" I fisted my hands, shoving them

out to the sides, and flexed my back—which was when I hit the peak of my arc and started falling again.

"Noooo!" I went back to flapping my arms.

A heavy *throp-throp-throp* caught my ear, almost like a helicopter, the rhythmic noise was so powerful. I couldn't see where it was coming from.

A brown gargoyle—Alek—rolled away on my far right, moving through the air like a tumbleweed in the sky. A stream of light soared up through the trees, aimed at me. It would be too late, though. By the time it reached me, I'd be a smear of red pulp on the rocks.

"C'mon, wings," I pleaded, seeing none of my people. Not able to properly look around, not able to look away from the mottled gray rock ten feet beneath me. Five.

I scrunched up my eyes, willing my wings to work, knowing they probably wouldn't, the rhythmic *throp-throp-throp* filling my world.

CHAPTER 10

S TRONG ARMS WRAPPED around me, bands of steel trapping me to a wide, heavily muscled chest, the skin basalt gray with a light sheen, the color gorgeous, the fact that I was alive to see it even more so. Huge, heavy wings strummed the air around us, mighty and powerful. They sped up, *throp-throp-throp*, lifting us into the air at an incredible speed.

A jet of light shot straight at us from the trees. The gargoyle tilted and spun, dizzying me with the maneuver so that the world seemed to circle us. He straightened, beating the air with his wings, and turned to face the attacker hidden within the trees, seemingly fearless.

I was terrified. If one of those zips of light hit him, it was back to the rocks for me.

"Go, go, at least get higher," I said, my magic pounding around us, doing absolutely no good.

Those incredible wings, mightier than any I'd seen thus far, their breadth incredible, had us a hundred feet above the ground in a blink with seemingly minimal effort. That was when I noticed the others.

Gargoyles streamed around him, some large and powerful, some smaller and incredibly quick, their skin in all colors and shades. One of them paused twenty feet away, its coloring overall a deep gray but cut through with tan in various places, and looked up at us.

One of the arms holding me peeled away.

"Oh no. No, no!" I tried to twist around and grab his neck. I assumed this was the protector sent by Ivy House, but even if I was wrong, I didn't care—I was going to hang on for dear life until our feet were on the ground. His one arm held me firm, though, absolutely no give.

He pointed with the other hand at the trees where the zip of light had originated. The gargoyles took off, flying for that spot, fast and effective in the air.

Zips of light met them, arching through the blue sky, the enemy seeing the coming attack and defending against it. The gargoyles tilted and spun, barely missing the magical assault. The one who was holding me pushed higher still, soaring out of harm's reach.

A neon-pink gargoyle reached the trees first, a blast streaking across his shoulder and punching through his wing. He tucked his wings in close and dove through the canopy.

Purplish skin caught my attention—Cedric, a jagged gash across his torso and his pants halfway ripped off. He stopped in front of us, his wings needing to pump faster than the gargoyle holding me to keep him afloat.

"Help," I said before I'd thought it through.

Ivy House's magical communication echoed in my mind. "You are with help."

"Never mind." I waved Cedric away as Niamh's alicorn body rose on black wings from the canopy of trees near the enemy's location, her crystalline horn and hooves catching the dying light. The struggle to rise was clear, one wing tattered and something dripping from her back leg. Blood, it must be.

A dual-colored gargoyle rose from the same area. A man dangled from his hand, held by the ankle, his body limp. A long cape swung down, clothing, not wings. More gargoyles rose around him, three of them also carrying a dangling person.

Niamh, the effort to stay in the air plain, reached us, her red eyes staring at the gargoyle who held me.

"It's okay," I yelled over the throbbing wings around us. "Ivy House sent him. Where are the others? Alek and Mr. Tom?"

She neighed and tossed her head. I wasn't sure what that meant.

I peeled away the block I'd put up to give her privacy, and a wave of pain, frustration, and impatience blasted me through her magical connection. She wanted to go home. Right now.

Fair enough.

As my gargoyle rescuer wrapped his other arm around me to further tighten his hold, I peeled the other blocks away to check on Edgar (obviously safe but worried) and Mr. Tom (wallowing in agony). There was no way I could get a reading on Alek, who hadn't been granted Ivy House magic, so I'd have to find him the normal, and much harder, way.

"Mr. Tom is there." I pointed, down and to the left, feeling him through our magical connection. "Hurry, he's hurt. Niamh, you go back to the house. These guys clearly have the danger under control."

She stayed where she was, annoyed now, her glowing red gaze accusatory. Thankfully, I could only pick up on her feelings, not her thoughts—I doubted I'd like the names she was calling me.

"Fine, stay. Hey—" I patted the large arm around my middle before pointing again. "Please help me. We need to get to Mr. Tom. Cedric!" I waved at him even though he was already watching me, flying in place ten feet away. "Go get Edgar." I motioned him upward. "We'll meet you back at Ivy House. *Stay there* until I get back."

But he didn't move, and nobody else did either. The other gargoyles had gathered, four of them holding their limp catches of the day, a host of flying creatures nearly stationary in the sky.

Ivy House's words thundered through my skull. *"You must lead, or you will be led."*

I gritted my teeth. I didn't have any freaking experience leading an army of magical creatures...

Or did I?

I'd been a PTA president for two years, I'd been a parent helper in classrooms, I'd had to take over for a drunk dad in Boy Scouts, and I'd marshaled my family through some hard times. If I could handle bored, passive-aggressive moms, pompous school staff, crazy children, and a bunch of mansplaining dads who thought they could do better but didn't want to step up to the plate, I could handle a bunch of gruff, stubborn gargoyles.

I steeled my nerves and pumped out a shocking blast of magic, rocking them in the sky.

"Cedric, *go get Edgar*," I growled, low and stern and promising pain if he did not listen. It was basically the grownup equivalent of counting to three. I hoped he could hear me through all the racket. Large wings were loud. To emphasize my point, I used my magic to hurtle him upward, the same principle as shoving him away,

K . F . B R E E N E

just in a specific direction.

He took off, flapping like I'd jabbed him with a hot poker.

"Big guy. Hey." I patted the arm around me again then pointed toward Mr. Tom. "Hurry. He's hurt. *Now.*"

I focused on spurring him on, like a swat to the butt. The electricity I'd felt earlier, the surge of magic that had not, unfortunately, resulted in wings, rolled through my body again and skittered across my skin. He jerked, his arms spasming, squeezing me tightly enough to force out my breath.

Right. Probably the wrong magical trick—

But then his wings beat at the sky, moving us forward, parting his waiting people. He tilted us until our chests were pointing at the ground, our bodies aligned so his wings were like a hang glider on my back. In a moment his wings curled inward and we pitched forward, gaining speed in a fast dive.

"Oh crap, oh crap, oh crap," I said between clenched teeth, my nails digging into his rough gargoyle skin, my stomach trying to evacuate through my mouth.

Flying wasn't just about flapping wings, clearly. Flying was maneuvering and diving and rolling through the sky with confidence. What had I been smoking, thinking I was prepared for something like this? It took everything I had not to scream.

The canopy jiggled in my vision, rushing at us like I was falling again. I squeezed my eyes shut, unable to take it, pointing in Mr. Tom's direction so we stayed on course. The snap of his wings surprised me, and I jerked against his constricting arms, a scream slipping free. I blinked my eyes opened as we hovered just above the treetops. Slowly, his control excellent, he lowered into the branches until his wings flapped just above them.

"Tu-*rrn.*" He loosened his arms a little and then altered his hold, coaxing me to twist within his embrace. His arms tightened again when my front was pressed against his thick chest, his gargoyle skin tough and a little scratchy.

He tucked my left arm in against him, then my right, before nudging my head under his chin, getting me to curl up into his big body. Once done, everything happened really fast. One arm kept squeezing me close and his wings snapped inward. We dropped like a stone.

"Oh sh—"

His free arm lashed out and grabbed a branch, jerking us to a stop.

Crack.

The branch broke under the weight.

Incredibly fast, he let go and grabbed another, slowing us again. The first branch continued to fall, headed straight toward us, but he bent forward, curving around me, and the branch struck his shoulder instead of my head.

He let go of the stronger branch and grabbed another, then another, one wing half curled around our sides, protecting me from the foliage, while he kept me tucked within his protective embrace.

Near the ground he let go of the last branch, his wings snapping back behind him again and his free hand hugging me tight. His feet slammed into the ground and he bent with the impact, loosening his hold and then swinging my body around so I hardly felt the jolt.

My butt bumped the ground, and all I could do was stare up into his face, his eyes bulging unnaturally, his jaw pushed forward, and his large teeth protruding over his leathery lips. In that moment, I could well understand why beauty had fallen for the beast. It wasn't about appearances in times like these—it was about appreciating the creature that had not only saved your life, but also tried to keep you in perfect condition while he did it.

"Thanks," I said, and wiped my arm across my forehead.

Branches cracked around us and leaves shivered

down onto the ground. The other gargoyles landed, followed by Niamh, touching down in a rainstorm of leaves and branches.

I scrambled up and looked around, sensing Mr. Tom twenty or so feet away. He lay in a crowding of brambles, one wing torn along a vein and the other cinched in tightly to his body, embedded with hundreds of thorns, I was sure. A jagged cut slashed across his chest, and blood oozed from his forehead.

"Mr. Tom?" I stopped just outside the brambles and looked around, lifting my arms in that way people did when they were getting ready to wade into really cold water.

He grunted, the mouth and teeth of gargoyles not quite conducive to talking.

"Can you be moved, Mr. Tom? What do we—"

"Here, Earl..." Niamh came over in her birthday suit, wincing with each step but clearly not ready to give in and limp. Thick crimson rivulets ran down the milky skin of her leg. "Either change into stone so you can heal, or change into a man so we can see what's wrong with ya."

"His wing is torn, that's what's wrong with him," I said, looking for a path into the middle of that patch of brambles. "He's got a—"

"There's some damage, yes, but we need to know if

there is anything that will jeopardize his healing."

A sound like boulders moving through a canyon caught my attention as Mr. Tom shifted into his solid form. I made sure to think about what I wanted—*change into a man and be okay*—so that we could get him out of there. This was another eccentricity of gargoyles. When in stone form, they awakened more quickly if they were called to do something. Hopefully Cedric hadn't had any trouble with Edgar, but there was still Alek to find.

While Mr. Tom was doing that, I turned back to the enormous basalt-gray gargoyle, the tops of his arcing wings adding five feet of height to his already wide and brawny shoulders. A wicked claw protruded from the top of each wing, joined by a claw at the end of each vein, where the leathery material gathered when the wings were pulled in. His thick arms hung loose at his sides, ending in large, clawed hands that could rip my throat out in one swipe.

He was magnificent, huge and imposing, an obvious force to be reckoned with.

And I was somehow supposed to lead him. I nearly laughed.

You got him here, Jacinta, I reminded myself. *You summoned him, and when he didn't want to rescue Mr. Tom, you forced him to land. You got him here, which means you* can *lead him—you just need the confidence.*

I wrapped my magic around me to ward off the cold and surveyed the gargoyles around him without really seeing them. It was a stalling tactic and something that looked really good in movies.

"Do you have all your men?" I asked the basalt gargoyle. "Did you lose any?"

"No," he grunted, his speech a little clearer than Mr. Tom was usually capable of in gargoyle form.

"Right, okay. We have one—a little smaller than most of you—missing. Brown form. No idea where he could be. Send a few people to fly over the treetops and look."

"That missing gargoyle is going to try to blend in. He won't want to be seen if he's hurt," Niamh said, her hands on her hips, her leg bleeding freely. "He won't know these are friendlies."

The lead gargoyle grunted, and it felt like an affirmation.

"Crap," I said, looking out through the trees. "Well, we can't leave him."

"Ah, sure, it'll be grand," Niamh said. "He'll heal and come back, or he'll not heal and he won't come back."

The large gargoyle grunted out another affirmation.

"That's…" I shook my head at her. Magical people

had a very different view of fallen soldiers than their non-magical counterparts.

A pulse of magic concussed the air before the idea even coalesced in my head. There was one guy who *did* understand the need to bring everyone home. A guy who wouldn't blink if I asked him to hunt down a fallen man.

Austin, I need help. Please come.

I hoped he'd know the request was from me and not Ivy House. The more I thought about it, the more I knew he was the perfect person to help. Gargoyles couldn't smell like shifters could. They couldn't hunt or track. They weren't good on the ground—not like Austin.

"Yes, miss, here I am. You wanted me?"

I turned back to the brambles, peering in to see Mr. Tom's face. He lay still, making no move to crawl out.

"Mr. Tom, are you okay?"

I sent another pulse to Austin, pulling down the block on our connection to see if he was responding. Immediately his location hit me—he was headed my way and coming fast, probably halfway between where I stood and town. He'd somehow known I was in trouble and had left before receiving my summons.

Relief coursed through me. "Okay, good." I brushed the hair away from my face. "Austin is on his way. He'll find Alek."

"That lad made a right balls of the battle," Niamh said. "Sure, he flat-out got in the way when Cedric was zeroing in on the enemy shootin' that magic. If you ask me, yer passin' up a grand wee lesson for the lad. What happens when you are not helpful? Left for dead, that's what, and good enough for ya."

"Not much of a team player, then, ye eld bag?" Mr. Tom said from the brambles, his words a little slurred and his fake Irish accent utterly terrible and therefore hilarious.

Niamh blew out a breath and walked away. "Speaking of letting the weak links die off…"

"Mr. Tom, can you get out of there? Will you heal?" I paused, then added, "Could you not crawl out in your other form?"

"No, miss, I'm okay. I was just taking a little break before I headed back into the fray. This seemed as cozy a place to land as any. A little poke-y, but nothing like a pea under my mattresses, right?"

"Donkey," Niamh muttered. "He's clearly cracked his head. He's going to have to be carried home."

"Oh no, I don't want to be any trouble."

"Should we send someone to get a truck, and we can haul him home that way?" I asked.

"One of the others can carry him," Niamh replied.

"Mind you, one of 'em will need to drag him out first. There isn't enough room to fly over him and scoop him out."

"I'm not going to make them cut themselves up. He's my responsibility. I'll do it," I said with a sigh.

Of all the days not to bring a metal suit. Not that I had one, but still…

"Okay, Mr. Tom, I'm going to come in and get you, okay? I'm going to take your hand and drag you out. It won't be pleasant." I reduced my voice to a mumble. "For either of us."

After walking around the perimeter and finding a smallish break on one side of the brambles, I steeled myself and shoved the branches aside, making room for me to work my way in. Given my escalated healing rate, this would merely be painful. Tolerate that for a bit, drag him out, and I was done.

"No." The large gargoyle stepped forward, his wings opening just a bit more, the ends dusting the ground. "I. *Go*."

"It's fine, honestly. It'll just be—"

"No." He gently placed his hand on my shoulder, the warmth sending a wash of goosebumps across my flesh. "I. *Go*." The pressure of his touch made me step back, out of the way. "Me."

Given his skin was coarser than mine, and he

seemed tough and no-nonsense, I stopped arguing. Brambles shouldn't hurt him as much as they would me.

He didn't enter the mess of thorns gingerly, like I'd planned to. He marched in, thorns scraping across his arms and crushed under his feet. Red lines opened up along his skin, blood welling quickly and dripping down. He turned his head to the side and reached. His arm flexed, and then he was turning and walking back out, dragging poor Mr. Tom behind him.

"Not as fun as exfoliating with a Brillo pad," Mr. Tom said, his wings catching and the split one leaving a trail of blood behind him.

The large gargoyle dumped Mr. Tom on the ground, looked down on the badly torn wing, grunted, and resumed his place in front of his men.

"Ouch." Mr. Tom didn't bother getting up. "That was mostly unpleasant."

Another peek into the connection, and I saw Austin was almost here. As soon as we found Alek, we could all head back. I'd about had it. World's worst flying lesson. I wished I could just throw in the towel. And now we had yet another problem on our hands—the attack, and how these mages had known where I'd be.

Suddenly exhausted, I didn't have it in me to be nervous about the future. I'd get to that later.

"Mr. Tom, change into stone so you can start healing. Who volunteers to carry him?" I lifted my eyebrows as I faced the gargoyles. "He is the caretaker of Ivy House, and I am its mistress. Really? None of you want the honor of carrying him?"

The bright pink gargoyle stepped forward, his chest shimmering with an electric sheen of blue. I hadn't known they could come in disco colors. I quite liked it.

"Thank you." I nudged Mr. Tom with my foot. "Come on, change. Hurry up now."

"Of course, miss. I am just now summoning the energy. It is not easy, I assure you. I feel rather like a wad of gum that has been swallowed and has since been worked out the other side."

I frowned down at him. That wasn't a great image, but it did seem accurate.

In another few moments, the pink gargoyle lifted off with the stone version of Mr. Tom, the weight not seeming to affect him at all. The gargoyles who were toting our possibly alive but maybe dead attackers left with him. Only the uninjured stayed behind.

"We don't have long to wait for my friend," I said as the gargoyles stood in place. They didn't seem impatient, but then, they didn't really have facial expressions.

A moment later, I heard the soft rustle of something coming through the trees, something that sounded about half the size of what I was expecting. My connection said it was Austin, though, and a moment later he edged out from the dull green foliage, a massive polar bear bigger than any such creature in the wild. Standing on all fours, he was tall enough that his shoulder nearly reached the top of my head. His own head was full of sharp teeth, and each of his claws could rip a person apart with a single swipe. When he stood on his hind legs, you just really hoped he was on your side.

Head low, a deep growl in his throat, he advanced on our group slowly. His focus was on the basalt-gray gargoyle, who, upon seeing the enormous predator suddenly in our midst, turned quickly and snapped out his wings, the claw on one ripping bark as it passed a tree trunk and the other punching into a wall of bushes. He didn't have the space to maneuver, though. If there was a fight, Austin was much better equipped to handle it. As the gargoyles' hands came up, though, revealing his claws, and his mouth opened to expose his long canines, it was clear he wouldn't let that stop him.

"Whoa, whoa, whoa." Despite my survival instinct instructing me to get out of there, I jogged between them, my hands held high. "Whoa, whoa. Friendly fire. Austin, this gargoyle and his people saved my life. He literally plucked me out of the air. They took down someone shooting magic at us. Four people, actually.

The threat is gone. What we need now is to find one of the fallen. Alek—remember Alek? He went down, and since he's not a part of Ivy House, I don't know where to find him."

Austin's intelligent blue eyes regarded me from within his awesome beast form. His head swung slightly until he was looking at the large gargoyle again, that stare enough to unnerve even the most courageous. The gargoyle stood his ground, though, his muscles still flared and his wings fully expanded.

With a huff, Austin took a step before dropping down to his belly, making himself vulnerable in a way that showed an incredible amount of trust in me and my ability to control the gargoyles. I ran and jumped onto his back, not making it all the way up and scrambling. He reached back with his large paw and pushed me the rest of the way.

"Thanks." I reached into his fur, coarse on top and baby-soft within, as he rose to all fours. "Try not to thwap my face with the branches. I don't want to go flying again just yet. I've had enough of that for a while." I turned to the others. "Follow us in the air. When we stop moving, one of you can come down and get Alek, yes? Niamh, go home. I have more than enough protection. I don't need you bleeding out."

"I'll be—"

"Go home. You'll only slow us down." I stared at her, brooking no argument.

"Fair play to ya," she muttered. "See ya at the bar. I need a drink."

"Go, Lassie, go! Find Timmy!" I motioned us on, grinning at his sudden burst of speed. At least if I fell off him, I wouldn't go splat.

After we found Alek, we could get to the bottom of who'd wanted me captured or dead.

CHAPTER 11

NIAMH WAITED IN Ivy House, her leg pounding like the bejesus and Earl hunched down in his stone form beside her. She'd made him very comfortable by decorating him with doilies and potted plants. When he came out of his healing stupor, or when Jessie called him, needing something, he'd shake everything off and create a big mess that he'd then obsess over.

It was the little things.

The host of very polite gargoyles waited in a few of the other sitting rooms in the house, mostly dead quiet. Their kind didn't say much. Where had Earl gone wrong?

That crew had taken out the attacking mages without much hassle, which was good news. Bad news was that those mages had gotten Alek before they'd been taken out. He hadn't made it. Jessie had insisted one of the gargoyles take the body back safely to Ivy House. She'd wanted to ride home with Austin. She'd clearly had enough time in the sky for the moment.

"They've been gone a long time." Edgar, standing in the corner like the creepy vampire he was, tapped the wall for some reason while looking at the grandfather clock. "Are we sure they're coming back here? Maybe they went to the bar. Or Austin Steele's cabin."

"Not a hope. Austin Steele got a good look at yer man, but he didn't get a chance to assert his dominance. He'll want another chance to size him up." She steepled her fingers, calling up the memory of the largish basalt-gray gargoyle. She'd seen bigger, tougher, and more advanced fliers, but he'd do fine for the current situation. He shouldn't be too hard to control either. If he got too rowdy for Jessie, then Austin Steele could handle him, Niamh had no doubt. She hadn't yet met someone the vicious shifter couldn't take down. She rued the day when she did. "It was a tense couple of minutes. You missed it."

"It couldn't have been more tense than being dangled below a large gargoyle over incredible heights for a very long time."

"Ah, stop yer moaning. The standoff would have been even tenser if Austin Steele had thought Jessie was in any real danger—"

"Are you sure he didn't? I saw the gargoyle alpha from the very high cliff. He looked huge compared to the others."

"The whole host of them were standing there, Jessie off to the side. If Austin Steele had thought they were a threat, he would've approached from behind and barreled through them all, taking on the largest last. Otherwise the rest would have piled on him while he tangled up with the big 'un. Honestly, Edgar, how have ye lasted this long?"

"Hiding in holes and shadows, mostly. People seem to forget about me pretty easily…"

She scratched her nose, then knocked on Earl's head. It was nice when he was quiet, but it was also nice when he served her beer and snacks. Although, when he came to and realized she'd bled all over the rug, plus pulled off the trick with the doilies and potted plants, he'd probably need a cooling-off period.

She reached down and checked the leg wound, a nasty affair. The mage who'd hit her had attacked with some sort of healing-resistant spell. She'd leaked out her leg all the way back to the house. Thankfully, as soon as she touched down onto the property, Ivy House had patched her right up. It still hurt like a Texan's butthole after a chili contest, but the blood had stopped pouring. She'd mend.

She'd mend, and she'd hold a grudge.

Someone had sent those clowns after them, and that someone was going to die slowly and painfully. She'd make sure of it.

"Well, ye can believe me when I say Austin Steele knew they were no threat. Still, I half thought he was gonna launch himself at that big el' gargoyle. He wanted to, I could see that. He wanted to give that gargoyle a nice el' slap," she said, thinking back with a grin. She shivered. That had been a nice little treat, all that hostility. Too bad the pain of her wound had blocked out the rush of adrenaline.

"Why do that if he knew there was no threat?"

Niamh knocked on Earl's head again. She really did want a beer. Or a cuppa with a biscuit. She hated sitting around empty-handed. It wasn't right.

"Because they are two alphas, that's why." She grinned. "They are two alphas who can each handle a large territory without blinking, and this is a very small town."

"Oh. Yes, that is a problem. Austin Steele doesn't like competition."

"It's not competition he's worried about, it's insubordination. And this other guy won't like that someone is trying to make him submit, especially someone that doesn't hold the actual title of alpha." She rubbed her hands together. "And here I wanted to retire before Jessie came along."

"This is the danger Jessie felt coming."

"Must be. Those two together will be trouble, ye mark my words. Very astute, our Jessie. Very emotionally in tune. It's probably because she's a mother. Mothers seem to sense things normal people don't. If it wouldn't have meant looking after a carpet shark, I would've had a bebe just to get the extra powers."

"I don't know that they are exactly powers…"

"A little extra patience for dealing with you and Mr. Tom could certainly be counted as a power…"

"Yes, I see what you mean."

A presence interrupted the plane of Ivy House, immediately morphing into the feeling of Jessie and Austin Steele.

"Speak of the devil and the devil doth appear," Niamh murmured, wincing as she stood from her chair. "Come on, Edgar, let's go watch the fireworks."

The front door swung open as Jessie neared, Ivy House welcoming its mistress home. Her hair formed a fuzzy halo around her head, and her tired eyes drooped. A smudge of dirt darkened her rosy complexion, and her disheveled clothes revealed a little more side boob than she probably realized.

"Hey," she said when she saw Niamh. Glancing around the empty front entranceway, she added, "Where is everyone? Where's Cedric?"

Jessie had the ability to feel everyone in the house,

but she was clearly too exhausted to bother.

"In one of the sitting rooms. I didn't pass any remarks about which they chose." Niamh looked behind her at Edgar, wondering if he'd paid any more attention to the strangers.

He shrugged. "They're intimidating. I figured I'd make myself scarce."

"Excellent protection of the house, Edgar, yes," Niamh said, nodding as she turned back. "It's well sorted with you around."

"What did you guys do with the body?" Jessie asked quietly. Austin Steele stood at her back, looking with hard eyes deeper into the house. "Alek's body?"

"Oh, that." She glanced back at Edgar again. Grounds burials were his department.

"I thought it best to drop him in the incinerator," Edgar replied, entwining his fingers. "If someday someone digs up the grounds of Ivy House, we don't want them to find a supernatural body. It would raise questions."

A crease formed in Jessie's brow. "How would they even know? The wings? Because, I mean…we buried a ton of supernatural bodies a couple months ago after that battle…"

Edgar leaned forward a little bit, his eyebrows crawling up toward his hairline. "Oh yes. I forgot about those. Well…" He hesitated, clearly searching his pea-sized intellect for another, more believable, excuse.

Niamh saved him the trouble. "He got lazy and was too afraid to ask the gargoyles to dig a grave." She waved it away.

"Yes. That's the way of it. But don't worry, Jessie, no one will miss him." Edgar crossed the room to stand just beside Niamh. "He wasn't all that bright and he wasn't a great flier. Why your magic called someone with training wheels, we'll never know, huh?" He smiled, his teeth still stained red.

Jessie's mouth fell open and she pointed at him. "Oh my God, Edgar, did you drink from him before you disposed of him?"

Edgar's mouth snapped shut.

"Waste not, want not," Niamh said. "Don't worry about Cedric, Jessie—he and Alek weren't close. They were both summoned, sure, probably because you were *just* thinking about flying and not someone useful in other things, but they were more associates than friends. They both came here knowing the risks. Besides, he's found…new friends."

Austin Steele's cobalt gaze slid to Niamh, wild and vicious and sending chills down her spine.

She'd be damned if she took a step back—

Her back bumped into Edgar, who'd retreated

quickly, neither fighting his fear nor attempting to hide it.

Bollocks!

Jessie nodded, looking left. "What's the story with Mr. Tom? Is he—"

The sound of boulders rolling drifted to Niamh. Porcelain crashed to the ground.

She couldn't help a smile.

"That insufferable woman. She did this, I know it," Mr. Tom muttered.

The chuckles were unavoidable.

"Yes, miss. Coming! Coming, miss."

Niamh cleared out of the way as Earl emerged from the room, stiff, wincing, a doily on his head, and one wing still nearly torn in two.

"Oh no, Mr. Tom, are you okay?" Jessie reached out to him, compassion soaking through her eyes and a pout pushing out her lips. "You should be stone, right? Doesn't that help you heal?"

"I am completely fine." He jolted forward, a lot of effort for one step. "It's perfectly all right. You need something to take the edge off, and I need to prepare for company. Don't worry, I will see to it directly. I just need a bottle or so of painkillers, and I'll be at your service."

A man with a compact frame and short, spiky, pink-

and-blue-dyed hair stepped out of the room across the way.

"Oh. Hi." Jessie stepped forward with her hand outstretched. "I'm Jessie. Welcome. Thank you for helping earlier. You guys came just in the nick of time."

"Thank us?" he said with a huge grin. "No, thank *you*! We're honored you called us." He motioned back at the room. "We've been waiting for you." He looked at Austin Steele, his eyes not losing their sparkle. "Hey, bro." He bowed, the movement casual but poignant. He was registering Austin's superior status as the dominant male.

Austin Steele nodded at the pink-haired man, his posture large and imposing, but then turned slightly toward Jessie and grazed his hand across the small of her back. "Would you mind if I used *your* restroom?"

Niamh barely stopped herself from grinning and nodding in approval. Austin Steele had accepted the gargoyle's acknowledgment of his status and rank, and then passed it on to the holder of the establishment. By asking about "her" bathroom, he'd made it clear that this house was Jessie's, they were there with her permission, and he was just a player in her game.

They'd been incredibly lucky that Austin Steele had been tricked into coming on board, no matter his bellyaching about getting the magic. So few truly powerful people were willing to share their status and prestige.

"Sure, of course," Jessie said, absently patting his chest, the house sweats much too small for his powerful frame. Mr. Tom needed to up his ordering game.

Austin Steele left, and Earl stepped up beside Jessie, his arms rigid at his sides in a way that spoke of his incredible pain. Niamh had to hand it to him for holding it together.

"Oh, excuse me. Where are my manners." Jessie pouted at Mr. Tom again, like she would've an injured child. She rubbed his arm. "This is Mr. Tom. He's the caretaker—"

Edgar jabbed Niamh's side with a claw, making her jump. The magic of this place had restored much of the vampire's strength and vigor, but maybe the years of being TOTF (too old to function) had gotten to him— he constantly forgot to retract claws and fangs after feeding.

He pointed at Earl's wing as Jessie rambled on.

A shimmery haze floated in front of the leathery skin, slowly rotating around the tear. The magic sparkled, some of it soaking in while the rest continued to slowly revolve. Little by little, the tear stitched back together, as though unseen hands were sewing it.

"I'll be buggered," Niamh said quietly, watching the

magic work.

That wasn't Ivy House. Ivy House sped up the healing of the magical creatures attached to it, but it didn't do the work itself. This magic was actively fixing his torn wing.

This had to be Jessie. This right here was proof that mothers developed powers. Right now, Jessie was ignoring her incredible fatigue and the recent attack on her life, while making a complete stranger feel welcome, comforting a man-child, and mending a boo-boo, all while making it look effortless. Not actually powers, her arse.

"If you don't mind, I'll just quickly go change. I'll be down directly." Jessie smiled at the pink-haired man, ran her hand down Mr. Tom's arm for comfort, and jogged up the stairs in a hurry. The magical haze lingered, continuing to do its work.

"I'll go get some refreshments." Earl lurched away, his wing already half mended but still flopping as he moved.

The pink-haired man grinned at Niamh. "So you live in this creepy old house, huh?"

"No," she said, not caring to make other people more comfortable. "I thought your kind didn't talk much?"

"Most of us don't. I'm the exception."

"Pity," Niamh said, finally getting his grin to fade.

"And which gargoyle are you?" Edgar asked, inching closer.

"He's not the thinker of the bunch." Niamh patted Edgar's shoulder.

The grin was back. "The pink one." The man pointed at his hair. "I got picked on mercilessly as a kid. Before guys wearing pink was cool, obviously."

"Oh no, I'm so sorry. Bullying." Edgar shook his head. "It's not acceptable, even between shockingly violent creatures such as yourselves."

One to talk, him.

The man shrugged. "I survived." He put up his hands. "It made me tough."

"Tough and probably emotionally imbalanced, I'd expect." Edgar nodded sadly. The man's smile slipped again.

"Well, anyway, I should get back before... Jessie? Do we call her by her actual name?"

"No, she was just being polite. Call her madam or master." Niamh kept a straight face. "For special occasions, queen. But you knew that."

"Do no such thing." Earl walked back in with a silver tray laden with tea and water, wearing a somewhat wrinkled tux. He had his head held high, clearly fighting the pain, or maybe Jessie had numbed that. "She detests being called those names."

"Kill-joy," Niamh murmured.

"You may call her miss when in a professional setting, and Jessie when in a casual setting. Now, come along. Let's all assemble in the large drawing room for introductions and lively chatter before we figure out sleeping arrangements."

Niamh followed Earl. She didn't care for introductions or the nuts and bolts of a company this large descending on Ivy House, but she did want to see Jessie's face when she saw that other alpha's human form. He was a fine thing if ever there was one. A real looker. If she'd finally abandoned her plan to date strictly Dicks, she'd do well to get her feet wet with a guy like that.

CHAPTER 12

I STEPPED INTO a pair of slacks before shrugging into a nice sweater. Being that I'd called these people with my summonses, only to order them around, I figured I'd better look at least a little presentable. Not to mention poor Alek hadn't made it.

My stomach swam as I checked my face in the mirror, something I immediately regretted. I looked like I'd been rolling around in the dirt.

It hadn't taken Austin long to find Alek, both pieces of him. His head had rolled a good ways away from the body, and I'd thrown up a good ways away from that.

One of the gargoyles had taken Alek's body back so he could have a proper burial—joke was on me there— and the large lead gargoyle had gestured me closer so I could get a ride home. I'd turned it down so I could ride with (or on) Austin, something the guy hadn't seemed to understand, probably because I was supposedly made to fly. He hadn't just nearly died from falling, though.

Hair brushed and in a ponytail because it was much

too messy to stay down, I made my way back downstairs to officially meet my saviors. My limbs shook with the memory of those rocks rushing up to meet me.

I'd been ten feet from death, something I hadn't properly freaked out about yet. On Austin's back, I'd closed my eyes and pushed all thoughts from my mind, comforted by the rhythm of his soft steps and the muscles bunching and releasing under my body. Relieved crying could happen later, in the privacy of my own darkened closet with a bottle of wine and brick of chocolate. Immediately afterward, I'd slide into frustrated crying, pissed that I couldn't get my stupid wings to extend, or my magic to do anything even remotely useful except for calling for someone to save me. I was supposed to be a badass, and instead I kept ending up being the damsel in distress. It was driving me nuts.

Austin waited for me at the base of the steps, his thumbs hooked in the band of his tight white sweats, awkwardly showing off his prominent bulge, and his muscles flared under his wrinkled, too-tight sweatshirt. Mr. Tom had clearly gotten the sizing wrong.

He nodded at me in greeting when I neared. "They're all waiting for you in the—"

"I know. I can feel them," I said.

He nodded again. "I'm going to head out. I want to gather some information about those mages they took down before I do a perimeter check and then head back out to the battle site. I want to make sure no one escaped, number one, and get some idea of whether we should expect more trouble from this faction, number two."

"Don't you want to meet the others? Speak to them about what they know?"

"I was just in there. They told me what I needed to know." He paused, then added, "I don't belong here, Jess. This is your jam. I need to get back out to the town, make sure it's secure. You can take it from here."

"You have Ivy House magic and a seat in that Council Room if you want it. You belong here more than they do."

He shook his head slowly. "I don't want it, you know that. They do, though, and they all seem to have your best interests at heart. Whatever you did when you met Damarion—"

"Who?"

"Damarion. Their alpha. Your second-in-command, if you choose him."

"Ah. The biggest one."

"Yes." A growl rode the word. "The biggest one." His biceps and pecs popped, straining his sweatshirt. He rolled his neck, something bothering him. I had a feeling it was the memory of walking into my vicinity and thinking Damarion and his people were trying to kill or capture me. "Whatever you did set you up as their top badass." A sparkle of pride glimmered in his eyes. "Their alpha might have carried you around like a damsel, but you proved yourself in their eyes."

I hadn't voiced my frustration, but somehow he'd picked up on it, figured out how to recast my weakness as strength, and made me feel amazing about myself, all in the same breath. How the hell did he do it? The guy had a gift.

I leaned toward him without thinking, closing my eyes and sighing when he wrapped his arms around me and hugged me close. Now more than ever, I needed a friend. I needed a solid rock in this storm of uncertainty. I had to know he'd be by my side the next time someone came for me, because I knew it would happen again.

"You okay?" he asked softly, rubbing my back.

"Sure."

"They'll follow you. As long as you keep the status quo, which is easier than getting status in the first place, you're head dick. You can pick and choose who you want on your team. But listen…" He pulled me back, his face not far from mine, his breath smelling of spearmint and honey. "If you leave these grounds to train, you call me, okay? You shouldn't have had mages waiting in the trees to take a shot at you. I'm your ground man. My job is to take out the problem before there is a problem. But you need to *call me* so I know what's going on. If it weren't for those gargoyles showing up in the final moment..."

"Ivy House sent them...somehow, but yeah, I hear you. We don't even know how people knew where I'd be."

A vein jumped in his jaw as he clenched his teeth. "That's one of the questions I'll be trying to answer."

"How'd you know to come? You were on the way before I called you. How'd you know?"

The vein in his jaw jumped again and fire kindled in his eyes. "Ivy House knows the trick to get me moving. Or at least checking in..." He shook his head. "This damn house is too adaptable for its own good."

With that, he strode past me and out the door, not looking back.

"What'd you do?" I asked Ivy House quietly, a little embarrassed by my tendency to talk to the house like it was alive. Talking to myself was one thing...

The wooden carvings along the arch formed by the meeting of the stairs started moving. The house did this sometimes—it sent me messages via moving pictures in the carvings. I didn't talk about it much with the others. If this whole thing turned out to be an elaborate joke one day, I didn't want a stack of evidence against my mental stability.

A woman with a bare bust and flowing hair galloped across the scene on horseback. Ghastly creatures swooped down at her with long claws and sharp fangs. Animals lunged for her war-horse, its head leaned forward with speed, not distracted. She turned, spear in hand, and looked down at me, the battle raging around her.

I stood transfixed, feeling fire spread through my blood, watching as wings sprouted from her back, snapping out to the sides and moving faster and faster, beating at the wind. She rose from her horse, and then it dropped out of view as the wooden scene shifted from ground to sky. Spear still in hand, one leg bent and one down, her posture proud and magnificent, she gave me a thumbs-up, and I felt rather than saw a little smirk and a wink.

"Tricky little bitch," I said with a grin, unable to help laughing. Austin was being dominated by a house, and while I didn't know how, I knew it pissed him off. It pissed him off, and Ivy House was gloating about that fact.

"I'm definitely going to the loony bin," I said as I tore my gaze away from the triumphant woman in the wooden carving and went off to join the others. "I'm rooting on a house in a battle of wills with a man that turns into a polar bear. Somewhere along the line I've hit my head and now I'm living in fantasy land. I'm probably in a straitjacket in a padded room as I mutter about knives named Cheryl…"

My mumbles dried up, along with all the spit in my mouth, when I walked into the sitting room they'd chosen for the meeting.

My gaze immediately went to the man at the back of the room. He had dark, tousled hair, a midnight five o'clock shadow, a strong jaw, and a straight, narrow nose. His eyes, the lids naturally heavy, as though he were plotting something, flicked my way. In the next moment, his body position shifted minimally, enough to alert everyone in the room that he'd torn focus away from them and was now devoting it all to me.

A hush settled on the room as the others followed his lead, and in that moment I knew. He was the large gargoyle with the incredible wingspan. This was the guy who had saved my life, protected me from the reaching branches, and cut himself up in the briars so I wouldn't get scratched. This was my knight in shining armor. This incredibly hot guy, in his mid-thirties, was under my command.

The breath left my chest and a tingling warmth spread within my lady-drawers. Usually a man got the position of power and the underling was an implausibly sexy young woman. The role reversal was a little hot, making me want to do things that were a lot naughty, and oh my God, where were these thoughts coming from?

I cleared my throat, trying to scrub my mind while I was at it. I might have to work with this guy—you never got involved with someone you worked with.

"You need to live a little. When the pants come off, make sure he's the one on his knees."

I blocked out Ivy House's magical communication and thus her voice. She wasn't helping.

"Well now, this is nice, everyone just standing around, staring at each other," Niamh said, cutting through my frozen thoughts. Mr. Tom sighed much too loudly.

There went any semblance of classiness, gone with one comment.

"Hi," I said to the room at large, not able to tear my eyes away from the tall man in the back. He was Mr. Tom's height—six four or five—but he looked much larger by virtue of his perfect posture. His broad shoulders and muscular chest was nearly as robust as Austin's, and his wings fell so low that they nearly dusted his ankles.

A surge of heat blistered through me, making me

want to fly with him again. To see those incredible wings snap out before they pounded against the air. Something in me craved it. And I didn't just want to see it—I wanted to join him, to meet him in the sky so we could tumble down together, our bodies entwining, reaching our finish and separating before we crashed into the ground.

I belatedly realized I was fanning my face while staring at him. A sheen of sweat covered my brow. Live a little, indeed. I'd gone completely off the rails.

"Hi," I said again with a sheepish smile. "Welcome. I'm Jacinta—Jessie, if you like." Mr. Tom sniffed, and I wasn't about to stop and question why. I forced my gaze away from Mr. Hot Guy, looking over the others gathered in the room. Fourteen new faces. The guy with pink hair smiled at me, but the rest of them stood or sat with straight faces and patient gazes, living stone. "Thank you for showing up today. Really. You saved the day. We're going to have to be a lot more careful now that we know people are infiltrating this neck of the woods. If not for you, I would've been splattered on the rocks."

My gaze slid back to those serious, deep brown eyes in that handsome face, letting him know that last thank you was for him in particular. His nod was succinct— just another day saving damsels in distress.

"I'd like to go around and get all your names, if I could," I said, taking another few steps into the room. "After that we'll order some pizzas, I'll give you a little history on my situation here, and we'll figure out what we're going to do with all of you. You won't all fit in Ivy House."

"At least one of them sure will, though," Niamh murmured, and my face burned hot. This was not the time to return to blushing.

Or fanning my face.

Or agreeing with Niamh.

It certainly wasn't the time for all three…

CHAPTER 13

"**O**KAY, WELL..." LATER that night I stood in front of Damarion's chosen room like a geeky teenager who didn't know how to flirt.

He and two others, not including Cedric, who was also staying, had been given rooms in Ivy House, Mr. Tom insisting at least that many resident gargoyles were needed to protect me after the attack. Damarion had pushed for more, but I didn't want to feel like I was walking on eggshells in my own home. Four strangers were bad enough, especially when one seemed to cause hot flashes of the lustful persuasion.

My God, the guy was hot, though. Hot and intense and I couldn't push away the fact that he'd saved my life and thought nothing of the act. It made him that much more desirable.

I was crushing. Hard. I'd forgotten what it was like. I kinda liked it, though I could do without all the embarrassing remarks from Niamh and the goading remarks from Ivy House. I didn't need one pimp, thank you very much, let alone several. Good grief.

Damarion waited just inside the door, his gaze rooted to mine, a man of few words.

"Thanks again, for everything," I said, prone to babbling around him. I wasn't a master at small talk, and with him, it showed.

"I am glad I came," he replied.

"Awesome."

Oh man, had I really just flashed him a thumbs-up?

I tore my hand out of the air. "Anyway, if you need anything, I'm in the master suite at the end of the hall." I pointed at a wall. "I mean... You know." I did finger acrobatics, as though he'd find his way through the halls thanks to my pointer finger tracing the invisible path. "So..."

"Thank you," he said, stepping forward, his direct gaze intimidating, mostly because I was thinking impure thoughts. "This house—your magic—is a legend among our kind. It is a great honor to be summoned here."

"Oh." I smiled at him and then tucked a lock of hair behind my ear.

"I can help you. I can feel your magic, pulsing within you. I can help you release it. That is why you summoned me, is it not? You require...release?"

His eyes sparkled devilishly. My chest felt tight, like

I wasn't getting enough air.

"Y-yes." I cleared my throat, trying to play it cool but *so* out of practice with all this. I hadn't expected to be this fervently attracted to someone so quickly, especially someone much younger and way hotter.

"Power trumps beauty," the walls whispered. But this was not the voice of Ivy House—it was a woman's voice, the same one I'd heard before accepting the magic—Tamara Ivy, the creator of this place, if I had to guess. *"But just like you wouldn't trust someone who only valued you for your beauty, trust no one who only lusts after your power. Trust no one who doesn't see you for* you. *Your life depends on it."*

Fair point, but a depressing sentiment. She wasn't the happiest of women. Being murdered would certainly do that to a person. I really needed to find out the story behind that so I had a little reference for her words.

"I mean, I need help controlling the magic," I said. "I can do some things, but I have a lot to learn. I need someone to help teach me."

He took another step toward me, his head bowed to look down into my eyes. I licked my lips, trying to hold my ground. "You know all you need to know," he said. "You merely have to release the information from your mind, and the magic with it. Slowly at first, to get used to it, but then in wild, hard, pleasurable gushes."

Okay, that was a little much with the double entendres. I knew that logically, anyway, but my body hadn't quite gotten the memo, because I shivered hot and cold.

"How do you know that?" I asked.

Another step, right in front of me now, leaning over me so our breath merged, the air between our mouths heating. "I don't know," he whispered, his voice not much more than a hum. "I just do. The second I landed on Ivy House soil after rescuing you, I felt it. I felt it as hard as I felt your summons. Just like I can feel your magic, which isn't something I can normally do. I am meant for this role, Jacinta. I am meant to help make you our queen."

Like Edgar finding the book because he was meant to read the old scripts. Clearly Ivy House had deemed Damarion worthy, and given him a few tools to help him train me.

She couldn't somehow superheat my blood within his proximity, could she? Because that was just wrong on so many levels.

"Okay, well…" I took a nice, big step back, just in case. "O-kay. I'm going to go. I'll see you tomorrow. Flying, right?"

"Yes. I'll take you flying after your training, and then to dinner." He put his forearm in front of his waist and bowed. "If you'll allow me to escort you."

My belly fluttered. "Uhm, sure. I should warn you, though, I haven't been lucky on the dating front. Zero for two. Well, zero for three if you count the failed marriage…"

What was wrong with me? He'd said dinner, he hadn't said anything about dating! Even if he had, my response shouldn't have been to knock myself and call out my divorced status in the same breath. *Abort, abort!*

"Anyway…"

"Tomorrow, we will end your streak of bad luck." He took hold of my hand gently, his palms baby-soft, and brushed his lips across my knuckles.

I wanted to swoon, but instead all I felt was awkward, especially since his pants had tented, I couldn't stop from noticing, and this situation was escalating a lot quicker than I was comfortable with.

"Good night." I yanked my hand out of his grasp, turned like an army captain, and strutted away.

My first breath came after I turned the corner. Holy crap, that had been intense. He'd been super forward. His confidence was off the chain, so that was probably why, but still, that whole exchange had blown the doors off my comfort zone.

The door on my left opened, and I jumped, startled. The door slammed shut.

"Oops." I magically pushed it open again. I might not have mastered much of my magic, but I did know how to work with Ivy House. "Sorry about that," I said as Ulric, the guy with the pink and blue hair, jumped back from the door, looking at it, then me, with wide eyes.

"Hey," he said, running his hand through his hair. He pointed at the door. "You can do telekinesis, huh?"

"Yes, supposedly. Edgar says so, at any rate, but I don't know how yet. That wasn't telekinesis, though, that's just the power of Ivy House."

"Uh-huh." Tilting his head with squinted eyes, like he was processing that uncomfortable fact, he stepped out of the room. He was compact, not much taller than me, and leanly muscled, like a dancer, his physique less brutish than many of the others. He pointed the way I was headed. "That next room has a bunch of dolls in it. I accidentally walked in there thinking it was my room. It is not."

"Yeah. They aren't mine. I mean, technically they are, but Mr. Tom won't let me burn them, so…"

"Ah. Well, you know, some are nice…and normal. Some, though, are a little…"

"Screwed up?"

"Nightmarish, I was going to say. Made from a warped mind. The jar of doll eyes floating in liquid is also a little…" He put up his hands. "I'm not judging. My sister had a ton of dolls—not *that* many dolls, but a lot. I mean, a lot for a normal house. I don't mind them, I was just surprised, is all." He grinned at me, his signature facial expression. "Just didn't peg Her Royal Highness for a doll lover."

"I hate them, actually, especially since they come alive and kill people."

His smile dripped away. "What?"

"Don't worry, they can't open doors. Ivy House can, but they can't."

"If I get on Ivy House's bad side, I should get out of this house as quickly as possible, huh?"

"Yes, but you wouldn't make it. The house would kill you before you reached the door. If you did reach the door, even more dangers would await you on the grounds—dangers you'd never see until you were dying from them." I smiled at him. "Welcome and sweet dreams."

"A female alpha…" he said as I walked down the hall. "I don't think I'm cut out for a female alpha. Clearly they are a helluva lot more creative with their scare tactics. I'm going to have nightmares."

"Welcome to the club."

"Nicer to look at, at least," he mumbled, not returning to his room. "Hey, quick question…"

I stopped and turned back, waiting.

"Are you and that enormous polar bear an item?" he asked.

"No. Just friends."

"Sweet. Wanna bang? Quick or slow, up to you. I can pull your hair if you like. Or you can pull mine— whatever you're into."

For a moment, all I could do was stare while trying to process his offer. At least he hadn't hit me up with innuendos and unasked-for intimate intensity. I kinda liked this approach better. Answer was the same, though.

"No, I'm good," I said, my frown somewhat masking the lightness of my mood. I didn't know whether to laugh or shake my head at him.

He made a gun with his fingers. "You sure? I can knock out a quick orgasm for you, if you want. You seem stressed. A little tongue tickle between your thighs might be just the ticket."

The laugh won. He was so carefree and blasé about it. He put me at ease while propositioning me. That was talent.

"Nah, I'm good, thanks. Wine works, too."

He dropped his hand and shrugged. "No worries. When you realize that wine doesn't, in fact, work better, my door is always open. Mostly because you can apparently open it yourself. I'm good to go at any time, day or night. Just come hop on."

"Oh my God, good night." I laughed again and turned, happy to hear an answering chuckle.

"I'm looking forward to working under a female," he called after me, laughter in his voice. "It'll be a fun ride…"

There it was. Wow, these guys would take some getting used to.

I sighed as I closed my bedroom door. My pace slowing, I crossed the room to the little table by the window, looking out into the darkness. I could just make out Edgar by the labyrinth made of hedges, opening and closing his garden shears. Even after the day we'd had, he was tending to his duties, helping Ivy House stay beautiful and uncharacteristically weird.

I sat in a chair and allowed the memories to rush over me—plummeting through the air, landing in that spiderweb clearly meant to detain me, falling through said web and nearly splatting against the rocks, and being launched back into the air by Mr. Tom.

I hadn't thanked Mr. Tom for saving my life. I hadn't even remembered until this instant. He'd been hurt, under fire, and still he'd thrown me out of harm's way, if only for a moment. It was his actions that had kept me alive long enough for Damarion and Ivy House to come to the rescue.

My heart swelled. Then guilt ate at me. I'd repaid his heroics by accidentally rousing him before he'd fully healed in stone form. He'd served drinks through the pain, then proceeded to make pizza for everyone because he couldn't suffer for a paid establishment to do his job. At least Ivy House had helped heal him, but still, I'd been so mesmerized by Damarion that I'd forgotten about poor Mr. Tom. That wasn't right.

"I'll do better tomorrow," I said to the quiet room as my phone chimed.

I pulled it out of my pocket.

A text from Austin: *A mage escaped that fight. He's dead now. I have some information to talk to you about. Can you stop by the bar tomorrow?*

Yes, I texted, leaning against the chair back, watching Edgar work. *What time?*

Niamh's usual drinking time is fine, he replied.

I nodded, as though he could see me, and noticed the three dots saying he was writing more. Looking out of the window while I waited for him to finish, I flinched a little when Edgar let go of one side of the shears and waved, his claws glinting in the moonlight from the nearly full moon. The light was out, but he'd noticed me anyway, because of course he had. He was a vampire.

Feeling a little stupid, I glanced at the phone. The dots had disappeared, only to flare up again, no text coming through.

Hurry up and spit it out, I texted. *I'm tired.*

The dots disappeared. The phone rang a moment later, his name coming up.

"Yup?" I said by way of hello.

"Hey." His deep voice was soft and slightly raspy. "Just wanted to say...credit where credit is due. I covered more ground today than I ever have in my life, but I had enough energy left over to take down a pretty tenacious mage. I have as much strength and endurance as I did in my twenties, but I'm ten times smarter and more experienced. It matters. Knowing when to save energy, when to cut corners, when to go hard—it all matters. It makes me, right now, better than I've ever been in my life. It's like the perfect storm of amazing."

I laughed, my head lolling against the chair back. "Oh yeah? That good, huh?"

"Better. I never did thank you for making this possible."

"Probably because you didn't ask for it, and it came at a price you weren't comfortable paying."

"Still. Thank you. That's all I wanted to say. The explanation was too long for a text."

I laughed again, grateful for this return to normal

before I went to bed. "One got away, huh?"

"Yes. It makes me nervous that the gargoyles didn't catch him. This guy was mediocre at best, so they should've. He wasn't good enough to entirely disappear."

"Clearly, since he is now…you know."

"Dead, yeah. I got some information out of him, but he tried to kill me."

"He tried to kill you?"

"Of course. I'd captured him, so what else do you think he was going to do? I couldn't get his boss's name out of him, though. It leaves us with a blank spot. But given Elliot Graves's interest in you in the past…"

He let the sentence linger.

Elliot Graves was apparently a big to-do in the magical world, someone like a top crime boss. I was told that he had magic in spades, and given he'd sent a couple of guys to grab me, he was definitely interested. I was pretty sure he was also the mysterious guy who'd shown up outside of Ivy House the night I'd claimed the magic, indicating he'd orchestrated the attack on the house to get me to accept my magic.

He'd said he would meet me soon.

I hadn't told anyone about that. I'd meant to, trying to find the right words. I worried that the extra pressure might push Austin into thinking he had to accept the house's magic in order to protect me, further forcing him into a role he didn't want. Or Mr. Tom stressing to the point of trying to strip away all our freedoms. A day had passed, then a week, then a month, then two... Nothing had happened. We'd just bumped along in safety. I figured that the second something looked suspicious, I'd definitely fess up.

I would, too. I would tell all. Just not on this call. Not right now, when I was dead tired.

"I'll talk to you about this when Niamh is around," he said, and I figured that would be a good time to share my info as well. "She'll want to know the details. Earl, too, I guess."

He did not sound enthused about that last one. I laughed, then remembered my plans. "I agreed to have dinner with Damarion tomorrow. I'll stop by afterward. He should probably be in on the talk, anyway."

Silence filled the line for a moment. "Sounds good." But his tone said otherwise, and I rolled my eyes. He'd need to get over the way they'd first met. "What's the plan for training tomorrow?"

"Training on the grounds and then flying over them. Ivy House will have our backs. If anything crosses the threshold of the grounds, I'll know. Your time is your own."

"Sounds good." This time I wasn't sure what his

problem was. I'd expected a thank you for not wasting his time. I could have asked, but I was also too tired for curiosity. "See you at the bar," he added. "If that doesn't work out…I'll…come there."

I frowned, looking over the grounds. "Why wouldn't it work out?"

"Who knows. Night."

"O-kay, good—" But he'd already hung up.

I shook my head and placed the phone on the table, letting my mind drift for a moment, ending on a handsome face and a nice pair of eyes. The memory didn't linger, though. Almost immediately, the feeling of falling helplessly rattled my nerves.

I had to learn to fly. I also had to harness this magic.

A handsome face and nice body aside, I sure hoped Damarion had been right. I hoped he had some sort of key to unlock what was inside of me. My future depended on it.

CHAPTER 14

HERE I WAS again, staring at the woman in the mirror, this time in a slinky navy-blue number with a fun shimmer. It didn't squeeze me like the last dress, but instead hugged my curves and draped over my chest, not revealing too much of any one thing or making my body shape too obvious. It was modest, but in an alluring way that sent the imagination under all those drapes and folds. Truth be told, I was still getting used to looking like this again.

"Own your space. Grab life by the balls."

I let out a slow breath, eyeing my makeup and hair, and reached for a sweater. Then hesitated.

I was going to be with a magical guy this time, so I didn't have to pretend I felt the chill. I didn't have to pretend about anything, actually. He knew all the magic and magic-adjacent things I would have needed to hide from a Dick. In fact, he'd spent much of the day helping me train.

It had been kind of exciting...and fun. Instead of

standing around, waiting for Edgar to translate a sticky bit of magical instruction that no one really understood, Damarion had attacked me in gargoyle form, moving very slowly and exaggerating all his strikes, fully allowing me to smack and hit him with any weapons at my disposal. With Mr. Tom standing behind me, rooting me on, I used weapon after weapon, dodging blows, working in close, and smacking him with Ron the bludgeon or Carl the war hammer. As I did so, I felt flutters and fire radiating from my middle, shooting out in fits and starts, bursts of potent magic that blasted the sky or raked across Damarion's middle, leaving angry red gashes. He'd taken it all, although he'd backhanded me a few times on reflex. Or, at least, I assumed it was reflex—those magic attacks had clearly hurt.

"You need to know that is coming, miss," Mr. Tom had shouted multiple times, disappointment plain in his voice as Ulric helped me up. "You need to develop some reflexes. Rolling across the grass like a weed in the wind is embarrassing for you. Get up and go at him again!"

"Or hell, just duck," Ulric had said, laughing. "Now, go give him hell. Make him bleed."

"Welcome to your new life, Jessie," I'd muttered, squaring off with the enormous, lethal gargoyle yet again. "Anytime, Edgar. We can start the magical lesson anytime."

"The magical lesson has already begun," Edgar had replied, not looking up from the large book, his long, bony finger moving across the page. "Damarion is clearly a great instructor. You've made more progress today than you have since we started. But we don't want you covered in bruises for tonight—the non-magical people will think you're a victim of domestic violence."

"I *am* a victim of domestic violence," I'd grumbled.

"You've barely scratched him, Jacinta," Niamh had yelled from the sidelines, her fists balled and her desire to join the fight evident. "You have a fecking war hammer, girl. Use it!"

Back to the present, standing in front of the mirror, I turned to look for those bruises. Just like the one across my cheek, where I'd thwapped a tree with my face, they were all gone, the only traces left in my memory.

In comparison to Damarion, I'd gotten off easy. That poor guy had been smashed with very heavy battle weapons, poked with a spear, blasted across a clearing, tossed into the sky, and the torture had only worsened once Edgar got his act together with the book— Damarion had been slammed with solid air, gouged with invisible claws, and forced back into his human form, which had left him curled up and panting, waiting to heal.

I'd felt horrible, running to his side and crouching down to put a hand on his large shoulder, asking if he needed ice, or maybe a tourniquet. Everyone else had clapped. The man was a saint.

"Here we go. Number three." I headed downstairs with a wrap draped across my shoulders. I couldn't go out with nothing at all, or the non-magical people in the town would ask questions.

I'd already decided that if this date didn't go well, that was it for a while. This whole process was for the birds—so much time and preparation went into it, especially online dating, and for what? It was usually a total letdown, or in the case of Gary, an actual horror show. The pressure of finding "the perfect match" was messing with my head, even though I wasn't in the market for anything serious. It was all just a lot of hassle.

A long, low whistle dragged my attention down the hall. Ulric walked toward me, an appreciative smile on his face.

"You look a picture. Wow." He bowed deeply as he reached me. "Gorgeous, milady. You'll have kings and princes fawning all over you."

"Who are these kings and princes, anyway?" I took his outstretched arm as we reached the stairs. "There aren't many of them around anymore. I think all the royal men in the modern world are married and/or don't speak English."

"Magical kings and princes. They only hold titles in the magical world, but most of them have extensive companies and holdings in the non-magical world. They are kings of their domains in magical society, and kings of capitalism in the non-magical world. A good chunk of the filthy rich people of the world are magical royalty."

I lifted my eyebrows as we reached the bottom of the stairs. I couldn't feel Damarion in the house or on the grounds. I'd be really put out if he'd decided to cancel and hadn't mentioned it. It would be ten times worse than the run-of-the-mill version of getting stood up.

"That's...interesting," I said as Mr. Tom met us in the foyer. His tux was freshly pressed, his chin raised, his air important, and a white towel was draped across his bent forearm. He looked like a caricature of a butler instead of an actual butler, especially with his "cape."

"Miss, if you'll please wait in the sitting room, Mr. Stavish will be with you directly." Mr. Tom gestured to the doorway.

"Mr. Stavish—"

"Damarion." Ulric led me that way. "It's lame to pick up a girl for a date in the hallway. He has to come to the door. That's part of the whole process."

"So he's waiting out there on the sidewalk?"

"No." He left me standing at one of the chairs, stepped around a random doily that Mr. Tom had clearly missed, and took a chair on the other side of a small table. He didn't offer any more information.

"Okay, then."

Mr. Tom entered with a tray holding two glasses of wine as I felt Damarion's feet touch down on Ivy House's property. Mr. Tom stopped, about-faced, and left the room with the tray.

"Wait, but…" It was useless calling after him.

"He's an odd one, isn't he?" Ulric whispered.

"You're just now realizing that?"

Damarion used slow and purposeful steps up the walkway until he stopped at the front door. The knock was light and subtle, the knock of someone who'd clearly known I would feel him coming.

"That's my cue." I stood as Mr. Tom passed the sitting room, headed toward the front door. When he saw me, he stopped, back-pedaled, and pointed at me.

"You are to remain seated until I come for you."

"This has gotten out of hand," I muttered, doing as I was told. Only then did he continue to the door. "I'm a forty-year-old woman. The need for all the dramatics got old twenty years ago."

Ulric whistled. "Jaded much?"

"I'm still newly divorced. Yes, jaded is a good term."

He grimaced. "Probably should've given Damarion a heads-up."

The door swung open, and I heard Mr. Tom's grandiose tone but couldn't make out his words.

"So…" Ulric rested an ankle over a knee and leaned back. "Why do you call him Mr. Tom, and the puca calls him Earl?"

They'd all apparently encountered pucas before, or at least knew of them. I still hadn't had a spare moment to do any research on Niamh's kind. Given I'd seen her in action, I had a good idea of what the description would say. I just wanted to see if being cranky and drinking like a fish were normal traits, or her specific flare.

"His name is actually Earl. When he met me, he…changed it—it's a long story. Just roll with it. There is more weird to come."

Mr. Tom filled the doorway, the wine gone and his posture indicating he was at his most pompous. "Miss Evens, if you please." He put out his hand. "Your guest awaits."

"Well…" I moved to stand but was beaten to it by Ulric, who then helped me up as though I were fragile. The last thing I needed was a younger guy, in his early thirties, helping me around like I was geriatric. "Thanks," I murmured, hoping it was the dress and heels he was responding to instead of the age.

Once standing, I looked at my feet pointedly before putting out my hands. "Where's my red carpet, Mr. Tom? All this hullabaloo and no red carpet?"

"Nice word choice." Ulric laughed.

Mr. Tom sniffed. "I sure hope you liven up your jokes for tonight." He led me out and then peeled away.

My chest tightened up, and I forgot to breathe for a moment.

Damarion stood just inside the door holding a bouquet of long-stemmed roses. A navy blazer showed off his broad shoulders and perfectly followed the contours of his body to his trim hips. A cream dress shirt peeked out, the first few buttons undone, hinting at the defined chest underneath it. Dark, distressed jeans hugged his legs, ending at his shiny black dress shoes. His tamed hair shone with product, perfectly framing his handsome face.

Upon seeing me, he took a hand from his pocket and offered a slight bow, his face tilting up to me as he straightened, his forehead lined and eyes a little squinted, and holy crap this guy was really, really attractive.

I blew out a low breath. Who needed a red carpet when you had this waiting for you? I'd take a pile of loose dirt or an obstacle course if this guy waited at the end, no problem.

"Hi," I said, closing the distance.

He pushed forward the flowers, the gruffness of his—our—kind showing in the gesture. His wings draped down his back on the outside of the blazer, and I realized he'd had his jacket custom-made to work around his wings rather than wearing clothes over them. That was why it fit so perfectly, and probably the shirt beneath it as well.

How did he get them off, though?

Heat pooled in my core as I imagined it.

Down, girl, I thought.

"Thank you." I took the flowers and did the customary smell and smile, pleased down to my toes to receive them. It had been a long time.

Except...what did I do with them? I couldn't very well just lay them down on a table, could I? He certainly wouldn't want to wait for me to put them in a vase—it was arduous work, especially with stems this long. I'd have to measure them against the vase and then cut them down...

Mr. Tom saved me, as usual.

"Absolutely gorgeous, miss." He stepped up next to me and put out his hands. "Allow me to put them in a beautiful crystal vase so that you may best show them off."

"Oh, thank you." Delighted, I handed them over. "They really are beautiful, Damarion. Thank you."

He nodded and the door opened, Ivy House butting in. She *really* wanted me to get laid. If he was startled, he didn't show it.

"Shall we?" He gestured me out.

"Yes, of course." I took my clutch from the little table by the door and led the way, Damarion falling in beside me on the walkway.

Waiting by the curb was a silver Lexus, a sporty sedan model that I'd never seen before. The lights flashed, Damarion unlocking it while crossing to the driver's side.

"Is this your car?" I noticed the sticker in the window, indicating it was brand new.

"Yes. With so many non-magical people around, I decided a car would be necessary for transportation."

"Right." I sat into the cream leather interior, doing a quick check to make sure everything was still safely tucked into my dress before he got in. "So you just…went and bought a car, huh?"

He closed his door. "Yes, of course. The non-magical police frown on stealing."

I smiled, about to laugh, but then realized he wasn't joking. Which then made me laugh harder. "Too true.

Pesky non-magical police."

He revved the engine, and then we were on our way. Closed in the car together, I caught a hint of his cologne: subtle and sweet, somewhat floral.

"Where do you live?" I asked as we headed toward the highway. "Oh. We're not having dinner in town?"

"No. There's a nice restaurant in Franklin I think you'll like."

"Oh, great. I haven't really explored the area."

Once on a highway, trees and signs zipped past, his speed *way* over the limit.

"So…where'd you come from?" I asked, having to unclench my jaw to do so. "What's your hometown?"

"A small town in Pennsylvania, about four times the size of this one. Only magical people reside there."

"Oh, really? That's interesting. And…" I tightened my hand as he swerved around a car, our speed still climbing. I gritted my teeth. I didn't want to be *that woman*, the one who bosses or nags or tells a man on the first date that he is doing something wrong, but I also didn't want to be dead. It was a very fine line at that moment. I tried to ignore it, knowing he also flew at a jaw-dropping speed. His reaction time probably wouldn't be that much different on the ground, would it? "How do you keep magical people from—Watch out, *deer!*"

He glanced over when he really should've had his eyes facing forward.

"What is wrong?" The car swerved around the frozen animal at the last moment, the right tires rolling off the shoulder and into the dirt before he maneuvered us back into the lane.

"Not a thing." I sucked in a lungful of air, adrenaline firing. "I'm just calmly watching my life flash before my eyes. It reminds me of when we went flying earlier. Remember when you suddenly dropped me, let me fall, and then scooped me up at the last minute? This is kind of like that."

"Yes. I've seldom heard a woman scream so loudly. I hope to get that volume out of you again, but in the bedroom next time."

I widened my eyes, not sure what to say to that. I went with the eloquence of "Yeah."

"You screamed through the whole lesson."

"Well, yes, mostly because I thought I was going to die. For a while there, I thought you might make me have an 'accident' for magically knocking you around earlier. I made it, though, so that's good news."

"I do not have accidents in the sky." His tone was haughty. "My purpose is to protect you, Jacinta. I would die to do so."

Warmth flooded me. For the second time, I didn't

know what to say.

"Why do you flap your arms when you're in the air, though?" He turned abruptly off the highway, not slowing nearly enough before he did so. The tires screamed around the corner and the back end of the car whipped out.

"Oh God." I squeezed my eyes shut. "Please slow down a little. I'm just starting to really like my life. I don't want to lose it."

"I am in complete control." He took another corner too fast, very nearly hitting a tree with the back end of the car as the whole vehicle slid off the road through the dirt. "I'd expected the car to handle a little better, however. Must be the roads."

He slowed just enough to get traction, then we were on our way again, speed limits be damned.

I cracked an eye open. "I flap my arms because I'm dropping through the air without wings."

"You shouldn't think of arms as wings."

"Yes, thank you. That hadn't dawned on me."

"Didn't it?" He looked my way as we approached a glowing establishment with a large wagon wheel affixed to the outside. Steakhouse, I'd bet.

"You're not one for sarcasm, huh?" I asked.

"No."

I took a deep breath when he parked, his car easily

the most sporty and upscale vehicle in the lot.

"Oh, I forgot to mention…" I climbed out of the car and steadied myself. "After dinner, we need to stop by the bar."

He waited for me at the back of the car. "The one the bear owns?"

My heel caught a divot and I wobbled, clutching his arm, my fingers not able to wrap around his forearm, not even close. He stopped and let me regain my footing. "Sorry, heels and gravel do not mix. Austin's bar. He's the polar bear, yes."

I wasn't great at reading grunts, but he didn't seem pleased.

"He found someone who escaped the attack yesterday," I said.

He opened the door for me and waited for me to go in. A little hallway led to a scuffed-up wooden podium, currently unoccupied.

"Escaped?"

"Yeah. Apparently there was one more attacker that your guys didn't grab."

"Impossible. We're very thorough."

"He tracked down the guy."

"I don't know who he found, but it couldn't have been from that battle. My people assured me the threat had been extinguished."

"Well...I mean...they weren't lying. The guy took off, so the threat *had* been extinguished. It's just that not all the attackers had been extinguished with it."

The host, who would have given Sasquatch a run for his money with his thick beard and shoulder-length hair, showed up at the podium in a black vest with a white shirt layered underneath. He lifted his eyebrows at us.

"Stavish," Damarion said, his arm encircling my shoulders possessively.

The awkward feeling of a stranger being too close crept through me, but I ignored it as the silent host led us to our table. We sat in the back, the table built for two, our menus laid sideways because of their size and the little wagon holding the condiments between us. The host nodded once and walked away.

"Real chatty, that guy. I kept waiting for him to shut up." I opened the enormous menu, the words big and spaced far apart just to fill it all up. "This is a man-sized menu, huh?"

Silence greeted me. A quick peek told me Damarion was still there, his fingers gripping the edge of the menu and the rest of him hidden behind it. He wasn't much of a joker, clearly. Pity. Hot guys were so much hotter when they had a sense of humor.

"So..." I hunted for small talk as a strange feeling

washed over me. I couldn't place it, but it persisted. "Do all the guys you came with live in the same town as you?"

"No. None of them. I arrived with them, but I did not come with them."

"Oh, really? How do you know them? Like…how'd you meet up if you didn't come with them?" Because they'd clearly known one another at least a little.

I was still trying to tap into that feeling, to pin it down, as it were. Buoyancy was as close as I could get. It made me feel lighter than normal, almost like I might drift into the sky. This couldn't be normal. Damarion was hot, but he wasn't hot enough to make me float.

"We all felt the summons, and I met them on the way."

"Mmm. Mhm."

My thoughts turned to the attack yesterday. They'd been magical workers. One had gotten away, a mediocre mage, and if he'd escaped, wasn't it possible a higher-caliber mage might have gotten away too?

I glanced around at the couples and families, spying nothing out of the ordinary. No one glanced up out of curiosity or from darker intentions. No one within my view was sitting alone.

In fairness, why would someone who was out to cause me harm or capture me make me feel as light as a feather? What would be the point?

"How'd you meet them, then?" I asked absently, taking in more details of the scene, just to be safe.

We'd been given a fairly private table, with a wall behind Damarion's chair, plus a half wall directly to my right. Behind me, four of the five tables were taken, two couples, a group of three with a young girl, and a group of older ladies.

"What's the matter?"

I lowered my enormous menu, thinking about who was on the other side of that wall, when my stomach fluttered and the feeling died away, like getting over nervousness.

I frowned, pausing. Maybe it had been the adrenaline from the car ride mixed with nervousness. It hadn't felt threatening, in any case.

Before I could think further, the waitress approached us, a woman in her mid-twenties wearing the same black vest and white shirt as the host. Lust flashed in her eyes the instant she noticed Damarion.

Something tight and uncomfortable lodged in my belly, and it wasn't magic this time. Despite the upgrade to my physical level, I wasn't nearly as attractive as this girl. And although I was once again flexible in a literal sense, I wasn't bendable to other people's whims in the way I'd been at twenty. What would a hot, younger guy like this want with a woman walking through the door of forty?

Power. Prestige.

The words floated up from within me, popping like little bubbles in a glass of champagne, but a dark mood had already settled on me. A mood that questioned what, exactly, I thought I was doing showing myself off in a sparkly dress and running around with a man in his prime. It pissed me off that I felt that way—that I bought into the notion that certain things were "improper" for a woman my age, but it was harder to shake off society's shackles than I would have liked.

"Did you get a chance to look at our wine list?" the waitress asked, and I belatedly noticed a little booklet tucked between a little cowboy figurine and the half wall. They'd gone a little far with the Wild West theme, truth be told. If Austin had been my dining partner, I would have said so, but I had a feeling Damarion would just grunt or nod.

"Oh no, I—"

"We will have a bottle of the Migration Pinot Noir," Damarion said. "Water, please, as well, no ice."

"Of course." The waitress flashed him a winning smile that he didn't notice.

"Mr. Tom mentioned that Migration was your favorite," Damarion said, his eyes traveling over my face. "I called ahead and made sure they had it."

CHAPTER 15

MY DARK MOOD hadn't lightened too much through dinner. Damarion had ordered for me again, steaks for each of us with a baked potato, butter, sour cream, and no chives. Apparently Mr. Tom had said I liked that dish. Which was mostly fine, since I'd intended to order it anyway, but also a little annoying.

"We won't stay long," Damarion said with grim determination as we pulled up to the warm glow of Austin's bar.

The familiarity of it came as a relief, even more so because Niamh sat in her usual seat. The spot beside her—the one I always sat in when I showed up—was still empty even though the bar was otherwise full.

"Hey," I said to Niamh as I stopped behind the empty chair. Paul stood down the way, shaking a silver drink mixer, but there was no sign of Austin.

"Well, how'r'u? What's the craic?" She caught sight of Damarion, his expression closed down into an uncomfortable mask and his biceps pushing at his blazer, clearly flexed to match his fists. How he and Austin met hadn't seemed to weigh any lighter on him. That, or he didn't like Niamh. It really could've been either. "Damarion, how was dinner? Did she let you order fer her?" She zeroed in on my best buddy, sitting next to the open seat. "Sasquatch, ye dirty bollocks, ya. Go down to the end. Open up that seat."

He scowled at her, no doubt annoyed she wasn't using his real name. Unlike Mr. Tom, he hadn't asked for the change.

"I was here first," he grumbled as Austin came around the corner from the back, two bottles of vodka in his hands. He caught sight of me, but his small smile slipped away when he noticed Damarion at my side.

"But ye won't be there last, will ye?" Niamh said. "Jessie will make you leave, now ye know she will."

"She has a seat right there." He nodded down at the open place.

"Yes, but her very large, fine man would also like to sit, or didn't ye notice the grumpy gargoyle standing at yer back?"

Sasquatch's shoulders tensed as he slowly looked over his shoulder. His eyes widened when he caught sight of Damarion, who was in some weird, silent standoff with Austin.

My nemesis hunched in his place but didn't move.

"I don't care. He can't do anything to me. Neither of them can. I didn't insult her or bad-mouth her or push her or anything. I didn't break any rules. I was here first, so I get to stay."

Damarion's eyes came around. Finally realizing the issue, he reached forward, grabbed the back of Sasquatch's shirt, and yanked him. Sasquatch's shirt ripped but held, pulling the guy back and off the stool, and he rolled across the floor.

Niamh jumped up and grabbed me, pulling me out of the way, and not a moment too soon. The next events happened so fast that at first I couldn't do much more than widen my eyes and blink stupidly.

Austin lunged forward over the bar and grabbed Damarion with both hands, dragging him up and over the barrier. In a show of dizzying strength, he then lifted the huge gargoyle over his head and slammed him down onto the bar, crushing glass and spilling drinks beneath him.

Damarion grabbed Austin, twisting in such a way that he threw him over the bar. But Austin hadn't released his grip on Damarion, and he pulled the gargoyle with him.

Their bodies knocked people out of the way, sending them reeling, before they both crashed onto the floor. Austin punched Damarion square in the face, the *crack* making it clear he'd broken Damarion's nose. The gargoyle was already throwing his own punch, though, and it landed on Austin's jaw with a pop that made my knees weak.

Adrenaline blasted through me.

"Go," I yelled at everyone backing away from the two men. A pulse of my magic sent everyone scattering for the pool area. *Everyone* this time, including those on the outskirts.

I magically yanked the bar doors closed, apparently not needing to be in Ivy House for that sort of trick to work anymore, and slid a magical barrier between the pool area and the bar to keep everyone put. Well, everyone but me and Niamh.

Austin smashed his fist across Damarion's face. But Damarion didn't look like he felt it, as he threw Austin off him, sending him crashing into the wall. Austin slid down halfway before bouncing up, but he wasn't on his feet for more than a moment before Damarion was up and plowing into him.

They hit the wall, shaking the whole place, exchanging punches faster than two boxers in the ring. Fear gripped my guts. I'd never witnessed this kind of intense brutality close up between people I knew and cared about.

My mind snapped back to the million or so

schoolyard fights I'd broken up. Other mothers would scream and wring their hands, leaving me to wade in and shove everyone aside. Of course, those kids had been weak and easily controlled—these man-kids were a force to be reckoned with.

Screw it.

I pushed forward, determined. Niamh plucked at my dress to keep me still, but I shrugged her off, hoping none of my lady bits fell out.

Austin landed a punch to Damarion's ribs. *Crack.*

"Enough!" I shoved my hands apart, magic blistering within the room.

Austin's hand flung sideways, and he jerked back from an invisible force—me. Damarion struggled to push through and get at Austin, but he only hit hard air.

"Stop!" I kicked off my shoes, needing to be grounded, and stepped up to the dueling alphas. They kept fighting my magic, and it felt as though they were scratching my flesh.

"Enough!" Electricity crackled. Sparks flared. My rush of anger filled the room to bursting. "You're acting like children! Knock it off."

Damarion stepped forward, shoving the wall of my magic. Austin slashed the air, shattering my hold entirely for an instant.

I gritted my teeth and strengthened the magic

wedged between them, the wall now spitting fire if they reached forward and touched it.

Damarion, his whole body flexed, his eyes on fire, dropped his arms to his sides, responding to my force. But Austin pushed forward, his jaw broken, his determination unshakeable, his power still trumping mine. I hadn't learned enough to best him.

My jaw ached from how hard my teeth were clenched together.

"Please, Austin," I said, appealing to him as a friend. "I know this is your bar and you have the right to enforce your law, but please stand down just this once. For me. I need him."

He cocked his head, cracking his neck, his gaze never leaving Damarion. His fists clenched and his pecs popped. The dark side of his beast had emerged, and I knew he felt the compulsion to sink down into it and fight until a victor emerged.

I could not bear to see him destroy or badly wound a man who had saved my life.

"Please," I whispered, the bar dead silent, my words carrying.

A tense moment trickled past, adrenaline still coursing through me. I wasn't sure what I'd do if he refused.

"Get. Him. Out. Of. Here," Austin said at last, each word clipped as though it had cost him great effort.

"*Now.*"

The dam burst, and I pushed my way out of the bar, shoving Damarion in front of me with my magic. As we left, I released the spell holding everyone else in the pool room. I needed them to rush back into the bar so Austin had something else to focus on. He wouldn't lose his mind and chase after Damarion if his customers, his *friends*, needed his attention.

"There are rules here," I yelled when we got outside, my anger and fear boiling over. I grabbed Damarion by the lapel and shoved him backward. Only my magic made it possible. "There are rules in this town. Is that why you took me somewhere else for dinner?"

His nose still bled, dripping blood down his lips. He didn't speak.

"You may not like Austin, and I kind of get it based on how you two met, but he is incredibly effective at protecting this town. He's done it for *years*. It is not hard to follow the rules. Do you know what they are?" I paused for a beat. "Don't be a dick. That's it. Those are the rules. Don't start trouble. Well, guess what you did tonight?" I paused again. "That's right, you broke the single rule of O'Briens. You were a dick to Sasquatch. He's the worst, but he was right—he didn't do anything wrong. You can't just push people around because you're stronger. That's a bullshit thing to do, and that's why Austin is here—to prevent that sort of posturing. His reaction was extreme, I'll grant you that, but so was your counterreaction. This is on you. I had a nice time, thank you for dinner, but you need to leave for now. We need to cool things down here. I'll see you tomorrow."

I couldn't see his eyes in the dark. I had no idea which way the wind blew. After a beat, though, he took a deep breath, his large chest inflating and deflating.

"I'm from a place that does things differently. Please accept my apology. I acted out of turn."

My eyebrows climbed toward my hairline. In as much as I'd expected anything from this near stranger, I'd thought he'd be stubborn and standoffish—two traits distinctive of gargoyles, or so Niamh had said. This was a nice surprise. I appreciated his apology, more so because I believed it. I felt the sincerity in it.

I nodded.

He pulled a handkerchief from his back pocket and wiped his face, which had already stopped bleeding.

"Your magic is coming along," he said, cleaning up. "After just one afternoon, you've grown in power."

"Thanks to you for taking my beatings."

It was the first time I'd seen his smile, and it was a thing of beauty. "It was nothing." He let out another breath and tucked his handkerchief back into his pocket. "You will dwarf the world with your power. It is my honor to have been summoned, my queen. You will make our species proud." He took my hand gently and, connecting eyes with me, grazed his lips across my knuckles.

This didn't feel like the night before, with his over-the-top double entendres. This time, the heat in his eyes sparked a similar heat deep in my core. It burned hot, searing me, making me ache for his touch. It had been a really long time since a man had looked at me like that. Since he'd let his lips linger on my flesh. Since I'd accepted the vulnerability of losing myself to the fire.

"I know you need to go back in there"—he nodded to the bar—"but I will wait up for you." His other hand blazed a trail along my jaw before hooking around my neck. The pressure was subtle but firm, pulling me in slowly, his eyes hooded and head dipping.

I licked my lips, logic warring with desire. I knew I should take this slow, but part of me wanted to get in the boat, without oars, and let the river current take me where it would. All I could focus on were those lips, a little parted, his breathing speeding up to match mine. And his eyes, filled with desire.

His lips finally brushed mine, and dynamite exploded within me. His hand slid around my back, pulling me in a little tighter, his body now pressed against mine, his desire clearly evident in his hard heat. I rested my hands on his chest and angled my head, letting him take the lead. It felt so good to have his strength and power wrapped around me.

His kiss deepened and his tongue thrust in my mouth, swirling. His other hand left my jaw, and then his fingers splayed across my back, spreading tingles across my skin. He slid it down slowly as his kiss increased in fervency. That hand reached my lower back and still didn't stop, not until it reached my butt, squeezing.

A moan escaped me, and I pushed my hands up his chest and hooked them around his neck. His hand was on the move again, though, down my side until he hit the bare skin of my thigh, and then back up, pressing, his fingers slipping underneath my hemline, heading for goal.

"Whoa, whoa," I said, leaning back and pushing his hand away. His labored breathing matched mine, merging as he lingered near my lips. "Let's… That's… We're in public."

"Let's go home, then," he murmured, and kissed me again. "Let me coax those screams out of you."

CHAPTER 16

MY BODY WAS on fire, pounding, and desperate to be touched. I wanted to know the feeling of being desired again—not for the sake of a release but because a man wanted to relish in my body. The way Damarion was moving his hands across me, thrusting his tongue into my mouth, it frazzled my mind.

But not enough for me to forget that I wasn't ready yet. I had a hard enough time wearing nice dresses that showed off my figure—I wasn't sure I could comfortably be naked around someone. My body was revved up, but my mind wouldn't stay in it once clothes hit the floor. Insecurity would come raging in, and I'd make it awkward, which would make things weird. I didn't want the first time back to be weird.

"You're right. I do need to go in there. I have to exchange information with Austin," I murmured, backing off. "My safety is on the line. I'll see you tomorrow, okay? We can have another flying lesson—you'll get another opportunity to make me scream." I belatedly realized how that had sounded. It was like the whole "Netflix and chill" debacle all over again. "I mean—"

"I'll take great pleasure in it," he said softly, his voice the equivalent of liquid sex.

I shivered from my head to my toes, about-faced, and walked back into the bar. Best to just abandon ship. I'd climb into that boat another day, when I was feeling a little braver. Maybe it would help if he'd take things slower. The man was stuck on *full speed ahead*, that was for sure.

Only when I was separated from him could I take a deep, desperately needed breath.

"I take back the whole wanting-to-date thing," I muttered as I threaded through the people standing around, making my way to Niamh. "I'm too old for this."

"Too old for what?" Niamh asked, two full bottles of cider in front of her and a third in her glass. An empty wine glass and a bottle of wine waited at the top of the bar in front of my usual place.

"Has this turned into a self-service bar, or..." I looked down the way, catching Austin's eyes as he looked toward me. His gaze dipped, hitting my lips, before rage and then frustration flashed through his expression. The look was there and then gone, and when he looked away, his face was a flat mask of disinterest.

"This place is wedged!" Niamh gestured around us. "They heard about the attack and everyone wants the gossip."

Fancy that. I hadn't even noticed anyone entering the bar.

"So yeah, help yourself," Niamh continued. "Austin is mostly keeping up, but poor Paul is run ragged. He's useless when it's busy like this."

"Austin seems pissed at me. How was I supposed to know Damarion would throw his weight around?"

"You've got lipstick all over your face. Got a snog off that hot gargoyle, did ye?" She grinned at me as I grabbed a bar napkin and started wiping. "No, Austin's not mad at you. He's struggling with having another alpha in his territory without being able to force submission."

A wave of uncomfortable fear washed through me. Their fight had been so brutal...the violence of it uncontrolled.

"They would've ruined this bar. I wouldn't have thought Austin would jeopardize his place of business."

"Allowing Damarion to treat the patrons badly, without recourse, *would've* been jeopardizing this place. It was bound to happen. If the circumstances had been different, they would've rumbled right when they met.

Instead, they had to do their jobs and make sure you were safe and your people were secure. Ye pulled rank then, and ye did it again now." She smiled with pride. "The best bit? They are both happy to let ye do so. They are happy to let a Jane with new magic push them around. I regret ever having thought about retiring. This is a good laugh. I am absolutely tickled, so I am. I bet Austin never, in a hundred million years, thought he'd end up in this situation. He says he wants to leave town, so he does, but I bet you he's also desperate to stay. I got a tenner on it with Edgar."

My mood darkened for the second time that night, dragging me low. "It doesn't sound like a good laugh. The last thing I want to do is create upheaval."

"Ah, you're grand. 'Tis good for him, you'll see. Anyway, what were ye mumbling on about just now? What are ye too old for? Sex on the first date? Because I'd beg to differ. You've been on the merry-go-round and ridden enough horses by now to do as you please. Don't even go on a date. They're a load of bollocks anyway. Just fashion yerself a cowboy, grab a ride, and see how hard he bucks, eh?"

I smiled through my mood. "He's young. Damarion, I mean."

"What are you on about? He can't be more than six or seven years younger. Yer just not used to it because women usually have to date older men if they don't want an eejit. But that's for younger women—we've enough troubles that we'd do better being *less* mature, not more. Yer not lookin' for a long-term thing anyway, right?"

"God no. I just need someone fun to take the edge off…being lonely."

"Is that code for needin' to get laid? I can't tell."

I could feel my face heating.

"Ah right, yeah. Thought so." She nodded. "Yer just findin' yerself, you are. You don't need to go worrying about nothin' t'all. All you need right now is a willy that stands up as long as you need it to. Trust me, younger is better. Maybe aim for twenties. It's never fun when they're done before you've even gotten goin'."

I blew out a slow breath, her talk greatly helping. It felt like the clouds of doom had parted, letting in a little sunshine. That sunshine was cutting through all the crap I'd been brainwashed to believe about what "proper" women could and could not do.

"Thanks," I said, reaching for the bottle.

"I got it." Austin strolled up behind the bar, ignoring someone waving to grab his attention. He wrapped his large, scarred hand around the wine bottle.

"Are your hands soft, Austin?" I asked without meaning to, my mind running away from me.

A crease worked in his brow and his body tensed. "When they need to be," he said, his voice deep and rough.

"She means soft, not gentle," Niamh said. "When does your shift end? We need to talk before she can't function anymore."

"Good Lord, my tolerance isn't that low," I grumbled as Austin pushed the glass of wine my way and affixed the cork.

"Ye still do, yes," Niamh said. "As soon as ye grow into that power of yours, it won't wear you out so. I have faith ye'll be able to hang on a little longer."

"I've got help on the way," Austin said, pointing at someone further back in the crowd to get their order. "And no, they aren't soft to the touch. I've never... That's not something..."

"My hands aren't either." Niamh analyzed her palms.

"Shut up, yes they are. So is your face, I can tell." I slid my fingers across her palms.

She yanked her hands away. "Janey Mack, do you wash yer hands with sandpaper or something?"

I huffed out a laugh. "Clearly I need to invest in some magical skin cream. Damarion's hands are really super soft."

"That'll feel nice when you finally take off that chastity belt." She winked at me.

"I just have no idea how he does it. Mine keep getting rougher and rougher as I work with the weapons. I hope he doesn't care…"

"If yer hands are in the right place, he won't even notice." Niamh chuckled.

As I took a sip from my glass, I finally noticed Sasquatch to my right, hunched over his beer and half turned away from the bar, showing me a little of his back.

"A glutton for punishment, huh?" I asked Niamh, ignoring him.

"He's making a statement, the eejit. He's putting his faith in Austin to protect him—meaning he's declaring Austin as the stronger alpha. He doesn't realize that we don't need to resort to violence to make him regret waking up this morning."

"He's been through plenty tonight. We'll leave him alone."

"Sure, say that now when yer on the sober side of that bottle. Once yer a fan of the el' gargles, your tune will change."

Donna, the cute twenty-something who worked in a wine-tasting room on the main strip and who turned into a rather gross rat, practically danced down the inside of the bar, a big smile on her pretty face. "Hiya,

Jessie." She waved as she hustled by. "Quite a night, huh?"

From right behind me I heard, "Hey."

I jumped, spun, and blasted out a pulse of magic. The room at large groaned, someone shrieked, and the chatter died away. Everyone doubled over, as though a bomb had gone off and they were dropping for cover.

Everyone except for Austin. He didn't flinch, but every muscle on his very impressive body was clenched, including his jaw.

"Sorry," I said, shaking my head. I lifted my voice. "Sorry! Austin startled me. My bad."

After a silent beat, movement and chatter picked back up again, and Austin rolled his shoulders. "Ouch."

"Why would anyone in their right mind want to attack her?" someone said into the din, everyone straightening up.

A little glow infused my middle. That was a nice thing to say—it meant I was getting better.

"I didn't even feel it." Niamh took a sip. "It's good to be on the inside, Austin Steele. You should try it. Then she'll protect you instead of battering you around. She's getting stronger. That el' gargoyle is doing his job."

"Sorry," I repeated, trying to scoot over to make some room and bumping into Sasquatch. He scowled but didn't budge.

"It's fine, I'll stand." Austin pushed in a little closer.

"Hey, listen, sorry about what happened earlier," I said, wanting to clear the air. "I didn't realize about you and Damarion. You know, the whole alpha thing. I didn't know he'd cause a problem."

"It's not your fault. Thanks for giving me a good reason not to destroy my bar."

"What reason was that?"

"No one would begrudge me for granting a beautiful woman her request, now would they?" He smiled at me, and his hard exterior thawed. "I can't have him coming in here anymore, though. If we have Ivy House or town issues to discuss and you need your whole team there, we'll have to do it on Ivy House soil."

"Sure, yeah. No problem."

His gaze flicked to my lips and then he looked away, his jaw clenching. "You still have some lipstick…" He pointed to his upper lip. "In case you want to fix it."

"Of course I want to—" I grabbed another bar napkin. "Really, Niamh? You couldn't let a friend know that she looked like a clown?"

"Oh sorry, I wasn't payin' attention." She put an empty bottle at the edge of the bar. Donna swept it up as she passed by, then dropped it in the recycling bin, delivered a drink, and grabbed an order—all with quick economy.

"Hire that woman full time," Niamh said. "Fire that donkey that works on Wednesdays and hire her."

"Listen, Jess..." Austin moved in a little closer still, his side bumping my shoulder, heat shivering through my body. The gravity of his voice set me on edge. "I'm one hundred percent positive those mages yesterday were trying to capture you. They wanted to get rid of your team and make the grab when Ivy House couldn't protect you. The mage I caught was shocked as hell I was there, meaning they didn't expect any ground interference, and I'm sure they didn't expect the gargoyles to show up—"

"Speaking of gargoyles showing up..." I recognized Ulric's chipper voice. "We're directly behind you, alpha. Thought you should know. We're here to watch the miss."

"The miss?" I asked, trying to look around Austin to see Ulric's face. I couldn't tell if he was joking or not.

"That clown Earl put that nonsense into their heads," Niamh grumbled.

"I know you're there and why," Austin said, "but this town doesn't use the title of alpha for me. They call me Austin Steele."

"All due respect, you're not the sort of guy that can hide his status, but if that's what we're doing..."

"I'll be with you in a moment," Austin said, and my small hairs stood on end at his rough tone.

"Yes, sir." I could just see Ulric shifting behind Austin, his hands clasped in front of him.

I wasn't used to seeing this side of Austin, the one ready to subdue anyone who created turbulence. His gruffness sparked a strange excitement deep within me, an unexpected thrill, primal and unguarded. It invigorated the hidden part of me that wanted to fight for dominance—and also to let go and feel the rush of being dominated.

"You okay?" Niamh asked me. "You look a little flushed."

I cleared my throat and dabbed at my face. "Just hot. Forgot to control my body temperature with my magic."

"They had a good plan yesterday, and a poor execution," Austin said, reaching between Niamh and me to grab a beer Paul was offering. His scent, clean cotton and something spicy, grabbed me.

Freaking Damarion had gotten me all hot and bothered, and now I was noticing heat and smells and things I'd rather ignore.

"Oops, ye seem to have turned the dial the wrong way again." Niamh's look was shrewd. "Yer face is practically on fire. Is the thermostat broken? Yer too young for menopause…"

I rolled my eyes at her as Austin frowned at us.

"I'll say they had a poor execution…" I put my drink down, my mind coming back online. "Their magical net broke in midair. If not for Mr. Tom and Damarion, I would've died on the rocks. Some plan."

"If I may…" Ulric stepped closer to Niamh's back. "They might've assumed she would be flying. Or at least floundering. Gargoyles are born with wings, and because they're present at all times, at least for us men, we have a certain affinity for them. As soon as we shift into gargoyle form, our wings are mostly ready to go. Flapping them is natural—you don't have to learn that. Controlling them isn't easy, at first, but it would be reasonable to assume a new gargoyle could at least slow down enough to prevent herself from dying on the rocks."

"So it's harder for me because I'm not a true gargoyle?" I asked.

"Jess, do you mind?" Austin grabbed the back of my stool and the base before pausing to look at me, his face inches from mine.

"What?" I leaned away, against the bar.

"I'm just going to turn you to make more room."

"Oh sure, yeah. Have at it." I meant to get up, but he'd already pulled the stool up off the ground with me on it, his muscles barely flexing with the weight. He set me down so my back was to Sasquatch, my side to the bar.

"I should've just done this in the beginning," I said. "My peripheral vision is much nicer this way."

"Without that dirty bugger by your side, you mean?" Niamh looked around me. "Yes, I did mean you."

Austin resumed his place at my side, now allowing Ulric into the circle. "Beer?" he asked the smaller man.

"Bud, thanks. Now, miss—"

"You can call me Jessie," I said.

"Mr. Tom was pretty clear about what you should be called." Ulric grinned at me. "The fact that it annoys you is just a bonus." Niamh huffed out a laugh. "I'm sure someone has told you natural female gargoyles are immensely rare, and have been throughout history. They can be created magically by a powerful mage sacrificing a male gargoyle and…whatever spell they use to transfer his magic to a female mage or Jane, but the transformation of species doesn't enhance the power. In fact, it shrinks the wings and hinders the ability to fly."

"And they did this why?" I asked, but the answer came to me in a flash of intuition. "To try to breed more natural female gargoyles."

"Based on the records, that was the reasoning behind creating the female version—they hoped a male and a female gargoyle would have a better chance of producing a natural female specimen than waiting for the genetic lottery. Maybe if the mages engaging in this practice had been female, they would've gotten things right and the female gargoyles they created would've been able to reproduce. But they didn't understand the complexity of female anatomy, so they were left with sterilized versions of male gargoyles who couldn't fly half as well."

"Who do gargoyles typically mate with that might create a female version? Humans, mages...?" Austin asked.

"Who we mate with doesn't seem to matter with the outcome of our kind. A male child will typically turn out to be a gargoyle, and the female will inherit their genes from their mothers, except every once in a great while." Ulric waited for Niamh to hand his beer across the counter. He took a sip. "It's very rare, as I said, but the females are everything those mages were hoping to create. They do have smaller wings, but it's a tiny grievance considering the power at their disposal. Every single female gargoyle in history has been mighty. They are more powerful than mages, hardier than shifters, more cunning than gremlins, and better leaders than all the famous battle commanders throughout time. Or so it is said."

"But I'm not natural." I palmed my chest. "I was magically created."

"Tamara Ivy was a natural female gargoyle," Ulric said, his voice taking on a storyteller's cadence and rhythm. "Her power was legendary, drawing the most powerful magical workers in the world to call on her. She wanted for nothing, ever. Eventually a handsome young mage caught her eye, one powerful and great in his own right, but his ambitions got the better of him. Or maybe it was his jealousy.

"While he was great, Tamara was exceptional and truly rare. She was sought after above him, had more power, more prestige. After a while, it began to chafe. *He* wanted the prestige. *He* wanted to be the most powerful in the land."

"Swap this for beauty and you have Snow White," I mumbled. Niamh nodded.

"He reckoned that if he could harness the power of her magic, combining it with his own, he would be unstoppable. She fell into his snare because she trusted him, but he had underestimated Tamara's might. As he drained the life from her, intent on stealing her magic, she used the last of her strength to pour her power, everything that made her great, into the foundation of the house she loved. The house she'd built. She gave it a piece of her soul too, and it's that piece that chooses the heirs of Ivy House—each of them a woman sound of heart and logic, filled with fire and strength of character." He bowed at me. "A person just like you."

"Right, okay, but why did she transfer the magic to the house instead of using it to kill him?" I asked. "It seems like a missed opportunity."

Ulric paused in sipping his beer. "I don't know? Maybe she didn't realize what her beau was doing until it was too late, and by then he'd siphoned enough energy or power to render her incapable of getting herself out of it? Love sometimes makes us do stupid things. Maybe she couldn't bring herself to kill him even to save herself."

"And so maybe the house was waiting for a jaded spinster who just wanted to get laid once in a while," Niamh said. "That solves that. No history repeating itself there."

"Well, maybe you're not far off," Ulric said, and before I could poke him, he continued. "A spinster was a weaver back in the day. A woman, since sewing and whatnot was considered a woman's job. A spinster could make enough money to set herself up without a man. Everyone gives spinsters a bad name, but they were smart, if you ask me. They were career women who didn't need to marry to have all the things they wanted, including their own money and free license to spend it as they wished."

Niamh turned around to get a look at Ulric. "Well, aren't you a fountain of knowledge."

He shrugged. "I can be."

"Even if those mages thought I'd be able to flounder in the air, that net still wouldn't have held me," I said. "I fell into it. There was nothing keeping me from flying out of it—assuming my arms worked for wings."

"It was a magical net. They clearly misread the situation," Niamh said.

Austin and Ulric nodded.

"I heard you caught another one?" Ulric asked Austin.

He nodded, finishing his beer. "He'd holed up in Greenville." Seeing Ulric's blank stare, he added, "The town to the east. He didn't have a computer on him and his phone wouldn't unlock with his face. His magic level was mediocre, but I got the sense he was working for someone high level. Whenever he tried to say his boss's name, he choked on the words. I've seen that kind of thing before. Whoever he is working for is watching Ivy House, and they want an easy grab. Their goal is Jess, not that house."

"We missed that mediocre mage," Ulric said, his expression troubled. "I looked all around. A few of us did. We don't have a shifter's sense of smell, but we found everyone else, even after they scattered."

"I picked up the trail about fifty yards from the attack site. He'd only managed to eliminate his scent for that distance, which was how I knew what level of magic he was working with. And he also came at me when I barged into his hotel room."

"Ah." Ulric nodded. "Your experience wins."

Austin shook his head, turning so he could look past the people and to the far end of the bar. "Without knowing who exactly the boss is, we—"

"So, there's this thing I didn't tell anyone…" I clasped my hands. "Maybe it is nothing, but…"

I told them about seeing the mysterious man in the black suit, with the dark goatee and slicked-back hair. Most importantly, I told them that he'd just up and vanished.

"That might've been helpful to know," Niamh said, and sipped her drink.

"He said he looked forward to meeting you again soon?" Austin asked, an inferno glimmering in his cobalt eyes.

"Yeah. He was all the way across the street, but I still heard him as though he were whispering into my ear."

"Ye had this hanging over you, and ye decided it would be a grand time to start dating and meet a bunch of strangers, did ye?" Niamh lifted her eyebrows at me. "If you needed to get laid, I could've just grabbed someone off the sites that would've worked for you and Edgar both. Run them through you, and when you were done with them, toss them at Edgar. There's a lot of weird people in the world, I'm sure I would've been able to find someone easy-like for that sort of setup."

"Good Lord," I groaned. "That's one of the reasons I thought dating a Dick might be a good idea."

"If that's all you need..." Ulric grabbed fake lapels and waggled his eyebrows. "How about a massage with a happy ending?"

"Enough." Austin held up his hand. A crack of power had all of us clicking our teeth shut. Niamh and I grimaced. "What happened yesterday was not headed up by Elliot, I'm sure we can all agree on that. Even on his worst day, he wouldn't have created such poor spell work. However, the mediocre mage who got away had plenty of time to make a call. If his boss *is* Elliot, we can now assume that Elliot knows Jess can't fly. He'll also know she has backup, so he'll send better mages next time. There *will* be a next time, we can be sure of that, and if Elliot takes part directly, we'll all need to fight him together." He turned to face me. "I know you are independent and you don't like to be governed, but I also know you'd rather not be kidnapped. You'll need protection outside of Ivy House property, and all of those gargoyles should be in the air whenever you are. Do I make myself clear? We have to be prepared. If we aren't…"

His voice drifted away and a growl laced his words, drifting up my middle.

If we weren't, I'd be taken, and he'd be pissed. That was about the sum of it. I'd rather be the one left behind in anger, but given that I didn't have a choice, it looked like I was about to lose what was left of my privacy.

CHAPTER 17

THE SCREAMS CUT through every fiber of his being. They quickened his heart and doused him in fear. He ran with everything he had, sprinting through the light snow, cutting through trees and felling anything in his way.

Another scream, closer now and higher. Jess was in the air, and it didn't sound like it was going well. His range of motion restricted by his animal form, he could not yet see her. Pushing harder, he burst out through the trees lining the cultivated area of Ivy House, circling the flowerbeds that bloomed despite the winter chill. He ran along the maze made of tall bushes and shrubbery until he could see her, way up in the sky, free-falling.

A sound like a sail snapping in the wind caught his attention. A shape with a large wingspan descended out of the clouds, spiraling through the air with incredible speed. The gargoyle angled his flight at the last second and scooped Jess out of the sky, cradling her gently and fondly within his shining gray arms.

Damarion.

Earl in gargoyle form hovered closer to the ground, watching what went on above him. He was the safety net in case Damarion or one of the others didn't catch Jess. Earl had shown he could pull her out of dire straits in the nick of time.

A bright pink gargoyle swooped around Damarion. In a move that stopped Austin's heart, Damarion tilted and launched Jess into the air. She kicked her arms and legs, screaming again, and was grabbed by Ulric. Another gargoyle swooped low, and she was tossed again, and again to another. They were playing catch with her in midair, her screams sounding with each hurtle.

Rage bubbled up through Austin, not pushing away the fear. Not watering down his desperation to pluck her out of the sky and deposit her safely on the ground.

A comforting feeling sifted down over him and tried to worm its way inside. A feeling of acceptance and confidence.

Ivy House, trying to tell him how to feel.

He gritted his teeth and forced it away, turning toward the house. He couldn't watch what was going on in the air, not if he wasn't ready to give in to the urge to charge the large gargoyle the second he touched down. Niamh, Edgar, and Earl had always done right by

Jacinta—they'd always done what was best—and Earl knew what it was to be a gargoyle. If they had put their rubber stamp on this atrocity, he'd let it go. It wasn't his call.

He didn't have to watch, though.

Nearer the house, he shifted into human form, hoping the return to two legs would soften a few of those screams. His hearing wasn't that different across forms, truth be told, but maybe…

"Help! Please, help!"

He spun, eyes searching the sky, seeing Jess falling again, head pointed toward the ground. A shock of adrenaline nearly had him sprinting toward her. He'd never make it in time, not even in animal form, but seeing her in danger strummed at every protective instinct he possessed. He couldn't reason. He couldn't focus…

Damarion once again burst through the low cloud cover and thick haze of the frigid day, grabbing her before she reached Earl, and then snapped his wings, stopping nearly in midair. She jostled within his grip and fell free. Her ragged scream cut off as he beat his wings once, grabbing her again and regaining his position. His hold was possessive, declaring to everyone that she was his.

He would claim her as a mate the second she'd allow it, Austin had no doubt. And why wouldn't he? Jacinta was the complete package. She was witty and smart and fun and beautiful. She knew her own mind, got her way when she needed to, and happily went with the flow otherwise. Her company was easy to keep, and her smiles made any hardship worth the effort.

A lead weight settled in Austin's gut, and he turned away again. It had been four days since her first date with the gargoyle, and apparently they'd gone out to dinner a second time, to the restaurant in town. Austin had promised Niamh he'd leave them be, and Jess had promised she wouldn't make the mistake of taking Damarion to Austin's bar again.

This town wasn't big enough for the both of them, though. A visiting alpha not appealing to the territory holder for right of passage was...

It was a challenge, or at the very least, a flagrant disregard for how things were done. In any other situation, Damarion's behavior would demand retaliation. Jess didn't know that, of course, but the gargoyle understood the line he was walking. He was taking advantage of the fact that Austin would not risk hurting Jess, physically or emotionally, to make a point.

One of them would have to leave in the end, and *that* decision would come down to Jess. If she needed that big male, or wanted him, Austin would find greener pastures. There could be no other option. If the situation went on for too long, Austin and Damarion would have a run-in, and the tougher alpha would have to be decided. Austin wasn't sure if the fight would be to the death, but given what he knew about gargoyles, he assumed it would be.

"Would ye put that thing away? *Jay*sus, Mary..." Niamh met him at the back door, holding one of the dolls from upstairs. It flailed in her left hand and she pointed at his crotch with her right. "If you swing that thing around, yer liable to take out the whole house."

"I need some sweats."

"Well, all we've got are the white ones, and every single spare pair has an old bloodstain on it. Edgar keeps switching them out and thinking we won't notice, and that gobshite Earl won't buy another color."

"Why don't *you* buy another color?"

"I hate shopping. It's much easier to bitch about it."

She led him back into the house, the closed door thankfully cutting out the echoes of Jess falling.

"What's with the doll?" he asked, following Niamh into the laundry room.

"It was thumping down the stairs and teetering around the place. It got on my nerves. I was about to rip off its head and drop-kick it outside when I saw you. No idea why Ivy House let the thing out."

"Me, probably. Last time I was here, it communicated with me through one of the dolls. They're creepy."

"They're just dolls, for heaven's sakes. They're tiny. Even if they've got a knife, you just give 'em a kick and go about your day. Look up, though. Some of them know how to climb. They drop down on you when you least expect it."

He jerked his head up to hunt the ceiling.

Niamh smirked as she slapped a pair of sweatpants on his chest. "We don't have a sweatshirt your size. Earl can find you a T-shirt."

He slipped into the sweatpants. "What's with all the screaming?" He tried not to take a tone, but he wasn't sure he succeeded.

"Eh." Niamh chucked the doll in the dryer, shut the door, and turned it on. "See how you like that."

"Isn't that going to melt the plastic?"

Niamh checked her watch. "Not before Earl comes in to rescue it. They're almost done. Want a beer?"

"No, thanks."

"Will ye have a cuppa?"

"No, I'm—"

"Ah sure, ye might as well." She led the way to the kitchen for some tea. "The screaming, yeah. The goal is to get Jessie acclimated to all parts of flight, including having no control when something goes wrong and you're falling. The fact that she hasn't gotten over the screaming is...troubling."

"There's a difference between adjusting your strategy because something's gone wrong and having no control from start to finish. She clearly doesn't trust them. If she trusted them, she wouldn't be so obviously terrified something could go wrong."

Niamh flicked on the tea kettle. "Ye've got a point there, so ye do, but I don't know that these guys know another way. Most of them learned by being pushed off something high and then figuring it out."

"Maybe they should work on helping her change into her other form." He paused, considering, then asked, "Does she change into another form?"

"Not like yer thinking. Her skin texture and color will change when she extends her wings, but just a wee bit. She'll look like a human sprite or something, they say. Her power is in her magic, not in another form. She's stronger and faster than a human, but she's no match physically for the males or a shifter or something like that."

"Are they at least teaching her how to fly—what to do?"

"O'course. Damarion does that in the beginning, then he speeds up, then they toss her around. Every time the same. Every time you'd think she'd get a little more used to it. Nope. They're starting to wonder if she's got wings at all."

He shook his head, frustrated on Jess's behalf. Clearly this method wasn't working. Maybe the problem was that she still thought like a Jane—the idea of flying was fantastical to her, and it was a huge leap of faith to believe she could fly without having ever seen her wings.

"She needs to believe she can do it before she's dropped," he said, hearing talking from the direction of the back door. "She needed to see Donna change to believe magic was real. She should work on extracting those wings before she takes to the sky, and she needs to trust the people who bring her up there. Throwing her around like a doll isn't going to establish that trust."

Niamh poured water into the teapot. "I'll mention it to Earl. He doesn't have much sway with Damarion when it comes to flight, for obvious reasons, but he can appeal to her. What she says goes with that crew."

"Oh, hey, stranger."

He looked up at the familiar voice, something in his middle leaping, and then the world went dizzy. He saw red.

✦   ✦   ✦

"WHO DID THIS to you?"

Niamh jerked with the drastic change in Austin Steele's voice, a rough growl lacing his words. Power whipped around the room and pressure bore down. Her small hairs stood on end, warning her that danger was at hand, a predator in her midst.

Austin Steele stalked forward, his bare torso ripped with muscle. His grace and fluidity of movement did nothing to hide the brute strength contained within that robust frame, coiled power ready to be unleashed. Jacinta's eyes widened as he bore down, one of them half swollen shut from a hard punch not long before, a glimmer of fear sparkling in their depths competing with her obvious excitement.

Only a lunatic would be excited by this beast coming at them. If he put his mind to it, he could be the thunder of a god.

Then again, Jacinta must know, or at least sense, that he would never hurt her. This hardhearted alpha had wrapped her in a blanket of his protection, and he would become the devil unleashed if harm ever came to her.

Which made this situation dicey at best. Niamh wasn't *directly* responsible for the bruises blotching Jessie's face, her swollen lip, the lump on her head, or the scrape on her neck—those were the results of her training session with Damarion and the other gargoyles—but she'd allowed it to happen. Even urged Jessie to continue with the rough training. Austin Steele could very easily blame Niamh for letting harm come to Jessie. If there was one person in the world Niamh didn't want to go toe to toe with, it was the uncrowned alpha.

"She's okay," Niamh said from right where she stood, not daring to go any closer. "It looks worse than it is."

He stopped in front of Jessie, the muscles flaring across his back. His voice reduced to a low, rough, barely contained growl. "Who did this to you?" he repeated.

Niamh edged around the kitchen island, keeping that big block of wood between her and Austin Steele while she tried to gauge the situation.

He grazed the fingertips of one hand across Jessie's black-and-blue cheek, and used the other to lightly trace her eyebrow, a cut marring its perfect arch. She flinched when he reached her discolored temple, and a shock of power bled through the room, his rage clearly on a very, *very* loose leash.

Despite that, Jessie's eyes fluttered closed and a slow exhale tumbled out of her open lips, like she was relaxing within his touch. In contrast, Niamh's knuckles had turned white as she gripped the edge of the island.

"We were training. It's fine," Jessie said, bringing up her hands to rest on his popping biceps. Her eyes opened slowly, hooded and lazy. The woman had no idea how much danger the rest of the house was in. "Austin, I swear, he gets it way worse, trust me. The guy is a saint for what he has to put up with. I'm getting better every day."

"Damarion." It was more of a growl than a word.

As if on cue, Niamh felt Damarion enter through the back door, followed by Earl. The rest of them would be filtering in after that, winding their way past the kitchen and heading to the showers. They might not stop in, but it wouldn't matter—Austin would be able to see them through the arched kitchen entryway.

In this situation, one glance at Damarion would be all it took.

For both of them.

"It looks worse than it is," Niamh said again. "He's allowing her to all but cripple him. He's conscious of her pain."

His body tensed. She'd just aligned herself with the bad guys.

Bollocks.

"He is incredibly restrained until she hits him with the very worst of it." Niamh thought about edging around the island a little more, getting closer so as to give her words a personal, comforting touch, or maybe even pat his arm, but she decided against it. His responding personal touch might be to crack her in the head. "The rest of them are joining in now, trying to help him fight her. She heals within hours. It really does look worse than it is."

"Being flung around like a plaything in the air might look worse than it is, but *this...*" He turned slowly, his icy blue stare cutting right through her, making her bowels watery. This might get a whole lot worse before it got any better. "You're calling this *restrained*? Has he so little control that mere pain prompts him to batter a beginner?"

"It really does look worse than it is—"

"She needs real-life lessons, Austin Steele," Niamh cut in. "She needs to learn how to get back up after she's been struck down."

Austin Steele swung those meaty shoulders around, facing her now, his intensity and size daunting, even for her. His power sent nervous tremors through her body.

Maybe it was good Damarion was steadily walking closer, drawing ever nearer—it would take some of the heat off her.

"This is *training*, Niamh. She is a beginner. You don't toss beginners around without protection. You're treating her like you would an advanced fighter. Besides, if she's used to getting physically knocked around every time she lands a good blow, she may flinch or hesitate at the worst possible moment. That could kill the element of surprise she gets from her magic. It could make her lose. And all because a sad-sack excuse for an alpha couldn't handle pain when it really mattered."

"I don't think you understand what kind of pain we're talking about—"

"I don't give a shit what kind of pain we're talking about," he barked. "Ensuring her safety is worth handling whatever she can dish out. We heal, Niamh. We all heal, especially on Ivy House soil. If we black out from the pain, then we come to and start again. That's the job."

"Ah, but it isn't your job, is it now, Austin Steele? Ivy House chose Damarion to draw out her power, not you. He has become instrumental in unlocking what is inside of her—slaps, air drops, tosses, and all." Niamh noticed his shoulders slumping, just a little. Was that regret? She pushed her advantage, feeling Damarion walking down the hall, just about ready to turn the corner and come into full view. She had a chance to deflate Austin Steele's sails a little before that happened. "Ye won't set foot in the Council Room, but he is desperate to be accepted in it. Ye dislike that Ivy House gave you the magic and keeps summoning you, but he is eager for the chance to be a part of the team. This is *his* job, Austin Steele, not yours. When ye walked away, he stepped in to take yer place. You can't lead while sitting in the back seat."

Damarion turned the corner, not a scratch on him, already having healed from his training with Jessie. Whether it was true or not, and Niamh didn't know, it looked like Damarion was inflicting more pain than he was taking. That wouldn't go well.

Niamh kept from flicking her eyes that way, hoping she could keep Austin Steele's focus on her.

"More importantly, Ivy House chose him because it must know Jessie can handle it. And she is. She isn't flinching. In point of fact, getting return fire, so to speak, seems to surprise her every time. That's probably not ideal either, but at least—"

Damarion stopped in the wide hall just off the kitchen entryway. "What's he doing here?"

Niamh didn't have time to answer the fool gargoyle.

Austin Steele spun on a dime, a blast of power rocking the room. He charged toward Damarion, all that rage and coiled power exploding outward.

Jessie's eyes turned as big as the world; she was shocked out of whatever stupor she'd settled into. Earl had already reacted, though, diving between the two alphas and slamming into Jessie, forcing her out of the way.

"No, waaait—" Jessie yelled, falling to the side.

"Don't let them at each other, Ivy House," Niamh roared, grabbing a kitchen knife off the counter and dashing forward. If she had to poke holes in them to get them to slow down so Jessie could pull them apart, she would. With glee.

A white door flew out of the wall, closing off the kitchen from the hall. All these years, and Niamh hadn't even known the door existed. It slammed home just as Austin Steele barreled into it. Any other door would've split beneath the onslaught, but this one didn't even splinter. A dull thunk said Damarion had reached the other side and was trying to get through just as fiercely.

Light flared, followed by a shock of air. Austin Steele flew back, lifted off his feet by invisible hands and thrown. He crashed into the island, punching through the wood and cracking the tiles. Pots and pans contained within it clattered as he rolled out of the debris.

"Get him out of here," Earl yelled, bracing himself over Jessie with his bony arm out, trying to protect her in case the fight moved her way. "This isn't the place for him right now. Get him out!"

"Austin!" Jessie scrambled up, out from under Earl. Earl grabbed her arm to keep her put, ripping her back much too aggressively for the situation.

A pat on the back was probably too aggressive for the situation.

"No, Earl, don't touch her—" Niamh started.

Austin Steele was there in a flash, grabbing Earl by the front of his sweatshirt and almost lazily flinging him away. Earl flew across the large room and onto the table, busting it beneath him and sending a table leg skittering across the floor.

"Austin, please stop. *Please!*" Jessie smacked her palm against his chest, determination on her face and fire in her eyes. She was going to unleash magic on him.

She wasn't strong enough yet, though. She'd only fuel the rage.

"No, Jessie, leave him be—"

Niamh dashed forward with the knife and sank it into Austin Steele's back, a nice, big target. Not a fool, she then leapt back and over the island, putting distance between them, ready for his attack.

Banging sounded from the other side of the door, Damarion still trying to get in.

And then all sound ceased, like Niamh had suddenly gone deaf. Everyone froze, but if Niamh's situation was any judge, it wasn't by choice.

"What in the hell has gotten into everybody?" Jessie asked in exasperation. She glanced at the kitchen door, her voice the only thing Niamh could hear. "There'll be no fighting here today. Walk it off, okay? I'll check in with everyone before dinner." Given her focus, the words were obviously meant for Damarion. A moment passed, then Niamh could feel him walking, doing as she'd said. Niamh had no idea if that had been his choice or not.

Jessie turned back to Austin Steele and took a deep breath. "I can't let you free just yet, do you see why?"

Niamh wished she could've snuck around to look at his face. All she could clearly see was the blood leaking out from around the knife still stuck in his back. She'd hit the meaty part, so he'd be fine, but still, that had to hurt.

"You're in that dark place," Jessie said, stepping closer to Austin Steele, her voice soft and resonant, supportive and understanding. "I get why. I appreciate all the things you said a moment ago. Thank you for trying to protect me. Niamh is right, though—I'm doing okay. I'm giving much better than I'm getting. If I wasn't, I'd say something. I'd stop. The first time I was supposed to attempt flying, I backed off, remember? You need to trust me, Austin. You need to *listen* to me when I tell you I'm okay. I know it's in your nature to reduce harm to those in your territory, but I don't need it. When I do, I'll ask, okay? I promise you, I will ask. I know I haven't always been good about that, but I'm getting better."

Niamh stepped forward, suddenly freed.

Austin Steele took a deep, shuddering breath. "Would you mind taking the knife out of my back?"

Jessie's brow fell and hurt flashed in her eyes. "Real mature, Austin. I tell you all of that, and you think I, what, betrayed you by saying I can think for myself?"

"No, no." He half turned, grunting with the pain. "The actual knife in my actual back. Can you take it out? I can't heal with it stuck in there."

"Oh my…" Her face blanched. She grabbed the hilt with shaking hands and yanked. "What the hell… Who stuck a… Niamh, did you… Why…"

"She was probably trying to slow me down," he said.

"By *stabbing* you?" Jessie asked, dropping the knife into the sink and quickly grabbing a towel.

"Did it work?" Earl asked, still lying on top of the broken table.

"Why don't you two go for a walk?" Niamh said, preferring to have Austin Steele out of the house. Jessie was clearly the only one who could calm him down when he was in a rage. "Go visit Edgar. He's always on about no one visitin' him. Don't accept the tae, though. Trust me on that one. You don't want a cuppa tae from his house."

"Let him heal first." Jessie put the towel to his back,

the deep crimson now flowing down his skin.

"It's fine." Austin Steele delicately moved away from Jessie's touch. "Going outside would be good."

With an incredulous look at Niamh, Jessie led him from the room, wisely choosing the side door.

As soon as they were out of earshot, Niamh said, "Get up, Earl, we need to talk to that thickheaded muppet. That gargoyle has the upper hand with this house—with Jessie—he should've been the bigger man and kept walking. He only stopped because he wanted to ride the rage of Austin Steele, the dope." Niamh stalked to the door and paused, waiting to see if Earl would get up. "Did you know this door was here, by the way?"

"There are doors everywhere." He groaned as he rolled onto the floor. "It's the way Ivy House traps people in rooms."

"I see that." She waited for him to slowly stand. "Austin Steele had a lot of good points about how we're training Jessie. She's handling the battering, but does she need to be?"

"No, but we don't have much choice. Damarion was... *Oh*, that is stiff." Earl rubbed his neck as he cocked his head. "Austin Steele is like a tornado when he gets going."

"He sure flung you something good."

He grimaced and massaged his back. "Damarion was chosen, just as we all have been."

"A protector is only chosen when he is given the magic and a seat. Damarion has been given neither, despite asking Ivy House for them."

"Jessie isn't sure about him yet, that's why. She has the final say, not this house. But there can be no mistaking that her ability has grown in leaps and bounds in a short time."

"Except in flying. She isn't getting any better there…"

"No." A troubled expression crossed Earl's face as Niamh slid open the door without a problem. It fit seamlessly into the wall, as though there wasn't a door in there at all. This house was tricky. "You don't suppose she didn't get that facet of the magic, do you? Surely she should be exhibiting some of the signs of flying by now…"

They made their way up to Damarion's room by silent agreement.

"Austin Steele seemed to think we were going about it the wrong way…" Niamh said, thinking back over their conversation.

"Austin Steele wasn't chosen to train her," Earl replied.

"How could he be? He doesn't want any part of

this."

"There you have it."

Frowning, unsure about all of this, Niamh knocked on Damarion's door. "I feel like we're missing something. Maybe this is a test for us somehow?"

Damarion pulled open the door, his hair still wet from a shower and a towel cinched around his hips. My, but he was a looker. Jessie could certainly do worse on that front.

"What?" he asked, having fashioned himself Jessie's second-in-command from the moment he'd set foot on the grounds. At first no one had blinked because he'd just saved her life and the other gargoyles naturally followed his command—this despite having only just met him, something she'd been surprised to learn—but now, after hearing all that Austin Steele had said, Niamh was starting to wonder if they'd been wise to accept him so readily. Maybe he wasn't the best for Jessie, he was just the best that they had. Maybe she needed to send another summons.

Niamh suspected she'd get a better read on that after this conversation.

"What were you on about down there?" Niamh asked him. "You were trying to cause a row."

"A what?"

"A fight," Earl said. "This is not the place for a battle

of dominance, especially when Jessie is standing between you two."

Damarion straightened a bit more, full of righteous indignation. "This is exactly the place for a battle, and Jacinta is the person who must witness it."

"And you think you'll win, do ye?" Niamh asked with a chuckle. "Have ye not heard the stories about Austin Steele?"

"Stories grow bigger as the years grow long."

"Not in this case," Earl said.

"He's a distraction to her," Damarion said. "She won't give in to me completely with him coming around. She needs to see me force him to submit so she can recognize the true alpha."

"She doesn't give two shites who is the true alpha, you muppet," Niamh replied. "The girl is a Jane in her bones—she doesn't even know what true alpha means."

"I'm not sure he does, either," Earl mumbled. Damarion bristled.

"Regardless, it doesn't matter," Niamh said, waving it away, "because they're friends, that's it. There is nothing romantic between them. He's not your problem. Yer problem is ye've got limited game and you can't read the situation. She's too confident to give in to ye just because it would make you happy. She's not on this planet to please you, ye donkey. Ye gotta try a new tactic besides drooling all over her and calling it kissing."

"You should watch yourself, old woman."

She laughed. "Don't challenge me, kid. You don't want to know the nightmare you'll wake up."

CHAPTER 18

"YOU KNOW HOW to freeze air and sound now, huh?" Austin asked, rolling his shoulders.

I grimaced at the blood still dribbling down his back and soaking into his sweats. "We should probably wash this off before we go into a confined space with Edgar."

"I'm not worried about that vampire."

We stepped out of a hidden side door, having gone through the secret tunnels to exit the house. I didn't want to chance another encounter with Damarion or the others. "You're not worried about a distracted vampire talking nonsense while he stares at you longingly, imagining sucking that blood off your back?"

Austin stopped walking. "You have a hose around here, don't you?"

I laughed, leading him to the right. "It appears so. About the freezing air and sound thing, I mean. Also about the hose."

"You hadn't done that before?"

"No. Regardless of my advancement lately, I still do

most things on the fly. That's why it's going fine with Damarion." I ignored him stiffening. "He's rough, yes, but trying not to get pummeled opens up my mind for creative evasions."

"Look, this needs to be said." He paused as we reached the green hose wrapped around the black spindle. He grabbed the metallic tip and tugged. The hose gave a little and then caught. He sighed. "I hate these kinds of hose holders. I always end up breaking them in a frustrated rage."

Wincing, he gripped both sides of the black roller and pulled, turning it enough to get another foot of hose free. He gritted his teeth as he repeated the movement, his muscles flaring, probably from the strain of not ripping the whole thing away from the wall and throwing it.

I laughed, braced a hand to his arm, and waited until he stepped out of the way.

"I got this. You just focus on not bleeding out."

"Thanks." He looked out over the trees at the edge of the yard. "I'm not going to apologize for losing my cool earlier."

"I didn't expect you to."

"I don't like seeing you hurt in a way that I don't think is necessary because—"

He gritted his teeth, biting back what he was about

to say. I knew what it was, though—because Damarion couldn't control his reaction to pain.

But he shifted gears. "Because Ivy House thinks you can take it. Even I started slow, Jess. Slower than I would have liked. But the whole pack worked as one to train each of us, at a pace that made sense for that person, and they did it right. I'm a bad example of their training, but I did learn what works, even if I didn't apply it in my own situation."

"You're apparently known throughout all of the magical community. I don't think that's a bad example of anything…"

I yanked on the wheel of the hose roller, only getting another foot.

"What the hell is the point of this thing? To make sure no one uses the hose?" I yanked again, using all my strength. It wouldn't budge. "Screw this thing. Rip it out and toss it."

Austin laughed and bent, bumping me to the side with his big shoulder. "Lemme try again." His yank cracked the plastic, breaking it from the base. He ripped the hose off the side, tearing it from around the spindle, and got enough out to reach his back. "There. See? Nothing to it."

"If Edgar asks, we have no idea how this thing got broken."

"Agreed." He pushed down his sweats, and I ripped my gaze away, my face heating and my heart quickening. I breathed through the heat worming through my core. Wrong guy for this reaction. I had a willing partner upstairs. Hell, I had a whole host of willing partners. This guy was off-limits.

I just wished my mind and my body would get in sync for once. I was still hesitating with Damarion, although I had no idea why. He was hot and nice and a gentleman and insistent—boy was he insistent—but I never got further than the roaming hands before I freaked out and pushed back. I wanted to close the deal while at the same time wanted a longer ramp leading up to it.

The poor guy was probably frustrated, though he didn't show it. I just didn't know what my problem was.

"Can you get it?" Austin turned and showed me his blood-slicked back, the wound newly closed and the edges already starting to crust. The top of his muscular butt was smeared red from where blood had soaked into his sweats.

"Why on earth does Mr. Tom insist on white sweats?" I asked, turning on the water. Austin didn't react to the frigid air or the cold liquid washing down over his defined back. He turned into a polar bear—ice was kind of his thing; it was intense heat he probably disliked.

"There is one thing I would like to apologize for, Jess," he said, his voice sending shivers racing across my skin. "You're right—you're your own woman. A smart woman, at that. I need to trust that you know what you're capable of."

"When you're not flying off the handle because of a few bruises, you mean?"

He let out a slow breath. "I'm not sure I can control my reaction to seeing you…like this, especially knowing who's doing it. We won't ever get along, him and I. It will never be peaceful between us, not until one of us submits to the other."

His voice turned harsh, a growl riding his words. He'd die before he'd submit, that much was clear. I knew without needing to ask that Damarion was the same way.

I struggled to control a sudden surge of emotion. The writing on the wall was entirely too clear. They could not coexist. This town was too small, and this house smaller still. If they'd flipped out this much just at the sight of each other, they'd end up rumbling one way or another. If I kept interceding, eventually they'd figure out how to get at each other when I wasn't around. It was only a matter of time.

I swallowed down a lump in my throat. I could not

bear to see Austin leave. He'd been my first real friend in my new life. My first normal friend, at any rate. I'd come to depend on him, as much for his easy conversation and comforting presence as for his ability to keep the magical world from completely going off the rails. I'd almost died, for heaven's sake, and someone wanted to kidnap me. Those things should've given me nightmares, but they hadn't—because I knew Austin was watching the property. Because I trusted that he'd keep this town, with me in it, safe.

But I also trusted Damarion. He'd saved my life, and I needed him for training. Ivy House had given him the ability to draw out my magic, and without him, I'd be back learning at a snail's pace. With mages sniffing around, I didn't think I had that kind of time.

And yet...I couldn't help but wonder why Ivy House had chosen Damarion as my trainer over Austin. It wasn't the wings, because Ulric or any of the other guys could've helped with the flying thing, no alpha required. They weren't as strong or powerful in that department, but I wouldn't be either. They were probably more my speed than the breakneck diving and rolling that Damarion did.

I knew why, though, didn't I? Austin didn't want to be a part of all this. He didn't want to answer to anyone, especially Ivy House's magic. He wasn't a sure bet, and so Ivy House couldn't trust him. It had chosen the next best option.

I trusted him, though. Even though he hadn't taken a seat in that Council Room, he still checked in. He still helped. I had but to ask, and he'd see me through all of this.

"About that…" I said, turning off the water.

"Do you mind if I air-dry?"

"Do you mind if I accidentally look?" I laughed, picking up his sweats and handing them over.

His eyes were steady on mine, and I quickly looked away. I really needed to get over this embarrassment. It was getting downright ridiculous. I'd seen plenty of naked men. I'd raised a boy, for God's sake.

False equivalence, I thought.

Boy, wasn't that the truth.

"Just kidding," I said, staring forward. "I won't look."

"No, I don't mind," he said quietly.

"Where does that leave us?" I asked. "I mean, with Damarion, not with your very appropriate confidence in your body."

He didn't answer for a moment as we crossed the lush green grass, the garden as lush as ever despite the chill air and dusting of snow.

"I don't know, Jess." I could hear the regret in his

voice. I could hear the resolve.

I could hear the sound of a man taking the harder road, being the bigger person, and leaving.

"We will work this out, okay?" I clenched my fists. "This is your home. You're staying here. I haven't been trying to free you from the magic, and that's my bad, but I will, okay? We'll get that worked out, and then—"

"The magic isn't the problem..."

"Just shut up." Magic infused my words. This time, it was his jaw that clicked shut. "Sorry. Sorry, I didn't mean—Just, let's not talk about it right now. I'll sort it out, okay? I'll make this work. I'm a mother, damn it— I'm used to accomplishing the impossible."

"Okay," he said, and bumped me with his shoulder.

I wanted to turn and hug him, or grab his hand, or maybe slap him, I wasn't sure. I settled for bumping him back.

"I wanted to ask you..." I bit my lip, thinking about the feeling of danger I'd felt with the second summons, as we passed the maze and turned left toward the little cottage at the very back of the grass, nestled into the trees. Edgar's little sanctuary. I'd never asked why he didn't live in the house, and given I didn't really want to extend an invitation, it seemed better to continue avoiding the topic. "Remember when you said you were good at reading people?"

"This is the second time you've started a conversation like this."

"Oh, right. Well...as a man, and not as a...whatever it is that annoys you about Damarion, what do you think about him?" I paused. "Is it okay to be asking you this?"

"You can ask me anything." He was quiet for a moment, though, his pace slowing as we walked. "It would take a decent effort to subdue him, but I would. He will never tolerate us being friends, you and me. It will never sit right with him. He is loyal, though, and he'll protect you with his life. If it can't be me watching out for you, as much as it pains me to admit it, it's good that it is him, regardless of my views on his training methods."

"And it does pain you to admit it."

"It absolutely does, yes. I hope to never think of this moment again."

I could tell he was only half joking. We slowed even more, nearly at Edgar's front porch, one chair overturned next to the door and another lying at the far edge on its side. I frowned at the setup.

"Do you think this is normal?" I asked, putting out my hand to stop Austin's progress.

"Why don't you text him to make sure he isn't...otherwise unoccupied? Because normal and that vampire are not two words that should be said in the same sentence."

I huffed out a laugh and patted my pockets. "Oh. I don't have my phone."

"You know I don't."

I sure did. I'd taken in his flat, muscled stomach and the happy trail leading down to its well-maintained destination before I could stop myself.

Before we finished our approach, I said, "I don't want you to leave. That needs to be said. I will find a way to make this right, but in the meantime..." I shrugged. "Just figured you should know that."

His gaze was heavy on my face, but something stopped me from turning and looking at him. Thankfully, there wasn't a chance for it to get awkward. At least not between us.

The door swung open and Edgar stepped out, a red-fanged smile stretching across his face.

"Hello! You finally came to visit. And Austin Steele, too? Wow." He rested his fingers on his chest. "This is a treat. Come in, come in!"

He stopped beside the door like he was nervous about a cat escaping. But instead of shooing an animal, he nudged a man's leg, ending in a hiking boot, out of the way. Given its stubbornness in moving, it was thankfully still attached to the—hopefully living but definitely unconscious—source.

I hesitated. "Is it too late to turn back?"

"Yes," Austin answered, "and unfortunately, this sort of weird isn't something I can protect you from."

CHAPTER 19

"WHAT A TREAT. Sorry I didn't clean up a little more." Edgar led the way into a cheery though incredibly cluttered living room just off the entryway, with bright yellow walls, sky-blue curtains, and large white barrels lining the walls behind the furniture. Little canisters of all kinds topped the barrels, as well as squirt bottles with the labels either peeled off or mostly disintegrated.

He waited by the door for Austin to pass, Austin's sweats in a balled fist at his side and his body tense as he sussed the place out.

"How embarrassing. You caught me after a light meal." Edgar lifted the owner of the leg—a youngish guy in a flannel shirt and loose jeans—and stashed him further behind the couch by the front windows. "He won't wake up for an hour or so. We have plenty of time. Worst case, I can just bite him again, right? It takes a lot more than two bites for someone to sustain brain damage from the magical coma. He'll be fine. He did want to come back to my place, after all. Mistake number one. Stranger danger."

He closed the door and followed Austin, stopping at the threshold to the living room.

"I feel like we are walking a morality line right now," I mumbled, edging toward a couch choked with doilies. They were everywhere—lining armrests, spread across cushions, stacked on the windowsills... Where Niamh's house was over-decorated with them, Edgar's house was drowning.

"Where did you find him?" Austin asked, stopping beside me as I looked down at the doily-covered couch cushions. They looked like haphazardly knitted spider webs, all slightly oblong, with their interior webs far from symmetrical. I wasn't sure if we were supposed to sit on them, or carefully stack them up and shove them to the side, so I remained standing until I could get a further clue.

"Oh, he was just on the road outside of town, walking along the edge of our property. I stopped to say hello and one thing led to another. Back he came for a sandwich and to rest up before he went on his hike. I jumped him before that, of course. He looked strong and capable, I didn't think it necessary to give him a meal to sustain him."

"Still treading that line," I murmured. "Thank God I

didn't get vampire magic."

"You weren't watching Jess train?" Austin asked, and the growl was back in his voice.

"He was there for training, but he doesn't stay for the flying," I said, touching Austin's arm with the back of my hand, hoping a physical connection would keep him from losing it again. Poor Edgar wouldn't be able to handle Austin in a temper.

"Correct, Jessie, yes. The flying scares me. I'd rather not watch. I'm always afraid she'll fall." Edgar nodded gravely, and because I didn't want the conversation going any further along that track, I veered back to this issue with the hiker. Magical morality aside, it was still a weird situation.

"So...this guy you randomly picked up in the woods..." I shook my head, needing a moment to process this insanity. "He planned to go hiking...but he was out for a stroll in the cold before that?"

Edgar sank into the old-fashioned chair facing us, doilies now trapped between his butt and the seat. Cue received.

"I think that is what he said," Edgar replied. "I wasn't really paying attention. It's so rare I see people so easy for the grabbing this time of year. I've been getting lucky lately, what with the two people trespassing through the woods the other day, and now this guy, just on the outskirts of the property. No witnesses, no fuss, and in the end, they wake up none the wiser. I always just tell them they've fainted."

"Riiight." I slowly lowered onto the mess of doilies.

Austin hesitated and held up his sweats. "These have blood on them. I'm not sure if they are still wet."

"Oh. How silly of me. Stay right there." Edgar pushed out of his seat and left the room, back a moment later with a new pair of sweatpants. "There you go. I'd let you sit directly on the doilies, but the yarn is a little rough and I wouldn't want it to chafe." He smiled and lowered back down, bending an ankle jauntily over his knee.

"Good looking out," Austin mumbled, taking the new pair and holding them up to his body. At *least* two sizes too small. He struggled into them, although they squeezed his body like a sausage casing and ended well above his ankles. His look clearly blamed me for this whole situation.

I stifled a laugh.

"You collect doilies, then, or…" I motioned around the space, trying to get a look at those large barrels or even the canisters on top, both curious about what they were and wary of finding out.

"I make them." Edgar was up again, opening a cabinet on an empty entertainment center displayed proudly against the wall. The furniture layout would have made a lot more sense if there had been a large TV in that setup. He grabbed a few doilies out of a stuffed drawer and held them out. "Would you like some? I know Mr. Tom is dead set against decorating with doilies, but Niamh has been able to sneak in a few. Since you're now the owner of the house, you can probably decorate any way you want."

"Oh." I gave him what I hoped was a regretful smile. "I don't want to go against Mr. Tom's wishes so soon. I'll need to work him around."

"Austin Steele, how about you? I'd be mighty proud to have my work displayed in your home."

"No," Austin said.

"Ah well, maybe you'll come around." Edgar placed them gently into their drawer before sitting down.

I picked one up from the arm of the couch, studying the gaping hole on one side, the bulging yarn on the other, and the small spot that looked okay in the otherwise terribly executed design. "Wow, you make these?"

"Yes." He held up his long fingers, sporting even longer nails, one of them tipped with blood. I could feel the grimace on my face. "My goal is to create the *perfect* doily. I've always found that a perfectly symmetrical doily is as beautiful as it is calming. I haven't been at it for very long, but one day, I hope to enter that perfect doily into the town craft show. It will be a thing of beauty, you mark my words."

I gingerly returned the doily to its spot, a smile wrestling with my lips when I noticed Austin's look of pure bewilderment and confusion.

"How long have you been at it?" I asked, clasping my hands on my lap.

"About fifty years or so. It started as a hobby, but it has become one of my life's great passions."

"Have you ever considered, maybe, a different color besides cream?" I asked, strangely fascinated.

"Oh now, Jessie, whoa." Edgar chuckled softly, putting up his hands and leaning back a little in his seat. "You give my prowess too much credit. Those of us in the doily biz need to walk before we can run. I need to nail the perfect doily before I can dress it up a bit, otherwise I'd just be distracting from something not quite perfect."

I nodded dutifully, trying not to laugh.

"What's with the..." Austin gestured at the barrels and tubs.

"Oh! That is my life's other great passion. Well spotted." Edgar turned, leaning heavily on his right so he could get a better view of the closest barrels. "Those are gardening elixirs. I get them from Agnes. You know, the town witch? The real one, not the Jane who looks at palms and pretends to know things. She really is terrible for the false hope she gives young lovers. Anyway, I order the elixir in moderate increments during the spring and summer, when the ingredients are at their best, and then apply it during the winter when it is nearly impossible to naturally keep flowers in bloom. It keeps us with a lovely home year-round."

"Why don't you keep all this in a shed?" I asked.

"What, and have Marg from 856 Maple Drive snoop around and find out my secret? Not a chance, Jessie. No, I keep them in here, nice and safe. Do you want to see all the trophies I've won over the years? I win the wine and garden festival every year, without fail, and Marg has been driven mad with jealousy. She's resorted to trying to cheat, of all things."

"But…Edgar…*you* cheat."

"I do not. I just use better growth serum than she does. If Marg didn't look down her nose at Agnes, she could use the same serum and not rely on pig or cow poop or whatever it is she uses." His grin was sardonic as he shook his head. "She wants to grow beautifully smelling flowers…with poop. It makes no sense."

"Is Marg magical?"

"Oh no, she's a Jane. She doesn't believe in magic at all. It gives me a slight edge." He grinned at me, his stained chompers on full display.

"Right."

"Do you want some coffee? A soda, maybe?" He placed his hands on the arms of the chair and leaned forward, as though ready to sprint to the kitchen. "I think I might have leftover meat for a sandwich, if you want that? I know how much you like Niamh's sandwiches."

"No, no, that's okay. We can't stay long." I waved my hand as a scuffling noise caught my attention. Austin turned a little on the couch, his knee bumping mine, his focus on the body stashed behind us.

"He's waking up," Austin said, turning back around. "We should probably let you deal with this, Edgar." He scooted forward, ready to leave, and then stalled at the edge of the cushion. "Wait a moment." A groan sounded behind us, but Austin didn't seem to notice. "You met him on the edge of the property, and you found two others in the Ivy House woods?"

"Not all today, no." Edgar leaned back. "The other hikers were a couple of days ago. It's a lovely area. I usually get a few people passing through for one of the local festivals."

"Why didn't you mention this?" Austin asked.

"Mention what?"

I heard the sound of a body sliding against the wall.

Austin stood in a graceful rush of power. "Festivals are on in the summer and fall, when the weather is nice. They don't put on events in the winter. There aren't a lot of tourists around at this time of year, and those who do visit typically don't spend their time outdoors. Not Janes and Dicks, at any rate."

I pushed forward to the edge of the couch, half turning around. Doilies fell to the floor. I remembered Edgar talking about those hikers the other day, but I hadn't thought anything of it. Most of the time I tried to ignore any and all talk about his feeding habits. Maybe that had been a mistake.

"Oh, well, they didn't put up any kind of fight," Edgar said, also pushing to the edge of his seat, looking up at Austin. "Magical people would've known what I was right off the bat—I keep forgetting to try to hide it. They wouldn't have offered to be a snack—they would've fought back. Jessie even fought back before she became the chosen."

Austin walked around the couch and bent. When he stood, he was clutching the gently flailing man's flannel shirt. The guy's face came around, and I recognized him immediately. The younger guy who'd been sitting at the bar of the Italian restaurant the night of my botched date with Ron. The one with the young face and those old-soul eyes.

I opened my mouth to say as much, but his eyes snapped open and his body went taut, straightening within Austin's hold. His hands jerked up as Austin let go, dropping him.

Too late.

A jet of magic exploded out, punching into Austin's bare chest and flinging him back. He hit the wall, sticking into the plaster, his eyes widening before fluttering closed. He sagged, sliding bonelessly to the ground.

Terror kick-started my heart and adrenaline flooded my body. There wasn't any blood—maybe it had just knocked him out?

Another jet of magic flew out, catching the edge of the couch and exploding the back. I dropped to the ground in a hail of doilies. The guy popped up, his eyes focused, his movements reeking of confidence and experience.

Edgar dashed forward at incredible speed, but he wasn't fast enough. Magic slammed into him, tossing him back against one of his barrels. Canisters thumped forward and fell off, drenching him with plant juice.

An invisible weight dropped down over me, covering my body and sticking me to the ground. It shimmered within the afternoon light, hazy gray, similar to the net that had caught me—and then let me go—when I was falling, but translucent.

Clearly this guy was much better at his craft than the others had been. He'd done what they could not.

He'd trapped me.

CHAPTER 20

A SMILE SLOWLY spread across his thin lips. "This is such a backwoods town. Dormant. Anyone at all can walk in here and hang around. If you stay away from that big alpha and don't cause any trouble, no one bothers you. You even get welcomed into homes with open arms. All you need to do is sustain a little bite and there you go, no one suspects you." He walked around the couch, his old-soul eyes sparkling. "I didn't even have to go find you. You came right to me. Is it my birthday?"

"I hope so. Not many people get to exit the world on the same day they came in. It'd be a real treat to make that happen for you."

Anger raged through me, fueled by fear for my friends who'd just been taken down, and I sent a pulse through the very fiber of Ivy House, rumbling along the ground, flowing through the air, hopping from tree to tree and flower petal to flower petal. Across the expanse of garden, within the house itself, I felt my team stir. I felt them move, first to the windows and then to the stairs, running to get the gargoyles.

"Big words for such a young little thing." He bent to me, his eyes roaming my face. "A pretty little thing, too."

"Young? I could be your mother."

He laughed, delighted, and then made a motion through the air. My translucent cage lifted from the ground, and me with it. "You see? So young and inexperienced." He continued to lean toward me, his face right in mine, his stinking breath making me cringe. "Magic can give us any kind of face we want. Young, old, male, female? We can be anything at all."

"Except a good person. Magic can't make you likable."

He tsked. "Of course it can. It is human nature to crave power. The more you have, the more everyone wants to be in your company."

"Sure, but that doesn't mean you're likable. People might tolerate a dickhead, but it doesn't make you any less of a dickhead."

"Well." He straightened and lifted me a little higher. "Maybe so. Let's hurry now, before your winged friends try to follow us."

I laughed, closed my eyes, and reached for the power of Ivy House. "There is a reason those others tried to capture me when I wasn't on this property."

All her defenses were at the ready, waiting for me to call out which ones I wanted. Ready to play with him like a cat plays with a mouse. She hungered for it.

Not yet, though. He had information, and the grounds were extensive. I had time.

"Yes, I know," he said. "Afraid of a house. The actual house, not the people in it." He laughed and lifted his hands. "They were afraid the house would stop them, and yet here I am. I didn't burn to ash the moment I set foot on the grounds, and I have the chosen in my possession."

We passed Austin, who lay unmoving on the floor, and I reached out to him, my heart lodged in my throat. My hand hit somewhat pliant magical bars. The memory of falling through that spidery web flashed through my mind again. The magic felt similar—did that mean this prison was breakable too?

"Many of my colleagues studied the ancient texts about this house and the chosen, and they were naïve enough to take them literally. It didn't occur to them that history evolves over time, and lore and myth often get confused for fact. A magical house with battle defenses does make for a good story. Not quite a believable story, but a good one. Now…" He opened the front door, peered out, sent a pulse of magic, and then walked out the rest of the way, pulling me behind him in my floating prison. "What *I* found helpful was the information about the chosen. She is the heir to a wealth of magic, yes, we know, but she doesn't have access to it all at once. She has to learn it, little by little, until she's experienced enough to handle the large dumps of magic she is given. You are awarded the magic you can handle. The other night was enough to convince me you can't handle much, hmm? And thus, here you are."

"You have got to be, and I don't mean this kindly, the biggest know-it-all I've ever met, and I've met a few. You are never invited to parties, are you? All the droning on and on. Is that why you weren't working with that other group? Do you have to skulk around alone because no one wants to listen to you?"

He sniffed, walking fast now, heading for the trees. I could feel a ripple of magic flowing behind us, magically covering our tracks. Austin had said that a mediocre mage could do that for fifty yards or so. The woods here were much bigger than that, except Austin wasn't awake to find us. It would be a long walk back if the gargoyles couldn't figure it out, and given the mess they'd made of things the last time, they might not.

Thinking of Austin made me throb with worry. I closed my eyes, breathing deeply for a moment, seeking out Ivy House.

"*Can I heal him?*"I asked. "*I know I am supposed to find my own way, but in this… Can I heal him? Please help me.*"

"*You already are. You do not have to touch to heal. It began when you tried to reach out to him. You can use your magical connection to give him energy. Love strengthens the bond and quickens the pace.*"

I ripped away the privacy blocks from my connections to Austin and Edgar, annoyed that I hadn't thought about that myself. Edgar's strength came through immediately, the blast he'd gotten clearly not as severe. I focused on Austin, thinking about my desperation to help him, to heal him—trying to touch him this way as I'd tried to physically touch him through my magical prison.

"Ah, here we go." The man walked us into the woods, the trees reaching over us, concealing us from anyone flying overhead. "Gargoyles battle, they don't search for prey. The big alpha hasn't been coming to the house much—I didn't think he'd be here. Lucky stroke for me how it ended up, huh?"

"Where are you taking me?"

"Well, if you must know, to the holding cell where the contract holder will collect you. He put a high price on your head."

Whoever was behind this had sent out multiple teams of people, not just one group, and he'd clearly set it up like some sort of bounty-hunter situation. That wasn't ideal.

"Where's this holding cell? You people have magical prisons?"

"Ah. If I told you that, I'd have to kill you." He chuckled to himself even though his joke didn't quite fit the situation.

"Mhm." I nodded, seeing that I obviously had to switch gears or he'd likely clam up with more off jokes. "Aaaand you never commented about your lack of teammates. You were picked on in magical school, weren't you? Always the odd man out. I hear this tale a lot. Do you hold a grudge? Is going out on your own, sticking your nose up at the other team, your way of saying *nah-nah-nah-nah?*"

He looked back at me, annoyed. "A Jane becoming magical. What a strange turn of events. I doubt they'll mention that in the history books."

"I doubt they'll mention you, either."

He puffed up. "If I bring you in, I will earn a coveted place on one of the most elite magical teams in the nation. I will earn a highly desired spot at a master's table. The money I earn from bringing you in will allow me to hire a bard, if I want, or marry from within the magical elite."

I didn't know what the most elite magical team was, but someone surely would. This guy was just shedding hints, likely because he didn't think I'd be able to escape.

"Whoever you buy for a wife won't want to sleep with you. That's got to be dick shriveling, huh? Remember what I said about being a dickhead..."

His shoulders tightened. Anger crackled in his gaze when he turned around. I was walking a fine line—if I pushed him much further, he'd do something to knock me out. I hadn't made it this long in life without seeing the signs of a man on the verge of violence.

I tried to pump energy through the connection with Austin, hoping it was happening, and hoping whatever I'd done subconsciously was having an effect. But I didn't want the mage to get me much closer to the border of the property. Time to act.

Magic built within me, feeding on my anger at being trapped. I pulled a magical blanket of darkness over us, shadow crawling across the crisp blue sky. The ground rumbled, rocks shivering around us, and leaves waved without a breeze.

The man looked at the sky first, and then his head dipped as he watched a rock slowly roll across his path.

There was so much I could do, but I didn't get the

chance. Ivy House, impatient, took over.

Fog rolled in as though driven by cowboys on horses, tumbling through the trees, so thick it was swampy. It pushed in around us, making the man startle. Menacing laughter echoed around us, up high in the tree branches, down low in the bushes. A foot-high body ran out in front of the man, a lovely little doll face looking up with a smile, a knife in its animated hand.

"Oh God, oh no." I balled up. "What the hell, Ivy House? You're doing this on purpose to mess with me!"

"What is that?" The man peered down at it like a moron.

"You got your myths wrong, Mr. Know-It-All. Ivy House is very much a threat, and you will not make it off this property alive. You brought this on yourself!"

A little plastic body dropped from the sky. It fell on him, its hands out, holding two needles.

"Oh, gross." I pushed back against the web, this assault not intended for me but terrifying nonetheless.

"Gah!" He reached up to grab the doll as it swung its chubby little arms down. The needles dug into his face, and I rolled over, my stomach swimming.

"There are other ways to crack a nut, Ivy House," I said, seeing a little creature running up behind me, one of the Halloween dolls that had given me nightmares. It passed under my thankfully suspended cage. "*There are other ways to crack a nut. Use the other ways!"*

The man screamed, flinging the doll off his head. The magic around me faltered.

"No, no, keep me in here until they're gone," I said, not trusting Ivy House to give me control of those dolls. I didn't want to wander around in the mist with an unseen army of dolls. Talk about my worst nightmare. "How'd they even get here so fast?"

A barking cough sounded out of the dense white to our right. Another to our left. Needles sprayed, silver glimmering in the dim light. They dug into the mage's clothes and embedded in his skin.

He sprayed out jets of magic, one zipping past me, and another coming head-on.

I screamed and magically pushed outward at my cage, bowing then breaking it, falling to the ground. But I didn't escape quickly enough to dodge the spell. I threw up my hands—the spell-blocking equivalent of flapping my arms to fly.

A skeleton jumped in the way just in time, the magic hitting it and exploding the bones outward. I stared for a solid moment, unable to understand what had just happened.

Dirt moved in the trees to my right, hard to see through the rolling, tumbling mist, but I thought I saw something jutting up out of the ground. Then I was sure of it when a torso interrupted my field of vision.

"Oh my God," I breathed out as a lumbering stack of bones approached from the left, teetering toward the mage. The other skeleton rose from its unmarked grave, stepped up onto the dirt, and headed toward the man.

"Of all the options at your disposal..." I said as the first skeleton bent over the flailing man and dug bony fingers into his eyes. His screaming wilted me in place. "All the options, like spears and darts and gas... All that, and you chose to unleash the biggest nightmares you have? This is a joke on me, isn't it? You think my fears are stupid. Well, your humor is terrible, Ivy House."

The jubilant feeling soaking into me was the house's mirth, rubbing it in.

"We'll see who's laughing when I set you on fire," I grumbled, hopping to my feet.

Through our now-open connection, I felt Austin rouse and then his sudden gush of terror. Incredible pain bled through as he struggled to stand. He knew I'd been taken, and he intended to come to me even though he was hurt.

"Keep him there, Ivy House—we don't need him making himself worse," I said.

I felt the door swing shut, something I probably could've done myself if I wasn't so completely distracted by the little doll bodies competing with animated skeletons to swarm the enemy. Boy had he been wrong in his assessment of this house.

Frustration ran through Austin. A moment later, I felt something weird and wondered if the magical connection had gone haywire. But then I felt his huge body slam into the front door, bursting it to bits. He'd shifted into his polar bear form. So much for Ivy House keeping Austin put.

A doll ran by me, laughing like a mad thing.

I hadn't known they could speak. That was disturbing news.

The doll took a running jump at the mage, who was fighting with the two skeletons, his magic slapping into them uselessly. The doll's weapon lodged into the man's back, and it hung there for a moment, dangling.

The mage's scream cut right through me. Horror movies had never been my thing, and now I was witnessing the real thing. The word *shocking* couldn't fully describe it, especially when the doll grabbed another knife from a holster on its frilly dress. It pulled it out and stabbed it into the sinking man, trying to climb him like a mountaineer.

"Nope." I popped up, adrenaline fueling me, about-faced, and ran like hell. Ivy House had this covered, clearly, and someone else could grab the mage's body if they wanted it. This whole scene was a nightmare, and I didn't want any part of it.

I could sense Niamh and Earl flying overhead, and I sent a wave of magic so they'd know where to find me, just in case Ivy House had kept my location a secret in order to continue tormenting me. A snap of great wings said Damarion hadn't been left behind.

I felt Austin before I saw him, a great lumbering beast through the rolling, swirling mists. When he neared, he dropped and slid to me on his stomach, clearly wanting me to hop on.

"Run away," I said, pointing behind him. "They got him. That guy is dying a gruesome death. Go the other way!"

I climbed on and sank into his fur.

Thankfully, he listened. He turned around and started lumbering back to the house, his pain unmistakable but his determination pushing him on.

That could have been a close call, but the mage had made the fatal mistake of attacking me on Ivy House soil. And he hadn't felt the need to knock me out—another mistake.

In short, I was lucky. Very lucky. If that mage hadn't been a self-important idiot, things could've gone much differently for me.

I was two for two on lucky escapes. There was a

price on my head, though, and the person organizing this sounded like he had a lot of money, a lot of power, and probably a lot of prestige. He'd have mages of all types trying to cash in. Soon my luck would run out.

CHAPTER 21

"**D**O YOU NEED anything, miss?" Mr. Tom stuck his head into my favorite sitting room, tucked away in the back corner of the house. Smaller and cozier than the other sitting rooms, it had lovely wooden carvings at the base of the ceiling that moved in pleasing ways. It was the room I used to decompress, Ivy House helping by changing the carvings as befitted my mood. She was currently attempting to make up for the horror show with the mage by showing me ocean waves and softly swaying trees and flowers.

I still hadn't forgiven her.

"No, thanks, Mr. Tom, I'm okay." I leaned back in the recliner, my feet up and my head turned so that I could look out the window at the side yard, alive with beautiful flowers from our award-winning (cheating) gardener. "How's Edgar?"

Mr. Tom fully entered the room and took a seat by the door, not getting comfortable. He usually left me alone when I was in this room.

"He's a bit down in the mouth," Mr. Tom said, resting his hands on his knees. "He committed a grave error yesterday and jeopardized your life, not to mention we still don't have any information about those hikers that he dined on before. It doesn't matter that you've forgiven him—he's gone against his duty to the house, which is to protect you. He thinks it is time for you to retire him."

That kind of punishment felt much too heavy for an honest mistake. "Where would he even go?"

"Oh, they don't go anywhere. Unless you're talking about the ash from their burned bodies? That's hard to collect, so usually the magical community just lets it float at will…"

"Do you mean retire like…kill him?"

"Kill him is always a bit confusing when it comes to vampires, isn't it? He's basically already dead, so you can't really kill him again. You just retire him from being a vampire. Make him stop existing, like should have happened the first time he died."

I rolled my eyes. "You knew what I meant, and no, we are not going to retire Edgar because he wrongly chose a food source. You guys have been idle in this place for years. The change is hard for all of us. That mage had been lingering in town for…days, at least. Probably much longer. Austin never noticed him. I saw him and didn't know what he was—Edgar did me a favor by bringing him onto Ivy House property, where we have defenses. If that guy had grabbed me outside of Ivy House…" I shivered, that little sticking point a big reason for my downer mood. I might still have been able to best him, but I didn't want to hang my future on a "might."

"Have you spoken to Austin Steele?" Mr. Tom asked, standing again.

After returning to the house yesterday, Austin had waited with me in polar bear form. I hadn't wanted to be alone, and he'd sensed it—or maybe he hadn't wanted me to be alone either. The others had come back a while later with the news that they'd buried the mage's body, reburied the skeletons, and roused Edgar. The dolls had apparently seen themselves home, which I didn't relish thinking about. Once everything was sorted out, Austin had lumbered back out of the house, and I hadn't heard from him since. I said as much.

"He probably blames himself, as well. That mage was in his territory all this time without him knowing."

"That mage knew just enough to purposely stay away from him."

"That won't matter to Austin Steele. He holds himself to unrealistic expectations. It won't be easy for him to get over the fact that the mage got the better of him."

I turned my head, back to looking out the window. "This is ridiculous. I can't stay on this property forever—I will have to leave sometime. With a price on my head, I'm going to need a team around me to guard my back. Everyone blaming themselves and licking their wounds is not helpful. It's not going to make things safer going forward."

"Agreed, miss."

"What do you think about bringing some of the gargoyles onto the team?"

He sat down again, as awkwardly as before, and said, "Honestly, I don't think they have proven themselves yet. None of them have meshed with the established team. Right now, there are two teams, rather than just one."

"Damarion's team, and yours and Niamh's team."

He hesitated. "Basically, yes. The summoned gargoyle team, and the house team. Despite being the same species as the others, I am not viewed as part of the gargoyle group."

"But Damarion said that they didn't even know each other before they came here."

"I wager that is how the summons works. They collect along the way, finding each other, moving together, and establishing the pecking order *before* they arrive. Once they arrive, they are ready to assimilate."

"Except they haven't assimilated."

"They have, just not with the house team. They have assimilated with one another, and with you."

Frustrated, I pushed to standing. "That's not going to work for me. Does Damarion need to be brought into the Council...seating thing in order for all of you to work together? Are the groups only separate because he's not connected with the magic? Those gargoyles will follow me, sure, but my default setting isn't as commander. When I need something, I take charge, but otherwise I don't think of it. It'll take time for me to grow into that role. In the meantime, I need someone to handle the day-to-day..."

A memory jogged for position. Austin speaking to me.

I have experience in leading. Obviously you don't need my help with Niamh and the others, but if new people show up, you can count on me. I will put them in their place until you're ready to step up and take over. You know my past—you know I won't try to usurp power. Eventually, hopefully, I wouldn't be able to.

My frustration bubbled a little higher.

"Damn Austin for not wanting to be involved in this. *He's* the missing link. He's the ace in the hole. *And he doesn't want the job.* Not officially, anyway, and if he won't officially take it, it's a hard sell to outsiders."

"Yes, the situation is certainly grievous."

I huffed out a sardonic laugh. "Grievous…yes, it is. So what I'm looking for is a replacement for Austin. Right now, the only candidate is Damarion."

"He certainly has the right materials. Strong, sure, loyal, born to lead…"

"He's an elitist, though, who hasn't made an effort to connect with the nut cases of this house."

"True, he hasn't taken to Edgar and Niamh very well…"

That didn't warrant a comment.

"I wonder if I could talk him around," I said, bracing my hands on my hips. "Maybe he just doesn't understand that I need my second to handle day-to-day issues that involve the whole house. If he knew that, he might be more inclined to treat everyone as a group."

"He'd certainly need to welcome non-gargoyles, because you can't just have gargoyles on your team."

"Yes, exactly. He seems a little green—maybe he just needs some training, like I do." I paused, thinking, then added, "And if he's more secure in his footing, he may treat the Austin situation like a professional instead of a competition for dominance."

"I was with you until that last bit."

"It's worth a try. I don't have much choice."

"But you do have a choice. You can send another

summons and see who you get, like fishing. Catch and release. You don't have to settle for your first couple catches."

"Is it too late to quit and choose a different life?"

"And stay alive and free? Yes, miss. That ship has sailed. You have the magic now, and only death will change that."

"I owe it to Damarion to give him a chance. He showed up in the nick of time and saved my life. He's been taking beatings from me. The least I can do is talk to him. This is all new to him—the town, the people, us. I'm sure we can get him on the right track."

"Of course, miss. There's the spirit. 'Beating a dead horse' wouldn't be a saying if people didn't love to do it."

"That's not why…" I let it go as I passed him, headed for the kitchen. I'd grab a bottle of wine and invite Damarion to one of the larger sitting rooms for a chat.

I was in the kitchen, having just opened a bottle of wine, when I felt Damarion approaching the room from down the hall.

"Hey," he said, coming up behind me. He slipped his hands across my hips and gently pulled me back until my back was against his front. "I was just coming to do the same thing."

"What's that?" I asked, coaxing myself to relax within his arms, wanting to just get over this hump of anxiety and let myself be touched by someone new. I knew if I just buckled down and made it through the first time, I'd realize it wasn't such a big deal. Plus I'd get a little…exercise that I was starting to crave with more urgency lately. I just needed to stop getting nervous and running for the hills.

"Grab the wine." He bent and ran his lips along my neck, lifting a hand so he could pull down the edge of my silk housecoat (Mr. Tom had insisted I have one), exposing the spaghetti strap of my singlet. The wet warmth of his kiss left a trail until he got to the strap, then he hooked his fingers underneath it, about ready to pull that down, too.

In the middle of the kitchen.

"Let's…" I slid away a little, hitting the edge of the counter with my hip as I half turned. This would all be so much easier if he didn't come on so strong. It was like he didn't have a "warming up" setting. He went from normal guy to Mr. Handsy in one second flat. "How about we—"

He dropped his finger to my lips. "*Shh.*" He pulled his finger away and planted a kiss on my lips. "I know what will help you forget about that bear."

I paused. "What?"

He reached around me and took the bottle of wine.

"You need me to show you how I feel, right?" He grabbed two glasses. "You need romance?" He gave me a sultry smile. "Give me ten minutes, and then look in on my room. You have the ability to see into any of the rooms, right? Ulric said the house lets you look in on anyone. I'm sure you've been using it to check on me..."

I tried to keep a straight face, but a furrowed brow might've broken through. Not only would I not do that because of the creepiness factor, but the thought honestly hadn't crossed my mind.

"Give me ten minutes, and then I will show you. You can come to me whenever you want."

I let out a held breath and smiled—he'd finally landed on the perfect words. *I* could go to *him*. I could choose when and how. Being able to set the pace and apply the brakes sounded really good. Especially as it concerned him. I wondered if he'd consent to just being tied up and letting me work the whole thing out without his digits searching for every available orifice.

"Yes, that's right." His kiss was urgent and needy. "That look in your eyes. I like it. Ten minutes. Come see me."

His new approach had certainly derailed my plan to talk to him. But maybe this was a good thing—maybe it would help me overcome whatever was holding me back with him.

I was standing in the same place, biting my nails, when Mr. Tom drifted in a few minutes later.

"When you try to talk him into leading the whole group," he said, "you might give him some romancing pointers."

"Why? What do you know?"

"That he is very bad at it. Clearly he has never had to try with women."

"How do you know that?"

Mr. Tom stopped between the still-ruined island and empty area where the table had once been. "You are standing in the kitchen, by yourself, while he is off…doing whatever he is doing. This is, apparently, his new tactic in romancing you. He reminds me of a great many boys I knew growing up. Knuckle draggers. I'd thought the younger generations would have more of a clue, but… Well, I do not expect a great outcome from this effort."

I opened my mouth, intending to make some kind of a rebuttal, I was pretty sure, but nothing came out. I really didn't know where to go with this. Talking with Mr. Tom about romancing was about as awesome as talking to him about his stuffing condoms all over my room.

Instead, I just nodded and made my way out, having

decided I'd head straight into the secret passageways and take my time getting up to Damarion's room. When I got there, a minute or so early, I took a deep breath, butterflies fluttering through my belly, and approached the little viewing hole that allowed me to see—and hear—the goings on in most of his room.

Candlelight flickered within, a great start. The bottle of wine waited on the dresser to the right, the two glasses next to it, their rims shimmering in the glow. His headboard was pushed against the wall opposite me, but the small footboard didn't obstruct my view.

In a moment, I wished it had.

"*Yes...*"

My eyes popped wide, and it took me a moment to make sense of what I was seeing.

Somewhat hairy legs were bent and spread wide, creating an "M" shape on the fluffy white duvet, the middle being thighs and a bare butt. Candlelight flickered off his ripped body, slanted slightly upward because his head rested on a stack of pillows, but there was no way in hell his muscular chest could hold my attention.

His hand, wrapped around his naked shaft, slowly stroked up and down, timed to his soft moans.

"*Yes*, girl."

My mouth dropped open. I couldn't look away. I

didn't know why, but for some reason—disbelief maybe, horror probably—I could not tear my eyes away from this train wreck.

What the hell did he think he was doing? *This* was his response to my need for romance? This was showing me how much he wanted me?

Okay, sure, logically it was pretty clear that he did, indeed, want me. But really?

No, it had to be a joke. There was no way he could be serious with this.

His hand sped up as the other reached down between those spread, hairy thighs and cupped his danglers. I thought maybe he was trying to cover them, because this view of a man had to be, without a doubt, the grossest view possible, maybe second only to if he bent over and showed off his bells and tackle from behind. But no, he was not covering them.

"Yes, yes…"

He was massaging them.

"*Yes!*"

"Oh, ew." I spun around, shocked mute for a moment.

I stood corrected. *That* was the worst view—the conclusion.

I stared at the opposite wall for a moment, the passageways lit by a magical blue glow…and cracked a smile.

Since my start in online dating, I'd gotten my fair share of dick pics, but this was the first time I'd caught a live performance. Dick pic live, coming soon to a peephole near you.

Laughter bubbled up, overtaking me.

I had to tell somebody. I couldn't keep this to myself. If I kept it to myself, it would just be icky and unfortunate. Telling someone meant there was a punch line, even if it was me.

I hurried away through the passages before emerging into an unoccupied room that looked out over the front yard. Niamh's lights weren't on, which meant she was probably at the bar. I hurried back to my room through the passages, not wanting to be seen, and changed quickly before jogging down the hall to Ulric's room.

After a couple of light knocks, he opened the door with a "Yup?"

White sweats hugged his thick thighs and a sports jacket fit his upper body perfectly, even though it was over a bare torso.

"What the hell is wrong with gargoyles?" I asked, taking a step back.

He looked down at himself. "Oh, I was just trying on the jacket Mr. Tom ordered for me. What do you think?"

"Looks good. Get dressed; let's go to the bar. Bring the jacket."

"Your wish is my command, milady." He left the door open as he hurried to change, and I turned around, just in case I got another show I did not want.

"What's the occasion?" Ulric popped back out and closed the door behind him, wearing jeans and a white shirt under the jacket.

"I need to speak with Niamh."

He noticed the phone in my hand, then shrugged and fell in step with me. "Cool. This place gets pretty boring after we finish practicing. We should play some board games or something."

"We need to grab another person, probably. Not Mr. Tom. I don't want him hearing...certain things."

"I'm sensing Damarion is a no-go, so what about Jasper?" Ulric asked, pausing in the hallway.

"Who? Oh, the deep gray one with the brown lines? I don't think I've ever actually spoken to him."

"He's not much of a talker. Damn fine guy, but he can be creepy. How about Cedric? You remember him—you got his friend killed?" He paused with his hand on his chest. "Too soon?"

Laughter burst out of me, which only made me feel guiltier, but not guilty enough to wipe away my smile.

"Cedric is good. Let's get Cedric."

"Least you can do, right? After making him a solo unit?"

"Oh my God, you have to stop. I feel really bad about that."

I knocked quietly on his door, only two doors down from Damarion.

"In all seriousness, don't feel bad—"

I put my finger to my mouth to quiet him.

"Cedric and that other guy weren't friends any more than I'm friends with the guys I showed up with," he said in a softer voice. "If you kill them off, I'll give you a cookie. I could use a little less competition. Why are we whispering?"

"I want to let Damarion get his beauty rest."

Cedric opened the door, also wearing a sports jacket over a bare torso and the house sweats. His lifted his eyebrows when he saw me.

"Get dressed," I whispered. "We're going out."

"Good." Cedric turned back into the room, and I swiveled around, still worried about getting another peep show.

"I know, right? It's boring here," Ulric said.

"If you're so bored, why don't you go out? You all are clearly horny as hell. Go pick up a girl at the bar."

"Well, yeah, but you only go occasionally, and we're

supposed to stay with you, so…"

"We need to create a schedule," Cedric said as he came back out. "Picking up a girl sounds good. I'd hoped for some time with the queen, but it seems she has made her choice."

"Nope, I haven't made my choice, but correct, I'm not an option. Grab someone at the bar. That's your best bet, definitely—damn it."

Mr. Tom waited downstairs, already holding out my handbag, and his gaze flicked from Ulric to Cedric. "Ah. I was right, then, and you're trading up? Yes, probably wise. Both of these men listen to you. They'll make sure your pleasure is as great as theirs. Just make sure they give you time to enjoy yourself. Two at the same time might be a learning curve. You won't want to constantly be fiddling with something when you'd rather focus on something else…"

"Oh my God, Mr. Tom, you have got to stop with all that." I grabbed my handbag. "It isn't right. We're not that kind of friends!"

"Well…" He smiled at me, his face clearly not used to that formation. "I'm honored that you would think of me as a friend. Wait, miss, I'll be coming—"

I shut the door after me, Ulric and Cedric already down the steps, Ulric wearing a smile.

"I would, though," he said.

"What?" I said, distracted. We might need one more person, at least until we hooked up with Niamh and hopefully Austin. Only one mage had come for me yesterday, but there'd been a handful at the first encounter. I wasn't sure I could handle the embarrassment of Mr. Tom right then, though. What if he kept on about...stuff.

"I would absolutely make sure your pleasure was as great as mine, and then some. Get a woman where she's goin'..." Ulric waggled his eyebrows at me. "And she will want to stay for the next ride. Keep a woman happy, and she'll keep you happy."

"Yes," Cedric said.

I couldn't do much more than let out a breath like a leaking tire. Why did my life keep getting weirder?

Mr. Tom stepped out of the house wearing a sports coat like Ulric, a white T-shirt underneath it, also like Ulric, and a bright green ball cap, not like Ulric or anyone.

"Ready, miss, thanks for waiting. Here we go." He put his hands in front of me, urging me to get walking.

"Nice getup, bro," Ulric said with a grin.

"Don't encourage him." I nudged Ulric's shoulder to get him moving and checked to make sure Cedric was following. "We don't know what waits out there, so let's keep this speedy. If anything happens, one of you should get me airborne, and the others should fight. Or maybe we should all go airborne? I'm not the best person to come up with our battle-aversion strategy. I wasn't even good at Battleship."

All the humor fled from Ulric as we walked. "Because of my age and stature, I can change in a hurry. I'll get you in the air if Mr. Tom and Cedric can run interference."

"Yes," Cedric replied.

"I excel at battle," Mr. Tom said.

"Okay, then," Ulric said, his grin creeping back.

"Let's just hope it doesn't come to that," I murmured, peering into the shadows as we walked. The still night allowed for sound to carry, not hindered by the scattering of leaves in the wind or the groaning of branches, but not a sound drifted out of the trees. Houses, pushed back from the street, sat quietly, their lights either dim or dark. The crescent moon hung high in the sky, shedding weak light.

"Why do you dye your hair the same color as your other form?" I asked quietly, my footsteps the only ones that made a sound.

"I assume you are talking to me?" Ulric whispered. I couldn't tell if he was mimicking me, or if he was also on high alert.

"Mr. Tom's form is not white-gray, so I am clearly

not talking about him."

"I used to have lush black hair that was a *similar* shade to my form, thank you very much," Mr. Tom said. "I have now given up hope that you will do the right thing and change us all back to the glory of our youth, however."

"That ship has sailed, Mr. Tom," I replied.

"Wonderful, yes, using my words against me. How fitting," he said dryly.

"Oops. Sore subject?" Ulric chuckled. "I thought that was part of the deal, though." He bent a little as he looked right, the houses having ended and now just wood around us. This was the perfect place for an ambush, and had been used for that in the past. "I read that those who are chosen regain the power of their youth."

"The power, yes. We do have the power, and all the wrinkles to go with it," Mr. Tom grumbled.

"So it didn't work in your case?" Ulric asked me.

"It would have, and I definitely allowed some body upgrades, because why would I pass that up, but…" I shrugged. "I'm me. The world at large is always telling us women that we need to be younger, prettier…but I'm comfortable being me. There is nothing wrong with me. I've earned the right to look my age and still get taken seriously."

"And if they don't take you seriously, to hell with 'em." Ulric pumped a fist. "I like it. Well, if I make the cut, you can age me up if you want, I don't care. The pink hair is my way of owning who I am, to answer your earlier question." He gave me a small bow. "I didn't forget."

"Oh, good. We were waiting with bated breath," Mr. Tom said.

"I was a boy who grew up when pink was solidly for and worn by girls. Given my other form is pink...I was teased. A *lot*. Add to that my smaller stature, my chattiness, and my usual good mood, and I stood out about as much as you do in this town." He laughed when I frowned at him. "When I got older, being teased turned into being bullied. Then being beaten. I was jumped by four big dudes who left me for dead. That was a good time. I had to drag myself back home. I didn't have many friends, and those I did have wouldn't dream of sticking up for me and paying the price. Some of those years were pretty rough, but they taught me to accept myself. The only reason those people targeted me was because I didn't fit into their worldview, which made them insecure. People still react like that sometimes, but I just smile and nod. If it makes them angrier, then I ignore their anger, and if they decide to push the matter? Well, I'll make them sorry." He shrugged. "So I dye my hair to let people know that I'm comfortable in my own skin.

He pulled a face. "An unforeseen development is that it's become trendy for guys to wear pink. I got complimented for my hair the other day. People probably think I'm wearing my hair like this to be cool rather than celebrating being different."

"Oh, you're different, all right," Mr. Tom grumbled.

"He's a treat, I know," I whispered to Ulric, then jerked my head back at Mr. Tom.

"No," Cedric said. For a man of few words, he occasionally knew how to pick them.

The lights of Austin's bar glowed a welcome, and I felt the coiled tension around my chest ease slightly.

"Why do you want to be part of the twelve?" I asked Ulric as we neared, slowing as we passed the same light post where I'd seen that creeper in the hat a while back. He'd looked at me, but had it been for longer than a normal glance?

How long had people been watching me?

"What do you mean?" Ulric asked, the door to the bar closed for some reason. Part of me missed seeing my favorite friend outside smoking. At least that would have been expected. Of course, Sasquatch was probably in there on my normal seat, braving Niamh's irritation just so he could annoy me.

"You left your life behind so you could try to be one of the twelve people who protects me. One of my team. Why?"

He stared at me in confusion. "Because you're the Ivy House heir…" He shook his head as I reached for the door. "I don't think I understand the question."

"Female gargoyles really are incredibly scarce, miss," Mr. Tom said, reaching around me and slapping my hand away. "Remember what I told you? They are called to you. They would do anything to serve you, and mate you."

"Especially the mating. I would absolutely be in for that. Or even just—"

I held up my hand to Ulric. "I got it, thanks. Never mind."

"I would mate you, too, if we're putting our hats into the circle," Cedric said. "Or just pleasure you if—"

"Nope. No more. It's fine. Let it go." I stepped to the side so Mr. Tom could open the door.

"She's something of a prude," Mr. Tom said as he pulled the door wide and stepped aside with a flourish.

"Nah, she's just a Jane. They have different rules," Ulric said, and I wanted to throttle them both.

Instead, I stared dumbly at Niamh's seat for a moment, finding it empty. The person behind the bar was neither Paul nor Austin, but some woman I'd never seen before. Only three people filled the stools, and Sasquatch wasn't one of them. Neither was Niamh.

"Quiet, huh?" Ulric asked, staying by my side even though I'd slowed.

A groan sounded from the left, through the entryway to the pool area. From my vantage point, I could see part of a man who lay on the floor, his body as stiff as a board. His bulging eyes and straining neck made it look as if he were bound and trying to break free, but I didn't see any rope. Behind him, a glimpse of a woman's legs—her bare ankles pressed together and one shoe off.

My mind caught up to the situation at the exact moment Ulric grabbed me around the waist and threw me toward the door.

The door slammed shut before I got there. I rammed into it and bounced off, onto the floor. Ulric tore off his clothes. Mr. Tom didn't wait and ran forward, straight for the closest woman jumping up from her stool.

Cedric tried to step in front of me as a shield, but was torn to the side by invisible hands and flung.

A woman at the other end of the bar had bounced up, too, her arms out, her fingers aiming at me, and her face pinched with determination. A jet of color was the last thing I saw.

CHAPTER 22

"S O, HIDIN' OUT here, lickin' yer wounds, are ye?"
Niamh picked up the sack she'd carried around
the neck of her puca form, taking out some black sweats
she'd had to buy herself because Earl couldn't be
persuaded to veer from white. Her phone chimed, Jessie
wondering if she was at the bar. She wanted to share a
funny story.

That would be Niamh's next stop, right after she
tried to talk some sense into this big dope.

Austin sat in a lone chair on the beach, looking out
over the lake, his small, lonely cabin behind him. A
fresh kill, a skinned deer, hung from a nearby tree. Even
if it was bear season, no bear in its right mind would
come calling at this camp. They'd know a bigger, badder
predator awaited them.

He didn't look so big and bad now, though,
hunched in that chair, staring out at nothing.

She slipped into the sweats and took a seat behind
him, marveling at the ease with which she could lower

and get back up again. That blast of youth from Ivy House had been a blessing. One day she'd try to do a cartwheel again.

She let the silence sit between them for a while. A guy like Austin Steele didn't let you bully him. He responded best to logic and reason, especially when he was drowning in feelings that had nothing to do with either.

"You all healed up?" she finally asked.

"Yeah. Jess took care of most of it. I don't even know what that mage hit me with, but it was a good shot. I didn't expect it until it was too late."

"Yeah. That lad, whoever he was, had our setup mapped out. Couldn't get a face off him—or I should say, the dolls cut the face off him, so we're still not sure who he was."

"The dolls..." He turned to look at her, disbelief and a little horror crossing his face. He shook his head and faced the lake again. "Never mind. I don't want to know."

"Probably not. I took a picture, just in case we ever find out who his...the contract holder is."

Another beat of silence passed.

She had to throw it out there. "Have ye ever been saved by a Jane before?"

"You know the answer to that. I have been saved by

a woman, though. A little woman, protecting her daddy. My fierce little niece. Jess reminds me of her." He paused, then added, "I see now why no one batted an eye when that gargoyle knocked Jess around. She's fearless. She's unstoppable. A mage took two of her friends down, right in front of her, and then tried to kidnap her, but she still had the presence of mind to get information from him. That's…"

"She was chosen well, we know this."

"Yes, she was."

"You're not licking yer wounds after havin' been saved by a woman, fine. So why are you mopin' about? I sure hope it isn't to do with that fella the house took down. You don't run a military state here, Austin Steele. This is a tourist town, for heaven's sake. You can't ID everyone that comes through, and that lad knew about you. He purposely avoided you."

He sighed and slouched a little more. "I'm straddling a line, and it's making me do a piss-poor job of helping Jess. If I were in charge of her defense of Ivy House, that mage wouldn't have slipped through the cracks. That attack at the cliff would've ended before it had begun. Her people would be in line, and this whole town would be behind her. *Everyone* would be looking out, questioning, reporting back. I'm not in charge, though, which means I'm in the way. If I hadn't been there, that gargoyle would've been near her, and maybe he would've seen something I didn't. He's in this completely. He deserves to be by her side."

"Ah." Niamh nodded and leaned forward to brace her elbows on her knees. "So there's the reason for your pity party. Now I see."

He shook his head. "This is me finally realizing it's time to move on. That gargoyle was given the power to draw out her abilities, and that's the thing that will protect her the best. It's time for me to find a new territory and officially establish myself as alpha."

"I've thought about this a lot, now. Ever since you started shoutin' around the place yesterday. When you rebelled against Ivy House, Jessie took it to mean you didn't want any part of the magic, including helping her work that magic. She doesn't like asking for help, that one. Probably hasn't had anyone *to* ask for help in the last handful of years, so she got out of the habit. She's been a mother so long, looking after her family, that she stopped looking after herself. So when Earl fawns all over her, she relaxes, ye can see it. She appreciates it, which is great, because he's a useless ol' sod if he doesn't have someone to fawn over.

"Now, she's a fighter, and she's determined, and she's fierce, but she is in over her head, so she is. Ye know that. She's a Jane that is suddenly magical. She needs help in ways she doesn't even know to ask about. She didn't want to bother you, so what did she do? She called for help. Ivy House gave the magic to the best man willing, choosing that wanker because it couldn't choose you. Ye didn't give it a choice, Austin Steele."

"Ivy House has been trying to manipulate me from day one. I don't play that game."

"Yes it has, ye gobshite. It isn't competing with you, though. That house isn't trying to beat you in some elaborate game of dominance, Austin Steele. It isn't tryin' to rule ye. It is trying to protect *her*, and it knows that there's no one else on this planet that can do it better than you. *That* is why it is constantly at ye, messin' with ye, pokin' ye. Jessie won't ask for help, no matter what she says to the contrary, but it has been askin', on her behalf. You've just been too dumb and blind to see it."

His head drooped a little more. "Doesn't change the situation."

"No. Only you can change the situation." She sat back, bored out of her skull looking at the calm lake and the unmoving mountains and trees around it. She was tired of beauty. It was time for a few battles.

"I don't know that I can do that," he said. "I've chosen this life for a reason."

"Jaysus, lad, I'm not askin' you to mate her. I'm not

after a litter. Lord knows she wouldn't be into that, anyway. I'm just askin' ye to finally take on the challenge you were born fer. Things are just heating up. It will get worse. Much worse. Her type of power compels people to want it, by challenging, romancing, or stealing. We need someone that can bring us all together and create a cohesive army. That donkey of a gargoyle can't even unite the house. Jessie could, o'course—they all respond to her—but she has no experience. She needs a battle leader. That is you, Austin Steele. That can only be you. You have the organization, experience, and brutality to make that work, not to mention a soft spot for Jessie. Yer the man for this job. Ivy House is showing us what it looks like for the *wrong* man to be in that position.

"I think ye were right about the training. We've gone about it all wrong. Sure, she can take it, and yes, she is getting better, but...what you said made more sense. I don't think she trusts that wanker. She is certainly slow to bed him. Tonight must be another bust for him if she's wanting to meet me."

Niamh didn't miss the vein popping out on Austin Steele's clenched jaw, or the way he balled his fists when she mentioned the possibility of the gargoyle bedding Jessie. Jessie had somehow grasped the heart of this untouchable alpha. Oh, how the webs were tangling.

"I know she doesn't trust him like she trusts you," she went on, brushing it aside. He could ignore his growing admiration until the end of time, if he fancied being a stubborn fool, but Niamh couldn't let him ignore how much he was desperately needed both in this town and in that house. He was trying to run, but she needed him to stay. They all did, Jessie most of all. "I wonder how much better she would get if she was working within a trusting, safe environment. I think she needs more support than we are giving her, and until she has it, those wings and the next phase of her magic will be held back. This is a hunch, now, I can't say fer sure, and that clueless vampire can't get through that book, but…"

"I'm not the kind of guy you let off the leash, Niamh."

A growl rode his words, his past rising up to haunt him. Her senses all clicked on, feeling the predator in her midst. She ignored them.

"You can lose yourself to your animal around her, entirely lose yourself. She will stop you from going too far out of preservation *for you*. She is the only one in this world you would allow to magically cage you, like she did yesterday, without seeking retaliation as soon as you broke out. Do ye know why that is?"

"Because she doesn't know what she's doing."

"No. Because you trust her. Because ye know that she is not trying to control you, she is trying to help you."

He didn't comment, which meant he did know that. She was on the right track, quite amazing, since she usually had no idea what made people tick—nor did she care to know. This situation was dire, though. The episode in the kitchen had been weighing on her mind. Jessie had chosen a side yesterday, and she didn't seem to feel any regret about not picking her current team leader. That spoke volumes.

It also spoke volumes that Austin Steele, on the brink of passing out, had sat beside Jessie until everyone else had returned from taking care of the intruder. He was in this, whether he wanted to admit it or not.

"Even if I did agree to join Jess's council, the house gave the gargoyle the ability to grow her magic. He will not follow me until I make him, and he will not be at his best if I subdue him. He and I won't work. It's too late."

"This is the problem with talking to men. The lot of you are so dense, I wonder how you get through without someone holdin' yer hand." She ran her hand down her face. "Ye already have a place in that house. He doesn't. Ye already have the magic. He doesn't. If you give in and sit in a council chair, there is no doubt in my mind that Ivy House will give you what you seek—what you should have been given in the first place."

"Which is?"

"Have you not been present for this conversation? The ability to help her magic grow. Janey Mack, but I'm losing my patience."

He shook his head slowly, the stubborn ox, and went back to looking at the water. Niamh checked her phone again. No new messages, but a strange feeling was bleeding through the magical link. Wariness and anticipation. Jessie was on the move, and Earl was with her. No telling who else. She was probably heading to the bar even though Niamh hadn't responded. Time to go. She didn't want Jessie to leave before she got there.

She stood, about to tell Austin Steele to think on things, when she noticed his head tilted to the side and a crease between his eyebrows, as though he were listening for a soft sound.

The truth dawned on her. She smiled.

"Ye know…Jessie thinks that if she cuts out her ability to feel her team through the magic," Niamh said, "the link is severed. When she plugs her ears to us, so to speak, she doesn't realize we can still feel her unless we also block the link."

Austin Steele glanced up at Niamh, guilt in his eyes, before looking out over the lake again.

That was all the proof she needed.

"I've never corrected Jessie's thinking on this," she continued, "because I didn't want her learning to block the magical connection entirely. Eventually she'll figure it out, but now, when things are so precarious, we need to be able to keep tabs on her in case she gets in trouble. Don't you agree?"

He didn't comment, or look over again.

"She hasn't been keeping tabs on any of us, out of respect for our privacy. *Your* privacy, over everyone else." Niamh stepped a little closer, facing the lake to keep things light. "How strange, then, that *you* would be monitoring *her.*"

"I'm not monitoring anything. It's just since the trouble started. I'm…"

"Worried about her. What's going to happen when you move away? You won't be able to block her because of that worry, but what if something happens? How do you think you'll react if you feel that connection severed and know she died because you walked away?"

Muscles popped out along his frame, the air alive with power. Niamh's warning sensors turned up a notch. Her feeling of Jessie clicked off.

She frowned and looked back toward the direction Jessie had been, searching for that feeling. Was it because she'd been talking about it that—

Austin Steele pushed to standing, suddenly on alert.

"Do you feel that?" he asked, his deep voice rough with menace and terror. "Did you do something?"

"I feel a *lack* of something, yes. But it wasn't me. My giving ye a *what if* was not supposed to turn into a premonition." Her phone chimed.

A text from Earl. *Are you alive? You and Austin Steele aren't on bar premises. If you're alive, they took her. Four mages. Five tried, but I killed one and used her as a shield. The rest took Jessie and got out before Ulric could turn from stone to gargoyle and before Cedric could get his thumb out of his keister. They were incredibly effluence.*

"Effluence?" she said out loud. "Autocorrect for efficient, maybe?"

A phone chimed in the cabin, Austin Steele already running for it.

Niamh pushed her sweats down and then tapped Earl's name to call him.

"It's Earl," Austin Steele called out, jogging out of the cabin and tossing his phone at Niamh. "They've got Jess. Mages—"

"I know, I know."

"Hello?" Earl answered, out of breath.

"What's the status? Where are you?"

"Running back to the house. I didn't want to change until I could get ahold of you. Ulric is following them from the sky. He'll report back when he can. If we're lucky, they'll stop for food or rest. I've called Damarion, but he didn't answer. Jasper did, and he is going to knock on Damarion's door. Fine time not to be in that bar, woman. Where is Austin Steele? Those mages had magically tied everyone up. They only killed one of the customers, and the witnesses said it was an accident. Sadly, it wasn't that hairy creature that always gives Jessie a hard time."

"Austin Steele is here." She put the phone on speaker and bent to remove her sweats and stuff them in the bag. "He was at his cabin. I flew out to talk to him."

"Well, get to Ivy House. I'll get Damarion to call in all the gargoyles. We'll be ready by the time you get here. Hopefully, then we'll have word from Ulric. Blast it—I wish we had a way to magically track him. Jessie has got to pick some—"

Niamh clicked the red "end" button and tossed the phone into the bag. He was just babbling at this point anyway.

"Why didn't they kill anyone at the bar?" Austin Steele asked, shedding his clothes with quick movements and handing them to Niamh.

"Probably as insurance in case you descended on them before they had Jessie. Mages must be watching this town awfully close for them to marshal in the one night ye didn't show. We have'ta change that, somehow. We need a better system."

"Right now we need to get going. See you at Ivy House."

Heat and light blasted her as he shifted, making her stagger back. She wasn't long in following suit, the bag getting caught on her horn instead of her neck. It would do. In a moment, she was airborne.

A team of mages had snatched up the bar—and Jessie—under Austin Steele's nose. There was no chance they'd just randomly stopped for food and rest. If they were this organized, they'd have a safe place to hold Jessie.

Lord help them if they couldn't find that place.

CHAPTER 23

I CAME TO slowly, a hard surface below my aching body and throbbing head. Cold air slid across my face, the breeze slight but uncomfortable. Silence greeted me as I fluttered my eyes open, trying to collect my scattered thoughts.

Steel bars interrupted my vision, slicing through the image of a flat, stony surface nearly lost to the dim lighting. The bars rose all around me, bowing inward and connecting to a circular plate above me. The large, rusted chain attached to the plate connected to a high ceiling, anchored who knew how.

The ceiling stretched out until it reached a fissure. Light bled in from outside, diffuse but bright enough for me to see within the cavernous space. Something shimmered from the ceiling to the floor of the opening, as though it had plastic wrap blocking it off. Probably a protection spell of some sort, not that it was needed. The opening was much too far away for anyone to jump from it to me. Even if they managed, I was two stories down or so, out of reach.

I pushed myself to sitting, my head swimming. The platform beneath me swayed over a drop of at least a couple of stories.

A sea of spikes, each probably a person tall, good and thick, completely covered the ground below me except for one small path leading to a shadowy area that probably had an exit.

Swell.

Even if I could escape this rusty cage from yester-year, I couldn't jump down from that height without breaking something or dying, and if I missed the small landing strip, or hit it and bounced, I'd find myself not just broken, but impaled.

The haze cleared from my mind as I arranged my feet in a more comfortable sitting position and sucked on my lip for a moment. Obviously flying would fix several of my problems. I could safely land or even try for that opening.

What was the magic covering the opening, though? Could I handle it? Assuming it wasn't plastic wrap, of course. And if not, would that same magic be over the exit that was sure to be at the bottom of this place?

I pushed to standing, wobbled, and reached for one of the bars. Rough, cold steel greeted me. At least there wasn't magic on my somewhat rickety cage. That was something.

A rectangular block of steel interrupted the vertical bars, and I threaded my hand through the bars so I could feel it out. There was a keyhole in the other side. I shoved at the door and then wiggled it. Not much give, made of strong stuff, and there was no way my muscles were up to the task. Ivy House had made me stronger, but there were limits.

This was definitely a limit.

I'd likely found the prison that one kidnapper was talking about. The holding cell. Or to use a different name, the rendezvous point for the mysterious contract holder to come and collect me from whomever had managed to grab me.

"So okay," I murmured, sticking my finger into the keyhole and wishing the door open. Nothing happened. I'd half hoped my subconscious would take care of that. "I just need to learn how to magically pick a lock, tear down some sort of shimmery magical wall, and then finally learn how to fly and get out of here. Nothing to it."

"What?"

I froze as the voice floated through the air before waning.

"What?" I asked back.

A shuffling sound preceded a sort of large hominid

character hobbling into my line of sight, long strands of matted hair hanging off its head and down its body, like an upright shaggy dog.

A few feet from its starting location, it stopped and turned, hair and shadow draping its face, and a great mustache and even more impressive beard reaching down to its chest. Only the nose was visible, a large spectacle that hopefully meant a keen sense of smell or it was just overkill.

"What?" it—he?—asked again, that single word somehow managing to sound slow and deep and ancient.

"Oh. I didn't know you were there," I said, pulling my finger out of the lock.

"What did you say?"

Slower, I repeated, "I...didn't...know—"

"Yes, yes, I heard all of that. What did you say before? I missed it."

It clearly meant when I was talking to myself.

"Nothing. I was just...taking stock of my situation." I wrapped my fingers around the bars. "Why are you holding me?"

"I am not. I am guarding you."

I wiggled the bars. "From whom?"

He paused, staring up at me. "They didn't say."

"Right, fine. *For* whom, then."

"Your captors."

I rattled the door, ripping off the connection to my team so I could get their locations. To my horror, nothing registered. I couldn't feel any of them.

I used my magical Morse code.

"Ivy House?"

"Who are my captors?" I said through clenched teeth, waiting for a response.

"The people who put you in there."

Silence greeted me, not even a wash of feelings from home base.

Panic slithered across my mind.

"Are you trying to be difficult?" I yelled, losing control.

"No."

I leaned my head against the bars, willing patience. "Who are the people who put me in here?"

"Mages. Women. Very brusque, if you ask me."

I was going to ask for their names, or who they worked for, but at the moment it made no difference. I had to get out of here. The question, as ever, was how.

"How long will I be in here? What are they going to do next?"

"Yes, that is a good question. It has been a long while since I have been solely in charge of this mountain, and for the last…oh, many years, this holding cell has been nonoperational. I agreed to guard it because that was my job of old, and also because they surprised me with the task, but…" He scratched his hairy stomach with his furry hand. "Well, I never really cared for this job. My home is in the wild. In the woods. There are no woods within the mountain. Besides, I don't much like the problems of the magical world. Very dramatic. Did you know…" He tilted his head back up to me, and the hair on his face moved, as though he were smiling. "They think I am one of their Bigfoots. Absurd, I know. That's just a made-up creature. But…" He nodded at me, his hand still resting on his belly. "I'm something of a legend around here. Maybe not as big as my cousin up north in those redwoods, but I have a nice little following around here, hunting the trees for me, trying to get a peek. Sometimes I show them a little leg, as it were. Maybe dart between the trees, too fast for a photo. You have to be quick in this day and age, though. Their little cameras are so fast. Much faster than those old upright, standing cameras. Remember those? Better picture, too. I have to be on my game. It keeps me busy. Kind of slow in the winter months, though."

My knuckles were white on the bars. "You are welcome to haunt my woods. They're glorious, and I have a diligent groundskeeper. If you let me out, you can roam to your heart's content. I'll even let you flash the locals—whatever you're into. Or money. How about money? I can give you—"

He shook his head. "I have no need for money." He spread his arms. "I don't wear clothes. Woods, though, huh?"

"Acres and acres. Have you heard of Ivy House? Down in—"

"Oh yes, Ivy House. Now *there's* a name out of my memories. Ivy House, yes. Lovely woods, there. Enchanted woods, my favorite kind. I like the way the magic feels on my—"

"No, no." I pushed my hand out through the bars. I was worried he might start talking about his begonias.

He knew of Ivy House, though. We couldn't be too far away. Given his predilection for the woods and the size of this cave, we might be in the Sierras. Not far at all, in the grand scheme of things.

Not that it mattered if I couldn't get him to let me out.

"Lots of enchanted woods and lovely gardens," I pushed.

"I do love the taste of flowers. They are scarce this time of year."

"We have lots of flowers! Our groundskeeper, he's a vampire—"

The creature sucked in a breath.

"You don't have to talk to the vampire," I rushed to say. "You don't even have to see him. He's a little crazy anyway. I get it."

"Vampires are not the right sort. I used to try to capture them so I could pop off their heads and bowl them through the rest of their kind."

"Right." I grimaced. That was gruesome. "Well…he's pretty tame. He's really old. He got kicked out of his—"

"But I do so love flowers. Magical woods produce the best-tasting flowers."

"Yes. We have lots and lots. The…groundskeeper wins the local festival every year for his gardening. *That's* how good he is."

The creature dropped his hand from his belly and looked back at that shadowy area. "My duty is to guard the prisoner. I cannot go back on my duty."

"But"—hand still pushed through the bars, I stuck out a finger—"if you don't get paid for it, is it really your obligation? You don't even like the job. Maybe you should break the mold, let me out, and go back to—"

"I do love flowers," he murmured, still looking at the shadowy area. "I'm salivating even thinking about them."

"You could just free me and go." I shrugged. "We have trespassers on Ivy House that you could scare, and then you could feast on all the flowers. Bring me down, and—"

"Oh no. They might hear. The crank is very rusty. I nearly went deaf trying to get you up there."

That didn't bode well.

I resumed holding the bars. "How about a key? Could you throw up the key?"

He scratched his head in a way that made me wonder if he had fleas. "How about this? I will just…go on break."

I lifted my eyebrows even though he probably couldn't see that. It gave me something to do while I tried to make sense of his words.

"Yes." He nodded his great, shaggy head. "I used to get breaks, I remember. It isn't my fault that no one is here to relieve me. It is my break, and so I must leave."

"No, but—"

"And on this break, maybe I'll get delayed. Yes, maybe I'll sprain my ankle. That's not *my* fault. Hikers sprain their ankles all the time. One fell off a little cliff and rolled a ways after seeing me. No one blamed *him* for that. He and his friends had to make a splint before they all hobbled away. It took a bit of time. A lunch break and a sprain, that should be enough time for you to escape." He put his fist in the air. "Any mistress of Ivy House would have the magic to escape in that time, right? And if you're lying, and you're *not* the mistress of Ivy House…well, I'll see you back here in a while, saddened that you lied about the flowers."

"No, but you don't understand. I just got the position. I don't have all the magic yet!"

He turned for the shadowy area, his stride long and his speed surprisingly quick, and either those spikes weren't as tall as I'd thought, or he was huge.

"What if they come back?" I yelled in his wake.

But he just disappeared into the darkness.

Breathing quickly, I heard a phantom clock ticking in my mind.

A lunch break and a sprain, assuming the mages didn't return. That was all I had. Time for a lunch break and a sprain, plus a fake hobble back. His stride was long, though. It wouldn't take him as long as it would a normal person.

As if there were any normal people within the magic world.

"Okay, okay," I said softly, reaching out to Ivy House again. It was as though I existed in a vacuum, no messages or feelings going out or coming in. "Okay. I need to…open this door. No, wait, I need to fly. Flying is more important. Even if he does come back, he can't fly. He wouldn't be able to get me if I did."

With shaking hands, I worked at the buttons on my

shirt and pulled it off to expose my back.

"How do the others feel totally comfortable naked?" I whispered softly, putting my shirt on backward to cover things up. "Okay, wings, now is the time. Come out. Come out, come out wherever you are."

I thought about two glorious wings extending from my back.

I thought about soaring through the sky.

I thought about jumping.

"Come *on*." Eyes squinted tightly, I balled my fists, panic rising.

I hadn't been able to do this while falling to my death, why did I think I could pull it off now, especially without contact with Ivy House? I wouldn't be able to get myself out of this one.

CHAPTER 24

AUSTIN CHANGED BACK into his human form at the mouth of a small cave, the trees and bushes around it nearly obscuring the opening. Ulric stood to one side in his human form, his expression grim, having been smart and taken his phone so he could call the others and direct them. Having hands in the other form was a decided advantage. Speaking of, Austin could smell the others, the gargoyle host, most of whom he didn't personally know, and the three Ivy House guardians, their scents fresh but their forms nowhere to be seen. Traveling without wings, Austin had been the last to arrive.

He did not smell Jacinta.

He couldn't feel her, either. Although their link had been severed at the lake, the feeling hadn't sunk in until after they returned to Ivy House.

It felt like a hole boring through him, like a hollow absence he couldn't bear.

Given the house's constant blasts of panic and

pleading, it couldn't feel her either.

Austin swallowed a lump in his throat, feeling that dark brutality he struggled to contain stirring within him. Rising. If those mages had killed her…

"What's the status?" he asked Ulric, his voice rough with unshed violence.

"She's alive." His tone was flat, and frustration and guilt swam in his gaze. He blamed himself for Jacinta getting taken.

Good. That meant he cared. It meant he'd do whatever it took to get her back.

Austin didn't outwardly show his relief. But something loosened inside him. As long as she was alive, there was hope.

"Where is she?" he asked, a prompt to get the show on the road.

"In there"—Ulric gestured to the cave—"but they didn't bring her in this way. I lost them in the trees at the base of the mountain, so I flew higher to see if I could get a glimpse of them from a higher vantage point. I saw someone working their way through the trees. It must've been one of the mages. They were gone by the time I got down here, but I was able to find this entrance. We'll still need to find the other one."

Given Austin didn't smell this other person, it meant they'd magically masked their scent. Ulric was right—it had to be one of the mages.

"Why do we still need to find the other?" he asked, ducking into a small tunnel that his animal form would never be able to fit through.

"You'll see."

At the other end, the cave opened up significantly, about fifteen feet high and thirty feet wide. The dozen or so gargoyles mostly stood off to the sides, crammed together to leave as much space as possible for the three from Ivy House and Damarion, who waited in front of a shimmering magical curtain.

The mage had apparently come to erect a magical barrier.

As he approached the invisible wall, Austin got his first look at what they were facing.

Jess stood in the middle of a rusty cage suspended in midair, gently swinging over a sea of spikes.

"What's the status?" he asked this crew, ignoring the blistering, churning need to grab Damarion and toss him at those spikes.

Damarion stiffened, probably having the same thought, but their issues could wait.

"We're having a rather bad day, Austin Steele, thanks for asking," Edgar said, staring in at Jess. He cradled one badly burned hand to his chest, the skin blackened and blistered and peeling away.

"Edgar tested out the barrier," Niamh said, looking up at the ceiling, then down to the ground. He doubted it had given her any new insights. "Ye can see what it did to him. Vampire skin is more fragile than the flesh of a gargoyle, but wings are a different matter entirely. We can't fly through this thing, and without wings, no one is getting anywhere but dead."

"I offered to try anyway," Mr. Tom said, his chest puffed up.

"Who would clean the house if you died?" Edgar asked. "I don't like spiders."

"Have you seen the mages?" Austin peered into the shadows layering the room. Not even a flicker of movement caught his eye. "Is she being monitored somehow?"

"Through the years, I've heard rumors of a basajaun in these parts, the keeper of the invisible prison." Niamh shook her head. "I never passed any remarks on the story. The storyteller was always a drunk muppet. But…"

"I've run across the basajaun that lives on this mountain." Austin walked along the barrier, cutting in front of the others, to see if it completely attached to the rock along the sides. If not, there was a chance he could peel it back in his animal form, which had a degree of magical resistance. "I traveled through these parts without realizing it was his mountain, and he was all set to challenge me for it. I deferred and left it at that. I had no idea about the prison. No one mentioned those rumors to me, or I would've checked it out."

"How'd these mages know about it?" Damarion asked.

"Good question," Niamh responded.

"Going up against that basajaun would be a helluva fight." Austin crossed to the other side, and Damarion shifted in unease as he passed. "It would be a hairy situation."

"No pun intended," Ulric murmured.

"Not to mention the mages, who have some real skill," Austin said. "I could take the basajaun, but you all would have to handle the mages. I couldn't handle both."

"Except where are they all?" Niamh asked, putting out her hands. "They must have left Jessie here for safekeeping while they went to do...something, but they'll be back, sure they will, and we still don't know how they cut Jessie off from us."

Austin cracked his neck and then hovered a hand next to the barrier. It gave off no pulse or charge. He could feel no magic at all. Very fine work, indeed. Mages of this caliber would only work for a hefty sum or an important boss.

A boss who may or may not be on the way to collect

his or her prize.

A boss who may or may not be Elliot Graves.

They couldn't waste time trying to find the lower entrance. They had to get Jess out of there now, and the best way to do that was to help her help herself. It was to empower her to play hero. He might not be able to draw the magic out of her, but he could draw out her confidence and her faith in herself. He could give her the courage to face her situation. It was what a good alpha did.

Besides, he could not bear to leave her in that cage while he stayed removed, safe. His place was fighting beside her, and he'd be damned if he'd back away because of a little pain.

He licked his lips. He could get to that cage, he knew he could. It would take every ounce of power he had, but he could do it. He could even rip that door open. Then what, though? He couldn't jump down in human form—the fall would kill him before he could heal. And he couldn't jump down in animal form because the path was too small. The spikes would kill him before he could heal.

"Do you think that chain could hold the weight of my animal form smashing onto it?" he asked. The chain holding it off the spikes was thick and well made, but the rust signified age. It wasn't what it used to be. The last thing he wanted to do was make the cage fall—if it did, the path would catch the corner and tilt it so the spikes slid between the bars and impaled the person inside. Maybe Jess could hold the bars on the side of the cage and escape the thrust of the spikes, but she'd be trapped in there.

Damn good deathtrap.

"Even if it could, you'd be unconscious by the time you got to it," Damarion said, turning to see Austin's face. He held out blackened fingers, obviously having tried the barrier to get a second opinion. "The pain is excruciating for just a few digits. Putting your whole body through that will kill you. Maybe not right away, but you wouldn't have long. Don't get me wrong, I won't stand in your way. You're a distraction Jacinta doesn't need." He glanced back at the others. "We will search for the other entrance. We know what we are looking for—we have but to find it."

"They might've hidden the entrance," Mr. Tom said.

"They didn't hide this one," Damarion replied.

"Then there might be the same spell on the other, non-hidden, entrance…" Mr. Tom said.

"I won't black out from the pain," Austin said, "and Jess will heal me before I'm lost to it. That's not a concern. What about that chain?"

"Doubt it," Mr. Tom said, leaning forward and peering through the gloom. "It's not reinforced where it connects to the cage. That is probably on purpose. Rattle that cage too much and whoopsie daisy, down it goes."

"You'd need to jump in animal form to clear the spikes," Niamh said.

"I know," Austin said.

"But ye would need to change back into human as ye neared the cage, suffer the pain, and grab on to that chain, hoping Jessie remembers how to heal."

"I know."

"This is probably a fool's errand," she said.

"Probably."

"This is ridiculous." Damarion turned and made a circle in the air. "Have fun on those spikes, bear. I'll save her myself. Come on." He stalked to the cave entrance, almost all of the gargoyles falling in behind him.

Cedric watched them go, then he turned and faced front, his allegiance clearly to the few members of Ivy House.

Ulric blew out a breath. "I hope to hell you make it, Mr. Steele, because I'm about to burn a bridge by staying here with you all."

"What are you thinking?" Niamh asked Austin quietly.

"I'm thinking that today is the day Jess learns how to fly."

CHAPTER 25

T EARS OF FRUSTRATION in my eyes, I felt like kicking something. My wings would not pop out. They just wouldn't. I'd have to wait in this godforsaken cage until that hairy creature came back and tsked at me for lying about my access to magical flowers.

I stamped my foot, then froze when the cage vibrated under me. Best not to mess with my rusty hanging lifeline.

Puffing out a breath, I glanced at the shadowy area, terrified someone would come walking through it at any moment. Terrified they'd take me away, far out of reach of Austin and Niamh and the others. Seeing nothing, I glanced longingly at the other opening, and then widened my eyes.

People stood behind the filmy barrier, and I recognized their statures immediately. The thin, almost wilting frame of Mr. Tom; the comparatively short silhouette of Niamh, hands on hips; the hunching vampire, who looked like he was hugging himself; and the broad form of Austin, standing close, staring at me. If they'd been talking, I hadn't heard them, that barrier obviously locking me into a sound vacuum.

My heart surged with hope. They'd found me! Somehow, they'd found me, and there they were, looking in.

If the mages came and tried to move me, they could at least follow them. I didn't see Damarion, but he was probably there somewhere, or maybe still in the sky. With those powerful wings, he could fly for a long time without needing rest. He'd made it all the way here from across the country, after all.

"If there was ever a time for wings, it is right now," I muttered, facing them, my hands still balled. "Now more than a few minutes ago. I need to get to them."

Austin backed away from the shimmering magical wall, and I felt the frown crease my face. Hopefully he wasn't planning to leave and find the other entrance. If anyone could find it, he would, but that hairy creature would be back long before that. He'd only planned for that lunch break and a faux-sprained ankle. Even a real sprained ankle wouldn't keep him very long.

"Austin can probably take that creature, though," I mumbled to myself, willing my wings to pop out. Or grow, or whatever was supposed to happen. Of course, the creature had mentioned the mages might be alerted by the sound of the chain descending. That meant they were probably in the area. If they came back—

A burst of light filled the opening, and the hulking shape of an enormous polar bear pushed the others aside.

"What is he..."

My heart leapt when the huge beast launched through the barrier. His beautiful white fur instantly turned ashy, as though it had been on fire, and smoke trailed from his body. His skin under his fur had blackened as well, intense burns covering him, blistering the skin, some peeling away to show blood-red patches beneath.

My stomach dropped out and fear squeezed my middle—could he survive that type of damage? Would he be able to stay conscious?

His paws stayed splayed, though, and he soared toward me, aiming right for the top of the cage. Nearly there, a blast of light and heat pushed me back. His human form emerged right as he hit the metal top, jerking the cage to swinging.

He slid across the surface, all blood and burned skin, and nearly went off the other side of the bars.

I cried out and threw up my hands. He slammed into a solid wall of air, stopping his forward momentum and smashing his nose. Not missing a beat, he reached back and scrabbled for the chain, wrapping a horribly damaged hand around it and pulling himself to safety. He clung there for a moment, his whole body shaking, the pain clearly unbearable.

Still he held on, and I reached up, wanting to cure all of this. Hating that he'd done this for me.

His sigh preceded him dropping his head, and I latched on to his center with the magical connection I could once again feel, pumping magic into him. I didn't know if it was energy, or healing, or even if it was helping, but it was all I could manage.

"Thank you," he said in a wispy voice, laying his head down for a moment as the cage groaned and swayed and the spikes below us stared up hungrily.

"Why did you do that, you idiot?" A tear slipped down my face, and I reached up on my tiptoes for him.

He dropped a hand to catch mine, wincing as he did so.

"I couldn't leave you here on your own, Jess. Whatever comes, we'll face it together," he said, and though I knew it had to be agonizing, I gripped his hand tightly.

Tingles spread across my skin and prickled my scalp. My stomach felt like champagne bubbles fizzed up through it.

His moan bespoke ecstasy and his eyes fluttered, the patches of bloody red already gone from his still burned and blackened skin.

"My God, that feels good," he said in a breathy whisper. "You've taken away all the pain and replaced it with…"

I didn't need him to mention what I'd replaced it with. The evidence was currently reaching down through the bars at me, and I wasn't talking about his hand.

"Sorry, I don't know—"

"No, no, it's okay…" he said.

I nodded and bit my lip, trying to look anywhere but at his lower half. It was not easy.

"Did you get a look at your captors?" he asked, his voice already stronger.

"Just at the bar. I woke up in this cage. A big, hairy creature was down below. He wouldn't let me out, but he did agree to leave me alone for a while. I'm not sure how much longer he'll be gone. He's supposed to be guarding me."

"How'd you get him to leave?"

"Apparently flowers are his weakness."

Austin chuckled softly, the action turning into a haggard cough. "That mage did a helluva job on that barrier. It's a good one."

"You shouldn't have jumped through it! They probably don't mean to kill me, Austin. I can't say the same for you."

"We won't be here to find out."

"I admire your confidence, but I'm locked in here. I can't figure out how to magically unlock it."

"I got it." He dropped my hand and crawled forward, but stopped when his unmentionables bumped against the bar. "Oops. This is probably incredibly awkward for you."

I huffed out an unexpected laugh as he worked his way forward again, a little more careful than normal with a part most men didn't want to scrape up. Near the edge of the cage, which was still swinging, he grabbed one of the bars on the door and his muscles bulged. The door clicked, the deadbolt bumping against its frame, but it didn't swing open.

"You keep healing me. I'll worry about this," he said.

I grimaced, because I hadn't intentionally stopped.

I thought about his wounds and about his nervousness about his privates and the rough bars, trying to jump-start the magic I largely didn't know how to do consciously.

"Mmm...maybe don't work directly on...that part..." He groaned, stopping for a moment and lowering his head. "It's distracting me. We don't have that kind of time."

"Oh my God, I'm so sorry," I muttered, my face burning. "I'm just trying to—"

"After we get out of here, please feel free to practice that trick on me. I'll make myself available any time." He smirked as he readied to yank on the bar again. "*Any* time."

"This is no time to joke around," I murmured.

His muscles bulged again and he grunted. With a loud clang, the door to the cage ripped open. The top hinge popped off, and the door swung downward, the other hinge groaning with the effort of holding on. Unable to handle the strain, it tore free and the door went somersaulting down toward the spikes.

It hit and bounced a little before settling, part of it sinking into a gap between the spikes, the rest stuck on top. The sound reverberated through the room.

"That was loud," I whispered.

"I can't hear the others through that magical barrier. If there's another barrier of some sort down below, I doubt anyone will hear anything," he said, swinging his legs over the lip of the cage and slowly lowering himself.

"That hairy creature said he couldn't let me down because of the noise." I touched a healed part on his pec, his skin almost waxy in appearance.

He covered my hand with his and his eyes softened. "He was probably just saying that to save his skin.

Those mages would kill someone for less, I have no doubt. Nice fashion. That a new trend?"

I looked down at my backward shirt. "I was leaving room for my wings."

"Gotcha. About that, how's it coming?"

"Do you see any wings?"

"It's going well, then, got it." His chest rose and fell with a deep breath, and he looked down at the spikes below. "Your healing magic works incredibly quickly. Or maybe it just feels that way because you're numbing the pain."

"How are we going to get out of here, Austin? I don't know that you can jump down there without hitting those spikes, and even if you didn't, you'd probably go splat."

"I can't, no. That's out of the question." His gaze roamed my face. "I'm waiting on my knight in shining armor to save me. That's you, by the way. I figured you needed a damsel to live out your true potential."

I lowered my brow, my stare definitely hostile and probably unhinged. "This isn't a time to joke. I couldn't even get that lock to open, and my wings won't come. I'm dead in the water. I'm basically just waiting for the bad guys to save me at this point."

He spread his arms. "And then I came along and ruined your plans." His expression sobered. "I apologize. Whatever you're doing with your magic is making me feel like I've taken a happy pill. Listen, Jess, your days of being rescued are over. You have the ability to save yourself—and me. There's a reason Ivy House chose you above the Havercamps and everyone else. Mr. Tom, Niamh, and Edgar—they all know Ivy House chose correctly. *I* know Ivy House chose correctly. All that's left is for you to believe it. I need you, Jacinta. I need you to fly me out of here, because I am positive they will kill me when they find me with you. I'll make it incredibly hard for them, but there's not much I can do stuck up here in human form. They'll take me out. I've put my fate in your hands. I've put my *life* in your hands."

"But why?" I groaned out, dread overcoming me.

"Because I know you can do it," he said softly. "I believe in you."

I shook my head. "Even if my wings come out, they're going to be smaller and weaker than the guys'."

"They'll be big enough and strong enough to carry me in human form. I don't weigh that much. Mostly."

I blew out a slow breath, searching his eyes for a hint of doubt or nervousness, but all I found was unwavering support and conviction.

A soft metallic squeal interrupted my teeth grinding. My heart racing, I looked down at the shadowy area, wondering if someone was coming for us. Best-case scenario would be the hairy creature, but who knew what he would do with an intruder.

The cage jolted, dropping an inch.

Austin grabbed my shoulders out of impulse, looking up. Niamh and the others pushed closer to the barrier, something clearly sparking their worry.

"What was that?" I asked quietly, the cage shaking and my voice shaking with it.

"I might've put that chain under too much stress." Not letting go of my arms, he bent backward, looking down at the spikes below. When he glanced back up at me, any signs of mirth had completely dried up. "We're out of time. You can do this, Jacinta. Remember what I said? Grab life by the balls? Well, this time, grab your magic by the balls. You control it, not the other way around. Think about what you want, and *do it*."

The soft squealing preceded another jolt, dropping us a little further. The link connected to the cage was clearly pulling free. I didn't have to see it to know that. When it released, down we'd go.

It wasn't just Austin's life in my hands—it was both of ours. No one would come to save us.

I had to play hero, or die trying.

CHAPTER 26

"JUMPING OUT ISN'T going to work." I licked my lips, my mind running a mile a minute. "I almost died falling from that cliff and nothing happened." I turned my back to him. "Brush my... Brush your fingers right next to my shoulder blades. Maybe it'll help if I can feel the spot where the wings are supposed to be."

Another squeal from the chain made me flinch.

The soft brush of Austin's fingertips sent a ripple of heat through me, but the spot wasn't connecting. Something about it felt wrong.

"Smaller wings, yes, but I'm still a female gargoyle..." I clenched my teeth and squeezed my eyes shut when the cage jolted down. Austin's touch didn't speed up, nor did it become harder. He didn't show the fear he must be feeling...

Incredulity roared through me when I checked on him through our magical connection.

I turned around with wide eyes, finding his beautiful cobalt gaze completely open, and completely trusting. He wasn't afraid at all. Not even a little bit. He wasn't nervous or wary. He believed, with everything in him, that I could do this. He was just waiting for it to happen. I felt the strength of his conviction like I felt my own terror.

Something unfurled within me. Tears came to my eyes, and this time it wasn't frustration. This time I didn't even know what it was.

A thought occurred to me, like a lightning bolt crashing down.

"I don't just sprout wings, I change form. I'm a female gargoyle. I'm not human anymore, I'm a creature, like Mr. Tom and Damarion. I'm not human, I'm magical…"

Excitement and awe bubbled through me.

Austin nodded, a little smile tickling his lips. "So then, be magical," he said softly.

"Be magical," I whispered.

Hearing yet another squeal above us, I shrugged out of my backward shirt and pushed down my pants. I couldn't change fully dressed. I had to get comfortable in my birthday suit like the other magical people did. The time for modesty was over—I had a couple of lives to save.

"What if I get stuck in rock form?" I asked.

"It's simple—I need you to save me. You don't have

time to get stuck."

"Right. O-kay." I nodded in determination. "No time to get stuck."

"You're young for your kind, anyway. You wouldn't get stuck for long."

I grinned. Midlife for a human, young for a gargoyle, and I still didn't give a flying fig what people thought of me. I could live with that.

I just had to make this change so I *could* live with that.

"But still, don't get stuck," I said, standing naked before Austin, noticing he was standing at attention again.

"Sorry about that," he murmured, his voice deep and thick and a little embarrassed. "You're beautiful, and I don't have much control over that part of my body." He shrugged. "My turn to feel a little awkward— I didn't mean to look."

Not like I could complain—I'd been caught looking plenty of times.

I took a deep breath and closed my eyes, remembering Mr. Tom changing. Remembering Damarion snapping out his wings. Remembering how Ulric looked when he cut through the sky. Remembering what it felt like to soar high above the ground.

A sound like boulders sliding down a hill gave me a

thrill of anticipation and a little surge of fear. This wasn't natural for me. The thought of changing into something other than myself…

"I'm right here, Jacinta," Austin said, his words wrapping around me comfortingly. "We're in this together. Let's grab life by the balls."

Grab life by the balls.

I could do this.

I'd accepted the magic, I'd accepted the responsibility, Austin was counting on me…

I could do this!

The cage jolted down. That chain wouldn't hold us much longer.

Energy surged through my suddenly heavy limbs. My skin stretched and a shock of blistering heat boiled my blood. Before I could call out, euphoria took over, drowning me in bliss. A tingle sliced down two spots on my back near where Austin had touched me earlier.

Snap.

I felt the slide of the bars against my wings.

My wings! *I had wings!*

I opened my eyes to smile, and then stared down in shock at the purplish, luminescent skin covering my body. My fingers ended in sharp black claws, and unlike the guys, I had a pair of breasts with dark, budded nipples that currently had Austin's undivided attention.

"Hey."

That word didn't come out as "hey," though, it came out as "ha-aye" because a couple of fangs now needed room in my mouth. My pronunciation was better than that of my male counterparts, however, which meant my face and teeth probably (hopefully) didn't look as gruesome.

Austin looked up almost lazily, his eyes lidded and filled with awe. We might've been standing on Ivy House's front lawn for all the urgency he displayed.

I knew better, though.

My wings folded up with barely a thought, as natural as stepping forward and putting out my arms for Austin, which I also did. He shook himself out of his daze.

"The female of the species is *much* better looking than the male," he said with a smile, and wrapped his arms around me, one sliding under my wings and across my back, the other over my shoulder and diagonally down, so he'd have a good grip.

"Go," I mostly said, feeling drool slide down my chin. I couldn't grimace with this new face. It probably looked like a permanent grimace anyway, going off the others.

The squeal increased in pitch, the metal giving way. This was it. This was our last chance. We jumped and flew, or we jumped and plummeted to our deaths. It was all up to me.

I nodded and pushed forward, Austin moving with me in perfect synchronicity. He was probably an excellent dancer.

"Time to go, Jess," he said, his strength coiling around me, his lips near my ear. "I'll wrap my legs around you once we're in flight. I'll hold on. All you have to worry about is flying, okay? Sorry about the erection. First seeing you naked, then the brea… This is all very new to me. Hopefully I'll get used to it. I've never seen a female gargoyle. It's… You're…strangely erotic."

He wasn't the only one experiencing a first. I'd never heard Austin babble. And I'd never felt this deep, stirring heat burning in my core, so much more intense than anything I'd ever experienced as a Jane.

It would take some getting used to, indeed. Right now, I had to focus on getting us out of here.

Breathing fast, still scared out of my mind, I heard the loud *crack* before I felt the jolt. Out of time, I dove out through the door and hoped for a miracle.

Gravity reached up and grabbed hold of us. Austin wrapped his legs around my hips, his size and weight seeming too much. Too big. I wouldn't be able to lift him off the ground, how could I possibly fly with him?

I was still thinking as a human woman. Ivy House had made me magical. It had made me stronger. I *could* lift him in my human form, I was sure of it. And I could lift him with these wings. I had to.

We dropped through the air like a stone.

"Grab life by the balls," I tried to say. It came out a jumbled mess.

The spikes rushed toward us.

Now or never, I snapped out my wings. Lines of bright pink-purple wove through my deep purple, luminescent wings. As the wind billowed them, a shimmery glow and streaks of light swirled through the air.

"Good God, Jacinta, this form is magnificent."

I tried to smile, stretching my lips across those big fangs. Spit dribbled down my chin.

I really needed to get a handle on that.

We jetted forward toward the cave wall. I angled up, the maneuver surprisingly natural, and pumped my wings, gaining altitude. Not climbing so much as cutting diagonally upward toward the wall. I pumped harder, feeling the strain, still going forward. Nearly at the—

We slammed into the rock. Austin grunted. I tried to shove us off with my hands and feet, wings still pumping, but Austin's body was still bigger than mine, even in this form, and I just succeeded in scratching his back against the rock.

"Sor-reee."

Breathing hard, fear clawing at me, I closed my eyes and envisioned watching the other gargoyles soar through the sky. I watched their wings in my mind's eye, taking in the way they rolled and dipped, angled and flapped.

I turned a little to the side, shoved off with all my might, and tried again.

"Oops," I heard over the din.

The hairy creature stood just beyond the shadowy area, looking up at us.

"You must've been honest about Ivy House." His smile showed a lot of teeth. "I can't wait for those flowers. Oh, this makes me so happy. I am willing to overlook…whatever it is you are doing with that man. Seems complicated."

I flapped my wings, trying to counter Austin's weight and go straight up in the air. Except for some intense wobbling, I managed, but my stamina was wearing thin. I needed a lot more practice with these things, preferably without the extra weight.

"Well, as you can clearly see, I didn't wrap my ankle." The hairy creature shook his head. "I'd better go do that." He turned and walked back toward the shadowy area, disappearing.

He would deserve those flowers.

I turned in the air, which was surprisingly difficult, and beat my wings harder, climbing. My breath came in ragged pants. Higher still, I tilted forward, Austin's weight now propelling us toward the opening. I couldn't wait to get to those shadowy forms, waiting just beyond that shimmering barrier.

But how were we going to get through it?

Fatigue pulling at me, keeping us in the air harder with each beat of my wings, I managed to stop us next to that barrier, it having no ledge or lip to stand on, now trying to rip and tear at it with my magic. Trying to counteract it, or think it away. Whatever it was, though, it refused to respond to my attempts to dispel it.

"Just go through," Austin said, his voice hard with grim determination. "Go through. We'll survive."

We didn't have much choice. I was losing altitude.

Summoning a last bit of strength, clamping my teeth shut, I did as he said and dove forward. Fire ignited my body, starting with my head. It plunged into my blood and seared flesh and bone. Pain such that I'd never known washed over me, through me, became me, until all I was saw black.

CHAPTER 27

I CAME TO slowly at first, and then all at once. I snapped my eyes open, remembering the pain of plunging through that magical barrier.

Oh Lord, did I remember the pain.

A head loomed over me.

"Hah!" I struck out, my fist connecting with a face and my magic following it up.

A tall, gangly body flew backward, curving through the air and landing facedown on my red Persian rug. We were in my bedroom.

"Yes, miss, good point." Mr. Tom pushed himself to standing. "I should've announced myself after the ordeal you've had. I can appreciate you being a little jumpy."

"Sorry." I palmed my head, at the dull ache there. Weak morning sunlight filtered in through the window. The skin on my arms looked a little waxy. Although my skin had returned to its normal color, it was now devoid of moles, freckles, and blemishes.

"Not at all. It is quite all right. I should have been prepared for a quick punch from a sleeping woman. How are you feeling?"

He approached my bed again, somewhat hesitantly.

"Okay. A headache, but—"

"Ah. Yes. I have something here for that." From my nightstand, he picked up a clear bottle of purple pills. "These are still in beta phase—apparently that's what they call something experimental—but I have been assured they are very safe and quick acting."

"No, that's"—I pushed his hand away, bending my face the other way—"okay. I'll just grab some Advil."

"Advil is for blockheaded Janes who want to live with pain. No, no, try the magical variety." He pushed the bottle at me again. "Just one, mind. There is no telling what might happen if you take more."

I sat up and put out my arm to further avoid that bottle. As soon as my head stopped swimming, I reached for my magical connection with Austin—I felt him at once, his presence strong and sturdy. He wasn't dead, thank God.

"How's Austin?" I asked.

"Right as rain. *He* took one of the pills."

"He did?"

"Well…" Mr. Tom lowered the bottle a little. "He took one and threw it while giving me a threat, but…"

"Is he really right as rain, then?"

Clearly seeing that he wouldn't get his way, he pursed his lips and deposited the bottle back on the nightstand.

"He is, yes. Already out and searching for those mages who grabbed you. I've never seen him so worked up. He is taking the situation very personally, which is not good news for them. Too late now, eh? I'm forever glad he is on our side."

"He healed and everything?"

"Mostly. He has an amazing capacity for pain. I am, quite frankly, shocked. He stayed awake all the way home, asking for status updates on you. He didn't change form until he reached Ivy House soil and Ivy House started healing you both."

I let out a breath. "Amazing capacity for pain, yes. I couldn't handle it. It was…"

Mr. Tom nodded solemnly.

I tried to run my fingers through my tangled hair before giving up. "All my failures with flying, and he put his life in my hands because he had faith I'd figure it out in time to save us both."

"He's a remarkable leader. He brings out the best in his people. And look! You flew!" Mr. Tom beamed, his scowl morphing into a proud smile that would have scared children. "When Ulric saw you, he stepped forward in such a rush that he burned his face on that barrier. Everything about your gargoyle form is perfect. It is a thing of strength and beauty, and you carried someone as muscle-laden as Austin Steele with those tiny little wings! Oh, what a treat to watch. Horrifying, and you surely shaved decades off my life span, but majestic."

"Right, right." I swung my feet over the edge of the bed and reached for my phone. "How long have I been out?"

"Two days. You had a lot of healing to do."

"How long has Austin been on the hunt?"

"He's been working on it for almost a day. As I said, he has a pretty incredible tolerance for pain. Last I heard, he was only finding dead ends. Those mages are advanced in their magic, and he doesn't have a starting point because Damarion and his gargoyles couldn't find the lower entrance to that cave. Once you were freed, they came back here with you."

Damarion and his gargoyles.

They were supposed to be my gargoyles.

That problem would have to wait.

I sent a quick text off to Austin: *Where are you?*

To Mr. Tom I said, "I know a creature who can help us find the entrance." I headed for the closest, my skin feeling strangely crackly.

"Oh, that basajaun? No, I'm afraid that is out of the question. Austin Steele tracked him down, but the creature wouldn't tell him anything. He tried to subdue the basajaun, and Damarion tried to dominate it, but neither succeeded. Austin Steele worried he would kill the creature if it led to an altercation, and Damarion pulled back, which leads me to believe he feared he'd be bested. You have to be careful with basajaunak. They have large extended families and hold grudges. They are like a hairy, stinky mob. Kill one of them and their whole unit shows up and tries to claim vengeance. We don't need that kind of heat."

I shook my head, pulling on some jeans and a shirt. I clearly hadn't appreciated the full extent of Austin's prowess before. Handling that kind of pain not once, but twice, shrugging it off, and getting back out there to secure his home was... It was almost larger than life. It was unbelievable.

"Those two guys can't even be in the same room without going for each other's throats," I said. "Clearly that...what was it? The hairy creature?"

"The basajaun. He came in when you were flying. Hairy, stinky, wild, prone to hold grudges..."

"Right, that creature. Well, clearly he's cut from the same mold as Austin and Damarion. That, or the guys came on too strong, posturing and acting like macho idiots, and he wasn't having it. I've got something he wants, though."

"Really?" Mr. Tom followed me from the room. "What's that?"

"Magical flowers."

"I'm not following…"

My phone chimed, and I glanced at the screen.

Austin: *At the bar. Organizing sentries throughout town. You okay?*

My first destination was the kitchen to retrieve a huge glass of water. Maybe two.

I answered Austin. *My skin is waxy, but I'm good. Going to go find that hairy creature. I don't think it'll attack me. It let me escape. We have an accord.*

In the kitchen, I filled a glass, drank it, and then slugged back a few more.

"The thing is…" I wiped my mouth and headed for the back door. "He didn't seem to know much about the mages. I got the feeling that he'd always had the guard job, hadn't actually done it forever, and was doing it because that was his expected role. It didn't seem like he'd asked any questions of them. He might not know anything about them."

"When did you talk to it?" Mr. Tom followed me outside. Edgar stood on Niamh's porch, his hand up to knock. He turned our way when he saw us.

I quickly filled Mr. Tom in as I walked across the street to Edgar. A pulse of magic sang through my bones, and I felt doors open within Ivy House. A high-pitched scream made me look back.

Lights flickered in the windows. Smoke curled from one of the chimneys on the right side.

"What's…"

My speech dried up as the front door swung open and Ulric came running out of the house, followed quickly by Damarion, both of them wide-eyed and in a state of undress. From around the side of the house ran Cedric, holding up his britches as though he'd received the summons midway through getting dressed and hadn't paused to finish. Another body blasted from a second-story window, fell to the front lawn, turned the harried dive into a roll, and bounded up. Jasper, the gargoyle I hadn't talked to much. I really needed to make more time to get to know everyone. That was certainly part of the reason why they were Damarion's gargoyles.

Another pulse cut through me, Ivy House calling those in town, obviously summoning them to meet me. That was probably why she'd sent Damarion and crew racing outside. She wasn't one for patience, clearly. I'd woken up, and it was time to take down our enemies.

"What's the matter?" Damarion said as he reached

me, grabbing for my shoulders. I evaded and turned, catching Niamh opening her front door. A bright pink nightshirt hugged her torso and ended just below her upper thighs.

"This job requires pants, usually," Mr. Tom said.

"What in bejaysus are ye at this early in the mornin'?" Niamh hollered, scaring Edgar off her porch.

It was a good point—I hadn't thought to check the time.

Six in the morning. Did Mr. Tom ever sleep, or had he figured out how to sleep standing up, hovering over me?

"I'm feeling great, thanks," I said dryly, trying to hide my grimace.

My phone vibrated in my hand. Text from Austin: *Tell Ivy House to back off. I'm almost done. Meet you there.*

"Well, I can see yer feeling fine. Yer walking around and rarin' to go. That means you need to rattle everyone awake, does it?"

"Clearly the idea of working offends you, but did you forget there is still a job to be done?" Mr. Tom sniffed in disdain.

Niamh's eyes shot fire as she zeroed in on him. Edgar backed away a little more.

"Okay, enough." I held up my hands to forestall whatever zinger was sure to come. "Stop. Sorry, I didn't realize the time. I just woke up. We still have mages at large, though, and they know their stuff. I escaped them once. I doubt whatever they rig up next will be as easy to get out of. Spoiler alert, last time wasn't easy at all. It hurt quite a lot, actually. Clearly they won't be dumb enough to come for me on Ivy House property, so I will be putting myself out there, trusting Austin and Damarion to have my back."

Damarion stiffened, probably because I'd mentioned Austin first. I ignored it.

"First things first—we will find that basa...bas..."

"Basajaun," Mr. Tom said.

"Right, we'll find the hairy creature and ask him where to find the lower entrance to the cave. That should help us track them."

"Excuse me, Jessie, but—"

I held up a hand for Damarion. "I heard about you trying to talk him around. I'll approach it a different way." I turned to Edgar, surprised when he flinched and covered one of his eyes. "Edgar, please go grab me the best bundle of fresh flowers you can procure. Your very best."

"Basajaun eat meat, Jessie," Edgar said. "I'm sure I can find a haunch of pig or something..."

"Chocolate isn't strictly necessary for my survival, Edgar, but on occasion I'd gnaw off your hand to get some."

He pressed the hand not covering his eye a little tighter to his chest.

"We're going after them now?" Niamh hadn't moved to put on pants.

"Yes. Now. They've had two days to come up with another plan. I don't want to wait for them to spring it."

Gargoyle wings flapped above the street, flying low, coming from town. They'd beelined here instead of flying over the woods like we'd agreed. They were too big to be bats—any non-magical folks who were up at this hour would probably call the cops.

"Get them inside." I waved my arm and motioned them toward Niamh's house, the closest available enclosed space.

"No, no, not in here! They're gargoyles. They think they'll melt if they take a shower." She waved them away.

Mr. Tom puffed out his chest. "That is an old wives' tale, and your refusal to allow them into your house is discrimination. Really, woman, in this day and age?"

"The younger ones are a little ripe," Edgar said solemnly. "It isn't their species, of course, but just a lack of overall hygiene. Younger guys, you know—sometimes they'd rather not bother washing up. Niamh has a large collection of doilies in her house. They tend to trap smell. Then again, should we need to burn them, I can always furnish her with more. My newest batch—"

"Fine, put them in the back." I stepped onto the bright green front yard that Edgar must've made it his duty to keep up and directed them like I might an airplane. "Thanks for coming, guys. Just head back there, if you don't mind. We'll be with you in a moment."

"I'm a little lost. What's the plan?" Ulric asked.

"I can't allow you to approach that basajaun," Damarion said, his hand gently settling on the swell of my butt. I stepped away. Clearly we needed to talk. Now was not the time.

I felt Austin on the property, cutting through the woods and across the back lawn.

"Edgar, go get those flowers. Hurry."

"Yes, Jessie." He took off running, a strange sort of hunched lope with his elbows flared out, his long fingers dangling at his sides, and his head bobbing animatedly with each step.

"I hate to criticize, Jessie…" Niamh said, watching him go.

"If you couldn't criticize, you'd never utter a word," Mr. Tom said.

"…but you might've given that old vampire the gift of youth. Or even just shaved off a few years so he wouldn't look like such a muppet when he runs. I don't think his limbs work quite right. Look at the state of him!"

Austin loped around the house, passing Edgar, before he stopped and shifted into his human form. He stalked toward us, crossing the grass and then the street, like a predator about to take down a kill.

I put out my hand to tell him not to mess with Damarion, but I didn't need to. He gave Damarion a wide berth, clearly pushing aside their differences because of the situation.

"What's the plan?" Austin asked, having stopped in the place Edgar had just vacated.

"Find anything?" Niamh asked.

Austin shook his head, his gaze roaming my face and then body, probably sizing up the state of my health. His skin had the same waxy quality as mine, his freckles or sun spots also burned away, and his face looked a few years younger. Clearly we'd lost our top layer of skin and were still in process of growing a second coat, as it were. I hoped I'd never have to do it again.

"All the strangers around town have checked out," he said. "I have people working on checking the neighboring towns. The communities are small, so we should get some information soon."

I gave them a quick rundown about the basajaun as Edgar hurried back with the bouquet.

"I'm going to attempt to fly there." I took a deep breath. "I might not make it all the way, though. I didn't do great the other day."

"It was your first flight, but you held a mountain of muscle with those tiny wings," Ulric said, and I frowned about the wings comment. I didn't think they were *that* small. "You did great."

"I will carry you when you need it, but we should not approach that basajaun, Jessie." Damarion moved closer. "It is—"

"I'll follow in my other form." Austin didn't need to step toward me—he pulled my attention to him. Mine and everyone else's. "We'll be prepared to extract you if that basajaun decides you aren't so fun to chat with when you're out of your cage."

"This is a mistake," Damarion said.

"Doing nothing is a mistake," I said. Niamh disappeared into the house, and I called after her to grab a bag. "Waiting for them to trap me again is a mistake. Striving to protect myself is *not* a mistake. That basajaun will talk. Get ready to catch me if I fall out of the sky, though. That's the only part of this plan I'm not real sure about."

CHAPTER 28

NIAMH TOUCHED DOWN on the mountain right after an exhausted Jessie, who still looked great despite it. She had that beautiful, swirly magic streaking the air behind her wings, the effect incredible. Female gargoyles were worth all the fuss. If only Jessie could get her magic working like it should, she'd be on fire.

All they needed was time. After this, hopefully they'd have a little of it.

If not for Austin Steele, they would've already lost her, Niamh had no doubt about that. They would probably still be searching for the lower cave opening, long after the team of mages had already moved her.

Faster than the males, Jessie changed into her human form and then sank to her hands and knees, panting with fatigue. With a thrum of wings, the male gargoyles landed all around them, Damarion changing immediately so he could go to her.

He clearly hadn't gotten the—pretty obvious—hints that Jessie had been throwing out all morning. Whatever that gargoyle had done the other day, he'd completely lost her interest. Niamh could not *wait* to hear the story.

First, though…business.

Trees crowded in around them, cutting off their view, and hopefully the view of anyone in the area. That big ol' basajaun could smell them, though, if it was around. Those things had sharp senses and mean tempers. Niamh did not want to tangle with one of them. She almost couldn't believe Austin Steele was going along with this plan.

Then again, Austin Steele had changed. The shift had been subtle at first—Niamh honestly hadn't noticed it—but it had been as blatant as the nose on her face since the incident at the cave.

Something had clicked over for him. A switch had been flipped. He'd become more of an active leader—and not in the chest-beating sense. He was confident, strong. He didn't bother with Damarion anymore. It was like he'd stopped seeing the gargoyle as a threat. Niamh was very curious as to why.

There came the huge polar bear now, slinking in between two trees, stopping to stare as Damarion helped Jessie to her feet.

"Here." Earl handed Niamh's clothes over. "Though I'm not sure we should put them on. I fly faster than I run."

"That ol' basajaun isn't gonna chase us. If it chases anyone, it'll be Austin Steele or Damarion. Just trip one of those younger gargoyles to put more people between yerself and the beast, and cut in the opposite direction the others do. Ye'll be grand."

"Why Ivy House ever pegged you for a team player, I do not know," Earl muttered, shrugging into soft white sweats.

"Neither do I." Niamh put on her shirt. That oughta be good enough. Her lack of pants earlier hadn't seemed to bother Jessie terribly much. Earl was right, though she hated admitting it—running was not the way she wanted to go if that ol' basajaun got pissed.

"I'm good, I'm good." Jessie pushed Damarion away. "Thank you. Ulric, do you have those flowers?"

"Yes, ma'am." Ulric pulled forward the somewhat crushed bouquet of flowers. Stuffing them in his clothes bag probably hadn't been the best of ideas.

"Thanks," she said distractedly, taking the flowers and glancing back at Austin Steele. "Are we in the right area?"

He huffed affirmatively, and then worked around the gathered gargoyles, slipping through the trees and padding over the slushy snow that hung around this high up. Dark clouds slid across the sky, promising rain, sleet, or more snow. At this altitude, maybe all three.

Flying in that wouldn't be much fun. For Jessie, it would be downright life-threatening. She'd need to accept Damarion's help, although it was sure to be an awkward flight.

"Are you sure about this?" Earl asked Jessie as he caught up to her, his wings fluttering behind him in the wind.

Niamh pushed through the gargoyles to get to Jessie's other side. "Given enough time," she said, "we can find that other cave opening, Jessie. Ye don't have'ta—"

"It's fine. Honestly, this guy—basa... Why can't I remember that name?"

"Bigfoot," Earl said. "Dicks and Janes call them Bigfoot."

"Right. He mentioned something about that. He doesn't like being called a Bigfoot, though, since those aren't real. Honestly, I've never even heard of the basa..." She huffed. "I think it'll be fine. The reason I left Edgar home is so I could trade every edible thing on Ivy House property if need be. I think he'll go for it."

Austin Steele stopped and looked back at Jessie.

A trickle of adrenaline seeped into Niamh's blood. They were here. They were about to see if the basajaun would meet Jessie calmly, or if he'd take one look at the army of gargoyles and the shifter he'd already turned down and raise hell.

"Get ready to run," Earl whispered.

CHAPTER 29

"**S**TAY BACK," I said, really hoping I hadn't made a grave mistake, since everyone else seemed really put off by this creature. "Everyone stay back."

"This is a fool's errand," Damarion said through clenched teeth, pushing up between Niamh and Mr. Tom, who were drifting backward. "That creature has incredible strength. More so than me or the bear. It will tear you limb from limb. Reconsider."

"No. You weren't stuck in that cage, helpless," I said, fire rising through me. "I hated that feeling. I never want that feeling again. I *will* find those mages. That basa...ha...oon?"

"Very close. Good work." Mr. Tom gave me a thumbs-up.

"He knows the location of the cave mouth." I continued forward, my hand clenched around the stems of the flowers. "With that information, we have a much better chance of tracking those mages. We need to be on the offensive, Damarion. We need to be in a constant state of readiness. If we're ready, we're in control. I want to be in control of my fate."

"I applaud your desire to be in control," Mr. Tom said. "And when the time comes, I hope you will take control, and run to save yourself from this short-tempered creature. Let Austin Steele stay and fight. He's more able for it."

"Do you ever just think to yerself, if I wasn't such an eejit, I'd have more friends?" Niamh murmured to Earl.

"You should talk. The only people who willingly speak to you are paid to. They serve you cider so as to improve your personality."

"If only there was an easy solution for making ye more agreeable."

"Here we go," I whispered, tuning them out. A clearing lay up ahead, blotchy snow lying in clumps on the ground. Gray rocks rose away on the right, and I could see that was the way Austin's snout pointed. That was where the creature likely sat or hid.

Now or never.

I stepped out beyond the tree line, and Austin moved to block the others from following me. He pushed forward until he was even with the last line of trees, directly behind me, his head peeking out, showing his presence but not engaging. Hopefully that was what it meant, anyway. And if it meant something else, hopefully it wasn't something that would piss off the basa-whatever.

"She should've at least brought Susan," I heard Earl murmuring. "It's a fast little cut-and-thrust sword, great for sneak attacks. Get in, slash 'em up, get out."

"What's a small sword like that going to do against a basajaun?" Niamh asked. "It'd be like giving 'im a paper cut."

"Paper cuts sting. That'd make the brute at least pause before backhanding her across the clearing. You can get a good sprint in during a pause."

"*Shh*," I said. They didn't need to give the creature any ideas.

I edged out further into the clearing, and I wasn't going to lie: having Susan along wouldn't have been a bad thing, if only because it would have bolstered my courage.

Sitting on top of the highest rock sat a creature whose hair draped his body in dusky brown waves. He rose when he saw me, and slowly worked his way down to ground level, standing on the same plane as me. I had to tilt my head up to see his face and enormous nose, even from the distance across the clearing. He had to be nine feet tall, with ridiculously huge arms hanging at the sides of his massive upper body.

"This is, quite possibly, her worst idea yet," Mr.

Tom muttered from the trees.

I had to agree with him. The big guy looked a lot bigger when not viewed from above.

"Hi," I said, and gave a stupid little wave. All of my cool confidence had gone out the window in the face of this massive creature. Now, standing face to stomach with him, not even remotely on a level playing field, with a bunch of smooshed flowers instead of a sword, I was definitely having second thoughts.

"How do you hide from hikers?" I blurted. I couldn't help it.

"Oh." He tilted his head at me, his wide nose shadowing his mouth. "How nice of you to ask. It is an art, really." He looked behind him, found a flat part on one of the rocks, and sat. He crossed an ankle over his knee and put out his arms for inspection. "My coloring does help me blend in, but don't fool yourself—it's not easy being mistaken for a tree. I have no branches."

"Is he not very bright, or does he think *we're* not very bright?" Mr. Tom whispered much too loudly.

"The trick is standing very still. Also knowing where the hikers will pass you." The creature motioned in front of him like he was peering through the trees.

"If I had to guess, I'd say *he* is the one who is not very bright," Mr. Tom whispered, still much too loudly. "There are actual hiking trails, after all. It isn't rocket science—"

"Would ye stop, you donkey?" Niamh berated.

"But it wouldn't be enjoyable to go unnoticed. I wait for them to pass, and when I'm in their peripheral vision, I move *just a little.* Hardly noticeable. If I don't catch their eye, I move again, a bit more. Sometimes I am not obvious enough, and I lose them. This happened a lot in my youth. Or I move enough that they think I'm a bear, and there is great confusion and much screaming. But I have gotten pretty good at it, like I said. It is an art. I move a little, they glance over, and catch me looking at them. I stay there for the *right* amount of time—not too little, not too much. Enough for them to realize that I am an intelligent creature—"

"That's debatable," Mr. Tom muttered.

"—and then I move away, into the trees, out of sight." He slid his ankle off his leg and planted his feet on the ground, his body shaking with laughter. "You should see their faces!" He laughed harder, tilting his head up to the sky. "It is fantastic. They search frantically for their phones to get a picture. Or they freeze, as though they think I might not see them if they do not move. Or they take off running like the devil himself is chasing them! You just never know!"

His laughter shook his whole body, and I felt a smile crack my face.

"How is it I've never heard of you before now?" I asked, forgetting myself for a moment. With this new life, I'd learned to take the bumps of crazy and roll with it.

He stretched his arms wide. "Because I am the best at this! I am a myth! This is what diligent practice will get you. Mastery."

I couldn't make out what Mr. Tom had muttered this time.

"Well, that's pretty crazy, and I'd love to see it in action someday—"

"An audience. I've never had an audience, although I did have an apprentice or two in my day. Good kids. Fairly light on thinking ability, if you know what I mean."

"They must be as dumb as posts if *he's* saying that," Mr. Tom murmured.

"Shut it," Niamh hissed.

I shrugged. "Up to you. Listen, what I wanted to talk—"

"I can see how that might be fun. An audience. You would have to be very quiet. And very still."

I stared at him with my eyebrows up and my mouth open, really wanting to move the conversation along but not wanting to push him. Given he'd chased two alphas off this mountain, there were clearly hidden depths to him that I didn't want to see.

"If you dressed in brown, or maybe brown and green, you would blend in better." He eyed my outfit. "The white sweats would only do for heavy snowfall."

"Listen, Mr...." I paused so he could give me his name.

"You would not want to blend in too much, though, or they wouldn't see you at the end," he said, clearly in need of dynamite to get him off this train of thought. "Although you are just a human woman. Maybe you'd get a better fright if you changed into that purplish sort of rainbow monster from the other day."

"I would like to trade," I said quickly, holding up the flowers. Granted, I'd already promised the Ivy House flowers, but hopefully he couldn't call me on a technicality. Besides, I was delivering them. That had to count for something. "I am *delivering* some Ivy House flowers, directly to you...for a snack."

As if this was the first time he was noticing them, his focus zipped to the colorful array in my hand.

"You helped me the other day—"

"Oh no, I did not," he said. "It would go against my station to help a prisoner. No, I took my break, and tripped and broke my ankle. That was why I was absent, you see, and not able to sound the alarm when you defeated your confinement and escaped in a pretty, swirling light show. At first I thought I sprained it, of course, but upon reflection, it must have been broken, because I needed to be gone for longer than originally planned."

"Right. Did the—"

"So you see, my absence could not be helped."

"Gotcha. Did the mages come back to find me gone?"

"Yes."

I waited for more. He didn't give me anything.

"Did anyone else come—someone you hadn't seen or met beyond those mages?" I wondered if the contract holder had shown up.

"No."

That was a small relief, at least. "Were the mages mad?" I pressed.

"Yes. Very. They questioned my truthfulness. That is a grave offense, as you can guess."

"Right. And then they—"

"As the guardian of this mountain and the prison herein, it is my duty to secure those detained here."

"Totally. So did they—"

"But I am only one entity. I must take breaks. I must be able to eat, rest, and relieve myself. This is the nineties, for heaven's sake. There are rules."

"It's actually the…" I waved it away. "Never mind."

He'd catch up eventually. Or never. It probably didn't matter much to him, given his lifestyle. "Listen—"

"For their offense, I killed one of them. Justice was served on my mountain the other day. It is done."

I looked back at Austin. Another down, three to go, and as of yesterday, they were still in the area.

"Make note of that," Mr. Tom murmured. "Do not question the truthfulness of a basajaun, regardless of how big the lie."

I had to agree.

I held out the flowers, feeling a fresh wave of urgency. The mages had lost someone yesterday, and they were probably still scrambling. If we could find them now, we'd have a shot at stopping them permanently, before they came after me again.

"Can you please show me to the lower cave entrance?" I asked, holding the flowers high. "I'll trade you these flowers for it. I'm not a prisoner anymore. You don't have to guard me."

He stood, and I took a step back, his height incredibly daunting.

"Get ready to run," I heard Mr. Tom say.

"I will show you because you have asked nicely." He stepped forward. "Your friends may come, too, though they are not welcome on this mountain without you."

"I get it. Some of them are awfully pushy—"

"You are so pretty when you fly. I would hate to dull your luster by killing one of your friends."

I nodded and held out the flowers, doing my best not to scuttle backward the closer he got.

"I will show you as a gesture of good faith, in the hope that we can work together to give this mountain something it has never seen before. My family has never teamed up with a creature such as yourself. They will be red with envy. What name will the hikers make up about you, I wonder. Well…" He laughed as we walked, Austin and everyone else falling in silently behind us. "They would have to snap a picture first. Do you breathe fire, by chance?"

"Um…no. No fire."

"That is okay. Maybe they will still think you're a dragon because of your big fangs and the swirly rainbow colors that trail you when you fly."

I ducked under a branch, still holding out the flowers. "I brought these for you. A trade, a gift—either way, I'd like you to have them."

"Yes. Kindness. So very few people approach me with kindness. It is a nice change." Clearly Austin and Damarion needed to work on their people skills, which was rich, coming from me. "Unfortunately, I do not accept gifts from strangers. It makes one feel indebted, and that is not a nice feeling."

I wasn't sure where to go from there, so I lowered the flowers, too scared to drop them in case he thought that was some sort of offense.

"How did those mages rope you into guarding me?" I asked as we made our way, although my breath was coming quickly because I had to jog to keep up with his large strides.

"They entered the caves and lodged their prisoner. That act summoned me. I may not like the duty, but it is mine. I cannot find a way to get out of it."

"Right but...what if the prisoner isn't someone who did something bad? What if they were kidnapped, like me?"

"I do not pass judgment. I solely guard my charge."

"You guard your charge... In situations like that, maybe instead of guarding the charge *for* the kidnappers, you could guard them *from* the kidnappers?"

He looked down on me, not caring when a tree branch slid over his face. "That is a fun play on words, but that is not my duty."

"So...just so I'm clear, you don't have a duty to put me back in that cage?"

"The cage is broken."

"If it weren't?"

"No. You are not a prisoner. I do not have to guard you. The rules are pretty clear on that point."

We roamed down the mountain, traipsing through brush and bushes, weaving through large tree branches, and ignoring the deer and hiking trails that would make travel so much easier. A half-hour in, just as I was about to ask how much further we had to go, he slowed and turned, veering around a rock outcropping and stopping in front of a large stone slab. Trees pressed in on all sides, creating a blind.

I waited for him to speak. He stared down at me, not doing so.

"Is this it?" I asked dumbly.

"Yes."

"We found this rock," Damarion said, pushing forward.

The basajaun bristled, and his arms lifted just slightly away from his sides, like a bro in a bar getting ready to fight. "If you found this rock and did not find the way in, you are incredibly stupid."

"That means something, coming from him," Mr. Tom said.

"Walk through, Jessie." Niamh motioned me on. "'Tis a pretty standard illusion. A good one, don't get me wrong, but easy enough to find if ye know what ye're lookin' for. That rock has the shape of a door and doesn't blend in with the rocks around it, and take a look at the edges there, where they meet the natural rock. See how they are frayed, like fabric?"

I did see that, as well as a strange sheen that re-minded me of the magical barrier I had to plunge through in my gargoyle form.

"Just walk through," Niamh said again. "Or, better yet, have Earl do it. Give him a purpose."

"A purpose? I've been the only one speaking sense this whole time." Mr. Tom stepped forward, but I put my hand out to keep him back before passing off the flowers to the basajaun to hold.

"Given no trade has been initiated, I'll just put these down here for you." The basajaun placed them in a little nook at the very edge of the tree-sheltered area, protect-ed on one side by the rockface creating this area of the mountain, and on the other by a large boulder. He swooshed his hands, shepherding a pine cone and some leaves and pine needles in front of the bouquet to mask the colors, the objects moving without him actually touching them. Neat trick. There was more to him than just height, nose, and hair.

Austin stepped forward as I approached the large slab, palms up and out. The basajaun bristled again, but I shook my head at him.

"He doesn't mean you any harm. He's here to help protect me and our town, and Ivy House's beautiful gardens. Neither of us would do anything to hurt your mountain." I gritted my teeth as my palms neared the rockface. "Let's hope this doesn't burn."

"Oh no, it does not burn. Tickles, mostly." The basajaun continued to stand near the masked flowers.

"Our voices aren't echoing through that cave right now, right?" I whispered, the situation catching up to me. Those mages could still be in there.

"No. You will not hear anything of the outside world once you are in the cave," the basajaun answered, "and vice versa. It is magically sealed."

"Why?" I asked, not raising my voice beyond the whisper.

"I do not know. I did not make it."

There was no point in asking who had. If the creature knew, he'd spend the whole day talking about it, I was sure. We had to get going. My courage wasn't an indefinite thing.

A tingle worked through my skin as I pushed my hand forward, but the sensation stopped at the point of contact and did not travel up my arm. I pushed them further in, my hands disappearing into the rock slab, and the tingle left my hands and continued up my arms. Further still, I felt a familiar heat at my back—Austin had changed into his human form.

"I'll go in with you, Jess." He stepped up beside me, putting his hands out.

"Baaa-kk our-ff baa-re." Damarion's wings rustled as he neared, and power curled around us, the alphas about to square off again at the worst possible time.

"Not now!" I flung my hand back, frustrated and annoyed and entirely too keyed up. A rock-solid sheet of air slammed into Damarion, sending him flying backward.

It didn't stop, though. It crashed into the others and forced them back a couple of steps, pinning their arms so they couldn't lift their hands to protect their faces or ward it off.

"Ooh, I felt that." The hair on the basajaun's face contorted into what was presumably a smile. "That might be a nice trick to confuse hikers with."

"I think he has taken that hobby a little too far," I murmured, my heart starting to beat faster. To Austin I said, "You don't have to." I paused. "Which is just something I'm supposed to say to be polite. I'm not going to turn you away."

"We don't know what will be on the other side of that magical barrier." Austin's shoulder bumped mine as he got into position. "There's no way I'm turning away."

"The mages, probably." The basajaun leaned a shoulder against the rock and crossed its hairy arms over its chest. "They were not pleased that I killed one of their kind."

"Wouldn't they want to leave?" I asked, pulling my hands back quickly as everyone else pushed forward again.

"The mountain is my territory, not what lies beneath it. My duty is to guard the prisoner, and that is the only time I am below the mountain. I do not live there."

"He denied them access to his territory," Niamh said, "so they can't go up the mountain. Nor can they go into town or seek shelter in one of the surrounding areas—Austin has guaranteed that. And they know better than to seek ye out at Ivy House. We haven't been able to find the entrance to the cave, so they know this is their only sanctuary in these parts, so they do. Ye've got 'em cornered, girl—time to bag 'em up."

"Have we met?" the basajaun asked Niamh.

"No. I would've remembered all the hair."

I met Austin's eyes and saw the call of battle burning within them. I'd seen that look before, right before we'd stormed Ivy House a few months back. This was it. It was time to eradicate the vermin.

My limbs started to shake. A past battle in which I'd observed more than fought, plus a few skirmishes, weren't nearly enough to prepare me for rushing into the fray. I'd better get used to it, though. After these mages there'd be someone else, and someone else still, people coming after me until they were sure I could not be taken. Then the wining and dining would begin, and I'd be wary about poison and knives to the back.

"Why did I sign up for this?" I muttered.

"Because adventure keeps us young." Niamh rubbed her hands together. "Bigfoot, what sort of size can we expect these tunnels to be? Can we fit in with our other forms, like?"

"That name is hurtful to those of my kind," the basajaun said. "I don't call you grumpy old woman."

"Ah, sure, ye might as well. It's true enough. What about the size?"

"The polar bear can fit. The spread wings of these ugly creatures will not." He speared Damarion with a glare. "I will not be accompanying you—"

"Yeah, yeah, so ye said, we get it, quit goin' on about it. Jessie, let's go." Niamh motioned me forward again. "Like a Band-Aid. Should've brought some of those weapons, but we'll just berate *Mr. Tom* for that later."

"I have weapons. Claws." Mr. Tom hunched down, getting ready to change. "So do you—or did you forget how to change into your third form?"

"Ack." Niamh's face soured. "That one hurts to change into."

"Losing your nerve?" Mr. Tom asked.

"Why not? Ye've already lost yer marbles."

The sound of rocks rolling filled the little tree-enclosed area, the gargoyles who had shifted to human previously now changing back. Niamh stripped off her top, her body quickly morphing and reducing down into a small creature that looked like a cross between a goblin and a gremlin. With a hairless, bony head and huge eyes that sparkled like grayish gems, this form was literally what nightmares were made of. I gave those dolls a lot of heat, but now, seeing her, I could see why she'd never been afraid of them.

She opened her wide, gaping mouth to reveal two rows of sharp teeth, almost like a shark. Her bony hands ended in fierce claws, as did her webbed feet.

"What the hell is that?" I asked, knowing my face was screwed up in a grimace and unable to help it.

"It's the puca's third form, incredibly useful for small, tight places," Austin said. "Horribly ugly and quite scary in a place like a cave. She can see in great detail in the dark in that form, and hide in little crevices or hang upside down like a bat. I think it's also useful in water." He gently wrapped his fingers around my upper arm. "This whole situation has been sprung on you. We can always come back once you've had time to fully recover."

I shook my head, hardening my resolve. "They

might come up with another plan by then. Given they haven't left—"

"They might have left," the basajaun interrupted. "I really could not say. They might be in there, or they might have left. They might be trespassing on my mountain, hoping I do not find them. They might be trespassing in town, hoping the polar bear—"

"Right, right, okay. I get it. We'll act like they are in there, and be pleasantly surprised if they are not." I patted myself, half thinking of changing forms like all the others. Like Austin had stepped back to do. But even though it was easy to change, and I'd had enough recovery time to fly again, I wasn't used to fighting in that form. I didn't have any muscle memory as a gargoyle. It would slow me down, and I was already too slow.

Gritting my teeth, choosing to stay as I was, I stepped forward to walk through the illusion.

CHAPTER 30

B EFORE I MADE it, Austin nudged me to the side and took my place.

"Dang it, Austin." I followed him inside, Damarion at my back, his claws poking my shoulder.

I crossed the threshold. The second my head was through, the sights and sounds from the clearing were cut off—the raspy shake of pine trees, the shimmer of sycamore leaves, the call of birds, and the soft rustle of animals within the underbrush. Instead, a vast emptiness shrouded in darkness gave the space a hollow feeling, like we'd stepped into a vacuum and lost all of our senses.

A furry body brushed against my side, Austin moving, so I stepped closer, widening my eyes in a vain attempt to see through the pitch darkness.

Claw scraped stone, and I felt a brush of wing, the movement wafting air in the stagnant space. Damarion was on scene. He bumped me into Austin's big, furry body, and I found myself trapped between the two of them.

"I wish I knew how to make light," I whispered. I had no idea how well sound carried in here, but with just stone and air, it didn't have much to deaden it.

Austin moved away, the act making barely a whisper of sound. His grunt-growl wasn't so quiet. It sounded like he'd hit a wall. More wings rustled, the sound like a class of kindergarteners who had just been given construction paper.

"We need to do this quickly. They'll hear us coming," I whispered.

Scrabbling against the rock caught my ears, and then something grabbed my leg.

I let out a yelp and jumped, kicking my leg out. A critter crawled up to my thigh, needle-like claws poking me, before jumping off.

"Oh God, what was that?" My whisper had grown in volume. I expected jets of magic any minute now.

A soft growl, low and mean, cut through my middle and froze my blood. If it hadn't come from Austin, I would have taken off running blindly into the darkness to get away. A whine and a series of clicking sounds came from his direction, followed by more scrabbling against the wall.

"We need light or fire," I whispered, waving my hands in front of me and feeling forward with my feet just in case the floor dropped away.

Another whine and more clicks preceded the little critter grabbing on to my calf. I yelped again and tried to shake it off.

"Nee-vvvv," one of the gargoyles—Mr. Tom?—grunted out.

"Right, yes. That horrible little form. Boy did she get unlucky with her types of magic," I said, stilling as Niamh darted away.

"May-ch pear-soon-ahl-ty," he replied.

Match personality, it sounded like. Mr. Tom couldn't speak, but he still had something to say about Niamh.

The clicking carried off down the hall and stopped. I followed, assuming that meant she was leading us, still waving my arms in the empty space but not being so cautious with my feet. Ten paces along and she stopped.

Wings rustled. Claws scraped against stone. My feet scuffed and Austin puffed out a breath, clearly sniffing the air. We were anything but quiet.

"This was a bad idea," I whispered as the clicking sound traveled upward to my right. She had to be climbing a wall. "We should go out and get a lighter. From now on, we bring phones as well as clothes. Stupid not to bring phones, really."

Sound blasted down the corridor from somewhere

way behind us. After a moment I realized it sounded like rocks falling. I jumped and spun, stepping on a giant paw and falling forward, getting a face full of Austin's fur. It didn't taste great.

His leg came up and bumped me back, trying to help. I staggered, the guy clearly not knowing his own strength in that form.

Silence descended, even Niamh stopping with her scrabbling and clicks. Another sound, smaller than the first, like a small rock pinging against stone.

"This cave has clearly been here for a long time," I whispered into the silence, not a creature stirring, not even the wings of the gargoyles. "That cage was plenty rusted. There is no way this whole place would come down on us, is there?"

Wings did rustle this time.

"Someone needs to stay in human form from now on. I need someone to verbally panic with," I murmured, barely loud enough to hear myself.

Wood bumped my hand, and Niamh clicked—how was she making those sounds, anyway? Was it with her tongue, or was she gnashing her teeth? Whatever it was, she clearly meant it as communication.

I wrapped my fingers around the wood stick, and the clicking skirted beyond me to Austin, increasing in pitch and volume. The feeling of something large moving stirred the air, followed by four bright bursts of light sparking against the stone wall. Austin had raked his claws down it.

Niamh was with me again, dragging me that way, pulling at the stick. In a flash, I saw what she was trying to do—get the tip of the stick to the sparks. She'd given me a torch.

Another couple of tries, and the torch kindled, the fire growing large enough to create a glow within the tunnel. It branched off into two paths from the circular entry point, about a ninety-degree angle between them. More torches dotted the way, bracketed in old-school metal—iron?—holders.

The gargoyles were all clustered together, barely able to move, clearly not having tried to venture very far without their sight.

"Which way first?" I asked, looking each way.

Austin huffed and nudged me forward with his snout. Might as well go the direction we'd started.

I wasted no time, jogging, and Niamh scampered in front of me on all four legs, a horrible little ghoul who was, thankfully, on our side. Small shadows danced up ahead, the light playing off the uneven surface of the rock. Niamh disappeared into a room off to the right, the door roughly hewn in the stone and the dirt a mess of footprints.

Another crash from down the tunnel, the origin distant and the sound not unlike rocks falling. The idea of that made me incredibly nervous. The basajaun had killed one of the mages, and if they were pissed enough, they could've rigged up something to bring this mountain crumbling down.

"Hurry up," I said to myself, the torch shaking in my hand, making shadows jump in the small room Austin would somehow have to squeeze into, and then back out of.

A card table sat in the middle, surrounded by four metal folding chairs. Two candles had dribbled white wax onto paper plates in the center of the table, their wicks blackened and a box of matches just beyond one plate's lip. A black plastic bag leaned in one corner of the room, lumpy and half-full of what looked like food containers. A cooking stove with little green canisters for fuel crouched in the other corner, a can of unopened chili sitting on one of the cold circular burners. Two battery-powered lanterns hugged the wall next to those.

The funky smell indicated food had been cooked, consumed, and thrown away in here, which fit with the scene, but it didn't look like they'd slept in here. I couldn't tell how fresh everything was with the dim light, and Austin couldn't speak to fill me in. Regardless, they weren't here now, and given the chill and lack of smoke, they hadn't been here very recently.

I handed the torch down to Niamh. "Can you put that out?"

She chittered at me but didn't take the torch. Clearly that was either a "no" or an "I don't want to." I held it wide as I bent to grab one of the battery-powered lanterns, awkwardly tested it out without setting myself on fire, and then clicked it back off. I'd keep the torch until I could put it back, just in case... No, there was no real reason. I'd just gotten so used to putting things away that it was habit.

Judging by the orderliness of the room, I wasn't the only one.

Niamh quickly caught up to me as I passed Austin and then the gargoyles, probably frustrating Austin because he was now stuck at the back. I briefly stopped at the entrance area in order to put out the torch and stow it in its holder. If they weren't here now, they might come back, and while they might overlook a missing lantern, a missing torch *and* a missing lantern would probably be noticed.

I glanced out the doorway, half expecting to see a mage waiting outside, hands out, magic at the ready. The dark barrier waited, though, glimmering and seemingly solid. It looked like a wall. If a mage stood on the other side, waiting to get the drop on us, we wouldn't know until we walked right into them.

"What a stupid setup," I said, my adrenaline spiking. "Why would they wait in here blind?"

Niamh chittered. Why? Who knew, since I didn't understand a word of it.

Down the tunnel the other way, its size and shape uniform, I ended at the shadowy opening to the large cave with the viewing area at the top. The barrier up there was still in place, transparent and glimmering.

Maybe these mages could only create two types of variable: viewable or not.

But why make the other one viewable? So it could kill anyone who came to rescue me?

Thankfully, they'd underestimated Austin.

The cage lay where we'd left it, the door off and on its side. The chain dangled above. No one waited among the spikes. The mages weren't here.

I breathed a sigh of relief. That was bad news, probably, drawing all this out, but the relief was real.

"Let's head out," I said, turning around and weaving through the gargoyles. "They're not here. At least we know where here is, though. Maybe Austin can pick up the scent from here." I walked back to the trick door slowly, not really wanting to leave the protection of the stone walls. There only one way in, and we were walking toward it. Maybe they weren't lying in wait beyond it, but they could come back while we were exiting.

At the door, I checked to make sure everyone was set, turned off the lantern, and stepped outside, ready just in case.

Dead space greeted us—even the basajaun had taken off. The flowers were still there, though, in their protective little cocoon. He hadn't been kidding—he did not plan to take the basajaun candy from strangers. How odd. What could I have possibly done to flowers? Drugged them? Then what? The creature was too big for me to drag back to Edgar. And when he woke up, I'd probably have a dead Edgar on my hands.

Austin attempted to cross the threshold, but I was in the way, and he bumped me from behind. I moved as Niamh skittered through on all fours.

Something felt wrong. The wind in the leaves and pine needles were still present, but the birdsong had cut off. No animals skittered under the brush. It was almost like they'd sensed a predator.

But they'd all been active when we were here last. Maybe the basajaun's presence had put them at ease. Now that he'd taken off...

Movement in front of me caught my eye as Austin crossed the threshold. I looked up as a woman in a dark dress stepped through the trees with her hands up, flares of light erupting from her fingertips. Two more stepped out from the sides.

They'd been waiting for us after all. The basajaun waiting outside had given me a false sense of security, like he would watch our backs. How could I have been so stupid?

CHAPTER 31

AUSTIN LURCHED FORWARD, now knocking me to the side and trying to get in front of me. He planned to take the magical hit. From mages this good, it could be instantly fatal.

Terror bled through me. My own protection instinct, born of motherhood, flared to life—like Austin, I completely forgot my sense of self-preservation the moment someone I cared about was in danger.

But I also had more magic than Austin.

Drawing from the training Damarion had given me, I ballooned magic around us even as I kicked Austin out of the way, my magic greatly enhancing the strength of the blow.

He flew to the side, hitting the wall next to the flowers. The zip of light from the mage smashed against the balloon of magic I'd created, and then flowed along the periphery, lighting the arch of it up.

The gargoyles stepped out of the cave entrance, Damarion first, and he quickly realized what was happening. His wings snapped out, one hitting the rock wall, nearly spearing Austin, and the other pushing out through the trees, the span striking me as incredible regardless of how many times I'd seen it.

The mage on my right got a shot off. It slapped my bubble and spread along it, just as the first had done. This one, though, sputtered and fizzed, shooting sparks.

My magic dissolved under the pressure, leaving us open to their attack.

Niamh bolted toward them and leapt from the ground onto the face of the mage in front of me. That mage shrieked, magic erupting from her fingertips as she reached for Niamh, now clawing and tearing and biting at her face.

The magic zinged toward me. Before I could react, Damarion grabbed me and turned his back, his wing whipping around me for more shelter.

"No, Damarion!" I tried to struggle out, tried to toss magic between him and the attack, but my counter-strike must've missed, because he grunted and pushed forward from the force of the attack. Immediately he started to sink down, releasing me as he hit his knees. "No!"

I touched his shoulder, pain curling within me. He was terrible at romance, but he was a decent guy and a great warrior. He didn't deserve to go down on my watch.

The telltale fizzing in my belly—the feeling I attributed to healing magic—came as a relief.

His wings wilted, and I stepped out from behind them as more gargoyles tried to get out of the cavern. The mage in the middle was, thankfully, sinking to her knees, screeching, as Niamh bit into her jugular.

The one on the right waved her hands, probably creating a spell, but the one on the left already had her hands jutting out—open fire.

I slapped magic at her, deadening whatever bit of nastiness she was unleashing as Austin rushed forward, a deep and vicious growl riding his movements.

Another zip of magic pulled my attention right, and I braced myself to take the hit.

A snarl interrupted my flinch, and my magic sparkled to life in front of me, forming what I hoped to be another shield. I needed a lot more practice to identify all this stuff.

Arms swinging and vicious canines bared, the basajaun materialized just inside the pine branches, his hair reminiscent of an eighties hair band and his continued growls terrifying.

The mage recoiled, understandably, and her spell blasted the rock to my right. A pink gargoyle's arm wrapped around me, and he pumped his wings in an attempt to lift me out of there.

"Would you guys just stop?" I yelled, blasting Ulric back. "Thank you, but I can fight!"

The basajaun reached for the mage and picked her up by the head—and then I had second thoughts about being flown out of there. The splat of the body against the rocks made me retch. The way he then spiked her detached head like a football had me splashing the contents of my stomach onto the ground.

"Oh God, maybe I don't want to fight. This is too much for me." I struggled to stand up, trying to stay strong in the face of such unbridled brutality, only to see Austin rise up on his back legs, his height topping the basajaun's by three feet or more. He swiped with his huge paw, battering the last mage standing. She slapped the stone wall, something cracking. He lumbered forward, pinned her with his paws, bent, and ripped her neck out.

A tortured groan escaped my mouth. I burped up bile. "All right, then, sure. Yeah, let's fly away. Good idea."

But Ulric was no longer trying to save me. He bent over Damarion, his hand on the other gargoyles shoulder, checking in.

Damarion was healing, though—I could feel my efforts working. That part of magic I was close to having down.

The roar of victory from my right made me flinch. Austin's answering roar, delivered while he still stood on his hind legs, shook my bones. The gargoyles joined in, their wings flapping, their growls vicious.

The basajaun wasted no more time. He crossed through everyone, shoving gargoyles out of the way, and bent to the flowers. Straightening with them, he turned to me, and everyone fell silent to hear what he would say.

"We have reached our agreement. These will be a wonderful treat."

"But…" I put out a finger, happy for his help but hoping for a little clarity about the rules. After witnessing his display of violence, that seemed of the utmost importance. "The mages were on your territory when they shouldn't have been, right? Wouldn't you have…spiked her head anyway?"

"Yes. But I would not have waited around after you had gone into the cave. I did that to make sure no one snuck up on you."

"Riiight… But they did sneak up on us."

"The polar bear smelled me."

"Okay, but—"

"He knew that I could only be in that position if I was stalking prey. It was all the alert he needed."

"Except he wasn't—"

"Then I enacted my punishment for their trespassing. I only ever kill one for the first offense."

I couldn't do much more than stare. His smell alert would've been great if it had informed us of the problem *before* the mages had stepped out of the trees. His retribution would've been amazing if it had come before Damarion had been injured.

As if hearing my thoughts, Mr. Tom said, "Duu-mm azzz roc-ksss."

Dumb as rocks. I had to agree with him there.

"Right. Fine." I sagged with sudden fatigue, my stomach still churning. "They're dead. Clearly. Horribly so, even. Good day to you." I peeled away my meager clothing, changed to my gargoyle form, and took off flying. I needed a glass of wine. And maybe a sedative.

CHAPTER 32

B UTTERFLIES FILLED MY stomach. I didn't want to do what I was about to do.

My knuckles were white as I wrung my hands, perched on the edge of my seat in one of the large sitting rooms at the front of the house.

"He is coming now, miss," Mr. Tom said from the doorway, his tuxedo pressed, a white towel once again draped over his bent arm. His love of watching old butler movies was officially getting out of hand.

A week had gone by since the showdown with the remaining mages. Five had snuck around the area, learning my habits and those of the town. Four had successfully kidnapped me and imprisoned me within the mountain. Two had been taken down by Bigfoot's scary uncle. That meant my team had only taken down three of them—or really two, since Austin was technically still a free agent.

That was unacceptable. I needed to make some changes. I needed to bring everyone under one umbrella and get them working together. I could only make a decision about who should sit on my council if I knew which of them were team players. Baby steps.

Step one was this meeting.

The wooden carving on the mantelpiece moved and changed, a woman holding a sword emerging within the pattern, along with a large gargoyle who flew down to land beside her. Without warning, she spun and sliced with her sword. The gargoyle's head flew off, the body disappearing within the changing designs and the head bouncing along the ground. The woman stowed her sword and bent, picking up the head in a palm, and...

I looked away, my mood souring. I mention in the house, *one time*, how gross it was for the basajaun to spike a head like a football, and suddenly it was Ivy House's favorite joke. I really did question her sense of humor.

At least it was obvious she supported my decision. That meant a lot, since it affected her, too.

I stood when Damarion filled the doorway, his face hard and his eyes wary. He probably knew what was coming.

My stomach clenched with unease. I hated doing stuff like this.

"Hi Damarion, please..." I motioned to the chair that had been placed opposite me. "Have a seat."

"You're looking well," he said, his gaze sliding down my front. He stopped before me and bent to give me a kiss on the cheek.

Over the last week, he'd thankfully gotten the hint that any chance of romance between us had flown out the window. I was pretty sure he blamed Austin for that, even though Austin and I hadn't seen much of each other, what with him diligently working to better secure the town. Still, Damarion seemed jealous of Austin. And while, sure, Austin could sometimes burn my blood with a simple touch, it would forever be a no-go. Damarion had nothing to be jealous of. Regardless, the two couldn't be in the same room before, but now it seemed like Damarion was struggling with being in the same town.

I lowered into my chair and forced myself to cross my legs, as though pretending I was comfortable might make it so.

"Damarion, I know I've said it before, but I would just like to thank you again for helping me learn my magic, training me, and especially for saving my life. You've been a huge asset to this house and have been integral to my training thus far."

He nodded.

"Unfortunately," I went on, trying to keep the apology out of my voice. This was business. I couldn't worry about offending him or hurting his feelings, which was easier said than done, given the need to please people had been drilled into me—and every other woman I knew—my whole life. Before Ivy House, I would have preferred to endure my own discomfort rather than anger or upset others, even if the other party was acting out of turn. That made me a great host, but it really worked against me in terms of business. I had to harden up for this new life. I had to own being the boss lady. I couldn't apologize for the decisions I made. This wasn't personal, and Damarion had known the score all along. They all had.

But man, strapping on my iron panties was easier said than done.

"I have to make some structural changes to my set-up," I said. "You have excellent skills and a lot of very admirable qualities, but unfortunately, I'll no longer be needing your services at this time. I hope you can understand."

I just barely stopped myself from apologizing and telling him it wasn't personal.

He studied me quietly for a moment, making me want to squirm in my seat.

Finally, he nodded curtly and stood. "You are not ready for me. When you are, I will expect another summons. It has been an honor." He bowed deeply and his wings fluttered. After straightening, he took my hand and brushed his lips across my knuckles. "Until we meet again."

"Yes. Of course. I—"

He strode from the room, not looking back.

In his wake, I stood staring for a quiet moment. I wasn't sure what exactly he thought I wasn't ready for, his handsy approach to romancing a lady or his leadership style. Regardless, his delusions had made this conversation surprisingly painless.

One down, one to go.

"I doubt he'll get another summons." Mr. Tom stepped into the room. "He's a bruised apple at this point. Best to be tossed in the compost heap."

"Were you listening at the door?" I asked, sitting back down.

"Of course, miss. I wanted to know what he said."

I sighed. "He took it well, though. That's a relief."

"Yes. You are only excusing the one gargoyle, right—you haven't changed your mind?"

"Correct. I want to get to know the others. I want to see if, given the chance, they'll be better team players, like Ulric and Cedric have turned out to be."

"Right. And when will you call in Austin Steele?"

I looked out the window at the gloomy day, the dark gray clouds promising rain.

"As soon as Damarion leaves."

FORTUNATELY, DAMARION DIDN'T waste any time. He didn't even say goodbye to anyone. He grabbed the few things to his name (not including the car, which he left behind as if it were disposable), changed into his other form, and stepped out of the third-floor trapdoor. His huge and magnificent wings snapped wide and away he went, an amazing specimen.

His strength and power in the air would be missed. I probably needed to summon another flier with his abilities. It would have to wait, though. First I needed to get a handle on my team.

As the afternoon waned, I once again found myself in the sitting room, this time even more anxious. Austin's foot touched down on the property and the next followed slowly. His approach wasn't hurried as he made his way to the front door.

"I shall escort him in, miss," Mr. Tom said, pausing just outside the door.

Something thunked on the stairs, and he turned and looked at them as Austin opened the front door.

"Well, what in the world…" Mr. Tom stepped back.

The large doll head with eyes turned mostly white rolled by.

Austin swore and jumped back from the door.

"Kick it!" I shouted. "Set fire to it!"

"Now, miss, that is a little overdramatic, don't you think?" Mr. Tom tsked at me. "I wonder how the head got loose, though. How strange."

"What kind of a freak-show house is this?" I heard Austin say, and I remembered that he wasn't big on those dolls either. Big, tough alpha who could make an enemy cower got jumpy around dolls.

Something about that made laughter bubble up. It wasn't like I blamed the guy, but it was unexpected.

He stepped into the sitting room doorway. I could feel Mr. Tom jog out into the front yard, clearly intending to capture, and no doubt save, the doll head.

"Come in and close that door," I said, standing. "I need to burn that whole doll room. I'm not kidding. Ivy House, this isn't funny. No more decapitation jokes."

The wooden carving morphed into a sea of heads rolling by.

"She has a very sick sense of humor," I grumbled.

"You're telling me," Austin replied.

He stood in front of the newly closed door, watching me warily.

Remembering why he was here, I sat slowly. "Please…" I gestured for him to take the other seat. Breathing evenly, trying to keep my courage up, I waited for him to sit. "I want to thank you for saving my life—"

He shook his head. "You never have to thank me for that. It isn't a job. It is a pleasure."

My heart warmed, and I let a smile slip out. But I couldn't let myself lose momentum—I had to push forward.

"You were able to do what no one else could, even those with Ivy House's help," I said. "You helped me fully own my new magic and everything that comes with it. A thank you isn't enough for that. As you know, I've been having trouble controlling the house team. That's made us ineffective, and it's kept me from getting a good read on most of the new people. It is putting me and the town both in danger."

I clasped my hands in my lap and wet my lips, pushing myself to go on. Here came the hard part.

"I need someone that can unite this team. Someone that can help me lead it. For this reason, I've let Damarion go. I wondered…" I shifted within that focused blue gaze, close to squirming again. "You told me once that you could help me get people in line. I know you'd rather not deal with Ivy House, but I wondered if you might change your mind if I offered the position to you as a job, where I paid you. Will you help me unite these people? Help me learn how to properly lead people into battle? I mean, I'll still try to free you from the magic.

This isn't about that. I'll definitely do that. I was just wondering if you could help me with the other stuff…"

I let my words trail away, realizing I was babbling. Turned out it was even harder to ask for help and face rejection than to tell someone they were no longer needed. I had to work on all of this.

He stood, his gaze still rooted to mine, and turned for the door.

I deflated. That stung a little. I'd figured there was a fifty/fifty chance of him refusing, but I hadn't expected such an abrupt rejection. Usually he was a little more personable than that.

As he opened the door and walked out, I glared at the wooden carving on the mantelpiece. "Nice going, taunting him with the doll head. What's wrong with you?"

Doors opened and closed upstairs. I could sense the little doll bodies flopping around in their room.

I stuck out a warning finger, about ready to deliver a threat, when I felt Austin turn the opposite way I'd been expecting. I pushed up quickly and followed, catching him in the hallway headed toward the back of the house.

"What'd he say?" Mr. Tom called from the stairs, holding the renegade doll head.

I ignored him, my chest tightening as I watched

Austin turn the corner. He maintained his pace, and I stopped breathing altogether as he approached the door to the Council Room. There he hesitated, and I bit my lip, giving him space, disbelief and hope raging through me.

When he crossed the threshold, my heart thundered in my chest.

It felt like hooks lodged in my middle and pulled, reeling me into the room after him.

"I made a deal with myself," he said as he stood just inside the doorway, waiting for me. He didn't turn my way. "If you still wanted my help, I would accept the magic and a place on your team. I would accept the responsibility to guard and protect you, navigating all the strings attached to this weird house. I decided that if you gave me the honor of choosing me, I would unite this house with the town, and spread out my influence to the surrounding areas. I'd create and run a territory that would help secure you and your home. I decided that I would finally wear the title of alpha, come what may."

He turned toward me, his large shoulders stretching his white T-shirt and his handsome face showing his grim determination. It was clear he was sacrificing his earlier stance on the magic and this house because I needed him. The guy was as selfless as they came, and if

I hadn't needed him so badly, I would have shooed him out of the Council Room.

I did need him, though. We all needed him—this house, this town, even the tourists. When the crap rolled in, there were very few people who could balance everything effectively and maintain order. Austin was an incredible person and an incredible leader. No matter how many people I summoned, I didn't think I'd ever find someone better, not with his level of experience. Definitely not with his loyalty and sense of honor. He only demanded of the people he governed what he demanded of himself.

"I am honored you accept," I whispered, rapidly blinking away the tears clouding my vision. "Thank you."

He nodded, and his jaw and hands clenched. "The house is trying to make me walk to a specific chair."

"Oh, wait. Wait a minute!" Mr. Tom said, standing at the door. I hadn't noticed—he just blended into the scenery at this stage. He was the house's white noise. "Let me go get the others. Wait, what am I saying—Ivy House, summon the others! It's happening. Austin Steele is becoming one of us and getting a chair! It's actually happening!"

"I could've lived my whole life without hearing that I was becoming like Earl," Austin murmured.

Mr. Tom dropped the doll head he was still holding and ran from the room. "Wait for us," he yelled over his shoulder.

The doll head bounced and rolled toward me, its eyes moving and its stringy red hair flapping around unnaturally.

"No!" I made the door slam, trying to force it out. The edge hit the face and bounced back as if the doll were made of rubber. The head rolled until it was facing me, a little tilted, its eyes staring at me and a sneaky grin on its pink-painted lips. "Gross."

"I already regret this," Austin said.

"Ivy House, this isn't funny!"

Niamh approached the door wearing the black sweats she'd had to order herself, which was probably why they were two sizes too big, and stopped, looking down on the doll head. "What in the... Why is a doll's head lyin' around?" She squinted at me. "What's wrong witch'ye?"

"Throw that thing in the incinerator." I motioned at the head as Mr. Tom returned carrying a silver tray laden with glasses of champagne.

"Ivy House is taking the piss, is it?" Niamh stepped to the other side of the head and kicked it down the hall. "It seems to have a fascination with rolling doll heads lately."

"God, I hate dolls," I said, doing a heebie-jeebies dance. "I don't actually think your goblin form is worse than the dolls, now that I think about it. At least you know you're scary—those dolls are masquerading as lifelike babies, and then they come alive and grab knives and attack. It's just not right."

"Miss, don't take this the wrong way, but you're prone to hysterics when it comes to those harmless dolls." Mr. Tom set down the tray on the small round table by the window, its surface polished and sporting a high shine. "Many of them are cute."

"Some of them are creepy, though," Niamh said, walking into the circle.

"Don't you start," Mr. Tom said, straightening.

Niamh took a seat in the circle of chairs, the third from the top, the top denoted by a standing, woven flag on a pole that looked centuries old. Mr. Tom took the ninth chair, and when Edgar got there a moment later, his lips turned up in a ghastly grin, he took the twelfth seat. Apparently I chose my protectors, except for the three who had been here before me, and Ivy House chose their importance within the circle.

Austin stood, immobile. "There are ways to get something done, Ivy House, and trying to force me isn't one of them."

"Do I…stand anywhere in particular?" I asked, outside of the circle and close to the far wall.

"You wait until Austin's place has been chosen, miss," Mr. Tom said out of the side of his mouth.

Austin's muscles relaxed. His nod was slight, and then he walked forward, curving around the circle until he stood at the top behind the flag, which reached his nose. A shadowy, magical drape poured down in front of the windows, mostly cutting out the light. Candles flickered to life, the flames dancing slowly.

Austin glanced at me, and I saw the wariness in his eyes. After a deep breath, though, he stepped around the flag and between the chairs, entering the circle.

"I can barely breathe with the excitement," Mr. Tom said.

"Thank God this isn't a formal ceremony in front of strangers we needed to impress," Niamh said, watching Austin but addressing Mr. Tom, "or you'd just have outed yerself as a clown."

"Better a clown than a miserable old hag without a polite bone in her body," he grumbled.

Austin stopped in front of the first chair, the flag at his back, and slowly sat down.

I sucked in a breath, something stirring deep inside of me. Ivy House thought Austin was and would remain the most important member in that circle. She didn't plan to save the space in case someone better came along. She didn't have any second guesses.

Her sentiments lined up with my own.

My stupid eyes teared up again.

The pull forward caught me off guard, and I resisted at first, now knowing what Austin had been reacting to. A moment later, though, I took my place behind the long, thin flag, paused, and then walked into the circle, the air moving around me, the power building. I took my position in the middle and faced Austin.

"Welcome," I said, somehow knowing this was all that was required.

He didn't nod or verbally reply, just held my gaze for a long, silent moment. Candlelight danced and glowed around us. Magic and energy jumped between us as though sparks of fire, not sure which person to settle on.

My team officially had a new member. I half wondered if Fate had led him to this town, or Ivy House had called him in preparation for my eventual return. I doubted I'd ever really know.

He was here now, though, and relief flooded me that he'd agreed to join us. That he'd agreed to help us. With him on our side, there was no way we could go wrong.

"You know what this means, right?" Mr. Tom asked quietly. "If you're one of us, you have to call me Mr.

Tom. Or Tom, if the formality is a sticking point…"

Austin ignored him, not taking his eyes off me, like I was his lifeline in this new venture. He'd always been mine.

At least the new guy was already well versed in Mr. Tom's weird. Better and better.

EPILOGUE

"**T**URNS OUT THEY'D been there for the last couple of months." Austin leaned against the bar, his long-sleeved T-shirt hugging his currently flaring arm muscles. He seemed to find it humorous that my gaze always snagged on his various flexed body parts.

It wasn't like I could help it. His shirts were all kinds of tight because of some laundry snafu or other, and he put on a pretty amazing muscle show. Besides, I was a warm-blooded female who'd never gotten anywhere with Mr. Hot McHandsy, and I hadn't gotten to release the floodgates.

Paul bustled around him, the bar a little busier than usual for a Wednesday night. Word had gotten around that Austin had accepted an official spot in Ivy House less than a week ago. The magical people in this town loved to gossip, and everyone kept checking in to see how it was going. It was like they thought Austin might declare war on the house or something. They must've sensed the ongoing battle of wills, something I was happy to turn a blind eye to.

"Who'd been where?" Niamh asked as she returned from the bathroom. "Ah, bejaysus, what are you doing here, you filthy bugger?"

I turned back to find Sasquatch approaching the empty seat to my right. He hated me, I hated him, yet he always sat near me. Why, I had no idea. To make us both miserable, I guessed.

He didn't say a word as he took his seat.

Austin nodded at him, his way of asking Sasquatch what he wanted to drink.

"Usual," Sasquatch said.

Austin's shoulder flexed as he pushed open the door of the cooler that held some of the bottled beer. His bicep flexed as he reached in and took out a brown bottle with a silver label. His large and gloriously muscled back flared as he turned away from me to pop the top. When he turned back, his pecs popped under his shirt.

"What in the hell?" Sasquatch mumbled, catching the show.

"He's doing that for you," I told him as Austin set the bottle down. "He likes you."

Sasquatch scowled at me, but he knew better than to insult me in front of Austin. At this point in his existence, he was clearly tired of being punched and thrown off his barstool.

Yet he still kept sitting next to me. It made absolutely no sense.

"Those mages had been staying a town over basically since I accepted the magic," I told Niamh, running my fingers down the stem of my glass. "They'd been watching me the whole time. Probably most of the mages we encountered were doing the same."

"We're good now, though." Austin resumed his lean. "I'm setting up defensive measures and lookouts. There's a lot of work to be done before this town becomes a well-oiled machine, but that was obviously step one."

There hadn't been any sort of ceremony by which Austin had officially taken the alpha role. He didn't tell anyone or say anything about his change in status, but he *had* stopped correcting people when they used the title. Niamh said there had been a few other minor adjustments in the way he acted, but they were apparently too subtle for me to notice.

"What kind of work?" I asked.

He reached up to rub the back of his neck, his bicep flaring and torso hardening. Sasquatch jerked, leaned back, and scowled before shooting me an accusing look, clearly not liking the muscle show and blaming me for it.

"You chose to sit here. This isn't my fault," I said, chuckling.

"It's nice to look at, but aye, it is a bit strange, all right," Niamh mumbled.

"Just trying to get even," Austin said, his smile wide, showing his straight, even teeth, boosting his handsomeness tenfold. My stomach fluttered and I pulled my gaze away. "Just trying to prove that I'm not the only one who looks."

My face heated as I remembered his reaction to seeing me naked in that cave. Remembered the hard heat pressed against me.

I shivered even as heat pooled in my pounding core. "Little do you know, you're just making a fool of yourself," I said, and took a sip of my wine.

"That right?" He turned to help someone down the way, his muscular butt flexing.

Sasquatch flinched again and yanked his head the other way, catching me looking. He rolled his eyes and directed his gaze straight ahead. "You're the cause of it."

"You are as sharp as a tack, boy. Nothing gets past you, does it?" Niamh said to him.

"Austin means to replace the local Dick government with magical people, bring in magical people to buy out the shops and wineries," Niamh said, "and work a lot more closely with the local police. As the alpha, he needs to run the town, and to do that, he needs more magical blood in it."

"He can do all that?" I asked, awestruck. "The government and wineries and everything?"

"Ah." She tapped the bar with her finger. "That's the question, isn't it? We shall see."

"Yeah, he can." Sasquatch lifted his bottle in a salute. "Won't be a problem for the likes of him. You just wait. We'll be the most prosperous territory in the southwest. Maybe all of the west. Maybe—"

"Whoa, whoa, there, lad, yer startin' to sound absurd." Niamh leaned around me to shoot Sasquatch a look. "Go back to being friendless and mindin' yer own business. It makes the atmosphere nicer for everyone."

"What brought on the change, though, alpha?" Sasquatch asked as Austin worked his way back, more interested in hanging out with us than working.

Austin's gaze delved into mine. "Someone showed me what it's like to reach for the stars. She showed me that a new adventure is right around the corner—all you have to do is have the courage to answer its call. We can't be afraid of change, not when there are so many rewards from embracing it."

"Sounds like something you might read in one of them coffee table books or somethin'," Niamh said. "The ones you get on sale because no one wants 'em."

I smiled at Austin, warmth radiating through my chest. "Grab life by the balls."

"Hear, hear." Sasquatch lifted his beer again.

"Christ," Niamh said, clearly responding to Sasquatch. "So what's the story, then, Jessie?" Niamh pushed her finished drink forward, and Austin went to grab her another one. "Should I pick out another date for ye or what?"

"No. God no." I rolled my eyes as Austin deposited her drink. "I need a break from all that. I don't mind meeting new people and learning about them, but I'm not so much into the forced small talk and having the same date over and over—"

"What do you mean, having the same date over and over?" Austin asked, pointing at someone who'd just raised their hand to get a drink.

"Bud," I heard.

"I got it," Paul told Austin.

I tossed up my hands. "It's always the same kind of date. Get picked up, check each other out, have dinner, get weird about the check, and maybe go for drinks. Or in my situation, bomb out and say goodbye and then have drinks with your buddy. Repeat. I could probably plan something more interesting, but then there's that stigma about a girl being too pushy or bossy, so I just take their suggestions and... Boring. I suppose it's my fault, but it's still boring. I need a break. Maybe I'll find someone naturally. Like someone who comes here."

Sasquatch huffed, and I was pretty sure I heard, "Fat chance."

"I could do better." Austin flung a bar towel over his shoulder.

"That right?" I took a sip.

"Yes. I could take you on the perfect date."

"There is no perfect date."

"Each person has a perfect date. I bet I could figure out yours."

"Be careful about accepting a wager on this one, Jessie," Niamh said. "He's had more than a little experience with the ladies."

The sparkle in Austin's eyes dulled as he turned away to get a drink.

"Damarion had a lot of experience with the ladies, and his idea of romance was a live dick pic, so…" I brushed my hair away from my face, grinning. I'd told Niamh that story, and she'd laughed for ten minutes solid before making me tell it again. She couldn't believe even a guy as tone-deaf as Damarion had thought that display would work. Mr. Tom had been incredibly insulted.

"A hundred quid says you flunk out, Austin Steele," Niamh said, digging in her pocket.

"That's *alpha* now," Sasquatch corrected.

"Why doncha bugger off, ye maggot. Yer as *annoyin'*—"

"I thought you said not to bet?" I asked, exasperated.

"I did. But then ye got me thinkin'. You don't settle for second best, now do ya? An' I don't think he pays attention to women half so well as he thinks he does. A hundred quid."

"I don't think you guys saw how awkward it was to work with Damarion after it didn't work with Damarion," I replied. "Austin and I are magically stuck together at this point—dating would be awkward at best, and it would make things miserable at worst. No way. I can't jeopardize our working relationship for a muscle show. I need his help—things cannot get awkward."

"I didn't mean a *date*-date. I meant a friend date," Austin said, his eyes sparkling again, a challenge burning within them. He shrugged. "It'll be harmless fun. But it will still be perfect. I'll take that bet."

"Okay, but...no. No bet. It's not going to happen. I'll turn even a friend date into a disaster."

"A perfect date doesn't end in disaster." Austin's pecs popped again, catching my eye. I ripped my gaze away and scowled at his smiling face. "Come on. Go out with me, Jess. I'll buy you something nice with the winnings."

Those teasing blue eyes caught my attention and held it. Fire sparked to life in my core and burned white-hot in a way it wouldn't for a friend. I didn't mean to accept, and I certainly didn't mean to do it in such a sultry whisper. "Okay."

The same fire I felt deep within me flared to life in his hungry eyes.

Before I could come to my senses and back out of the whole thing, the bar quieted down around us. Warning flared within me—a predator had entered our midst.

"Jaysus, Mary, and Joseph," Niamh said in a release of breath.

The basajaun stood just inside the door, having had to stoop and practically crawl to get in, I wagered. Thankfully, the bar had really high ceilings.

A weathered red baseball hat sat crookedly atop his head, much too small. Two braids traveled from his chin to his chest, containing his beard. A little jean vest clung to his shoulders, the edges frayed, and a flannel sweatshirt was tied around his waist.

"Is this lad trying to fit in, or somethin'?" Niamh asked, the only one speaking.

Cedric stood just to the side of the basajaun, his

hands loose and his wings fluttering. My bodyguard this evening, he clearly wasn't letting his fear of the large and slightly unhinged creature get the better of him. I assumed the two gargoyles who'd been guarding the outside of the bar had taken up positions near the door in case something happened.

"Alpha," the basajaun said. "I ask leave to travel the hidden areas of your territory. In return, I will grant you the same courtesy within mine. A trade. Do you accept?"

Austin straightened up, his body tight again, although this time it was not a display. "A trade. I agree."

The basajaun bent to a knee and bowed his head. Austin bent his head in return.

"Hi, Jessie," the basajaun said in a loud whisper as he straightened up, offering me a little side wave. "It is me, the basajaun from the mountain. Remember me?"

My eyes had definitely rounded, I could feel it. I barely got in a nod. Dumb as rocks, absolutely.

"With the alpha's leave, I am here to reap the rewards of our trade. The broken ankle, remember?"

I nodded again, thankful he seemed to think Ivy House flowers on the property different than me bringing him the same flowers. I was starting to suspect Mr. Tom was dead right about his intellect, and that was okay by me.

"Ivy House lands are not part of my territory," Austin said, his voice hard. This was probably his professional face among very dangerous creatures. I was glad for it. I didn't want to accidentally break some obscure basajaun rule and get my head spiked.

"Oh. Well, if it is all the same with you, I would like to keep the trade. Just in case I'd like to wander, you know."

Austin nodded. "Don't get seen, if you can help it."

"Yes, of course." The basajaun pulled out a bit of his sweatshirt, as though it was the key to staying undercover. He and Mr. Tom clearly went to the same spy school. To me he said, "We should meet up to spook a couple of hikers. Remember when we talked about that? You can shove them with a little magic, and I can allow them to see me for a moment." He waved it away. "You are busy and I am late for my flowers. We will speak on it another time."

The entire bar was dead silent in the basajaun's wake. Mouths hung open, eyes remained wide, and someone had fainted.

"How'd he know my name?" I asked into the hush. "And who did he steal those clothes from?"

"See there?" Niamh looked over at Sasquatch. "He's *supposed* to be hairy, and since he lives in the wild, he's allowed to stink. Yer just takin' the piss, you are. Ye got the hair and the stench without the benefits. Now don't ye feel dumb? Maybe ye should wash once in a while."

"How does anyone stand you?" he grumbled.

"They don't. Which is why they don't sit next to me. Ye certainly got brains to match his, I'll give ye that." Niamh took a sip of her cider. "Wanker."

"How the hell are we going to hide his presence around town?" Austin muttered as he walked by.

I smiled and shook my head. God, my life was weird, but the people around me cared about my success and kept things interesting. Good or bad, dangerous or safe, weird or normal, I was choosing my own way, and it was about time.

LATER THAT NIGHT, after I pretended I was going to the bathroom and instead ran out the back door of the bar so Niamh wouldn't order me another drink, I made it home to Edgar screaming.

The gargoyles filed in around me immediately, not letting me into the house.

"It's fine, it's just Mr. Tom, Ulric, and Edgar in there," I said, pushing through.

Those three stood at the back of the house near the kitchen, Mr. Tom shushing Edgar while Ulric looked on with concern.

"What is it?" I asked, running to them. "What happened?"

"We've been robbed!" Edgar screeched. "They're gone. They're all gone!"

"What's gone?" I considered bracing my hand on his bony shoulder, then thought better of it. I swayed into Ulric. "Oops. Sorry, don't mind me. The basajaun came into the bar, and he spoke to me like we were old buddies, and then everyone was awestruck and bought me drinks—it was cah-razy. Anyway, sorry, Edgar, this is your show. Why are you crying? I didn't even know vampires could cry."

"Why wouldn't they be able to?" Ulric asked with a grin, his hand on my shoulder, stabilizing me.

"Shh, I'm good." I removed his hand and drifted into Jasper, who'd just shown up on the scene. He still lived at the house, and I still meant to get to know him, but he was so quiet that I constantly forgot about him. If Mr. Tom was white noise, Jasper was a potted plant that had just shown up one day, never seemed to need water, and seemed content to be part of the scenery. He was the gargoyle equivalent of a succulent. "I don't know, because water doesn't flow out of their eyes or something? They don't have emotion, maybe?"

"He's got plenty of emotion," Ulric whispered, back to focusing on a sobbing Edgar.

"He's downright hysterical. What is the meaning of

this, Edgar?" Mr. Tom demanded.

"We've been robbed, I tell you." Edgar grabbed Mr. Tom by the lapels and started to drag him toward the back door to go outside to check out the cause of his hysteria.

"Unhand me, vampire! This is a freshly pressed suit." Mr. Tom struggled out of his grasp.

Outside, following a wailing vampire, we finally caught sight of what had been stolen.

The whole back garden, from one end of the house to the other, had been picked clean of Edgar's award-winning flowers. Petals littered the ground, like the blood of the lost. The perfume of their crushed bodies, having met their end within the basajaun's teeth, still lingered in the air.

It belatedly occurred to me that I should've given Edgar a heads-up as to what was coming. Thankfully, he hadn't been outside and tried to stop the creature.

"Oh, for heaven's sakes, they're just flowers." Mr. Tom scoffed.

Edgar brought himself up to his full height, his fangs gleaming in the moonlight. "How dare you!"

"Sorry, buddy," I said, this time breaking down and patting Edgar's shoulder. I regretted it almost immediately. He felt like a bunch of sticks tied together with twine and overlaid with a rubbery mat. I definitely should've made an exception for Edgar when I made the call on the age thing. "Let's go look at your doilies and I'll explain everything. I'll help you fix it, okay? I'll put a couple of doilies in the house, even."

"No, you most certainly will not." Mr. Tom stomped after us. "Don't give in to this display, miss, it'll just encourage him."

"This is my life now," I heard Ulric say as he followed us. "I hope my mom never visits, because I have no idea what I would say to her."

I had to agree with that. I sincerely hoped my parents didn't get a wild hair to visit, either. That would be some mess.

It wasn't until the small hours of the morning that I made it to my bedroom. Mr. Tom followed me up shortly thereafter with a steaming cup of tea.

"There now, miss." He set the tea tray down, a black envelope resting on the outside lip. "That was nice of you to console Edgar, but really, you shouldn't trouble yourself too much. That vampire has long since gone Froot Loops. It's best not to get too involved in his lunacy."

He was one to talk.

I leaned back tiredly, the buzz from earlier having worn away. "I should've warned him that I'd traded away his favorite hobby. Poor guy will have to start over. What's that?" I pointed at the envelope.

"Oh. This came for you an hour ago." Mr. Tom handed it over before preparing some cheese slices on a plate.

An interesting sort of red seal stuck the flap down, though I couldn't quite make out the design. A cream card waited on the inside, and in a lovely delicate hand was written:

My dearest Jacinta,

Congratulations on acquiring your wings. What a triumph! I look forward to seeing for myself.

Sadly, it seems I have underestimated your polar bear alpha, or I might've already had the pleasure. How shortsighted of me. I must say, I am half delighted someone has been able to surprise me. It has been so long since that has been the case.

I assure you, however...it will not happen again.

Until we meet, I shall think of you fondly.

—Elliot Graves

I stared at it for a long moment before handing it to Mr. Tom and sending him away so I could change for bed. So Elliot Graves, Mr. Magical Mob Boss, was the one who had posted the contract. This didn't necessarily mean he was the man in black who'd waited for me outside of Ivy House a couple of months ago, but it certainly suggested it.

Life was about to get even more interesting.

THE END.

ABOUT THE AUTHOR

K.F. Breene is a Wall Street Journal, USA Today, Washington Post, Amazon Most Sold Charts and #1 Kindle Store bestselling author of paranormal romance, urban fantasy and fantasy novels. With over three million books sold, when she's not penning stories about magic and what goes bump in the night, she's sipping wine and planning shenanigans. She lives in Northern California with her husband, two children, and out of work treadmill.

Sign up for her newsletter to hear about the latest news and receive free bonus content.

www.kfbreene.com